TIGER'S EYE

BREEZY JONES

Also By
BREEZY JONES

Winter's Series

Winter's Rise

Winter's Rebel (Forthcoming)

Short Stories / Anthologies

Once Upon Academy, Vol. 1: Malefic Mixology

Once Upon Academy, Vol. 2: Magic and Mice

To all the mommies out there
struggling with toddlers that need
an escape into a world of magic and
hot tiger shifters...
XOXO
- Breezy

Tiger's Eye

One

I am *not* a werewolf.

It's just a fact. I'm not delusional.

But I've never felt exactly human, either... that is, not until now.

"Hey, are you listening?" Blake's voice sounds next to me. I pinch my lips together and shut my locker door. The ring of the final bell still hangs loudly in the air, signaling the end of the school day.

"Yes, I heard you," I say with an annoyed huff at my friend. "I just don't think I want to go this year." The slow trickle of students filling the hallway becomes a torrent, with clanging lockers and a rising tide of voices surrounding us on all sides.

"Fuck that, of course you're going," Blake says.

A boy pushes past her, making his way to the next row of lockers from my own. "Sorry," he says with a nod at her, then glances at me as he continues past. The hint of a smile ghosts his lips, making me do a double take. I politely smile back, but he's already made it to his destination, turning away from us and digging in his locker.

I tilt my head and decide to ignore it—clearly, I'm imagining things. Chad Danvers is on the football team, and his dad had been a huge real estate developer in Silas Creek up until he passed away a few years ago, so everyone knows him, even if they don't *know know* him. Like me, he's human. But unlike me, he has no idea the supernatural world exists. I shift from one foot to the other. I don't talk much to the other humans at the school. I've never really fit in with them. I almost laugh out loud at the thought. *But then I also don't fit in with the wolves anymore, either, do I?*

I shake off the uncomfortable thought just as Blake turns her attention from Chad back to me. "I've decided you don't have a choice in the matter," she says, continuing our conversation as if nothing happened.

I scrunch my face at her verdict as I grab my bag. I sling it across my shoulders as Blake and I walk away from the long row of faded silver lockers.

"Where are we going?" A high, delicate voice chimes in behind us. I don't need to look to recognize who it belongs to. Chloe, with her blonde hair and blue eyes, is the Barbie of our little friend group. The light to Blake and my darker features.

"Right now, shopping for a dress," Blake answers.

"For Halloween," I add in dryly. I try my best to keep the bitterness out of my voice, but I've got a deathgrip on my backpack straps as we weave through the crowded hallways toward the exit doors. I don't want them to know just how much it bothers me that I won't be a part of the Moon Awakening, on account of the *human* thing.

Chloe's squeal is piercing enough to have me cringing away from her. "You're coming, right? You need a dress, too!"

"I'll go dress shopping," I say, staring straight ahead, "but I don't think I'm going to the ceremony." I let out a resigned sigh, keeping my voice low. "I'm not... Moon-Kissed, remember?" I give her my best pleading stare as we continue walking, hoping she'll drop it.

"But it's your birthday, and we always go every year!" Chloe's voice takes on a wistful tone as her eyes drift past Blake and I. She's lost in dreams of flowing dresses, dancing under the full moon, and meeting her one, true mate. Her big, blue eyes snap back to meet mine. "You have to go! I can't do this without you."

Her words are like a knife to my gut. I want to go—so much more than I can ever tell her. The three of us have been dreaming of this day since we were old enough to understand what it is. The fact that I wouldn't be included in it had never really hit home before. In the past we had all sat on the sidelines, but this year it would only be me, watching my best friends participate in the age-old ritual. In *our* dream. Without me.

The Moon-Kissed Awakening is like Graduation for werewolves, raising you from child to adult. You get to find your place in the pack and if you're lucky, you might just find your mate.

I, however, will not be 'graduating' with my friends. I'm an outsider, a fact that could not have been plainer to me in this moment unless I had 'just your basic human' stamped on my forehead. The thought has my stomach in a knot and now I'm spiraling on a one-way ticket to depression-ville.

Blake grabs my arm, stopping me short. I turn to face her hard glare—her golden eyes bore into mine, making me realize how selfish I'm acting. Guilt rises in my throat. "Ari Jean. Just 'cause you're not being paraded in a fancy gown…" She lowers her voice as a group of freshmen rush past us in the halls before continuing, "…presenting to the pack that you're now open for business like the two of us have to do, doesn't mean you shouldn't be there." She flips her dark braided hair over her shoulder as she pushes open one of the double doors leading to the parking lot. "And it doesn't mean you're *not* dressing up in support of your two best girls." Blake leans her back against the door as she finishes, holding it open for Chloe and me.

I let out the long breath of air I've been holding in as I realize I'm not getting out of this one. Human or not, my besties are wolves and I have to support them. "Fine," I say, resigning myself to my fate. Blake answers me with a thin-lipped 'I won' kind of smile while Chloe hops up and down, clapping with an excited squeal.

I roll my eyes at their completely opposite reactions, and fight the smile that tugs at my lips. I just can't be mad around them. "Let's go then," I say, shaking my head and pushing past Blake into the cool, autumn air.

Chloe runs out after me, catching up quickly and looping one arm through mine. A smile beams from one side of her face to the other. Blake isn't far behind as the three of us march down the rows of parked cars toward Blake's enormous black Escalade. Blake's father, Jon, is the Alpha of the Lunar Falls pack and crazy wealthy from all the property he owns in town, even outside of the pack's territory. Like, 'fuck you money' kind of wealthy.

The sun is hidden behind low-hanging clouds and the wind rustles around us. It's a perfect autumn day—my favorite season, thanks to the bright colors of the changing leaves and the never-too-cold or too-hot weather. I smile, inhaling the fresh air and letting it fill me up, uncurling the knots that have twisted up my stomach.

Skipping a few paces ahead I pivot around, keeping my steps even as I walk backwards. "So, what kind of dresses are you guys…?" I begin before sputtering as my back slams into something solid.

My back goes rigid. I don't need to turn around to know who I've hit. I can feel his presence in a way that has my blood vibrating in my veins. There's just something about Dean Vargas that… calls to me. It makes me so uneasy. I've always tried to put distance between us over the years, dodging him in the halls at school and at pack meet-ups, and avoiding his hang-outs, and… it never works. His graduating last semester didn't even seem to help. Somehow, we always end up running into each other. Apparently, literally sometimes.

I whip around, finding myself inches from a broad, hard chest, covered by a thin white t-shirt. Slowly my gaze travels upwards as a round of giggles escape my friends. A shiver runs down my spine from a place I can't quite pinpoint. It's always like this with Dean. My body betrays me whenever he's too close.

Dean stares back at me, his bright eyes capturing my attention and pulling me in like they always do. There's something mysterious and beautiful about his eyes, a shade of greenish-blue I've never seen on anyone. Sometimes more of a mint color, sometimes more like turquoise depending on how the light hits them. I can feel my cheeks heating as I realize how much time I've spent thinking about those eyes. I try to force words through my lips. "S-Sorry," I sputter as my eyes impulsively trace the hard lines of his jaw and down the corded muscles in his neck to his broad shoulders. I lick my lips.

"My eyes are up here," Dean says in a deep, but silky, tone. I jerk my face back up to his. The embarrassment of getting caught gawking and the realization of just how close we are hits me all at once and I instinctively jump backwards. My heel catches on the pavement and I start to fall.

The air breezes through the ebony tendrils of my hair as the ground climbs up to meet me as if in slow-motion. Just as I know I'm going to hit the pavement my body jerks to a stop. Electricity zings from the touch of a firm hand on my waist, traveling through every muscle and vein in my body. Within seconds, Dean pulls me back to standing, a knowing smirk spread across his perfect lips.

"You know, if you wanted to be in my arms..." Dean starts, his gaze dipping to where his hand still grasps my waist. *I wonder if he can feel the electricity, too.* "You just have to ask." His words slip through the autumn wind, stirring a feeling in me that no voice ever should.

I push myself free of his arms, putting the distance between us that my mind is begging for. The breeze picks up and I inhale his masculine scent—sage and eucalyptus, blended with subtle notes of mint. I try to ignore it.

"Damnit, Dean," I say, taking another step away from him. "That's not..." I start but can't find the words. Frustration wells in the pit of my stomach. Being too close to him always does this to me. "Why do you always have to be so... so...?" But I'm lost again.

"So... sexy? Charming?" His eyes smolder. *As if my entire body isn't still on fire from the few seconds of contact moments ago.*

I growl in frustration. *What exactly is it about Dean that always has my blood boiling and my tongue tied?* Trying to act quickly to save myself from further embarrassment, I brush my hands across my jeans to get rid of the dirt I'm *not* covered in thanks to Dean, and give him a hard glare before turning and stalking back over to my friends.

"Next time, then?" Dean says with a laugh. I throw another glare at him over my shoulder before linking my arm into Chloe's and moving on. I hear him chuckle under his breath, followed by his retreating footsteps.

Blake whistles low as she falls into step beside Chloe and I. "Damn he's hot," she says, her voice sounding husky and breathless. She stops, turning to watch Dean.

I follow her gaze, watching as he approaches the driver's side of his white pickup truck.

"Dean?" I ask, raking a booted toe into the gravel as I try not to stare too hard at tall, dark, and way-too-sexy. "He seems to think so," I add, more to myself than anything.

Dean's younger brother Eli appears on the other side of the truck with a wave, making his way around to his older brother. "Hey, bro," Eli's voice carries to us across the parking lot. "Thanks for the pick-up."

Chloe nudges me with her elbow and nods in the brother's direction. She leans into me with a sigh, laying her head on my left shoulder. "Eli is like... my weakness."

Blake shoves Chloe, and the two of us shuffle sideways a few steps laughing.

Eli is like an exact copy of his brother, if only just a few years younger and maybe a couple inches shorter. But as tall as Dean is, it doesn't make much of a difference. The two of them easily tower over all the other boys in school.

"I mean, they're both fire," Blake says with a snort before squeezing my arm. "But now we know which one you have the hots for."

I eye her with a sniff. "I do not." It's more to convince myself than her. The truth is I'd always had a strange pull to the man— a tingle that I just can't explain any time I'm within a few feet of him. "He's always given me a dangerous kind of vibe," I say, leaving out the fact that part of his danger is the intense vibrations I get anytime he's close.

"Dangerous, huh?" Blake shoots back with a raised eyebrow and a grin.

"It's too bad they're tigers," Chloe cuts in, her shoulders slumping at the thought. Tigers and wolves mating was considered... less than ideal. Though they're also weres, and strength-for-strength a match to any wolf, tigers are always seen as less than their were-cousins. Which isn't to say tigers never mated with werewolves, they do—and with humans, too—but a tiger-wolf match comes with a heavy dose of condemnation from the pack.

"You can still have fun with them," Blake adds, a mischievous quirk forming on her lips. "I mean, you don't have to *mate* with them." Blake is like that. Flitting from guy to girl and back. Nothing ever too serious, and perfectly cool and confident around all of them. I envy that ability.

"Ari could," Chloe says, giving me another nudge. I open my mouth to argue but she cuts me off. "Tigers get with humans all the time."

"He does seem into you," Blake throws at me, raising her brows.

"He's not," I say, scrunching up my nose. "Flirting is just his default setting."

Chloe crosses her arms, turning her gaze back to the Vargas boys. "Not anymore. At least not for the last month or so."

My brows narrow as I turn to my friend. "Oh really? " I draw out the words. "Are we talking about the same Dean Vargas? So, he's on good behavior for a month, and that's enough time to say he's changed his ways?"

"Well, I did hear he turned down like three girls at Jake's lake house party two weeks ago," Blake pipes in.

"No way. Dean is the type to say 'yes' to all three in a single night," I argue.

"Yep. Everyone's talking about it. Rumor *is* he's found a mate," Blake shrugs as all three of us gaze at the two men. I allow my eyes to drift over Dean's perfect features again, drinking in his blond, short-cropped hair and perfectly chiseled jaw. His shoulders are thick and lined with muscles that make my fingers itch to touch them. *He has a mate?* My stomach rolls at the thought.

I only meant to steal a quick glance at him, but his eyes are now trained on me from across the parking lot. The same prickly, tingling feelings I get from the grit of his voice I'm now getting from the deep blue-green of his eyes. Its hold on me swirls there, within their depths. The piercing sight of them pins me in place as I hold his gaze longer than I should.

Chloe and Blake giggle, shocking me out of my trance and making me jump. Pushing down the feelings he's sparking in me, I turn and pull away toward Blake's car. I glance at him over my shoulder one last time and wonder if he feels the pull, too. A slow grin stretches at the corner of his lips, and his eyes glint with something I can't quite interpret. I swallow the lump in my throat and force my eyes forward, shaking the thought from my mind. He is only staring me down because I got caught checking him out… There's no way he feels the same. Especially if he's found a mate.

That would be stupid.

help beaming, too, and Chloe squeals again before heading back to the dressing room.

Alone now, I lean back against the couch cushions and once again find my head turning wistfully toward the front doors. The shuffle of fabric coming from my friends' dressing rooms as they change does nothing to discourage my mind from drifting back to the freedom beyond those doors. The fresh air is calling to me.

I don't belong here with all these beautiful fabrics, gushing over dresses for a festival I won't be a part of. At least not really. My chest is heavy with the want to join them, to be a part of the pack. One of them.

A group of kids appear beyond the glass, snapping me away from my dispiriting thoughts. The five of them are all laughing, and one of the girls smacks a tall, curly-haired, freckled boy on the shoulder. He's the football player, Chad, from school. Definitely the boy-next-door type. *Cute*, I think to myself—and human, like me.

I pull myself away from regular, normal human Chad and face forward once more, running my empty hand across my face and down my neck to soothe the muscles there. I set down my glass of water on the table to my left with a deep exhale. *Just like regular, normal human Ari.*

"Your turn," Chloe says as the heavy curtain from her dressing room swishes and pulls to one side. She's back in her jeans and pink top, holding the long gown between her arms.

My eyes grow wide and my lips part, preparing to argue as she stops in front of me, pulling my hand and forcing me to stand. "I don't need a dress," I groan. "I will be there in full support of the two of you, but there is absolutely *no* need for me to buy a new dress. I'll just wear something I already have." It's not as if I don't have a couple gowns from past years that should still fit.

Chloe frowns, "But this one is special! We're all finally *sixteen*, Ari."

I narrow my gaze on the blonde. I don't want to burst her bubble and point out that it's only special for her and Blake.

"Oh, don't pout," Blake's voice interjects as she comes to stand in front of the two of us, this time in a flowing blue gown that looks as if she's called the ocean itself to dress her in its soft, satin waves.

I gape in awe at how beautiful she looks. "That's the dress!"

Blake's smile widens as she flips her hair over one shoulder, turning toward the mirror to admire her reflection. The blue princess-style gown, radiant against the chocolate hues of her complexion, makes the gold in her eyes really shine. My smile widens even more.

"Yeah, I think so, too," she replies with a strong nod, "Blue was mom's favorite color." Blake gives a wistful smile to her reflection then turns on a heel, sashaying back into the dressing room to change while Chloe whirls toward the racks. I flop back onto the couch, keeping my mouth shut and hoping that Blake's stunning display has distracted them enough that we can get out of here.

My hope is short-lived however, as Blake appears from behind the dressing room curtain with a narrowed glare and drawn eyebrows aimed straight at me. "Now then. You're getting a dress," she says with daggered eyes and a wicked smile.

"Oh no," I start, waving a dismissive hand and shaking my head. "I really don't see why I need one."

"Here, try this on," Chloe says as she emerges from the racks of glittering materials and throws me a lavender mass of tulle and lace.

My eyes grow two sizes as I catch the fabric between my hands. "Purple? Really?" I say with a frown. "Could you have found something more... *not* purple?"

Blake plops down on the couch next to me as Chloe pulls a hand to her hip. "What's really going on, girl?" Blake asks in her friend-vention tone of voice. "You usually love dressing up for this."

I let the purple gown settle onto my lap and look from one friend to the other, each giving me their version of a 'fuck around and find out' expression. "I'm excited for the both of you, really I am," I start and sigh.

"But..." Chloe adds.

Pursing my lips and taking a second to glance around the shop to make sure we're out of everyone else's earshot, I continue. "But... I'm human."

"And?" Blake asks.

"*And...* you guys are finally going to join the pack, maybe find mates, and live that werewolf life. And I'm going to be like... regular Chad," I shrug.

"Regular Chad?"

"Nothing," I say with a huff and sink back into the couch.

Blake softens next to me, laying her hand on top of mine. "Girl, we're not leaving you behind."

"You're still our bestie, wolf or not," Chloe adds.

I chew my bottom lip knowing they're right—or at least they think so right now—but still not sure how to explain all the different feelings pushing and shoving in my chest. "I've never felt like anything other than a part of the pack before, and now I'm suddenly reminded that I don't belong there. Not really."

Laughing sounds outside behind us, making me shift toward the boutique doors once more. Chad and his group of friends are out there with fresh coffees in hand, all laughing and giggling. My shoulders slump as I eye their perfectly human lives. "But I don't belong with them, either," I whisper, more to myself than anyone else. Chloe sits down on my other side, resting her hand on my shoulder as I turn back to my friends.

Concern miring both their faces makes the guilt rise in my chest. I'm being selfish worrying about myself instead of just being excited for them. I want to—I really, *really* do—but something just keeps nagging at the back of my mind that says my two lifelong friends will move on without me.

"Maybe you should try and make some human friends," Blake blurts out suddenly. My head whips toward her.

"What?!" I shake my head, "No! That's not what I want. I don't want to lose you two, let alone drop you for some humans," I say a bit too loudly, as a passing shop attendant shoots us a curious look.

Blake laughs before explaining in a lowered voice. "No, what I mean is maybe having a human friend or two will help give you a… human-wolf-life balance or something, and make you feel less excluded from either side."

"Oh! That's a good idea!" Chloe starts nodding and fidgeting in her chair.

I snort, shaking my head again, but this time more violently. The idea of pushing myself further away from my friends and into the human world is terrifying. I might not belong to it, but the supernatural world is all I've really known.

"You have this whole other side of yourself you've never acknowledged, or... explored. Maybe you should do some exploring. Try embracing this whole other half of yourself, ya' know?" Blake continues. "Listen, just think about it." Her eyes narrow on me. I deflate and slowly nod my head, biting into my cheek with worry.

Blake smiles then pushes the gown in my lap towards my chest. "Now go try this on," she demands. I roll my eyes, but don't argue as I push myself up from the couch and toward the dressing rooms.

When Chloe adds another gown to my hands from seemingly nowhere, I force down the groan that is nearly out of my throat. "And this one," she says with the sweetest smile. "What? You said less purple and this one is yellow." I sneer at her, which only makes her laugh, and the two girls sit back down on the sofa to wait. My shoulders drop, along with my hopes of getting out of this store without buying a dress.

THREE

The yellow glow of streetlights illuminate the sidewalk in front of me as I make my way through the small, gated neighborhood. A dress wrapped in a long protective bag is slung limply across both my arms. Blake had offered me a ride home from the boutique but I told her I wanted to walk. I needed the fresh autumn air to clear my head and help me figure out all the emotions roiling inside me. Envy of my friends and what they had waiting for them in a few weeks was currently winning over the guilt, sadness, and whatever else was banging around in my chest.

The Lunar Falls neighborhood has always been my home. Picturing the annual decorations for the Moon Awakening that will be going up little by little over the coming weeks is easy—Every year my friends and I get excited as the colorful banners and lights start appearing, hanging from streetlight to streetlight. Houses decked out in a way that puts most neighborhoods'

Christmas decorating to shame. It's not that different from traditional Halloween decor really, but Lunar Falls takes it to a whole new level. And then there's the festival itself. I smile at the memories of Blake, Chloe, and I watching our friends and neighbors dress up in the traditional festival garb, wearing decorated masks, and being presented at the stroke of midnight.

Afterwards, the men go off into the woods to hunt down and kill their first vampire, triggering the werewolf gene and sending them into their first Shifting. The girls don't shift. There are a few theories as to why—some claim it's something to do with the chromosomal differences, others with a bit of a misogynist streak just think it's a matter of strength that makes shifting deadly for females. No one really knows what the actual reason is, but everyone agrees it's fatal.

Then over the next few days, Blake, Chloe, and I always make bets as to which members will find their true mates right away, waiting with bated breath to find out which of us are right. We couldn't wait until it was our turn. It had never fully occurred to me that I wouldn't get that turn—That, when I turned sixteen, I would only be watching my girls, not presenting with them.

The well-lit front porches of each house I pass are as familiar as the streets to me, having walked them a thousand times before. The wind blows, raising goosebumps across my skin, and I wonder if it's really from the wind or this sudden feeling of not belonging. I'm not a part of the pack. Not really. I live here, and was raised here with the pack, but at the end of the day, I'm the adopted human.

It shouldn't bother me so much. It's not as if being a human is so much different than being a female werewolf. They can't shift any more than I can after all. But it nags at me nonetheless. They will ascend as full members of the pack, find mates, and be privy to pack information that I never will. They'll get to *fully* join that family in every respect while I'll always be on the periphery. A 'family member' in name only.

Humans aren't supposed to know of the supernatural world. There are always exceptions like myself, of course, or those few humans who marry into that world. Most of those relationships don't end well, though. Secrets will inevitably develop between those partners, just like they will between my friends and I. Ones that pack law won't allow them to share with me no matter how much they want to. Because in the end, I'm *not* a werewolf. Even human pack wives are more a part of the pack than I am.

Ahead of me looms my home—the house I've spent my entire life in and never once felt different or out of place. Is it because this is the month of the Moon Awakening that we've been waiting for since we were little girls that I'm suddenly feeling different? The truth is, I've felt out of sorts the last *few* months. Like something is stirring just beneath the surface of my skin. Chloe and Blake turned sixteen over the past summer and neither said anything about feeling differently or like they were changing somehow, aside from finally being old enough to participate this Halloween. I won't even turn sixteen until then, but I feel like something's different already.

I sigh at the thought as I make my way up the driveway. Dean's truck is parked in front of the neighbor's house, and he's busy hauling two boxes stacked one on top of the other toward the front door. The muscles in his arms stretch taut, giving me a clear idea of just how strong he is. I stumble forward, nearly falling but getting my feet back underneath me before the dress and myself spill all over the driveway. He disappears inside the house a few seconds later.

Regaining my composure, I turn toward my porch, keeping my eyes in front of me and hoping I haven't been spotted. I take one step forward and immediately catch the hem of the garment bag protecting my dress, tripping the way I had just narrowly avoided moments before. The soft laugh from the next yard over tells me my slip-up hasn't gone unnoticed.

Quickly, I right myself and set my shoulders. With my head lowered, I chance a look in his direction, and find him staring at me. "Hey," I manage, pushing some flyaway hairs out of my face. He takes a step toward me and I have to fight the urge to move closer to him, as if his very presence calls to me.

"That your dress for Halloween?" He tilts his head gesturing at my arms.

"Huh?" I look down like I don't know what I'm holding. "Oh, right, yeah." Turning my body so I'm fully facing him, I hope my cheeks aren't as flushed as they feel. "Blake and Chloe, you know. They wouldn't settle for less." I half shrug, eyeing the sweat slowly rolling down his neck before disappearing below his shirt. With what I hope is a silent clearing of my throat I add, "They wouldn't let me leave without one, even though I'm not presenting."

His lips tilt up into a smirk that promises to make me flustered. *He's good at that.* "I already appreciate their effort." The tone of his voice is like honey, making my stomach flutter with a field of butterflies.

His eyes rake over the length of my body as he takes another step closer and I shiver, a thrill speeding along my spine. "I'm sure you'll be the most beautiful one there." The upward curve of his mouth never lessens, as his eyes darken with what I think is want, mirroring what I'm sure he can see in mine. *Nope, I need to stay away from that.*

"I—um, thank you?" I hate that with a few unsubtle words I'm left floundering, but part of me also wishes he meant them. I know better, though. Dean Vargas is a fuck boy through and through, the kind that leaves a trail of broken hearts in his wake once he gets what he wants from them. And despite the rumors that he's stopped all that, I don't want to be the guinea pig to find out if they're right. "So, what's with the boxes?"

His smirk drops to an amused smile and he shakes his head with a snort at my clumsy change of subject. "Smooth." Before I can prepare myself, he closes the distance between us, making my breath hitch in my throat. "I'm moving in next door," he says with a nod toward the house now behind him.

"Into Mrs. Station's old place?" I ask, huffing the words out in a rush. *I need to calm down.* It makes sense, she's long since passed and that's the way things work in Lunar Falls. The pack stays with the pack. Tigers aren't exactly a part of the pack—obviously not the way wolves are—but they still answer to the pack. This is wolves' territory, and Djinn law—the law that governs the supernatural world—states all shifters have to associate with a pack. It makes it easier to keep track of them all, I assume.

But does he have to associate right next door? I glance at the sky for a second then back to him. I really can't keep any distance between us. I swallow, fighting to slow my racing heart beat. "It's been empty for a while," I say, focusing on the topic at hand and not losing myself in the intoxicating scent of him.

"Yeah, but it's all cleaned up now. I've done a bit of work to it already."

I nod toward the traditional-style house behind him. The lights are on and I wonder why I didn't notice that earlier. On the second level one of the windows is lit up as well. The one directly across from my bedroom window. A tingle spiderwebs down my spine at the thought of that room being his. "You should come check it out sometime," he says, snapping my attention back to him.

"I… uh… maybe." I shift my stance to the other leg. Curiosity nags at me, wondering what kind of work he's talking about, while big, bright red letters of warning flash in my mind. I glance at that window once more and swallow. The idea of him sleeping so close has my heart racing and my brain panicking all at the same time. *It doesn't matter*, I try to remind myself. Next door or a thousand miles away it doesn't make a difference. He is not the guy for me. Fuck boy or mated either way. Off limits is what he is. I shift a step toward my house putting some more distance between us.

"I should…"

"Do you…?" Dean and I start to talk over each other, and we both stop with a laugh. "You first," he says, motioning toward me. I shake my head just as a noise catches our attention.

We both turn toward my house just as my mom mercifully appears from behind the front door. "Hey, honey, you're finally home," she calls to me. I take the last few steps to the porch, her welcoming smile settling my frayed nerves.

"Yep," I say with a small wave behind me to Dean.

Mom smiles, then looks over me to where our new neighbor is standing at the edge of our lawn. "Are you moving in next door, dear?" she asks just as I make it beside her.

"Yes, ma'am," he replies, stuffing his hands into his pockets in a casual manner.

"Oh, how nice, I'd heard Jon had let you rent a house." She smiles sweetly at him and I fight the urge to roll my eyes. "You're still working up there at The Brew'?"

I shuffle from foot to foot, mentally willing my mom to end this conversation as I glare at the side of her head. My cheeks are on fire with embarrassment from being caught talking to Dean. My mom would encourage it. She likes Dean and his brother Eli. Always telling me what a cute couple the two of us would make. I don't want to give her the impression that that's even a possibility.

"Yeah," he says, running his right hand across the back of his neck, "I had tonight, off though." I could have sworn his eyes shifted to me with the last bit. *Does he want me to know he's free tonight?*

"I'm so happy for you, dear. You make sure to let me know if there's anything you need for your new place now, okay?"

"Of course, ma'am, thank you."

Seeing my moment, I grab my mom's arm and practically drag her inside. A low chuckle sounds behind us, but I ignore it, shutting the door with a deep exhale of relief.

Four

My back presses against the front door as relief washes over me. Having barely escaped without embarrassing myself further, I close my eyes for a moment and savor the feeling.

"I always liked that boy," my mom says, padding her way into the warmth of our living room. I push off from the door, following after her as she turns toward the kitchen. "You should ask him to the Awakening."

"Mom..." I groan out the words. Draping my dress on the back of a chair, I sit myself at the kitchen island that dominates the space. Mom stands on the other side, placing a kettle onto the flat stovetop. Her medium-length, blonde hair brushes the tips of her shoulders with the movement. "I keep telling you there's nothing there."

"So you say," she says, eyeing me with her chocolate-brown eyes. She's a petite—yet curvy—woman, with a look to her eyes that lets you know not to mess with her, despite her small frame. The same look she's pinning me with at this moment. "I can smell it, the two of you," she says, tapping her nose. Mom's intuition is nothing to joke about. Trust me. I always believed that if she hadn't been born a werewolf she'd have for sure been a Djinn instead. She just has a way of knowing things somehow. I can't help shaking my head. Intuition or not, she's wrong about this one. "The two of you would make such a cute couple," she finishes, turning back to the steaming kettle on the stove top.

I tilt my head, pinching my lips together. This isn't the first time I've heard this argument from her. "I don't need a date. I don't really even want to go to this thing."

My mom freezes, her eyes snapping back around to meet mine, burning a hole straight through me. "You have to go," she says, pulling her hands to her hips. Worry deepens the subtle lines already creasing her forehead. "You're turning sixteen."

I throw my head back in a mock whine. "Ugh, I know. It's just..." I start, before realizing I'm not up for a conversation about what's really eating me up with my mom just yet. I switch gears, "Blake and Chloe won't let me skip it anyway." I sit back straight as the kettle starts to whistle.

With furrowed eyebrows, Mom removes the kettle and pours us both steaming hot cups of water before adding her fragrant tea. "Good," she says with a firm nod of her head. "You always loved going before, and besides, your brother is presenting this year." *I hadn't even thought about my brother...* The guilty feelings are welling back up again to fight with the feelings of not belonging. She passes a mug across the wooden counter to me. I frown at her, my shoulders slumping. "Oh, honey, I know it's not the same for you like it is for your friends, but it'll be special all the same."

I shake my head, gazing into the contents of the steaming mug warming my hands. The bright, overhead light casts my shadow the length of the island. "I don't know about that," I sigh.

"The Moon-Kissed Awakening is always magical... and this year even more so with the full moon landing on Halloween night! Your birthday!" Mom says over the lip of her mug. She sighs, and makes her way around the island and takes the seat next to mine. "I understand how you must be feeling, though," she says quietly, placing her hand on my shoulder and giving a gentle squeeze.

I turn in my chair, meeting her tender gaze. The skin around the corners of her eyes crinkles with age. The look she's giving me makes my chest hurt even more than it already does, feeling like it might burst with all the mixed feelings that I've gone through over the past few weeks. I'm suddenly an outsider in a way I have never really felt before, even here with my close family. And at the same time, I also feel like I'm dismissing how much this means to my friends. Hell, I even forgot this is my brother's big year, too. But I can't shake the idea that I am no longer Ari, but the 'Adopted Human.' I open my mouth to say something and quickly shut it again, not knowing how to explain the hole slowly being gnawed open inside me. "I know..." Mom says, giving my shoulder another pat. "I know."

The sound of the front door opening and quickly shutting makes me look up, stealing my attention away from the conversation. "Hey, Mom," my brother says as he appears shortly after in the entryway to the kitchen. In a few short steps of his long legs he closes the distance to us, pecking mom on the cheek.

"Oh, hey, honey," she says as her hand leaves my back to hug my younger brother before he moves away to dig in the fridge. Koa takes after our dad more than Mom, with his shaggy brown hair, and tall, lean frame. But those brown eyes and freckles are all Mom. A second later he straightens with a soda in hand. "Your laundry is folded in the basket on your bed for you, dear," Mom says in her soothing motherly tone.

"Thanks, Mom," he says as he cracks the can open and takes a long sip. "Is that your dress for the festival?" he asks, tilting his soda in my direction. I nod. "I can't wait. It's gonna' be epic when I bag the first vamp." My brother wiggles his dark eyebrows, and I can't help but laugh at his cockiness. My brother and I are only a few months apart in age. *I need to be there to support him, too.*

Having watched the ceremony every year since I was a child I know the first transition is the worst. You can hear it: the cracking of bones, tearing of flesh, the howling of those going through it. The sounds will haunt you for the rest of your life, but at least they say it only hurts the first time. With the change, thankfully comes the ability to heal quickly. Afterwards, the 'graduates' are different—their childlike features firm up, muscling over as if they had been injected with some superhuman enhancement.

The image of Dean's fully muscled body flashes through my mind. His Weretiger gene was triggered three years ago. I was there at the ceremony. He went from being hot to godlike in the span of a day. My thighs ache just thinking about it and I quickly shake the thought from my mind.

"Yeah, good luck with that," I reply, starting to stand from my chair. I do my best to keep the images in my mind from showing on my face. "On that note, I think I'm going to head up to bed." I say before taking one last sip of my tea.

"But you haven't had dinner yet!" Mom protests.

I shake my head and set my empty cup on the counter. "I got dinner with the girls after dress shopping." Mom eyes me for a second like she doesn't believe me. Almost in answer to her stare my stomach growls, betraying me. I pretend not to hear it. I'm not in the mood to eat despite what my stomach has to say about it. The two of us have a silent staring contest before Mom finally shrugs with a heavy sigh.

"If you change your mind, there are leftovers in the fridge," she says, apparently deciding not to argue with me.

"Well, I'm starving," my brother interjects, yanking open the fridge.

Mom smiles gently at his back before turning it on me, and my whole body relaxes. All it takes is a smile from her to completely disarm me. "Goodnight, Mom." I kiss her on the cheek and then grab my dress from the chairback before heading toward the entry. "Goodnight, Koa." I give my brother a playful shove on the shoulder as I move past.

"More for me," Koa throws at me.

I roll my eyes at him and make a beeline for the stairs.

Taking two at a time, I reach the landing and turn left. Mine and Koa's bedrooms are directly across from each other. A Jack-and-Jill bathroom separating the two. Shutting the door behind me, I deposit my gown in the small walk-in closet and then turn to the full canopy bed taking up most of the space in my room. I plop down onto the down comforter with a heavy sigh.

The day's events play through my mind like a mini movie. *Maybe I'm freaking out over nothing*, I tell myself. So what if my friends are joining the pack... and my brother, too. Nothing's gonna change, not really. Right?

The sound of a door opening and shutting down the hall signals that Koa has made it to his room, no doubt intending on spending the rest of the night on his Xbox. We won't be seeing him until tomorrow.

Deciding a good book is what I need to get my mind off everything, I stand and make my way to the bookshelves flanking either side of the window seat that lines one of my walls. A light outside catches my attention and I lean into the cushions underneath the windowsill. That upstairs window I noticed before is illuminated again, and with no curtains, I can see directly inside to what looks like a bedroom. Dean stands directly in the middle of the room, pulling a shirt over his head.

My pulse picks up and I bite my bottom lip. I should look away—that would be the polite thing to do—but I can't force my gaze away. That is, until Dean turns directly toward me. He's discarded his shirt to the floor, and now the only thing he's wearing above the waist is a smirk spread across his lips.

I slap a hand to my face and jump behind one of the bookshelves, pushing myself as far back as I can. "Stupid, stupid, stupid," I say in a rushed whisper to myself when a muffled sound catches my attention. I peek around the corner to see Dean leaning out of his open window.

It's *way* too late to turn off my light and pretend I was asleep.

I chew my bottom lip for a moment and then, finally relenting, I open my window. "What?" I ask, trying my best to be quiet while also being loud enough for him to hear me across the way.

"Like whatcha see?" Dean calls back as he leans casually against the side of his window frame.

"Cocky much?"

"You were the one creepin'."

I snort, settling myself down onto the cushions in front of me and crossing my arms against my chest. "I just wasn't expecting to see you outside my window, that's all."

Dean laughs, throwing his head back with the action. The sound is beautiful and the motion transforms his whole face in a way I know will star in my dreams tonight. "You know if you want the full show all you gotta do is knock."

I roll my eyes, feigning indifference. "I'll pass thanks."

"You sure?" he asks with a lifted brow as he pushes off the window, straightening. I chew my lower lip just as he grabs the waistband of his sweats and tugs them down on one side just enough to show the line of his 'V'. My mouth drops open, my throat suddenly going dry. Not that I can see anything with his window seal in the way, but damn can I imagine. I yank my eyes closed, pulling both hands in front of my face. I should say something… but I can't seem to find any words. His echoing laughter has my cheeks on fire. "Sweet dreams, Ari," he calls out, laughing once more before a familiar click sounds and I know he's shut his window. I peek between my fingers to see that he has indeed left the window. Turning back to my room, my shoulders finally relaxing, I let a huff of air escape through my lips. I'm suddenly very sure I do not like the idea of Dean living next door.

FIVE

A sculpted werewolf and vampire figurine perch on Mrs. Hannely's desk—décor for the coming holiday, though I doubt she really knows the significance of them. I toy with one of the ears of the wolf while pretending to listen to my teacher.

"These run-on sentences keep popping up in your papers, Ari."

I nod, only half-listening. The vampire statuette is cliché and styled after Dracula. I want to tell her that real vampires don't look like that. They're basically blood junkies, so consumed with the need to feed that any bit of humanity is lost to them. Real vampires look more like the zombies you see in movies, with shredded clothing and ghost-white skin caked in dried blood and dirt. And they're fast—lightning fast.

Werewolves don't look like her little ornament either, for that matter. They just look like regular wolves, except... bigger. *Dire wolves then?* I snort under my breath. Mrs. Hannely doesn't miss my reaction to the thought, judging from the foreboding look that now thins her lips.

"I'm going to stop marking them for you and just take points off your grade from now on," Mrs. Hannely says, holding out a paper with a big red 'D' written across the top. I frown at the letter. Mom is *not* going to be happy. English has always been my worst subject—there're just so many rules that don't make sense to me. My frown cuts harder into my face. I don't bother to ask her to explain run-on sentences again. She never does.

"Sorry," I say, taking the paper and shoving it into one of the notebooks tucked between my arms. "I'll try to remember."

Mrs. Hannely swishes a hand toward the classroom door, giving me the go-ahead to leave, and I don't waste any time. Noise breaks around me as soon as I'm through the door, the hallways teeming with students. Compared to the quietness of the classroom, the hallways outside are pure chaos.

I reach the long row of silver lockers with mine at the very end, which is—thankfully—on the top row. I quickly spin my combination on the lock, and open the door, shoving my English notebooks inside and exchanging them for my next class's set.

"Ari!" An excited squeal erupts behind me. I turn to find Chloe's excited blue eyes alight and her blonde curls bouncing as she rushes across the hall toward me. "Did you see this?" she asks, holding up her phone.

I glance at the screen and then back to her, raising an eyebrow in confusion. "It's a snap invite to a party…?"

"Yes!" she cheers, pulling me away from the lockers and down the hall. "We should go."

Conversations soar around us as we weave through huddled groups of people toward the lunch hall. My stomach growls in anticipation. "Why?" I ask, glancing sideways at her. "We never go to those."

Chloe squeezes my arm and releases a frustrated huff of breath. "Because... there will be..." She pauses, glancing around before lowering her voice. "Humans there."

I snort at the obviousness of her statement. "And that's why we don't go to those," I say, enunciating each word as I eye her with a pointed stare.

Chloe juts out a hip, tilting her head. "But *you* should." She lets her statement hang in the air before turning toward the lunch line. We run through quickly, piling our trays with mashed potatoes, gravy, and Salisbury Steak that probably came from a box.

"Like we talked about the other day, you should hang out with..." She pauses again, waving a hand through the air to gesture at all the people around us. "Other people."

I frown, picking up a juice and handing the lady at the register my lunch card. Chloe does the same as we turn away toward the tables. "You know, people who have a... similar background," she says, nudging me in the shoulder.

"I don't know." I shake my head at the thought as we weave in between a row of tables. "I don't think jumping straight into a party is exactly what Blake meant." I have thought a lot about our conversation the other night, and while I don't think it's a terrible idea I'm also not sure I'm on board, either. I don't want new friends, but maybe I do need to find some balance with my human side. Maybe hanging out with them would help me be more okay with that part of myself… maybe. But would I even really be able to fit in with humans, knowing everything I know about the supernatural?

"Oh, come on!" Chloe gives me the 'puppy dog eyes' as we approach our usual table, where Blake is already seated. I hate when she gives me those eyes—it's impossible to resist when she pulls that card. I follow begrudgingly behind Chloe and sit down next to her, across from Blake. "I think it's the perfect place to see what the other side is like. Maybe make some human friends?" she finishes.

My frown deepens as I debate the idea. I've never been the 'party girl.' But Chloe has a point, some more human interaction might be nice. Especially with everything I have been feeling lately.

"Are you guys talking about that party?" Blake interjects, and I nod.

"Chloe, here, thinks I should go."

"But we never go to those things," Blake says, waving an apple in the air with a look of complete confusion.

I gesture toward her in agreement, adjusting the tray in front of me with my other hand. "That's what I said."

Chloe huffs, eyeing the two of us. "Listen, some new friends…" she draws out the 's' on the last word long and dramatically, making me snort. "…might help you feel a little less… excluded with everything going on. Maybe it will help you… bridge the two worlds you're standing in."

"You *were* saying that maybe you needed to find where you fit in with all of this. Hanging out with some, umm… typical… teens might help," Blake adds with a shrug of her shoulders.

Traitor.

Chloe jumps on the comment, pointing at her while glaring at me. "See! So, you should go."

My whole body slumps as I take another bite of mashed potatoes, mulling through the idea once more. "Fine. We can go," I finally give in. Silence follows my words, making the hair stand on the back of my neck as I realize I'm missing something. "What?" I ask the two of them, looking from one to the other.

Blake lets out a slow exhale, waving her hand to the side. "Maybe you should go… ya' know… alone."

"What?" My eyes bulge and my mouth gapes wide open. "I'm not going into that den of 'people' without you two."

"Yeah, but… you need to do this without us," Chloe says, the extra gentle tone of her voice only serving to deepen my scowl.

"Hear us out," Blake follows, putting up both hands. "You need to find where you fit, and you can't see the other side if we're there."

I shake my head. "No, that's not what I agreed to. I don't want to leave the pack," I say as my stomach jumps into my throat. "You two are my ride-or-dies."

"And we always will be. We know you fit with us, but you need to feel it, too. Maybe having some balance outside the pack will help with that."

"No," I say, putting my foot down. "I'm not going by myself." I fold my arms across my chest and lean back against the chair. I am not going to budge on this. Trying to make some human friends has crossed my mind, but I did not plan on being thrown into a totally new situation without the support of my best friends—that was never a part of the deal. They are coming, end of story.

After a few minutes of the three of us staring each other down, Blake and Chloe finally relent. I see it the moment the decision is made, as both my friends' shoulders deflate at the same time. I smile at the two of them, picking up my fork to dig into the mashed potatoes on my plate.

"So, what kind of party is it anyway?" I ask, shoveling in another fork-full.

Blake shrugs. "It's a costume party," she says with a sigh, waving her fork in front of her. "This close to Halloween what else would they do?"

Chloe giggles. "Humans are so original."

I snort, shaking my head. We've never been to a costume party, not since we were kids—I guess they just aren't popular with the supernatural world, or at least not with the Lunar Falls wolves. I mean sure, we got the chance to do the trick-or-treating thing when we were really little and timing allowed, but Halloween for us has always been about the Moon Awakening. You don't dress up as characters for that, it's a formal affair. A way of celebrating the Moon goddess and the new generation of wolves.

"What do you wanna dress up as?" Blake asks, and I lift my shoulders.

"I have no idea!"

Chloe falls into a fit of giggles suddenly. Blake and I watch her with raised brows, not catching the joke until she chokes out, "Werewolves!" And I start laughing alongside her until my sides hurt.

Six

I decided on jeans and a band tee for tonight's party. Cute, but basic—which is exactly what I want. The plan was to blend in and wear a costume, but I hadn't been able to run to a costume store after school. Mom had texted about wanting me to come straight home and help prepare some of the Moon Awakening decorations. Honestly, just going to this thing has my stomach knotted in every direction, and I can't make sense of where those knots start or end.

"I'm still not sure I even want to go," I say with a hand on my hip as I watch Chloe shuffle through the rows of clothes in Blake's massive walk-in closet.

"Well, I can't go anyway," Blake grumbles, plopping herself down on a huge fur ottoman in the corner of the room. "Alpha meetings suck." She rolls her eyes. "Daddy's been a hard-ass lately… I mean he always gets in a mood around this time of year 'cause of Mom, but… now that I'm presenting this year, it's all 'you're the pack princess.' on top of that." Blake's face pinches as she mimics her fathers deep tone.

Chloe whips around still holding a dress up to herself, her eyes growing three sizes. "He's not gonna 'negotiate' you to another pack, is he?"

"No… Goddess no," Blake rushes the words out, holding her hands up in front of her in surrender. "No, Daddy would never *force* me into a marriage. He just wants me prepared in case I find my mate, which he says will definitely be an Alpha. Though he's forcing the issue a bit…" She trails off, saying the last almost to herself. Blake picks at a stray strand on her frayed jeans. "Alpha blood runs too deep in these veins for you to pair with anything less,'" she says, again imitating her father.

I laugh at her mock impression. She's not far off the mark. Her father is a proud Alpha and, being the daughter of one, she would need to marry another Alpha. The pack would be disappointed with anything less. Marriages amongst the different packs are still widely used to create and reassert alliances, and to keep the bloodlines strong.

"Regardless, you two are going without me."

"So, does that mean we don't have to go?" I ask hopefully. Chloe shoves my shoulder in response. "Ugh… this sucks."

"Trust me, I would much rather get lit with some humans than sit through one of Daddy's Alpha meetings," Blake says with a pout. Then, shaking her head, she stands again and starts rummaging through her clothes. "That doesn't mean I can't help the two of you look hot A.F. *Annnnd* I was able to snag some wolf ears and a tail for you guys!" Blake yanks down a box from the top of her closet and pulls out two sets of wolf ears and tails. One is dark gray and the other white. I shake my head and laugh.

"Of course, you did," I say, taking the dark-gray set. Chloe snags the other. "Your dad's been dragging you to a lot of these meetings lately, huh?" I say, trying to keep my voice even. Things would already be different with Blake and Chloe fully joining the pack, but if Blake had to marry off into another pack, too…. They'd be drifting away even more.

Blake huffs and turns back to the clothes in front of her. "I'll never be an Alpha obviously, but I'm supposed to marry one, so Daddy thinks it's important for me to know the ropes." She pauses and I bite my lip. "He's invited all the eligible Alphas or soon-to-be Alphas to the Moon Awakening this year."

Chloe and I both turn at her words. "He's never invited other weres from outside packs before! The Moon Awakening is sacred!"

"Yeah, but since I'm presenting he says I won't meet my mate otherwise."

"Right," I say with a slow nod. "Because you have to marry an Alpha."

Blake nods. "He won't force the issue, but…" her words trails off.

"But he plans on throwing you in the path of every available male with Alpha blood he can, hoping someone will trigger the mating bond." Chloe says with a sad note to her tone. My frown deepens. In that way I guess I'm glad I'm not a werewolf. Women are still not quite equals in the pack, and oftentimes used as bartering chips. Like Blake's father, most

Alphas won't force their daughters or sisters into such an arrangement, but 'encouragement' is widely practiced.

"That's shit," I say, giving Blake a sympathetic look. She shrugs. "Won't work."

Chloe giggles at the certainty in Blake's tone. My lips tug at the edges, too. "I think it's romantic," Chloe sighs. "I hope I find my mate."

Blake and I both roll our eyes. Chloe is a hopeless romantic. Her parents, like mine do, had that storybook romance where they still hold hands and cuddle in the kitchen over a pot of dinner. Chloe's dad died a few years back in a vampire attack—the same one that got Blake's mom. She doesn't really talk about it, though, not that I can blame her. But she never shows the pain of it. She's always somehow focused more on the memory of her parents' happy marriage than its tragic end. I've always envied that positive demeanor of hers.

"That romantic heart of yours will no doubt find a mate immediately," Blake says to Chloe, who sighs wistfully before turning back to the mirror. Her bouncy demeanor returned. "So, Ari... you ready to see how the humans do it?"

"Yes... No... I don't even know any more." I stumble on every word as nausea rises in the back of my throat. I leave the closet, dragging my feet. "I feel like my life has become the *Jungle Book*," I say, throwing myself onto the bed. I grab one of the pink throw-pillows and hug it close to my chest.

"What? No, that's not true," Blake argues, still rummaging through her closet. She pulls out some dresses and hands one to Chloe, who holds the item to herself, shifting in the mirror from side to side.

"How's that?" Chloe asks, glancing at me before she hands the dress back to Blake with a shake of her head.

"Yes, it is. I'm the human—what was his name?"

"Ooooh, Mowgli!" Chloe says, holding yet another top in front of herself in the mirror.

"Yeah, him… he was adopted and raised by wolves." I pause thoughtfully, pulling my eyes to the ceiling and connecting the dots in my mind. "No one knows about the parents, right? They're not a part of the story apparently."

"Well, okay, yeah… but…" Blake says, her words followed by soft footsteps across the plush carpet floor. I turn my face to the side to give her a look of skepticism. Her shoulders slump as she tosses some clothes onto the far side of her massive bed then sits down next to me. "I still don't see how that makes you Mowgli. So, you have one *tiny* detail in common…"

I flatten my lips and sit up, staring her down head-on. "And now the wolves," I give my two best friends a hard glare before continuing, "are telling me to go find the humans."

"Girl, it's not like that and you know it," Blake says, twisting her lips into a scowl.

I roll my eyes, pulling the pillow back into my lap. "I rest my case."

"Oh, oh, oh! And now you have a tiger stalking you," Chloe squeals from the closet. I whip my attention over to her, my mouth gaping. "I heard Dean invited you to his new place!"

Blake's eyebrows disappear behind her dark bangs. "A tiger who wants you for your *fire*," she snickers.

"Ugh, no way," I huff, scrunching my face in response. "He's not stalking me," I say, throwing my hands up and then letting them fall onto the pillow in my lap. "He's just… playing with me like he does all the girls."

"I don't know, I think he seems pretty into you." Chloe grabs one of the dresses Blake has laid on the bed and takes it to the mirror. "Can I wear this one?" she asks hopefully, turning to Blake.

"Girl, you know you don't gotta ask—take it," Blake answers, waving a hand at Chloe who squeals between her teeth as she stares into the mirror.

"It doesn't even matter," I say, staring down at my hands. "I'm not into him."

"Yeah, okay…" Blake chuffs, shoving me in the shoulder. I fall into the pillows with a laugh. "You sooo think he's hot."

"Uh, have you seen him?" I ask, throwing a pillow at her. "I don't think there's a creature on this planet that wouldn't think he's hot."

Blake catches the pillow effortlessly. "Well… you're not wrong."

I shake my head, grabbing another pillow, then putting it in front of my face and groaning into it before bringing it back down to my lap again. "Maybe the humans won't be so bad… like in the *Jungle Book.*"

"Exactly! This party is just the thing you need," Chloe exclaims before making her way over to the bed, joining Blake and I.

"So much," Blake echoes her thoughts.

"I hope so," I sigh, pushing myself further up in the bed to make room. "We've never been to a full-on human party… with humans." I sigh again, my shoulders slumping as another thought crosses my mind, "What if I *do* like them, and fit in well, and..."

Silence stretches through the room at my words, the air heavy with the weight of them. I can almost see the internal battle raging within my friends. Part of them has to have considered the possibility—and what it might mean.

"Then there will be more people to love you," Chloe states finally, still holding onto the dress Blake is lending her. "And who knows... maybe you'll find your own true mate."

The skepticism washing across my face has to be obvious. "I doubt that," I frown at her, shifting uncomfortably with the thought. "Besides, I'm not looking for love. It's about finding myself. All of myself."

"Just saying—Dean hasn't found his forever love yet," Blake says, wiggling her eyebrows.

I snort at her, and just like that the mood has shifted again. "Because he 'loves' all the girls. Like, every single one. And besides, he won't be there anyway."

"Well, when you look like that can you blame him?" Blake deadpans.

Chloe scrunches up the dress in her hands, holding it to her chest. "That tiger could ravage me anytime," she says wistfully.

"Don't you mean his little brother?" Blake purses her lips in a teasing manner. Chloe throws the piece of clothing at her.

"Who do you think I meant?" she says, starting another fit of giggles. Blake and I follow, laughing alongside her, filling the room and my insides with giddy excitement. As nervous as I am, having my bestie there, I know I'll be fine.

"Wait, I thought you said Dean had found his mate?" I ask suddenly once we all calm down.

Blake shrugs. "Who knows. Some people seem to think so."

"I think he's just found you and decided he doesn't need any other girls," Chloe adds, standing again as she heads back to the closet.

I snort. "He's not into me. He's *always* flirted with me, but he never means anything by it." I don't get into the weird pull I've always had to him. The desperate want to wrap myself in his arms, his scent. Just standing near him makes my skin prickle. But that is exactly why I never let things get past casual flirting. He is dangerous… and sexy… and one hundred percent not for me.

I have no doubt he hasn't given up his fuck boy ways. Maybe he's just being more discreet about them? After all, he is a full member of the pack now. He'd be expected to find a mate soon. His playboy ways won't fly with the Alpha for long, not now that he's past eighteen.

A dress lands in my lap, pulling my attention back to my friends. Chloe smiles and points to the garment in my lap. "That's what you're wearing tonight." I frown and hold up the little black piece of fabric as my head bobs from side to side. Chloe is having none of it as she hands me a pair of matching heels with pursed lips. "Yes."

Blake snickers next to me but is nodding her head in agreement. "The two of you are going to be the death of me," I say, standing. With a sigh I hold my head up straight and begin to change. I'm not the type to wear such a short dress, but if I'm going into the humans' den I should do it looking snatched. Period.

Seven

The pale glow from the nearly-full moon illuminates the freshly manicured lawn Chloe and I stand on the edge of. Towering above us is a large house, Tudor style—exactly the type of lavish home you would imagine the kids of Silas Creek High would grow up in.

My throat feels thick, and my stomach is a jumbled mess of buzzing bees. I am seriously reconsidering this super tight dress. Music blares from behind the large double-doored entrance like it's a warning on its own. I hold onto Chloe's arm, my grip tight, as I try to mentally prepare myself for whatever lays behind them.

"I don't think we need to do this," I say to Chloe, turning slightly toward her without letting her go. "We could totally turn around and have a sleepover at my house." She smiles warmly back at me. Everything is written in that smile. Encouragement, understanding, and maybe a little bit of fear herself. Neither of us ever hang out with humans.

"Come on," Chloe says, sounding more confident than I feel, giving my arm a slight squeeze. "It'll be fun. You'll see."

I take in as large of a breath as my body will allow. In unison, Chloe does the same, and together we start forward. "Do we knock?" I ask, glancing at her for guidance I know she doesn't have as we approach the doors.

Her eyes are large and round as she gazes back at me, and then with a shrug she raps her fist against the wood. The door swings wide and a girl peeks around the frame, music tumbling out to us from inside. Her smile slowly drops.

"Oh my god! I know you two!" the girl exclaims, her way-too-chipper voice matching the way-too-bright pink of her hair. She is dressed as a Barbie doll and fits the part perfectly.

"We go to the same school," I say, before immediately hoping it didn't sound as sarcastic as I think it might have. Mentally I chastise myself for starting off so spectacularly.

"Right, yeah… Party's this way," she says, jacking a thumb over her shoulder. Chloe starts forward and I follow.

"I'm Missy," the Barbie girl says as she walks up beside me, taking my free arm, and guiding us further into the house. "You guys hang out with the Lunar Falls crowd, right?"

Missy takes us directly through the house to the other side and out onto the back patio, where a large swimming pool is lit up with multicolored glowing lanterns. "I guess so, yeah…" I answer, just as she finds what is apparently our spot. Letting me go, she seats herself on a cushioned patio chair. Chloe takes the other as I stand there for a second, wringing my hands, before finally taking the third.

"I just mean that everyone from there always hangs out with

each other. You guys have your own little Lunar Falls clique."
She casually laughs, but it sounds forced. Then, spotting someone across the patio, Missy waves, "Hey, Jess, over here!"

I follow her gaze to the girl Jess, who waves back before
heading straight toward us. Another girl I recognize from school
but have never really gotten to know. She has jet-black hair cut
into a bob. On the shorter side, but in a cute way. She's always
seemed nice. Tonight she is dressed as a ninja girl in dark blue—a
sexy ninja, of course.

"We don't normally get people from your side of town at our
parties," Missy continues, turning back to us.

"Uh, yeah, I guess," I respond nervously, not sure where
to take the conversation or any words other than 'yeah' and
'I guess,' apparently. Chloe and I know what she's talking
about when she mentions the Lunar Falls crowd: the pack. The
humans might not know about the supernatural world, but they
definitely know about social dynamics. Maybe they do have
some sense that we're different. Maybe it's a prey, predator-thing
they feel but can't quite put their finger on. I'm not sure, but
either way: the pack doesn't chill with humans, and humans
stay away from the pack.

"Well, we figured we'd break from tradition and come see
how the other side parties," Chloe replies quickly, picking up my
slack. I have no idea how to respond to Missy's comment, but
Chloe's save has me exhaling with relief. "Where's the drinks?"

"In the kitchen, obvi'," the girl Jess says as she approaches.
"I'll take you, c'mon."

"Sure," Chloe says standing. I give her a sudden look of panic,
hoping she'd read the 'please don't leave me alone' message I'm

trying to broadcast with my eyes. But either she doesn't get the message, or she thinks better of it, as she quickly falls into step beside Jess and disappears into the house.

"Well, I'm glad you two decided to come," Missy says, crossing one leg over the other as she flips her hair to one side.

"Really?" I ask with worried brows, peeking at her from beneath my lashes.

"Oh totally, I've always wanted to get to know you guys. You know, the 'other side' and all," she says, her whole face lighting up and somehow putting me at ease. I relax my shoulders and smile, thinking maybe this isn't so bad of an idea after all.

"Your vibe is giving…" she says, waving her fingers in front of me. I look down at myself realizing she means the costume. I smile with an inhaled choke.

"Oh right, yeah. Werewolf. Uh, sexy werewolf," I say with a clipped laugh. "Uh, you look amazing, too."

Missy smacks her lips then smiles as she poses for me in true Barbie fashion. I can't help but laugh. The whole costume seems to fit her perfectly.

A few moments later, Chloe returns with Jess and a few other people, drinks in hand. She hands me a red cup with a 'you got this' grin pulled across her lips. "Thanks," I say, taking a sip of the beer—I don't even mind the taste.

"Oooh I love this song, let's dance!" Missy shouts over the mix of conversations going on, standing and grabbing my hand at the same time. I glance over at Chloe, who nods excitedly. Our little group makes our way back into the house, cups in hand to find the music.

Hours or minutes later——my belly is warm from the beer and my thighs are killing me from the dancing. I can't remember the last time Chloe and I had partied like this. Pack parties are normally more laid back—mostly just hanging out. Alcohol isn't really a thing because it takes so much more of the stuff for wolves to get drunk. Even before their full transformation, they can out drink your average human adult. I don't have that luxury, and my first real experience with drinking seems to be catching up with me.

Missy and I stumble onto the back patio, both of us laughing so hard it makes my chest hurt. Each of us precariously holding up the other as we zigzag toward the patio chairs we claimed earlier. Missy hits the side of hers and falls to the concrete, and we both laugh even harder.

"Here," I say, holding out an arm for her to use to pull herself onto the chair. As she steadies herself, I glance around the pool patio for Chloe. A handful of familiar faces are around, and some of the same group from earlier are still here, but I can't spot Chloe's. Worry suddenly starts to claw at my chest, and I try to remind myself she's probably still inside, dancing or talking to someone. I take in deep breaths and pull an arm around my stomach to calm my rising panic. *She's probably just lost in the excitement like I had been.*

Brushing the thoughts away, I pull my attention forward as someone new approaches our little spot. "Hey guys," Chad says.

I glance up at the football player and smile, though it probably looks ridiculous in my weird, fuzzy state.

"Hey, I know you!" I say, then mentally slap myself for being so stupid. "I mean from school," I correct, hoping I didn't sound like a complete idiot.

Chad's face pulls into a knowing smirk. He's dressed in camouflage tonight for his costume and it looks good on him. I eye him up and down, admiring the fit. Uniforms are sexy as hell. The thought conjures an image of Dean in a military uniform and I have to lick my lips.

"Yeah, I know you, too," he says, taking one of the vacant chairs and snapping my attention back to him. "You're usually too cool to hang with the rest of us. What made you change your mind tonight?"

I choke on the sip of beer I'm currently downing. "Uhh, huh?" I manage as my choke turns into a cough. Patting my chest to clear my throat. "What? I'm not too cool... that's not..." I struggle to find the right words through the fogginess in my brain.

He laughs, but it doesn't seem pointed, which makes me settle some. "I'm just messin' with you." My back softens at that and I nod slowly. "So, you live over there in Lunar Falls, right?" he asks.

"Yeah," I reply, setting down my cup and pulling my hands together in my lap.

Chad leans back in his chair as his eyes narrow on me, sending a chill down my spine. I'm not sure if it's the good kind—I try to work out the feeling in my mind, but all I come up with is a headache. "You ever gone out into the woods back there?"

Slowly, I nod my head up and down as I try to predict where he's going with this. It's probably just the beer, but I have a nasty feeling growing in my gut. "I guess... sometimes," I say, taking my time to enunciate each word to keep the slurring to a minimum.

"My dad and I used to go out there a lot. He'd bought up a lot of that property, and was going to develop it or something. It's really beautiful back there."

"Don't you and Donavan go hunting out there sometimes?" one of the girls sitting with us cuts in. I'm pretty sure her name is Vivian. She seems to be swaying slightly in her chair, but that doesn't stop her from downing the rest of her cup. *Uck, or maybe I'm the one swaying.*

"Oh yeah," Chad says, a slow smile slipping across his lips, his eyes never leaving mine.

"That land is protected, though. It's illegal to hunt out there," I say with a snort, hoping I sound normal. I shift in my chair, my stomach swirling from the movement as nausea rises in my throat. I push it back down.

One of the guys hanging around us—Matt, I think—moves to stand behind Chad and pushes a fist lightly into his arm. "That's never stopped us, huh?" he says. "There's all kinds of game in those woods. Deer, rabbit..."

"Wolves," Chad cuts in, his eyes darkening almost as if challenging me to deny it. He gestures his hand toward me. "Love the costume by the way. Fitting," He says the last with a wink that makes my heart stop dead in my chest.

I inhale a deep breath of air and glance around again, trying to spot Chloe. "Has anyone seen Chloe?" I ask, attempting to change the topic and struggling to keep the panic from my tone. I'm hoping and praying that Chad meant nothing by his words. *He doesn't know about the pack, that would be crazy. He's human.* Maybe this whole 'playing human' experiment has me paranoid, reading way too much into his words. But then it wouldn't have been the first time either—it's rare, but occasionally humans find out about the Supernatural. Preventing that, and keeping the truth hidden, is part of a Pack's job. No matter what Chad meant, however, I'm ready to go.

Missy shakes her head at my question, falling back into her chair. "I think I saw," she pauses with a hiccup, "her leave a bit ago."

I pull my phone from my pocket, intending to send off a quick text to Chloe when I see she's already sent me one.

Hey girl, had to go. Mom needs me home. If you need a ride, call and I'll come get you.

Shit, she's already left. "I should probably get going," I say, glancing at the circle of people around me. Only minutes ago the atmosphere had been fun and light. I was making friends. Now I feel like I've suddenly fallen into a pit of vipers.

All around me the innocent faces from school seem to glow with venomous intent. Taking another deep breath, I try to calm the racing of my heart. I'm taking everything out of context, I'm sure. Blowing it out of proportion. It has to be the anxiousness and the beer giving me these queasy vibes.

I stand then, and the world goes sideways. Jerking one hand out to steady myself on the chair I pull my phone up to my face with the other. I dial Chloe's number but no answer. I try again a few more times. *Chloe still isn't answering. Shit.*

"Don't go," Missy hiccups. Her eyes are half-closed, as she slumps uncomfortably in her chair. She won't be making it much longer tonight.

I give everyone a close-lipped smile and turn away. "My parents are gonna' kill me," I say with a forced laugh, holding up the phone. "It's so late."

Chad stands. "I'll give you a ride."

I shake my head, quickly regretting the choice as pain slams from side-to-side through my skull. "No, I'm good. I have a ride." I try to think of who I can call to come get me, since Chloe isn't answering. Blake will definitely be asleep by now. I turn slowly to head back inside. "Goodnight, guys," I say with a small wave to the group praying no one follows me.

Chad rounds up next to me, taking my arm as I sway on the spot. "You sure you're good?" he asks. I wave him off, fighting back the urge to jerk free of his hand, I don't want to show how uncomfortable he's made me.

"I'll be fine," I say as I glance to my side at him. From this angle, he looks just like the Chad I've always known from school. Young, cute, and completely human. *Regular Chad.* "My ride is on their way." I hold my phone up for emphasis.

Pulling away from Chad, I walk across the patio, concentrating on every step to not fall. I don't want to give him any reason to come 'help' me a second time. As soon as I'm past the threshold into the house, I yank out my phone and, still seeing no reply from Chloe, I run through my contacts.

"Shit," I whisper under my breath when I come to Dean's name. The letters glow in the darkness of the room around me. He's not Chloe, but he also won't yell at me for getting so drunk. I'm not even sure that he'll answer, but I need to get out of here and fast. Quickly, I dial his number.

As the phone rings, I beeline to the front door and out onto the lawn toward the street. "Hey," Dean's voice sounds through the phone, and I swear I've never been so glad to hear that sexy tone of his in my life. My whole body relaxes, and I let go of the heavy breath I didn't realize I was holding.

"I need you to come get me."

EIGHT

Cracked gray pavement sways from side to side beneath my feet. I'm using every bit of concentration I have just to keep myself upright. I don't dare look behind me to see how far I've gotten from Missy's house. One foot in front of the other—I just keep going.

The sound of a truck engine makes me stop and look up. A white Dodge Ram pulls up along the curb just beside me. My shoulders deflate along with any fight I had left.

"Wow," Dean says leaning across the cab to the passenger side window before he pushes the truck into park. "You are *really* drunk." His laugh is light-heartened, but sounds laced with a hint of concern.

I frown at him. "Can you please just take me home?" I ask as I make a move toward the truck. The whole world spins before my eyes; my stomach heaves. *Please don't puke.*

Dean's arms wrap around me. I didn't even hear him get out of the truck, but I also don't care—he's warm and familiar. I inhale his masculine scent and lean into his hold, my body reeling as he lifts me into a basket carry. I briefly think to argue, but decide better of it as I wrap my arms around his neck.

It takes only a moment for him to carry me to the passenger side of his truck and set me in the seat. I yank on my short dress that has ridden up more than I'm comfortable with. I knew I shouldn't have worn something so short. The tension slowly leaves my muscles as he climbs into the driver's seat. "Thanks," I manage, leaning my head back against the soft leather.

"No problem," he says as he pushes the ignition button and his truck roars back to life. Dean pulls onto the road just as a raindrop hits the windshield, a second one following shortly after.

Within a few minutes, rain is pounding against the glass. I wrap my arms around myself and shiver. Dean leans forward, cranking the heat. I give him a grateful smile, though the shiver is only partially from the cold. "I take it the party didn't go so well?"

"No. Maybe..." I roll my head to the side with a defeated huff. "I don't know, it wasn't bad, just..." my words trail off as I peer into the rain-soaked night. Chad's talk of hunting races through my mind. *Should I tell Dean?* I decide against it. What do I really know, anyway? People hunting in the woods behind Lunar Falls isn't exactly new. They're not supposed to, but that's never stopped people before. I'm sure I'm just being paranoid, overreacting to the whole situation.

"Why didn't your friends go with you?" Dean asks, pulling me from my thoughts.

I turn to face him with a shrug. "Chloe did, but I guess she had to leave early," I say, hoping it sounds like no big deal. I can't blame her if her mom called her home, but part of me boils knowing she left me there without saying anything. I'm sure she did it with what she *thought* were good intentions, but nonetheless, I'm a bit pissed off.

"Ah. And she was your ride?" Dean questions with a raised brow.

I purse my lips together. "Yeah. I hope I didn't wake you up when I called."

Dean eyes me from the driver's seat, but in the darkness it's hard to tell exactly what his expression is. "Nah," he says with a tilt to his head before turning his attention back to the road. "I was just getting off work."

"Oh… good," I say, raising my hands to the heater and letting the warm air breathe life back into my nervous system.

"I'd have still come, though. Even if I had been asleep," Dean says as he turns the wheel pulling into his driveway. Unbuckling, I give him a small smile. "For you…" he adds, his honeyed tone emphasizing the words.

My heart speeds up and I open my mouth to say something but stop short when my brain freezes—his eyes are on me. Even in the darkness I can see the intense electricity behind them. My gaze flicks down to the shadow of his lips and I wonder, not for the first time, what it would feel like to kiss him.

Jerking myself back to reality, I lean away before I do something crazy—like actually try to kiss him. "Thanks again," I squeeze out. The overhead light clicks on as I open the truck door. I blink against the sudden onslaught of light. Dean is wearing a smile that has me second guessing my need to suddenly escape. I barely even register the rain misting the right side of my body with him looking at me like that. Like he's wondering what it would feel like, too. My mouth waters and I have to rub my thighs together to quell the need swelling between them.

"You should come in," Dean says, gesturing his head toward his house. "Sober up before you gotta face your mom."

I frown, still holding onto the door. The thought of following him into his house has my stomach in a knot, but confronting my mom drunk… that is so much worse. *This is such a bad idea.* "Yeah, okay." I relent as Dean opens his own door. A few seconds later he's climbed out and run over to my side. He holds his jacket out to shield us both from the rain, and I jump down from his truck and run alongside him into his house.

The warmth hits me like a caress I didn't realize I needed as we pass into the foyer. I sigh at its touch, and my shoulders drop as Dean shakes the water from his jacket. He chuckles low in his throat and moves further into the house toward the kitchen.

I take a moment to study the house around me and to slow my pulse down a peg or two. It's a small space, but nice. Dean hadn't been lying when he said he'd done some work to it. Mrs. Station was old, and most of the place had fallen into disrepair before she'd passed. But looking at it now, you wouldn't know what kind of state it had been in just a few weeks ago.

"Wow," I say. "The place looks good."

The living room is simple with very little decor. Definitely bachelor pad-y. Light colored walls, and dark furniture. No frilly pillows or any feminine touch to be seen. The notion makes me smile a little inside.

"Thanks," Dean replies, his voice carrying from the kitchen just behind the living room. It's an open floor plan with everything right out in the open, but it's nicely done. "Want some coffee?"

"Yes, please," I say and start toward him. The room spins slightly and I have to stop and start again slower. *Uck, drinking is not for me.* Mercifully it doesn't take long for me to reach the kitchen island and drop myself onto a plain black stool. "Thanks," I mumble as he sets a steaming mug in front of me.

Dean snorts. "You're not normally one to drink.;" He says it like a joke, which only serves to ruffle my mood.

I narrow my eyes on him. "I'm sixteen... or close enough. Isn't that what normal sixteen-year-old human girls do?"

He shrugs. "Maybe. But it's still not like you."

I huff into my mug before taking a tentative sip. It's not too hot thankfully, and I guzzle a good amount down. The taste is amazing, though it's probably just my drunk brain craving the caffeine to sober me up some.

"So... what happened tonight? Why were you even at a normie party?"

After a few more moments of savoring the hot liquid, I settle into an explanation of how I've been struggling with the whole Moon Awakening situation, about Blake and Chloe's idea that I should try and explore the human side of myself, maybe even find some human friends. "Find balance and all that," I say with an edge to my voice. I don't know why I'm spilling myself to this man, but once the words start I can't stop them.

I look up from my mug to find Dean has moved around the counter to join me at the island, taking the seat next to mine. When did he do that? I jerk straight, turning toward him. We're so close. I glance down to where our knees are touching and my breath catches. Electricity skitters through my skin at the contact and my body heats. I swallow the lump that's lodged in my throat.

"I get their reasons, but I don't think human friends are what you need."

I bite my lower lip. "What do you think I need?" I ask and instantly regret it, expecting some flirty comment about how all I need is some D.

"Patience," he says instead, surprising me.

Scrunching up my nose, I tilt my head in question. Dean laughs softly. "You're all jittery over this event that isn't actually going to change anything between the three of you girls." Dean shrugs. "You've all been inseparable since as long as I can remember. Nothing can come between that."

"How can you be so sure? I feel like a lot will come between us once they're members of the pack."

"You mean secrets."

My shoulders lift and drop once in answer.

"Sure, there will be things they won't be able to tell you... pack things. But really, it won't be anything that's important to you anyway."

"And if it concerns my family? My mom? Or my brother? And... it's just... friends don't keep secrets."

Dean takes a sip of coffee and then shoots me a sympathetic smile. "Like you said, they're your *family*. They might not be as close-lipped as you think. At least about the *really* serious stuff."

"But they're not supposed to..."

"Kinda like how teenagers aren't supposed to drink?" he interrupts with raised brows and an impish smile. I can't help the small laugh that escapes into my coffee mug. "I'm just saying… Patience. The way things play out might surprise you."

I glance away, mulling through his words. I hadn't expected something so genuine. I look back to see Dean downing the rest of his coffee and gently setting the mug back down. "Thanks," I finally let out, my voice soft. The pitch of my reply no doubt betrays my shock.

"What?"

"I just… wasn't expecting that."

Dean chuffs. "Oh, well, I'm sorry to disappoint you. What were you expecting?"

"Something more like… 'all you need is some of this,'" I tease in a mock tone of his, gesturing my hands into a 'V' at my crotch.

Dean's eyes smolder as he lifts his right brow. "Oh… well, I mean we could definitely try that, too."

"Oh, is that so?"

"Yeah. For science."

My brows jack and my hand flies to my mouth to cover a snort. "For science?"

Dean totally plays it cool and gives a shrug of his shoulder. "Yeah, of course. An experiment to see if it helps."

"Right, yeah." I sarcastically nod.

"I mean we may have to try it a few different times to know for sure. Validity of results and all…"

I laugh, falling forward with the hilarity of this conversation. Dean chuckles, too.

I can't say the idea isn't a good one. My mind conjures the image of the two of us tangled in his sheets and suddenly I'm squirming where I sit.

"What was it like?" I ask, desperate to change the subject. "Turning?"

Dean exhales slowly before replying, "Painful… terrifying… but exhilarating." He looks away, his eyes misting as if lost in the memory. "Running as a tiger is the most freeing feeling I've ever experienced. There's nothing like it. The killing, though…" he shakes his head as his words drift off. "Even though they're vampires and have lost any shred of humanity, it… never gets easy."

His face morphs from serenity to anguish then back to content with each word he says. My eyes move to the empty mug in front of me as all my problems seem suddenly silly. I laugh under my breath. Dean's attention snaps to me and I realize how my reaction must seem to him. "Sorry," I say quickly, moving to fix the situation. "I wasn't laughing at you. I just realized how incredibly small my problems really are."

Dean's normal cocky expression returns to his face and I almost roll my eyes even though part of me is glad to have eased his thoughts.

"They're not small. Not at all. I can't imagine worrying over losing Eli, even just emotionally. And that's exactly what you're worried about. You won't lose them, though. I promise."

"You promise?" I ask, knowing that's not really a promise he can keep. I can't help but wish it was.

"Promise."

"I should probably head home," I say after what feels like a lifetime of silence, still smiling. Dean shifts in his chair pinning me in as I stand and the butterflies are back in my stomach. "Thanks for the coffee and… you know… the laugh."

"Any time," Dean replies, and I wonder if he's going to reach out to me but he doesn't. Instead, he extends his knees away letting me pass. "I'll see you tomorrow."

"Tomorrow?" I ask, before realization hits and I almost smack myself. "Yeah… the Awakening. My birthday. Of course. I'll be there."

"Good," Dean says, his lips pulling up at the corners. "Goodnight, Ari."

"Goodnight," I reply, and make my way toward the front door. I brave another glance back at Dean and then step out into the rain. It pelts against my bare skin, soaking me in seconds as I shut the door behind me. Turning on my heel, I run across the yard to my front porch. Once I'm safely under cover, I glance one last time over my shoulder toward Dean's house and smile to myself. Then I remember I still have to face my mom, and that smile vanishes. At least I'm not as trashed any more thanks to the coffee. Taking a deep breath, I force myself to summon every bit of courage I have left after everything that's happened tonight. I am *so* grounded.

Nine

Stepping out through the front door, it's the perfect night for the Moon-Kissed Awakening. The full moon is so large it looks as if the star-strewn sky might not be able to hold its weight. It makes for a perfect Halloween, too. But while most people in town are handing out candy and dressing as their favorite monsters or characters, Lunar Falls is celebrating something else entirely: The night when the veil between the worlds of the living and dead is at its thinnest, when the lunar magic that fuels Weres will be even stronger. Which makes for even stronger wolves—or so everyone believes.

I woke up this morning to a small birthday cake lit with a single candle and a card waiting for me on the kitchen counter. My family had already left to help prepare for the festival. Mom probably figured I could use the rest. When I had finally worked up the nerve to walk through the door last night, she'd been waiting for me at the kitchen island. She sniffed the air once, and all I got was a curt, 'Go to bed. We'll talk tomorrow.'

I ate a small slice of cake with a fresh cup of coffee in the quiet of the house before showering and dolling up for tonight's events. I took my time with every little detail, but unlike previous years, it had nothing to do with trying to look my best or match the rest of the girls in the pack. No, the longer it took me to get ready, the longer I had to try and control these jitters rushing through my insides. Whatever verbal lashing Mom had ready for me was just background noise compared to the harsh stirring of excitement and dread in anticipation of my friends becoming full members without me.

My phone beeps with a notification as I shut the door, reminding me that it's six p.m. and well past time to be at the clearing. The air is crisp tonight, with a soft breeze threatening to turn the night chilly. Multicolored lanterns are strung from streetlamp to streetlamp and tiny jack o'lanterns decorate the sidewalks, the yellow light from their faces flickering in the moon's glow. Everywhere the trees are hung with tea-light candles casting an eerie white gleam. They sway in the breeze, and their lights dance like small ghosts through the branches. Our typically traditional neighborhood has been transformed into a spooky forest. My stomach churns, as if some of those ghosts have found a new place to dance within it.

Something feels off tonight, and I can't quite place why. It doesn't feel like excitement, or anxiousness, or dread—I've gotten really familiar with those feelings over the last few weeks. And I don't necessarily feel *nervous*, but judging from the heaviness of my chest, the jitters in my belly, and the way I can't stop wringing my hands, I figure that must be it. But I don't exactly have a reason to *be* nervous, either. After all, I'm not the one being 'presented, 'but nonetheless, I can't shake the weirdness that tingles through my veins.

The way to the clearing is easy enough for me to find in the thick woods from memory, and once I'm close enough the light and noise of the gathering guides me the rest of the way. I find a place at an empty table tucked in the back of the festival area. The ceremony has already started, and while I'm sure every full-Were here scented my late entrance, they all have the courtesy to not turn and stare.

This year our celebration is much larger than normal. With the daughter of the Lunar Falls Alpha presenting, there is an extra theme of diplomacy. Alphas or soon-to-be Alphas of several other packs are in attendance as well. A jumble of unrecognizable faces, all of eligible age, good looking, well-dressed, and eager to meet the newest Pack Princess on the market. I laugh to myself knowing just how disappointed they would all be to realize Blake isn't exactly over-the-moon about jumping into the mating pool. But finding a mate doesn't mean they always marry right away—sixteen is still young. Some do, though, and others wait for a few years, but they almost *always* enact the mating ritual. I'm not exactly certain what all that entails, but the glow of a mated couple the next day is always apparent.

That maybe-nervous feeling still simmers in my stomach as the ceremony continues, but Chloe and Blake seem perfectly at ease as they make their entrance from the woods through three massive archways of twisted branches and wood, each decorated with hundreds of different wild flowers and roses. Their hair is styled elegantly, their smiles perfect, and their gowns make them look like goddesses as they enter on their father's arms or in Chloe's case-mom's, and present to the pack. Magic shimmers around the space, making the wooded area seem to glow of its own accord, despite the light of the hanging lanterns. One by one, all the females coming-of-age don their elaborate masks and take a partner for the traditional dance.

I can easily pick out each of the pack members here from my table in the back. My brother is closest to me, and there's no mistaking Chloe, even with the mask, dancing a few feet past him. My eyes roam around the space to find Blake when a man on the edge of the clearing suddenly steals my attention. *He definitely isn't a part of the pack.* He's tall, with blonde hair and milky-white skin that almost glows under the moonlight. His features are sharp and angular, almost fox-like. He's not dancing, just standing with his arms held behind his back on the edges of the party, as if ready to dissolve into the forest at a moment's notice. Watching. *Probably another Alpha invited to meet Blake*, I decide, but something in my gut doesn't believe it.

I shake the thought from my mind but when I look again he's gone, as if I imagined him. I glance around the clearing, searching, but there's no trace of him. I spy Blake then, twirling on the farthest end of the makeshift dance floor from me. She's laughing and smiling with her partner, another girl with bright-red, curly hair. I sigh at the sight of how happy my friend is, the mystery man already forgotten.

"You look amazing," a husky voice sounds just behind me. I don't even have to turn to know that it's Dean. I smile just as he steps around the table to my little corner, holding out a glass of champagne to me. I run my hands down the sides of my lavender gown as I stand, squirming a little under his intense gaze. The lights in the clearing catch on the tiny, sewn-on gems, making the gown glitter and sparkle. I realize then, for the first time tonight, that I feel beautiful, too.

"Thanks," I say, taking the glass with a small smile while I eye his tux. "You, too… you look good, I mean." I shake my head and mentally curse myself for stumbling over my words. I can feel my cheeks burning. I stop any further embarrassing comments by downing my glass, the sweet bubbles tingling all the way down my throat.

Dean makes a low humming sound, forcing my eyes to meet his. They glow almost electric under the lanterns, pulling me in. "Dance with me?" he asks, and I realize I've taken a step toward him. *When had I done that?* Setting my empty glass on the nearby table, I take his outstretched hand, and let him guide us into the swaying crowd.

If I was nervous before, it's nothing compared to the instant sparks shooting through my entire body now as he wraps his hand around my waist, pulling me flush with him. Breathing becomes difficult—his scent, sage and eucalyptus, fills my nose, overwhelming me. The whole world seems to disappear around us.

Our bodies entwined sway and spin to the music, but I can barely hear it for the pounding of my own heartbeat. "I wasn't sure I would get you to dance with me," he says, his hard chest pressed against mine, I'm sure he can feel how fast my pulse is racing. I lick my lips and try futilely to settle my nerves.

"Why?" I ask in a breathy whisper.

His answering smirk nearly has me undone as every fiber of my being wants to turn that look into something else. Something primal. "You're always avoiding me."

I glance away, lowering my lashes. He's not wrong. There's a reason I keep my distance from this man. But for the life of me I can't seem to remember what that reason is right now. Lifting his hand to my face he turns me to him once more. My lips part at the need and want darkening his eyes. My breath hitches. "You scare me," I breathe, and bite my lip to keep from further spilling my guts.

As the music slows, my mind starts to clear. My gaze roams around the clearing to the different members of the pack, paired off, dancing, or talking in dark corners. Off to the side a group of girls are eyeing Dean and I, pointing and whispering to one another. Of course, I know exactly what they're thinking: Dean's next target. Like a ram slamming into my gut, realization dawns on me. I stop, dropping my arms and pulling away from Dean.

"I scare you?" he asks, hurt lacing his tone.

I take in a deep breath. "What are you doing...?" I ask slowly, closing my eyes briefly. "With me, I mean."

"Well, I thought we were dancing." I purse my lips and jack a brow at his reply. "Let's take a walk," he finally says, taking a step toward me.

I pull away. "I don't know," I whisper, shifting my weight nervously. I want to run as far from the twinkling lights, the romantic florals, and fairytale setting as I possibly can. How could I be so stupid and let down my guard.

Dean grabs my hand and like a balm to my system, I relax, letting him steer us away from the party, the lights, and all the whispers. The music stops and the booming voice of the pack Alpha starting his ceremonial speeches follows us into the woods, telling me the moon must be close to its apex. Dean glances over my shoulder with a frown. It won't be long now before the men will all leave, taking off into the woods to hunt.

Turning back to me, Dean guides us further into the trees and away from the party. When he stops his eyes bore into mine, holding me in place. I want to dive into them and get lost forever. "Ari. I like you," Dean confesses as he rests his hands on each of my arms, pulling me a step closer. His eyes search mine. My chest aches with the want to believe his words.

"I don't…" I stop my words, shaking my head.

"What?" Dean asks, his voice soft, worry creating little divots in his forehead.

I sigh and continue, "I don't want to be another one of your conquests."

Dean takes a step back with a nod. "That's fair," he says as I shift from one foot to the other. I start to turn away as Alpha Jon's voice fills the silence, and I know we don't have much time. His speech is coming to an end. It's time for the men to go. Dean's hands wrap around both of mine, stopping me short. I turn back toward him.

"You have to go," I say, knowing that however this conversation ends, it'll be soon. He's a Weretiger, and while tigers themselves might be lone hunters, being affiliated with the pack means he runs and hunts with the pack—it's the law. I give Dean what I hope is an encouraging smile. It seems to only defeat him. His shoulders slump and his hands drop to his sides as the sounds of clapping and cheering rise from the party. Excited howls follow as the men are no doubt heading toward the woods. Dean won't be able to resist the need to follow. The shift will happen either way.

I start again to pull away. Dean closes the space between us, his hands whipping to either side of my face. His eyes darken under the lights and in a single breath his lips capture mine. The world stops. My heart stops. I lean into him, burying my own hands within the silken strands of his blonde hair.

The kiss isn't soft or gentle, as if he's trying to say so much with the action. He devours my protests in an instant. All I can think is *more*. I want more. I need more.

"I'm not looking for a conquest. I'm looking for you," he whispers against my lips, then gently pulls away. My lips hang open like a fish out of water. I'm lost for words in a fog that has consumed my brain.

"O-oh," I say, my words stumbling out in barely a whisper as my body still sings, memorizing the feel of his lips on mine and his hands cradling my body.

A smile spreads across his lips as he releases me, taking off his jacket and wrapping it around my shoulders. I snuggle into its warmth just as he takes another step back.

Looking away, I'm unable to stop the grin that has now transformed my face. When I turn back, he is wearing a smile of his own. Not his usual smirk, but a genuine, gentle smile. The sight is disarming every fight I might have managed to summon. "Ari, I need to tell you—" Dean stops short just as a loud rustling of brush sounds to our left. A figure pushes itself through the trees.

Ten

Chad's face appears under the glow of the moon, the shadows drawing back like a curtain as he moves out of the brush. His brows are strained, his lips thin. That easy-going football player from school is gone, his boy-next-door face twisted with smug self-assurance and rage in his eyes.

He raises a pistol in his right hand, bluish-white light shining off the steel surface. I look from the gun back to Chad's face, not daring a glance at Dean beside me. My mind whirls at the scene unfolding before me, desperately searching for what to do. "Hellooo, Ari," Chad says, his words slurring slightly. My skin crawls while I stand petrified.

"Are… are you drunk?" I ask, regaining control of my arms and legs and taking a few slow steps backwards. Chad follows, his hold on the gun never faltering despite the slight drunken shake to his hands. I force myself to stay calm and still. I don't want to give him any reason to spook. Beside me, Dean slowly creeps forward, trying to position himself between Chad and I.

"I know. Whatyouare, and what you alldid," Chad's words drip like acid, sending my stomach rolling at the sound. My back stiffens—I should have trusted my intuition after that scene with Chad at the party... *I should have said something to Dean.* The pack seems completely unaware of the situation going down in front of me, only yards away from them. *How?* I know better than to scream, though. More howls fill the air as the pack must be taking off into the woods.

"You're wrong about me." I say the words slowly, my eyes never leaving the threat in front of me.

Dean is now almost entirely in front of me, rigid with tension. I can see his back muscles beneath his white dress shirt straining with effort as I realize he's struggling to keep his transformation in check. During the few moments it takes to shift a Were is most vulnerable, and doing so with a loaded weapon—held by a drunk and manic kid, no less—pointed at your chest could be deadly. *Shit, shit, shit.*

Chad's eyes narrow as he sizes up the man in front of me. Dean, though lean in muscle for his size, is larger and stronger than Chad, and it looks as if Chad knows it. But it's not enough to make him back down, not when he's got a gun in his hand. Determination sets in his pinched brows, shadowing the anger on his face.

"Chad... Put down the gun," I say, keeping my voice steady and soothing as I take another step back. I need to put some distance between us.

"You. All you... Lunar Falls freaks... are werewolves," Chad growls, his voice clipped and shaky as he pivots the gun from Dean to me and back. His eyes catch me with the accusation over Dean's shoulder.

"That's crazy, Chad. You're just drunk…" I say as the telltale snapping of a bone echoes in the small copse. Dean is shifting. Fighting it will only prolong the shift—and the pain.

Dean lets out a low, miserable growl as his shoulders pop backwards, followed by another snap as Dean's legs give out and he falls to his knees. He's transforming and there's nothing he can do to stop it.

Chad jumps back a step, aiming his gun at Dean's chest. "W-what the f—?" Chad gasps, wrapping his free hand around the grip of the pistol for a better hold. "Holy shit."

Seconds later, a tiger crouches low where Dean had been only moments before. A snarl curls across his lips, exposing deadly-sharp fangs. My breath hitches as my eyes swivel from Chad to Dean. *Please, Moon Goddess, protect him*, I pray silently.

"Chad. Put. Down. The. Gun," I say again, enunciating each word and hoping they will reach him. Dean's animal presence seems to feed my own courage.

The tiger stalks a step closer to Chad, letting out a low, rumbling growl through the clearing that would stand the hair up on even the hardest person. Chad visibly gulps, but finds his nerve again quickly, tightening his grip on the pistol. This whole thing is on a knife's edge, and what courage I had is starting to fade.

Dean is still in there, but I know right now the animal side of him is hard to resist. And that animal is cornered, protecting… me. He would reach Chad if he attacked, but definitely not before Chad could get a shot off. Dean has to know that, too, but I'm not sure if he'll be able to hold himself back. I slowly reach a hand out to his fur, hoping my touch might calm him down. *Think this through, Dean...*

His body hums like an engine underneath my hand and he crouches even lower. *Dean...* The tiger suddenly bucks forward with a roar, but stays in place. Chad's eyes go wide at the small lunge and he stumbles back a step, turning his attention away from the beast in front of him to look backwards and catch his balance. That fleeting moment is all Dean wanted. He goes low again, the muscles in his front shoulders bulging as he braces himself, then pounces.

Dean surges into the air as Chad turns his attention back around, shock suddenly razing his face. Time seems to slow. I see Chad's grip tighten on the gun as Dean's arms and claws go wide for a tackle. A shot rings out through the quiet space.

"*Dean!*" I scream, throwing my arms up in front of me.

Electricity sings from my core and out through my hands. I grit my teeth and my eyes snap shut reflexively with the vibrations wracking my body. I force them back open to find roiling, pink tendrils of smoke streaming from the palms of my hands. Or at least that's what it looks like. It feels like it, too. There's an indescribable *intensity* coursing through my arms, as if some internal force is surging through my veins to my out-stretched palms.

I yelp, yanking my hands back and turning them up to my face. They're clean, unmarked. Just normal hands. The pressure in my arms is gone, too. *What the shit is happening?* I don't have time to think it through, though, as I lift my focus back to the scene in front of me, and my jaw drops.

Pink smoke envelops both Dean and Chad, swirling around them in a silent vortex. *Dean!* He hangs suspended in the air for a few more moments, still in tiger form, then drops through the quickly thinning fog to the ground. Chad's body follows, crumpling into a heap ahead of Dean and I.

I maneuver around to Dean's side, kicking the gun away from Chad's limp form as I pass. The tiger pulls himself unsteadily from the ground, shaking his head from side to side. I bend down and run my hands along the soft fur of his back and chest, searching for a wound I knew had to be there. I heard the gun go off. I saw the flash from the muzzle. But after a minute of frantic searching I find nothing.

The moonlight catches on something inches away from where Dean sits and gathers himself. A perfectly intact bullet. A silver bullet. *How did he get something like that?* No blood coats its surface and I look back to Dean, whose eyes are locked on the fallen football player. I bury my hands in his soft fur as relief washes over me. Without letting go, I lift my gaze toward Chad.

His crumpled form lays only a few feet in front of us, but I can barely see him through my blurring vision. My cheeks are wet. *Goddess, what the fuck just happened?* Howls mixed with the vicious screams of hunted vampires pepper the air around us. They seem closer than they should have any reason to be, but I can't find enough of a care to focus on them. It's as if nothing exists outside of the pounding of my heart. I try to breathe deeply, but air is getting harder and harder to find. *What is happening?* I raise a hand to my chest, but it does little good to quell the panic squeezing my organs.

I give in to the weakness that's been threatening my knees. Hair whips at my face as I fall to the ground and my knee scrapes against something hard beneath me, but I can barely acknowledge it against everything else I'm feeling right now. I roll to my side and wrap my arms around my stomach. Dean's solid tiger form leans into me. "Wha-what…?" I try to ask a question but can't make sense of the words through the fog in my mind. The details of Chad's blank face slowly begins to fill in my entire line of sight. Is *he dead? Did I…* Pressure settles on my shoulder and back as someone pulls me into them. I don't fight it.

I can hear someone crying—loud, deep, sobs that seem to vibrate into my very own chest. My sobs, I realize, as my brain slowly focuses and takes in my surroundings.

Voices echo in the distance, or maybe they're shouting… I can't be sure as footsteps and snapping branches sound across the forest floor in all directions. I push away from the person holding me. Dean, I realize. He must have shifted back into his human form. "What happened?" I finally force the words through my lips, but they're barely a whisper against the violent sounds growing in the woods around us. The voices rise to yells and cries. I want to scream at them to stop.

A loud 'pop' sounds, and a large cloud of green smoke fills the space in front of us. I cough through the rolling haze. It begins dissipating as quickly as it came, and I pull my hands in front of my face again. It doesn't look like it came from me this time, and it certainly doesn't feel like before. *I imagined it, the smoke coming from my hands…* I laugh at myself. *Of course, it didn't come from me, I'm just losing my mind!* I'm certainly laughing like I have.

A man coalesces from the dissipating cloud in front of me just beside Chad's still body. "Not dead. Pity," the man titters to no one in particular. He is tall and expertly dressed in a tailored, dark-rust suit. His pale skin is almost opalescent in the moonlight, and his deep-set, hazel eyes are sharp and quick. He lifts them to mine and I recognize the man I'd seen earlier tonight in the crowd of our pack, looking very out of place. And now with him standing right in front of me I can see why he caught my attention. He doesn't look like any Were I've ever seen.

"This isn't Djinn business." Dean's voice is more growl than not behind me.

The stranger smiles a wicked, toothy grin. "*Everything* is Djinn business, kitten," he says, barely looking away from Chad,. "*Her* especially." He points a finger in my direction and cocks his head to the side thoughtfully. I glance at Dean over my shoulder. Outrage is evident on his features and I can feel the strain of his muscled arms around me, shielding me.

"Who are you?" Dean asks, his voice strong and demanding. The Djinn— apparently—just continues with that eerie smile. He waves his hand as if shoo-ing away a fly and Chad's body disappears in a green haze of smoke, eliciting another coughing fit from me. "He..." he pauses a moment, his eyes darting to somewhere else in the forest, "...and his silly little friends... are taken care of now," he says, voice smooth and casual like nothing crazy has happened at all. *Chad brought friends?* I didn't see anyone else with him; they must have been hidden in the woods.

"They'll wake tomorrow with a hangover and a memory of partying a little *too* hard—your boys should steer clear of the eastern woods for tonight." He shifts his attention behind us toward the party still going on and shrugs. "Though, it seems the dogs have bit off a little more than they can chew." I frown at his words. *What the actual fuck?*

I shift on the ground to get a better look at Dean, but his face is turned toward the party behind us, body tense. "What—?" I start to say, but before I can finish Dean is shifting once more, then takes off in an orange blur. *Shit!*

"I'm Joaquin by the way," the Djinn says, snapping my attention back. "We'll talk soon." And then he's gone.

Eleven

The loud '*pop*' signaling the djinn's exit is immediately replaced with howls and screams. Panic creeps into my chest as my eyes and ears adjust to the chaos filling the forest around me. Taking a deep breath, I start pushing through the brush after Dean toward the clearing. The metallic scent of blood and something rotten and dead fills my nose.

The scene in the clearing is sheer carnage. Human forms fly around the clearing, dodging and colliding in a hysteric rush of panic. Some of them are perched on top of struggling forms, ripping into their necks, arms… any place they can sink their teeth. Here and there, wolves are locked in vicious combat with things that are somehow matching their strength. Thick, crimson blood drips from mouths under soulless, red eyes onto ripped and torn rags of clothing. *Vampires.*

There are so many of them in all directions, so many forms rushing around, so many flashes of fur and claws… I move for ward in a daze, not sure how to make sense of it all. My foot catches on something soft and fleshy, and I look down to the lantern light catching on a familiar face. *Chloe!* "NO!" I scream, dropping to my knees next to her still body. Her neck is ripped and bloody, and her right arm is mangled. Even in the dim light it's easy to see how pale she's gone. *No, no, no… She can't be dead.* I reach two fingers up to her neck and hang my head over her nose. The wait feels like an eternity, and then, finally, the rise of a pulse and a warm flush of air. *She's still alive!* Hanging on by a thread, but still alive.

Without thinking, I shuffle around behind her head and lift from beneath her shoulders, then drag her back into the trees. Growls and snarls, snapping teeth, and screams surround me on all sides, but I block it all out. Only getting Chloe out of this maelstrom matters. I scan the area around me quickly as I drag us backwards, but there's no sign of Blake. *Goddess, keep her safe.*

Exhaustion eats at my legs and back but I force myself to pull Chloe further. A shadowed figure bursts through the brush in the corner of my vision and takes a wild leap toward us, fangs flashing in the moonlight. I whip toward it just as a mass of orange and black collides with it midair, sending both flying sideways into the shrub. The tiger's back on the vampire before I can even blink, pinning its arms with enormous paws and shredding the thing's throat with his teeth.

"Dean!" I scream as another form runs up behind him so fast my eyes barely catch it. It crashes into Dean, tackling him off of the vampire he had held down , and then lays into him with fangs and clawing nails. Pressure snakes around my ribs, choking the air from my lungs as I watch horrified and helpless to do anything. A powerful swipe from Dean sends his new attacker tumbling end over end, and again the tiger is on them in a flash. A blood-curdling scream erupts from the vampire's mouth, freezing the blood in my veins. Dean's teeth and claws shred skin from bone as the bloodied form claws and rakes against Dean's striped fur.

Dean takes down the vampire in a matter of seconds, tearing into its chest at its heart in a gory image I doubt I'll ever forget. The other vampire still lies where Dean had left him, body paralyzed but mouth still snapping at the air. The tiger strides toward it, then in one swift motion clamps down on what's left of its neck and cleaves its head from its body. The mouth stops moving. I exhale, not realizing I've been holding my breath this whole time as Dean turns his vibrant eyes on me. Stepping down from the lifeless form he's just finished, he starts toward me and shifts. In seconds my head lifts to see Dean standing above me naked as the day he was born. Every perfectly sculpted inch on display. But I don't have time to admire the sight. "We…" I start, and glance back down to my friend and then back to him. "We have to get her out of here."

He doesn't argue with me, doesn't tell me that she's probably dead and not worth fighting for. Dean takes an anguished look back at the sounds of the melee behind us, then nods once. He leans down and scoops her limp form into his arms in one swift movement. "Come on," he says, and I can not be more thankful for him than I am in this moment. I give him a weak smile, but I know it doesn't reach my eyes. I pull myself from the ground, not bothering to wipe the dirt covering my now ruined gown—Chloe is all that matters.

"Thank you," I say as he takes off through the trees. I follow after him, not asking where we're going. *As long as it's away from here.* All I can think is that Chloe has to be okay. She just has to. We pound through the forest, his pace still quick even with Chloe's weight. Branches and sticks scratch at my exposed skin, but I barely register it. All that matters is the howls and shouts are fading behind us, and the light of Lunar Falls is steadily cutting through the trees, growing brighter.

I'm out of breath and huffing as we cut through lawns and across streets to reach his house ten minutes later. My legs protest every step, but I ignore the stretch and pull of muscles not used to so much exertion as I run up the steps ahead of him to open the door. I thank the goddess it's unlocked as I twist the metal knob in my hand and push the door open, allowing Dean to step past me with Chloe in his arms. Silently, I follow him inside, shutting the door behind me. I rest my forehead on the door, close my eyes, and try to catch my breath. *What the hell just happened?*

When I turn, Dean has Chloe laid gently on the couch. He leans over her, one hand to her neck, his eyes scanning. I can't make out much from the door with Dean over her like he is, aside from an arm hanging lifelessly off to the side. I sink to the floor as the seconds pass. Minutes.

Dean straightens and stands stock still, then turns his face toward me. He doesn't need to say anything, it's all written on his face. Life leaves my chest.

"She's gone," he says the words quietly, barely a whisper, as if afraid to startle me. Tears flood from my eyes, soaking my cheeks in a matter of seconds.

"No," I say, shaking my head from side to side as if the action will change his answer. Dean turns, grabbing a pair of shorts from the back of a chair. He throws them on and in a few long strides covers the distance to where I'm sitting against the front door. My knees are pulled up to my chest, my face buried in my hands. He drops himself to the ground next to me and drags me into his lap. I don't fight him as his arms wrap around me, holding me hard against his chest. I bury my face into the smooth skin between his neck and shoulder. Dean doesn't rush me, doesn't urge me to move or do anything. He just rubs lazy circles onto the exposed skin of my back above the strapless gown.

I'm shaking with the torrent of tears wracking my body. I can't stop them, can't stop the pain spreading through my chest and carving a deep, black hole into my heart.

"She's gone," I finally whisper.

Twelve

I don't know how long we sit like that.

At some point, Dean had carefully moved himself out from behind me and gently laid me back against the door. He crouches next to me, then wipes the wetness from my cheeks and says something I don't quite catch. I nod—I think that's the right response—and he stands, taking a hard look into the living room at Chloe's still form, then heads upstairs.

She's gone.

I'm in a daze. The Awakening ceremony was only hours ago, but it feels like years, as if in the short span of one evening, a lifetime has passed. Hours ago the idea of not presenting with my girlfriends had been consuming me. And now one of those friends is staring at the ceiling, a red stain slowly spreading on the cushions of the couch beneath her. *Where is Blake?* Someone should tell her. *And Mom? Dad? Koa?* Are they staring up at the sky out in that clearing? Are they staining the ground, motionless out in the woods somewhere?

The awful thought jars me back to reality. I shake the thought from my mind—I need to move, to do anything other than sit here right now. I look down and take stock of myself. My dress is covered in a thousand little tears and caked in dirt and grime from our dash through the woods. My arms and hands don't look much better, with their own retinue of cuts and scrapes, dirt and blood... whose, I'm not entirely sure. I can hear Dean rummaging through a cabinet or something upstairs, and then a sink faucet turns on. *I should wash some of this off, too...*

I try to stand and almost immediately fall back down. My legs might as well be made of jelly from all the exertion tonight, and then sitting like I had for Goddess-knows how long. I grab the bannister of the stairs and slowly work myself up to standing, and try to work some life back into my legs. I use the railing to move forward, each step a little better, until I'm finally able to stand on my own.

I pass around the foyer wall into the living room toward the kitchen. Chloe sits with her head in her hands, her fingers rubbing tiny circles on her temples. *Poor thing probably feels worse than I do after her night.* I reach the kitchen sink and hit the water, then grab some hand soap and start scrubbing. I need to get this stuff off of myself and see if any of these cuts and scrapes need some attention.

I finish rinsing off my arms and hands, then grab a hand towel to dry off. It doesn't look like anything got me too deep and...

I stop.

Slowly I turn my head toward the couch.

"C-Chloe..." It comes out as barely a whisper. She doesn't

look up from where she still sits, head in hands. "Chloe!" I dart to the couch and wrap my arms around her in a bone-crunching hug, a swirl of joy and relief overwhelming every inch of me. "You're alive… you're alive!"

Chloe laughs beside me, the sound is as much a sob as a laugh. "Okay, okay… not so tight please," she chokes out, "and not so loud." She sob-laughs again. I pull back, looking her over. The wounds on her neck and arms look like they've closed up, but how well is hard to see through all the caked-on blood. Her eyes dart around the room and she looks confused, then seems to shake it off.

"I found you in the clearing and you were barely breathing and then Dean and I got you out of there and we ran back here and then he laid you on the couch and then Dean checked your pulse but he said there wasn't one and you were gone and then…" I ramble out the whole story to her in one breath. "The wolf genes must have kicked in, you must have healed."

"I guess… I don't… I don't remember much of what happened. Jon was talking, and then the boys started to go off into the woods… and then they were everywhere and I fell and…" Her big eyes go even wider as she speaks, and then she's sobbing again. I pull her back into a hug and hold her tight. She's shaking.

Footsteps sound on the stairs as Dean makes his way back down. He rounds the corner with his head down, looking over a clear case in his hands. He's still covered in cuts and bite marks, but they look days old. "I've got the first aid kit here if you need…" He stops dead as he makes it into the living room, setting the case on a console table and staring at the scene in front of him.

"Dean, look! Chloe hea—"

"Ari," he cuts me off. Every muscle he has seems to bulge with tension and his eyes fix on Chloe.

"Dean?"

"Ari. I need you to come over here please." His tone is uneasy and clipped. Chloe finally looks up at him, her big eyes still teary and full of confusion. She squeezes my arm nervously.

"Seriously, Dean, what the hell are—?"

"Ari. I need you. To come. Over here. With me. Please." There's something in his voice I've never heard before. It's still quiet, but there's an anxious demand, a mix of anger and worry. Chloe's squeezing me tighter now.

"Dean, what is your deal? Chloe is—" I look over to my friend who's staring back at me, but not at my face. A tiny rivulet of blood runs down my arm from a broken-open cut, and she stares, enthralled. "Chloe?"

She doesn't answer, her eyes slowly tracking the drip of blood. I hear a low growl rumble from Dean, and before I can even turn my head he's between us. He forces me backwards with his shoulder and in one swift motion grabs Chloe by the arms and tosses her across the room. She clatters over the small coffee table and crashes into the corner of the room, hard.

"She's turned."

"What are you talking about, Dean?" I speak the words out loud, but I know what he means. I don't want to believe him, though. *This isn't happening...* But something in my core tells me he's right. *No, no, no, no, no...*

He's already standing, putting himself between me and where Chloe is crumpled in the corner. "That isn't Chloe anymore."

Chloe raises herself up on her hands and knees. "No, no, no. I'm not... I'm not one... of those things." She's shaking her head wildly at Dean, using the wall to help herself stand.

Dean picks up the broken coffee table and holds it up, legs out towards Chloe, like a lion-tamer at the circus. I move closer behind him and lay a hand on his shoulder. "Dean... let's just chill out okay? She hasn't attacked anyone, her eyes..."

"It's still me! I'm still *me*, Dean... Ari, look at me..." Chloe holds her hands out in front of her and takes a couple steps toward us.

"Get any closer and I will drop you..." Dean cuts in over his makeshift shield, edging to the side a bit to block Chloe.

"Dean, *please*. Look at her, she's not—."

"She didn't have a pulse, Ari. She was dead. I could smell it. And now she smells... she's not a wolf anymore, Ari."

"She hasn't done anything to any of us Dean, she had plenty of opportunities to hurt me and..." And then I see it, the small white points pressing into her bottom lip. I know Dean sees it too. *Oh, Goddess...*

"Ari, it's me," Chloe pleads as she steps forward again. She gets one more stride in before Dean rushes forward, pressing her to the wall with the coffee table. His arm swings back, the muscles contorting and his nails elongating into claws, ready to dig into Chloe's throat.

"Dean! No!" I scream, desperate to stop this. *It's still Chloe...*

He rears back to strike, and the sound Chloe makes rips the air from my lungs. The fear and anguish in her eyes drops me like a punch in the stomach, and I fall to my knees. But Dean never finishes the blow. He stops himself, clawed hand hovering, staring at her and holding her against the wall while she gasps and sobs for what feels like ages.

He pushes himself away from her, letting the coffee table drop, and walks away with his hands gripping his hair. "Fuck, fuck, fuck…" He turns away like he's desperate to look at anything else, keeping his eyes off of me and Chloe, who's now curled up into a ball on the floor. I can barely look at either of them right now. Uncertainty and shock is written all over Dean's face, and a glance at Chloe is enough to shatter my heart. I'm not sure how much more I can take tonight.

"It's still Chloe, Dean…" I say softly, too emotionally drained to add any emphasis to my words.

"I know. I know…" he trails off, hands still pressed to his head, pacing. Chloe recovers enough to sit up, sniffling and leaning against the wall. I drop my head.

Silence hangs like an executioner's axe in the air. *What do we do now?*

Thirteen

Dean's constant pacing in front of me from one end of the living room to the other has all my nerves on end. I dig my nails into my hair and pull my knees up to my chest, seated on the floor in front of his recliner. Across from me, Chloe still sits in a daze against the wall. It feels like hours since anyone has spoken.

"We need to do something. We need to help her," I finally say, breaking the silence.

"How, Ari? I..." he trails off, shaking his head.

"I'm still here, guys," Chloe says hoarsely, attempting a smile that she can't quite seem to force herself to make.

Dean stops suddenly and glances sadly at Chloe, then turns toward me, his hair disheveled from running his hands through it so many times. His blazing mint eyes hold mine for a moment before he closes them with a deep exhale. "I've heard... stories... of vampires that don't turn completely," he says then, his voice quiet but hard with determination. He pauses, opening his eyes and turning toward Chloe. "Supposedly, if they never drain a human completely..." He sighs again and moves to the couch, sitting himself on the end. Chloe looks up, wiping what little tears she has left away with the back of a hand.

"I don't understand," she says, eyeing him and moving to the opposite end.

"I've heard stories from other tigers about vampires who... kept themselves 'intact,' I guess. Abel would know more..." he trails off again, shaking his head.

"I've never heard anything like that from the pack. Wolves are bred to hate vampires, and for good reason. They don't give vampires a chance to be different, they just kill them," Chloe cuts in, getting quieter as she speaks, as if realizing that now she'd be on the receiving end of that hate.

Dean shakes his head. "Tigers are a part of the pack, but... not. We answer to the wolves, but that doesn't mean we don't have our own beliefs and views on things. Me and my family answer to this pack, but we still communicate and work with other tigers. Tiger business isn't necessarily pack business."

My eyes widen as his words sink in. It wasn't as if I didn't already know most of this, but I'd never considered that weretigers might communicate within their own kind so much.

"Normally, it's on sight for a vampire that a tiger comes across, but my cousin has told me before that... Others have seen..." He pauses, glancing around us and lowering his voice. "Vampires that are able to hold on to their humanity. That don't kill."

"I'll do whatever it takes," Chloe says defiantly, a hint of hope in her voice. "I can hold onto it."

"But…" I start and stop. But what? There isn't another way. I want her to live. She's my best friend. I can't imagine a world without her in it. But a vampire? One of those bloodthirsty monsters that attacked our pack only hours ago, or one of the ones Dean's heard stories about? I start to shake my head, but the resolve in Chloe's eyes stops me. *No, we have to try. Something. Anything. She deserves that chance.*

"We have to try, Dean," I add in, piggy-backing on Chloe's optimism.

He sighs, "Either way, I know enough to know that you need to complete the transition tonight if you want to see tomorrow." With those last words his eyes harden, and he looks from Chloe to me and back.

"You need blood," I say through gritted teeth. "You'll die without it."

Chloe shakes her head. She knows it, too. "I don't want to be a monster." She chokes out each word through a pained expression.

"You won't be, Chloe, I promise we'll figure this all out… but this part… we have to do this part if we're going to try," I say, getting up and taking her hand.

Dean gets up off the couch and heads to the kitchen, toward the knife block by the stove. He pauses and takes a deep breath. "This is fucking insane," he mumbles to himself, then draws out a knife and returns to the living room. "I'm strong enough to stop you from drinking too much if you… lose control."

Chloe's lips part as we both realize what his intentions are. He's going to give her his blood, straight from the source.

"You're sure?" I ask. "Like this? She's… new… what if she can't stop, you know, right away?"

"Then you kill me," Chloe says, her body straightening with resolve as she sits up fully on the couch. Dean turns to her. "You. Will. Kill. Me," she says again, punctuating each word as she directs them at the man in front of her.

He nods once. "If you can't then… yes."

My head spins with everything in front of me. Chloe. A— I can't even think the word. I've never heard of a good vampire. Never heard of a vampire being anything other than a blood-thirsty junkie so consumed with their hunger they see everything and everyone as a feast to be devoured. Apparently, Dean has, but only in secondhand stories, if that. And now we're sitting in the living room, with Dean about to slice his arm open for Chloe to drink from. But what's the alternative? She dies. She can't die.

"Okay," Chloe says. Only the one word, firm. Certain in her decision. My eyes double in size as I watch Dean draw the knife across his arm. Quickly I dart into the kitchen, grabbing an empty cup from one of the cupboards. I take it back to him at the couch and hand it over to him.

"From a cup is better… easier," I say, and he nods, taking the glass from me. He pulls his arm above the rim, allowing the red liquid to drip inside. Chloe's entire form seems to freeze, her eyes drawn to the dark liquid congealing in the clear glass. Her fingers grip into the couch cushions as if she has to hold herself down to stay exactly where she is. I bite into the side of my cheek, poised and ready for anything.

Dean hands Chloe the cup and stands close. There's nothing casual about the way he still holds the kitchen knife. I stifle my gasp as two small fangs dart from the top row of her perfectly white teeth and she downs the glass in one swallow with a long, exultant sigh. Her eyes close and a look of pure ecstacy lines her features as she sets the cup down onto the coffee table, licking her lips. Dean still stands close, knife at the ready. Chloe doesn't look at him, as if she can still smell the wound on his arm and is disgusted by it. She turns away from him. "Thanks," she says, taking small breaths through her nose and out her mouth.

I glance from her to Dean. "What now?" I ask.

Dean shrugs as he heads to the kitchen. "We wait." A minute later, Dean returns with a washcloth pressed across his arm. He'll heal fast thanks to his Were genes. He turns his attention back to Chloe, still standing close, but not over top of her like before. I watch her intently, waiting for any of the telltale vamp signs—the blood-red eyes, the feral expression, the overwhelming smell of decaying flesh. "You'll have to learn how to control the hunger."

"We'll help you," I say, forcing a smile at my friend. She peeks up at me and her lips pull upward, but the light of her smile never makes it to her eyes. Fear shines like a beacon behind her blue irises. She doesn't look any different, aside from the tiny fangs piercing her bottom lip. I relax a little at the thought. Would she ever get those pitiless red eyes, or that savage look marring her gorgeous face? Maybe it takes more time? It's not as if I've had a lot of experience with these things. I've heard the stories, and the newly-turned Weres always come back with horrifying details of their kills, but until tonight I'd never actually *seen* any vampires. And now I'm sitting across from one.

"We will get you through this," I continue, keeping my voice firm. We have to. We have no other choice. I will *not* lose one of my best friends.

"I know we will."

Dean sighs as silence stretches through the room. The darkness beyond the living room windows begins to lighten. The sun will be rising soon. I sink back into my chair, and try to recap the events of tonight. *What the hell was this night?* First Chad, and then the magic. *My magic?* No, I can't think about that right now. Joaquin pops into my mind's eye and I quickly shake the image away. Can't think about that either. And then vampires, and running back here, and... But Chloe will be ok for now. That's what matters.

"I need to get home, at least check in with my family," I finally say, "My mom and dad are probably losing their minds worrying about me." *If they're okay.* I jump up suddenly at the thought. *This night has been too much. Too much...*

Dean nods once, as if he understands what must be a horrified expression on my face. "Go. Chloe will stay with me."

My lips thin as I eye him once more. My face softens at the hard expression set onto his chiseled jaw. He will protect her. I know that without a single doubt. "Thank you," I say with a small nod. I give my blonde friend one last glance. "What about the sun?" *Don't vampires burn in the sun?*

"I'll close the blinds and set something up for her in the basement," he says, pulling his hands into his pockets. "Easier to control the light down there." Chloe just nods drowsily to his suggestion, like she'll go along with anything as long as it means getting some rest. Exhaustion has me loopy, too, and I have to force myself to ignore the fact that Dean still has no shirt on, a full set of sculpted abs on display. *Now is* not *the time to simp.* I bite my lower lip and head to the door.

In a few short steps Dean moves across the room, and it's

as if I can feel him coming up behind me. His signature scent of eucalyptus and mint fills my senses, unraveling the tension that's been tying my insides into knots all night. I inhale the smell of him as his arms wrap around me and he pulls me into his chest. My eyes close with the want to stay here in his arms forever. The memory of everything he said tonight—before all of *this*—drifts through my mind with his body pressed against me like this. My lips part to say something but I shut them, knowing now is not the time. We can revisit that later. After I know my family is safe and Chloe is safely tucked away downstairs.

"Yell if you need me," he whispers into my hair and I turn in his arms. I wrap myself around him, allowing his strength to fill me up for a few seconds more before I pull away. I need to check on my family.

"I will," I say as his hands fall away. I turn and run from his house.

Fourteen

ater falls over me in blissful sheets as I massage shampoo through my hair. The need to be *clean* after the night's events is everything to me at the moment. Red-stained water pools at my feet as the dried blood washes off. I try not to think about where it all might have come from. Everything happened so fast. The cuts and scrapes I got weren't enough to cause all of this, so I know it can't all be mine. Images of the carnage drift through my mind. Vampires ripping into my friends—my pack—all around me. Screams and snarls that I'll have a hard time forgetting. I scour those thoughts away with my favorite coconut-and-almond body scrub.

Right now, I just need to focus on getting clean and making it through today.

I had gotten an ear full from my mom as soon as I'd entered the house—how worried she'd been, how worried my dad was…

I assured her a hundred times that I'm fine. I explained that I'd been helping Dean with some of the injured. That wasn't exactly a lie, but also not a good enough explanation for Mom as to why I didn't check in. But eventually she let it go, melting into a tearful hug with me. They are all okay, my mom, dad and brother.

We sat in the kitchen afterwards and talked for a bit. Dad was with Koa, and Mom definitely needed someone to talk to. Thankfully she did most of it, and let me get away with vague, non-committal answers. She explained how Dad had set Koa to clearing a way out for mom while he joined Jon and the older pack members to marshal some sort of organized defense. Dad had made it out mostly unscathed. Koa, however, had taken a vicious bite to his side in wolf-form. He would heal just fine, though.

One bit of worry had lifted from my chest after learning they were all okay, but it didn't take long for more to settle back into my body as Mom explained how many missing and injured there seemed to be. A good portion of the pack was still out in the woods searching, even now. Alpha Jon had called for a pack meeting today. One hour from now, to be exact, and I am even being ordered to attend. I'm not sure I particularly want to go, especially with what's going on with Chloe right now, but my concern for the rest of the pack won't allow me to skip it. I have to be there. I have to tell Blake about Chloe. She'll understand, right?

I shake the doubt from my mind and climb from the shower, wrapping a towel around my damp skin. The cool air sends prickles across my skin and I shiver. I dry myself quickly and yank on a long-sleeve shirt and some cozy boyfriend sweats. Scrunching the towel through my hair my mind drifts next door to where Dean and Chloe are. Is she still okay? Does he have a plan? What do we tell the pack? Can we tell the pack? So many questions run through my mind I don't even know where to start, and I pray Dean might have some answers. *He'll know what the right thing to do is, right?*

Once dressed, I glance at my phone. *Twenty minutes.* Slipping my feet into some warm UGGs, I grab a jacket and run out the door and down the stairs. My parents and brother are all waiting for me by the door in various states of gathering their own things. Each movement Koa makes looks pained, and Dad has to help him get his jacket on.

"Ready to go?" Mom asks, and I nod my head in answer. Dad lays a hand onto her shoulder in a gentle reassuring gesture, as if to wordlessly communicate that everything will be okay. It reminds me of Dean earlier this morning, and my shoulders relax, too. *Everything* will *be okay.*

A few minutes later, we are all gathered in the Lunar Falls Community Center near the entrance of the neighborhood. I'm toward the back, leaning up against a wall. I'm not a member of the pack—not really—so when I *am* allowed at these things I always keep to the back, as if no one will notice that I'm even here if I keep myself to the edges. Normally, Chloe and Blake stand with me, but today neither are at my side. I know where Chloe is, but where's Blake? Unease coils in my stomach like a twisting snake preparing to strike. I send a silent prayer to the Goddess that she's okay as Jon makes his way to the center of the room.

"Thank you everyone for meeting today. I know some of you haven't even had the chance to sleep yet, but after the events of last night there is much to be discussed," Jon begins as my eyes roam the room. The large space seems emptier than it should be, and there are a lot of unfamiliar faces here that aren't a part of the pack. *The Alphas from last night maybe? Are they still here?* "I want to start by thanking those of you who haven't slept, who have been out in the woods all night and morning searching for our missing brothers and sisters, and helping with our wounded. As well as the other Alphas and lieutenants who joined us, for their help last night and today. We are blessed so many of you were in attendance with an attack so large..." Jon stops as if searching for his next words just as a familiar scent fills my nose. I inhale deeply and relax a fraction as Dean leans against the wall next to me. I don't even have to look to know it's him, his presence is enough.

"Those of us not searching for the wounded and missing hunted down what vampires we could find, but from what we can tell there are still a handful that escaped. An attack this large is... unheard-of." There's an uneasy shift in the vibe of the crowd, and more than a few grumbles and murmurs. Vampires aren't social creatures and rarely congregate in large groups. Even on the Moon Awakening, it can be difficult to find enough vampires to hunt for those turning.

"As it is, we have many wolves injured. Some more seriously than others," he continues, then drops his head and pauses. "We also have four members we can confirm lost their lives in the fighting." *Where's Blake?* I desperately search the room again and still see no sign of her. Panic floods my chest. *There's no way*

Jon let something happen to his little girl... Dean must have felt something shift in me, too, as he moves closer and puts a hand on my shoulder.

"Jameson Moss, Damian Bennett, Avery Clayton, and Quinn Weaver." Jon's shoulders drop as he finishes his list. More than one person in the crowd has started softly crying. *But no Blake.* "We have two missing pack members as well." Jon says, taking in a deep breath as if preparing himself for his next words. That panic in my chest is making its way into my throat. *Two members?* "Chloe Hanshen and..." Jon pauses once more, shifting his stance before standing straighter. "And my daughter Blake. Finding them is our top priority."

His next words are lost to me as my mind whirls with the realization that Blake is missing. Chloe's a vampire and Blake is gone. *Was she turned, too?* Is she out there somewhere, turning, scared and alone. My chest aches and I'm suddenly glad for the wall at my back or I might have fallen to the floor right there. Dean's hand takes mine and squeezes but I don't look at him. My eyes flit from person to person in the crowd around me as if I'll still spot Blake amongst the members. Like it was all some big joke. But I don't see her. My shoulders crumple as all the hope inside me buckles.

The pack's gotten agitated, and the grumbles and murmurs are being voiced out loud now. *How did they get so close? How did they gather so many? We should never have allowed outside packs into the ceremony...* The anger and hurt from last night has boiled over, and they're not being coy about it. The other Alphas are looking uncomfortable, and Jon has his hands in the air trying to rein the crowd in civilly. If this keeps up he might have to remind some members where they stand, though. "That's one of the reasons we're meeting today, to…"

My eyes land on a red-haired girl I recognize from the ceremony, and I straighten a little. Blake had been dancing with her last night before Dean and I left to talk. Maybe she knows or saw something. I pull off from the wall, not releasing Dean's hand as if I need his strength to keep going. I drag him behind me as I beeline through the heated crowd. Alpha Jon seems to be gaining the upper hand in calming everyone down, but I hear none of his words as my entire focus is on the girl now only a few feet ahead of me.

She turns to me just as I reach her, a startled expression appearing on her face, but not an unkind one. A large man stands behind her, turning toward us at the same moment and taking a protective stance. *A brother maybe?* He looks too young to be her father. He's tall, almost as tall as Dean, with long, dirty-blond hair, golden eyes, and a hard expression set into a heavy, firm jaw.

"Sorry to bother you," I say as my eyes flit from her to him, and I'm suddenly wondering if approaching her was a good idea. This dude looks ready to hurt anyone he deems a threat to the girl. Dean's hands move to my shoulders and I glance back at him to find his chest is puffed out and an equally threatening expression is set across his gorgeous face. I relax a little at his protectiveness. "I noticed you were dancing with my friend last night. Blake."

The girl nods, a small, sad smile spreading across her face. "I did." Her smile grows then, as if remembering. "Blake is a wonderful dance partner," she says with a slight giggle and her cheeks redden. My brows rise, realizing she has a crush. The girl shakes her head, then her smile falls. "I'm afraid I don't have much to tell you. We were still dancing when the vampires attacked. It was... One of the vamps got close and knocked us to the ground. My brother jumped in and Blake and I scrambled away. Last I saw we were both heading into the woods, just in different directions... I'm sorry."

I nod, my eyes falling to my shoes. Of course, she wouldn't have any answers. It had been too much to hope for. No doubt Jon had already questioned the poor girl and here I am bothering her further. "I'm sorry, too," I say, bringing my eyes back to hers. "I didn't mean... I shouldn't have..." I fumble for the words and let them trail off unfinished. She seems to understand as her eyes shine with a kindness rarely seen in a pack princess. Most of the ones I've met over the years have been spoiled, self-centered girls. But this one is like Blake.

"I'm Lexi," the girl says, then gestures to the bear of a man behind her. "This is my brother Ryker. I swear he's not as mean as he looks." She says the last with a small laugh. I introduce myself and Dean. The men nod and smile to us, but only grunt in acknowledgement to each other, which makes Lexi and I both burst out laughing despite the atmosphere in the room. We spend a few more minutes talking about Blake before we say our goodbyes. It seems like the meeting is wrapping up, too—Jon has dismissed the pack but is asking the other Alphas to stay for a longer discussion. I find my parents and let them know we're leaving, then let Dean guide me through the crowd still milling through the room.

"Ready to head out?" he asks, and I nod. The fear and anxiety that talking with Lexi had helped ease, if only for a few minutes, is flooding back. *Where's Blake?*

Fifteen

The sun is high in the afternoon sky, the birds are chirping, and leaves rustle in the cool autumn wind. It'd be a gorgeous day under literally any other circumstances. I can't enjoy any of it. Dean walks beside me, neither of us saying a word as we head toward his truck in the parking lot. Breathing has become a chore with the weight on my chest. Alpha Jon's words ring on repeat through my brain: *...and my daughter Blake.* Blake. My other best friend. Rage and despair are fighting for top emotion in my mind over the thought. "It has to be Chad and his friends, right?" I ask, suddenly breaking the silence as I turn my face to look at Dean over the hood of the truck. His expressions spin so quickly they're unreadable, and then he motions to the cab of the truck. We hop inside and sit silently for a moment.

"Maybe," he finally says, shrugging.

I sigh, "Who else could have taken her? Vampires don't take

prisoners. And if she was… dead… the pack would have found her by now."

"There was that Djinn there, too."

"What would a Djinn be doing kidnapping some random pack princess? And he was with us when everything was going down. Chad's friends weren't," I say with a sigh. "The Djinn said he wiped their minds, though…"

"You can never trust what a Djinn says. Not really."

"Djinn don't lie, though," I say, turning my gaze in front of me once more and melting back into the passenger seat. None of it makes a whole lot of sense, but Chad's friends are the only group we can't account for *at all* last night. Dean leans back, too, throwing his arm over the headrest. "They don't have to lie to mislead. Do you remember his exact words?"

"I wasn't taking a transcript." I chew the inside of my cheek, wrapping my arms around myself, and we both fall silent. Djinn are tricky bastards, and also the ruling species of the supernatural world. Their word is law. I'd never met one until last night, and to be honest I'm not sure I ever want to meet another. He *seemed* genuine, but I've heard all the warnings before. 'Djinn have their own reasons, and they're never yours.'

"We should talk about the other thing that night," Dean finally cuts in from beside me. I glance at him from the side and find those turquoise eyes studying me. Does he mean what he said to me, or what happened after?

"Now's not the time, Dean. We need to figure out this Blake thing, and then there's everything with Chloe, and…" I say, prompting and hoping to avoid any talk about the pink smoke, or worse, his feelings for me. I'm still not exactly sure what my feelings for him are, and this really is *genuinely* not the time.

"I was shot," he interrupts, then runs a hand across his face. "I heard the gun go off. Hell, I feel like I even saw the bullet. Chad might have been drunk, but there was no way he'd miss from that close. I was basically on top of him. But I never felt it hit me."

I suck in a deep breath. *Nevermind, I'd rather us dissect our feelings.* I bite my lower lip as he continues. "You stopped it... The bullet. I'm not sure how, or even what exactly I saw, but you stopped it."

I tilt my head to the side, still biting on my lower lip. "I'm not sure," I say, then shake my head once. "I think so. I was panicking and threw my hands up, and then there was this pressure or something coming out of me and..."

Dean reaches over and takes my hand, giving it a gentle squeeze, thankfully stopping my ramble. Electricity zips up my arm from his touch. He just nods once, as if that was all the answer he needed. He almost looks relieved, as if me saying it meant he wasn't crazy. "We'll add it to the list of things to figure out," he says with a comforting smile. I release a shallow breath, glad that he's not pushing the subject further.

My thoughts turn back to Blake and Chloe, desperate to move on from the subject. One a vampire, the other missing. The Moon Awakening, all the other Alphas gathered, a giant vampire attack, a Djinn, and Chad and his stupid friends mixed in. He has to be a part of it, right?

There's something I'm missing. Some piece of the puzzle that I can't see. *Or nothing nefarious is going on, and the Lunar Falls pack just hit some bad luck of cosmic proportions.* There are just too many coincidences for me to write it off like that, though. Something was going on last night, and my best friends got caught up in it somehow.

"And speaking of figuring things out," Dean says after a moment, grabbing my attention before it runs wild with conspiracies. "Remember that cousin I mentioned last night? Abel?"

"The one you said you should talk to? The one who's… heard things?"

"Yeah. And I did, this morning. If anyone could help us with this, it'd be him."

His eyes are hard and full of certainty. "Are you sure we shouldn't tell Alpha Jon? Maybe, because it's Chloe…" I ask. Dean sighs and looks out the window.

"You know the answer to that. He'd kill her, or have someone else do it." Dean turns back to look at me, an uneasiness infiltrating his features. "He'd kill me, too."

A pregnant silence fills the truck cab, and I have to look away. He's right. For Jon and the other wolves this isn't 'helping' another pack member or a friend, this is treason. Aiding and abetting their mortal enemy, and giving them sanctuary right underneath the pack's nose. The full weight of what Dean is doing hadn't hit me until he said those words.

He turns back to look out the window again. The sunlight coming through the windshield catches his eyes and skims through his hair, making both shine. It traces his strong jaw and full lips and slides down his neck to his broad shoulders. That gorgeous face I've known since childhood is still there, but now there's a matureness I hadn't quite noticed before, too. Commitment lines his features just like the sunlight. He's made his decision, despite the consequences. For Chloe. For me.

Ugh, and now he's even more attractive… The same Dean who already invades my dreams. Dean who has somehow fallen into this comfortable thing between us. *Are we together now? Do I want to be together with Dean?* I'm not quite sure what we are. Maybe he is putting everything at risk out of some sense of nobility and 'doing the right thing,' not because of me or Chloe. With everything going on, now is probably not the time to figure it out, either. *Ugh, okay let's go back to talking about the gun and the pink smoke.* Feelings are not something I want to sort through right now. I just pray I'm not already too deep if it turns out I'm misreading all of this because of a pretty face.

"Anyways," Dean breaks in with a shake of his head. "More importantly, Abel works over at Summerfield Memorial. I didn't want to mention the Chloe thing over the phone, but I told him about the attack and kept things vague. He's going to snag some blood bags for us. She's going to need—food."

"Right," I say on an exhale. Blood bags are definitely better than the alternative, I guess.

"It's still hours before sunset, plenty of time to get to Abel's and talk and get back. I'll drop you off and then we can meet back at my place later."

"No, if he knows something that can help I want to hear it, too. I'm going with you." I turn toward him and set my shoulders, challenging him to brush me off. If there's anything that can help my best friend, I want to hear it firsthand.

The truck rumbles to life as Dean cranks the engine and shifts it into gear. "Okay," he says with a quiet laugh, "just be prepared."

"For what?"

"Abel's... a lot." He laughs again as he pulls the truck out of its parking spot, and we hit the road.

Sixteen

Tall oaks and pines line the two-lane highway we're taking out of Silas Creek. It dips and rises into the distance, cut here and there with mirages from the afternoon sun. Dean's eyes watch the road deep in concentration, but I doubt it's the drive he's absorbed in. I lean my head against the passenger-side window, incapable of stopping my brain from wandering between Chloe and Blake and… all the things. "So, why do you think Abel can help us?" I finally ask, broaching the silence less to talk and more to save my mind from spinning.

"Because I'm pretty sure Abel knows everything about everything," Dean answers with a soft chuckle. "Or at least more than anyone else I've ever met. He's kind of a… collector I guess. And he's always buried in a book or scrap of writing when he's not tinkering with whatever's caught his interest this week. He's the one who told me about vampires that can hold onto their humanity. Only in passing, but I remember him mentioning it."

"Just in passing? That's kind of a big thing isn't it?" I ask with an arched brow. That is the complete polar opposite to everything werewolves are taught, and as far as I know, what most of the supernatural community believes.

"Abel can get lost in tangents sometimes. Who knows what he was originally talking about. You kind of learn to tune him out sometimes." A regretful look crosses Dean's face. "Though now I'm wondering how much more I really should have paid attention."

"You couldn't have known."

"I guess not, but... everyone just kind of wrote him off as being strange, you know? Maybe we shouldn't have."

"So, he's not like all the other Weres?" I chuckle, trying to lighten things up.

"No, no he's not," Dean says with another laugh and adjusts his hands on the steering wheel. A green sign flies by the truck, letting us know we're only a few miles away from Summerfield. "But he will know something about Chloe's situation and what we can do. I'm sure of it. Just have to think of the right way to bring it up so he doesn't freak."

Dean's last comment sends a worrying thought bubbling up in my mind. "Can we trust him?"

"We can trust him."

I shoot Dean a skeptical look. "Are you sure? This is kind of a big thing to just cross our fingers over, Dean."

"I'm sure. Abel doesn't have the prejudices most Weres have. And we don't have to worry about him talking to anyone else in the pack about it."

"Wait, he's in the pack? Doesn't that mean he has to answer

to Jon and all that? And why don't I know him?" I rattle off, now with even more questions about this cousin.

Dean sighs. "You've probably seen him before once or twice, though I doubt you'd remember. Abel doesn't like to make an impression. He always keeps to the margins and would bolt as soon as the event was over." I try my best to think back to previous Moon Awakenings and pack meetings, but can't place him. I shrug. "Anyway, he's always been kind of a recluse, but he'd pop in for the required stuff. Then remember the vampire attack a couple years ago? The one that got Blake's mom and Chloe's dad and a couple others?" Dean asks the last gingerly, shooting me a sympathetic look before turning back to the road.

"Yeah," is all I can muster up in response. Up until recently, that would have been a contender for the worst night of my life. Blake and Chloe had been hanging out at my house while their parents and a few other higher-ups in the pack had a meeting out near the clearing. Blake was ranting about the orange dress her mom had gotten her for the upcoming Moon Awakening while Chloe and I tried to convince her it wasn't that bad. And then three soft, rhythmic knocks at my bedroom door crushed all of our naive illusions.

All it takes is one thought of that night to pull up a freeze frame of my mom's face as she comes into the bedroom. Shock and panic and grief were written all over her features while her red, watery eyes betrayed any attempt to look calm and in control. Chloe got quiet, Blake got angry, and I froze, not knowing what to say or what to do for my best friends. The pack had collectively boxed that memory away, and just one hard stare from Alpha Jon will shut down any overheard talk of that night.

I shake the thoughts from my head and throw Dean another—much softer—"Yeah."

"Well, apparently, he helped Jon out with something to do with the attack, and to thank him, Abel gets to do his own thing—no more required attendance or anything like that. Not that I think anyone has noticed or cared. It was probably Abel's idea," Dean says with a sniff.

"Huh. Jon's usually pretty strict on pack rules," I reply distractedly, a small part of my mind still reliving that night two years ago. It *is* odd for him to let someone off the leash like that, but then again, he had just lost his wife and several friends—maybe he was really just that grateful. "What did he help with?"

Dean just shrugs, "Don't know." He leans forward in the seat, squinting ahead up the road. "This should be it," he says as we approach a dirt road cutting off into the trees, marked by a faded, white mailbox and a few discarded tires. I shoot him a hesitant look that he must have caught, even with his eyes still on the road—"He likes his privacy," Dean returns with a smirk.

We turn off the blacktop and rumble our way back through the woods, curving here and there as the dirt road takes us uphill. Slowly, the trees and brush begin thinning out, until finally opening up into a large field, spotted with tufts of overgrown dry grass. An aged foursquare farmhouse sits in the center, complete with a full front porch and a large detached garage with an old blue Jeep parked out front. Four car bodies—along with a pile of parts—sit to its right in various states of rust, sprouting weeds and flowers from every crack and outlet. A figure leans against the open door frame of the garage, watching as we approach.

"Ready?" Dean asks as he pulls in behind the Jeep, shifting into park and turning off the truck. I suck in a deep breath.

"Ready." We both hop out at the same time and I circle around the front of the truck to Dean's side. We brush shoulders, and the electricity of his touch and closeness fills me with confidence. He throws me a reassuring smile and then sets his shoulders, looking ahead to his cousin, who still leans casually against the frame of the door. Abel pushes off from the door and takes a few steps forward, wiping what must be grease or oil off his hands onto a red rag before stuffing it into the back pocket of his blue jeans. In a lot of ways he looks like a slightly older version of Dean—tall and athletic, with strong, built shoulders put on display by the white tank top he wears. Shaggy blonde hair falls almost to his forest-green eyes, and his strong square jaw sports a healthy amount of stubble.

"Dean," he says with a relaxed drawl, giving him a curt smile and a nod as we approach. "You didn't mention you were bringing anyone."

"Yeah, sorry, it was kind of last minute. Abel, this is Ari. Ari, Abel."

"Nice to meet you," I stammer out, social anxiety getting the better of my voice.

"Miss," he answers with another clipped smile, before holding my eyes with a searching stare. The small wrinkles at the sides of his eyes deepen, and it seems as if he's trying to come to some sort of decision. His eyes finally lighten and a genuine smile returns to his face.

"Working on something back there?" Dean jumps in. Abel smiles wide and waves us into the garage. He doesn't wait to see if we're following, turning on a heel and heading into the lighted interior. Inside is wall-to-wall *stuff*. Vintage signs line the walls above various machinery and tools, and piles of metal parts lay here and there in organized chaos. Abel leads us to a battered wooden table set in the middle, itself covered in odds and ends in different states of repair.

"Know what it is?" Abel asks excitedly. Metal plates and a crank lay next to a chipped red metal casing and a glass sphere. *Pieces to a gumball machine*, I smile to myself, but before I can triumphantly respond, Abel answers his own question. "It's a gumball machine!"

Dean and I speak over each other with different versions of 'very cool' to his reveal, and it *is* pretty cool, but I doubt he hears us. Abel's already excitedly giving us the rundown on the machine. "It's from the 30's, from the Norris Manufacturing Company—they got the patent in 1923. See the original machines were all chrome; the red-casings didn't start showing up until…" He trails off, and turns around with a bashful smile. "Y'all just got here… Want something to drink?" He motions toward the house. "Oh, I got your blood for you, too. It's in the fridge."

Seventeen

Abel leads us through a side door into the kitchen and makes his way over to a refrigerator yellowing with age. "Let's see… I got water, tea, a few sodas… A little early for a beer," he laughs to himself.

"Water would be great," I answer, and Dean 'mhmms' in agreement. The kitchen appliances and aesthetic are all on the older side, but everything's clean and well-kept up with. The smell of old books and parchment is overwhelming even here, though, and I look around Dean toward the living room while Abel rummages around for a few water bottles in the refrigerator. It looks just like the garage, except the stacks of tools and parts have been traded for books and rolls of paper, strewn about on tables and bookcases, or just stacked right on the carpet. Shelves and cases of oddments line most of the walls. It's as if a library and a museum collided in his living room. *I guess that's what Dean meant by 'collector.'*

Abel turns from the fridge and hands us both a bottle of water, and we all pause to drink. "So, Dean tells me you work at the hospital. What do you do there?" I ask, trying to keep to small talk for now before I ramble out an avalanche of questions about vampires and Chloe and... everything.

"I work in the morgue."

"O-oh," I stammer out. I'm not sure what I was expecting, but it wasn't that. I'm suddenly hoping I didn't make a face.

"It's okay," he laughs, "I get it. Most people find it a little strange. Bothered by their own mortality, I suppose. But Summerfield is a small place, so there's usually not a lot going on. It gives me plenty of time to do some reading or writing, or some thinking. And the dead are quiet, which helps." He pauses thoughtfully for a second. "Usually."

"Usually?" I ask with a giggle. He just nods with an 'mhmm' and a straight face. *Oh, he's serious.*

"It also gives me the opportunity to steal some blood for my cousin here," he says with a pointed look at Dean. "Was the attack that bad? Were genes ain't taking care of everything?" he asks, and I can't shake the feeling that there's a bit of suspicion in the question.

"It was a... bad night. I don't think I've ever seen so many vampires together at once," Dean answers with a little hesitation. I wonder if he caught the same feeling I did. "Have you ever heard of vamps gathering up like that?" he asks, probably trying to deflect.

"Not since the Djinn took over, when those smoky bastards were directing whole hordes of them. At least from what I've read." Abel looks like he's ready to spit when he mentions

Djinn. The image of Joaquin's sharp, dark eyes leering at me over Chad's crumpled form floods my mind for a moment, and now I'm ready to spit, too.

"A lot of people got hurt. Some of them are still in really bad shape."

Abel nods. "Yeah. Yeah, I'm sure they are." He looks down at his shoes, and the briefest flash of disappointment crosses his face. When he looks back up, he's wearing a resigned smile. "But you and I both know if they had lost so much blood that the healing wasn't helping and they needed a transfusion, they'd already be dead."

The room goes silent as Abel pins Dean with another biting stare. *So much for 'bringing it up the right way,'* I think to myself, shifting my gaze between the two men. Abel crosses his arms and lets out a long, audible breath before continuing, "Now, I know whatever's going on can't be good or you wouldn't be calling me up askin' for *blood*. But whatever it is, we're family, Dean—you don't have to lie to me." He pauses, and lets his last statement hang in the air. There's a genuineness to the way he said it, and I can't help feeling like he meant every word. "Now why don't we all sit down, and you can tell me what's really going on."

Dean continues locking eyes with him for another few moments, then deflates and shakes his head. "Okay... And yeah, you probably should be sitting down." Abel throws him a curious and concerned look over his shoulder as he cleans up the kitchen table a bit, stacking a few papers to the side and then discarding a plate in the sink. Dean cocks his head to the side and gives me a half-hearted encouraging smile as we make our way to the table. Abel finally joins and holds his palms out to us, looking from Dean to me and back, waiting for someone to start talking.

"Well?"

I'm tired of being coy about all this—Chloe needs help, and Abel's probably our best bet to find some. If Dean says we can trust him, then let's see if he was right. *Time for that avalanche.* "Last night, the pack was attacked during the Moon Awakening ceremony by a huge group of vamps, just like Dean told you..." Abel and Dean snap their eyes to me, both looking surprised. The story of finding Chloe on the ground, the mad dash back to Dean's, the scene in the living room, and feeding Chloe the cup of blood pours out of me. Abel looks more and more incredulous with each detail, until he's got his hands running through his messy hair and his face scrunched up like he just tasted something awful.

"Okay. So. Your friend got turned into a vamp. Dean here sliced his arm open and fed her some blood. And now she's sleeping in the basement. That about sum it all up?" Dean and I both look to each other, and then back to Abel. Chad and the Djinn can come later—right now, I want to know how to help Chloe.

"Yep."

Abel opens his eyes and huffs, adjusting himself in the chair. He licks his lips. "Now Dean, you know I don't have a hard-on for rules and *tradition* like the wolves you have to goose step for, and beggin' your pardon, miss Ari, as we've just met, but I'd really just like to point out how incredibly stupid and dangerous all of that was." He fixes us both with another stare, "You had no idea what would happen when you gave her that blood, and even as fresh as she was, with you not shifted she could have ripped out your throat before you could say 'Oops.'"

Another weighted silence fills the room in a day that has already been full of them. It had been incredibly dangerous in hindsight, but he wasn't there last night. He didn't look into her eyes like we did. *It's still Chloe.* "Even so, what's done is done. Dean said you've talked about vampires that can control themselves, that can hold onto their humanity. So," I take a deep breath, "how do we help our friend?"

Abel purses his lips and studies my face. He's giving me the same look he had earlier, as if trying to make another decision. Then he shoots us both a wry smile, "I need to learn not to talk so much I guess…" He pauses. "Cei Reținuți."

Dean and I both look at each other and then back to Abel, confusion painting Dean's face just as much as I'm sure it's painting mine. "W-what?"

"Cei Reținuți. It's Romanian for 'the restrained,' and it's what they're usually called, academically at least. See there was this second son of a Wallachian noble named Marius Pătrașcu who wrote about them way back when. Supposedly, he himself had been turned and the majority of the writing comes from his personal experience." He turns to me, excitement shining in his eyes. "If you're interested, I have a french translation in the living room you can borrow and—"

"Maybe just the cliff notes, Abel," Dean cuts in with a placating smile.

"Yeah, it all sounds interesting Abel, really, but…" I take a breath, "So, what happened to this Marius guy?"

"Oh, he was burned at the stake."

"Abel…" Dean jumps in again, rubbing his eyes.

"Right," Abel sighs, looking a little abashed. "Anyways, your friend is going to basically be a recovering addict that still needs the drug to survive. Most people that get turned can't even last a day before giving in, but a rare few make it. Sheer force of will, I guess. Maybe it gets a little easier the longer they fight it." He shrugs. "Most everything I've heard and read is all theory and secondhand at best. Only ever seen one."

"Wait, you've seen one of these… Cei Ret-something… before?" I immediately lean forward in my seat. *There* is *hope for Chloe, then.*

Abel leans back in his chair and absent-mindedly plays with the edge of the table. "Reținuți, but yeah 'bout a year or so back when I was traveling. Pretty little thing. I trailed her for half the night—couldn't believe it. The scent was there, but… if not for that, I might not have even known. 'Til she fed, of course. Got some poor sucker in an alley. But… she stopped. It was nice and clean—no snarling or ripping or nothing. She said something to him and after a few minutes the guy got up and walked away like nothing happened. But the second she caught me snooping, she was gone. I'm actually kind of embarrassed she brushed me off so easily, though I suppose you get good at buggin' out fast when everyone wants to kill you."

Abel scans us both under furrowed brows from across the table. I don't even look to see Dean's reaction. I'm too busy trying to process all this information. I open my mouth to ask another question, but Abel cuts in first, deadly serious: "And make no mistake, pretty much everyone will be looking to kill your friend. You two want to go forward with helping your friend… it's very noble of you, don't get me wrong… but don't forget the situation you're in: you're hiding public enemy number one in a neighborhood full of people who're literally bred to kill them. And if they sniff her out, Jon's gonna kill her, and then he's gonna kill your friend Ari, here," he says quietly as his emerald-green eyes bore into me, "and once he's done with that he's going to turn your ass into a coat." He ends, holding Dean in the same stare he gave me.

My mouth works silently at his implication. "Jon wouldn't…" I trail off. Would Jon kill me, though? Killing Dean makes cold, logical sense—he's part of the pack, and there are *laws*. Even Chloe, one of his daughter's best friends, for the same reasons. There are laws. It had never occurred to me that I could receive the same punishment despite being someone he clearly views as outside the pack.

Abel's eyes go dark, and there's a simmering anger under his words that seems poised to boil over. "You have *no* idea what that man is capable of. None." There's something more than anger in his eyes and words. There's fear there, too.

He takes a long deep breath, followed by an equally long exhale, deflating back into his chair. His smile returns, "Which is all to say: be careful." *What the hell was all that?*

"Right. So, all we can really do is keep an eye on Chloe and keep her safe, make sure she doesn't fall over the edge."

"I wish I had more for you, but essentially, yeah. And a lot of it is gonna have to come from her. I hope you know this Chloe *real* well. Y'all are gonna be walking a tight-rope in more ways than one. Control her intake, control her movements. Make sure she stays inside. No visitors, understand?" Abel gives Dean a hard look. "You'll probably need to smell proof the house, too. How do you feel about taking up gardening?" Dean sniffs, but nods with understanding.

"So, we need to keep her prisoner?" I ask.

"That's my advice," he replies matter-of-factly. "You also need to start thinking about getting her out of Lunar Falls. Hell, out of Silas Creek for that matter. She can't stay here." We'd all already talked about as much, but it doesn't make hearing Abel's words any easier. He eyes me from under lowered brows, then turns to me with a disarming smile. "Hey, there's hope, though."

He looks deep in thought for a moment, then continues, "I've heard talk of enclaves for… people like her. Safe havens. They're called 'Nests' I guess. I don't know much other than that they're pretty much impossible to find—the second you think you have, they go to ground. And… that's probably not helping," He pauses. "I've got a pen pal—a friend—up north that would probably know more. I'll reach out to him as soon as y'all leave. He might know more about this whole situation, for that matter."

Dean shifts next to me, checking his phone. He sighs and turns to me regretfully, "We need to go, Ari."

"Right. Thank you Abel, for everything." We all stand in unison, awkwardly adjusting wrinkles in shirts and pants and muscles from such an abrupt end to the conversation.

"Of course," Abel says with a warm smile. "Listen, Dean's got my number if y'all need anything else. I'll see if I can work out a better way of getting your friend the… supplies she needs. I'll dive into the literature for you, too, talk to a few friends, see if I can't find anything else that might be helpful."

"That would be amazing, Abel," I answer half-heartedly. It was all so much—my thoughts ping-pong around in my skull: from the Cei Reținuți to the consequences of the pack finding out, to the woman Abel had seen who had held on, to having to sneak Chloe out of town, to the 'nests' to… everything. Hope. Despair. Hope. Despair. Back and forth until my head is pounding.

Abel steps forward and takes my hand. "Hey, girl, smile. Could be worse. You could be all mixed up with fae and Djinn and…" He trails off, seeing Dean and I shoot each other a nervous glance. "Oh?"

"There was a Djinn there, too," I offer quietly. He huffs out a laugh and rubs his temples.

"I mean, why not, right?" Abel chuckles again, but it definitely doesn't feel like he finds anything funny. He looks out the kitchen window toward the sun, hanging lower now on the horizon. I see it too. "That's gonna have to be a conversation for another day," he finally says, lips tight.

"Thank you again, Abel," I say as I shake his hand and turn toward the door. Dean steps forward and the two men hug, patting each other on the back before grunting a goodbye. We all take one last look around at each other, the gravity of everything settling over us. I say one last goodbye to Abel, and then we head out the side door toward the truck.

We're half-way there when the door slams open, with Abel jogging out to catch us. "Hey! Wait up! Y'all forgot your blood."

Eighteen

The night after getting back from Abel's felt like a blur. The ride back was mostly silent, both of us seemingly lost in our own thoughts while I held the white styrofoam cooler full of blood bags in my lap. Tiredness had been slowly creeping its way into my bones, and the ride back only made it worse. Chloe woke up not too long after we got back, coming up from the basement looking no worse for wear. That freshness disappeared after Dean and I gave her the rundown of our meeting with Abel, though. "That's… a lot," was all she had offered up in response.

Dean had given her one of the blood bags, and Chloe had greedily downed it without taking a breath until her chin was dripping crimson from the overflow. And then we did the exact same thing we had done the previous night—waited and watched in silence. At some point I started nodding off, the lack of a good night's sleep and the quietness permeating the living room catching up with me. Both Chloe and Dean, who already had dark circles alighting under his eyes, had told me to go home. I *had* needed to check in with my family, and truth be told, I was happy to be kicked out and sent to bed. My brain definitely needed the rest and, after several assurances from both Dean and Chloe, I complied.

It's mid-afternoon when I finally wake up and make my way back over to Dean's. Chloe would have been sleeping for hours by now, but for some reason I feel like I need to be there watching out for her. I shake my head. It doesn't make sense, but it seems like not much does anymore. I knock a few times on the door and wait, looking up and down the street. It's so strange to think that a few days ago, all these houses had been full of friends and neighbors, and now... Now I have to be on my guard with all of them. We're harboring a fugitive, and any of these people could be the one to turn us all in if we're not careful.

Dean appears at the door then, making me jump a little as I'm yanked from my thoughts. He's got on a brown suede jacket with a sheep-fur lining, a gray t-shirt, and jeans. Slung over his back is a small, black gym bag. "Hey, come in," he says, waving me inside.

"Going somewhere?" I ask, brushing past him into the foyer. He takes a quick look around outside from the door before shutting it and stepping back into the house.

"I was just about to head out, actually. I've got a few errands to run and I need to stop by work for an hour or two. Chloe's asleep downstairs if you were looking for her. Probably best to let her sleep, though. I'm not sure how vampires react when you interrupt their beauty sleep," he says with a muted smile. I get the feeling he's only half-joking.

"Yeah, I figured she would be, it's just... I don't know, I feel like I need to be here for her, watching over her or something." I shrug.

"You want to protect your best friend. It's cool, I get it," he answers. "You're welcome to hang out here as long as you want."

"Thanks." He gives me that smirk that always sends a shiver down my back, but it feels like more than a flirty smile this time. It feels like we're in this together.

"I'll try to be quick," he says, looking toward the door. "And if I'm not back before Chloe wakes up... Just be careful, Ari. It's still only been a couple days." I nod my head, sucking in a deep breath. He just wants me to be safe, but I know Chloe wouldn't hurt me, no matter what she is. She won't, not ever. I just know.

I keep that all to myself, though, and throw him a quick nod and reassuring smile. He gives me one last look with an unreadable expression on his face, then closes the distance to the front door and leaves through it, locking it behind him.

It's been exactly three hours and twenty-two minutes since Dean left. I know because I can't stop glancing at my phone, either to check the time or in the ridiculous hope that Blake will text me and tell me she's okay—that she's made it back home safe and sound. Shockingly, the latter hasn't happened yet. Chloe is still asleep downstairs, or at least I'm assuming she is. I haven't gone and checked, partly because I couldn't handle it if she's not there for some reason, and partly because I don't want to wake her if she is. At least I've got something to give her if she wakes up hungry now, aside from my own... Nope, not thinking about it.

I glance around the tidy house. Dean has done a nice job of furnishing it, though decor must not be high on his list of priorities. But he's a dude—simple makes sense for him. The color palette he's chosen is exactly what I imagine a guy like him would pick. I always pictured him as a black satin sheets and leather furniture type of guy. Apparently, I wasn't far off the mark. It's not as if I haven't seen the inside of his house plenty over the last couple days, but focusing on the details of his hardwood floor and plush white rug lets my brain focus on something simple rather than the series of unfortunate events that has been my life since the Moon Awakening. Simple is what I need right now while I wait for... I don't know what. So, I continue cataloging.

He has dark gray blackout blinds on every window—a great choice in retrospect. They look like the automatic kind that connects to some smart device, and I spot a screen display for one in his kitchen. A large flat-screen TV dominates the space above a contemporary fireplace. Built-in shelves connect on either side of it, filled with hundreds of books. I didn't know Dean was the reading type—He and Abel must be more alike than he lets on. I smile to myself as I make my way over to his shelves. You can tell a lot about someone by what they read.

A book also sounds like a good distraction while I pass the time. I'm still not sure what exactly I expected coming over here today. I've already run back next door and grabbed a bag of some of my clothes for Chloe until we can sneak over some of her own. I ate lunch a couple hours ago and already planned out dinner for later, but I won't be starting that for at least another hour or so. I'm left with nothing else to do but wait: wait for Chloe to wake up, wait for Dean to return… Wait to figure out what the hell to do next.

I run my finger across the row of books, reading the different titles printed across the spines until I finally land on one that catches my interest. I reach out to pull it from the shelf just as a loud 'pop' rings through the living room. I whip around to find the source and immediately start coughing through a haze of green smoke. Alarms blare in my mind as I remember this same entrance from a couple nights ago. The hazy tendrils of fog clear, leaving behind the figure of a man—a Djinn—sharply dressed like he was on the night of the Awakening.

"Joaquin," I say, crossing my arms, the book still held in one hand.

The tall man smiles a toothy grin, making his face crinkle around his thin lips. "Hello there," he says as he flops down onto Dean's sofa, throwing one arm over the back of the couch and crossing one leg over the knee of the other, reclining back into the cushions. I don't move.

"What the hell are you doing here?" I ask, not at all politely. You can't just burst into someone's home like this, and he is definitely not welcome here.

The man's face transforms into a wounded frown. "Well, that's rude," he answers with a scoff.

"No, 'rude,'" I reply with air-quotes, "is randomly appearing in someone's living room unannounced."

He cocks his head to the side, as if considering my words. "Fair," he finally concludes, pointing an agreeing finger at me before holding his palm out towards me and putting on an air of meekness. "But surely you would offer shelter to your kin."

My forehead crinkles in confusion. "What?"

"Your kin, another Djinn…" His words trail off and now it's his turn to look confused, though I can't tell if it's genuine or just more pageantry. "You're Djinn, obviously."

I move to put the book I've been holding down on a nearby end table, but keep him in my sight. His dark, penetrating eyes follow my movement while he sits completely still.

"Well, *half*," he says with a slight sneer I don't miss, as if the word itself insulted him. I can't shake the way those eyes following me has the hair rising on the back of my neck. My brain is shouting every warning it can think of at me… there's just something *implicitly* dangerous about this person. I need to get this man out of the house—and quickly—before Chloe wakes up or Dean gets back.

"You shouldn't be here," I finally say, forcing my shoulders to relax and adamantly ignoring the fact that he just told me I'm half-Djinn. *We can process that later…* I move to a recliner, feigning casualness. *I can't let him intimidate me. He needs to go.*

Joaquin shifts on the couch, re-crossing his legs and brushing an imaginary piece of lint from his impeccably ironed pants. "Interestingly enough… neither should you."

"I was actually invited." I retort, trying to sound confident in my defiance.

"Oh no, no, no. I don't mean here," he titters, gesturing to the floor, "in this home… I mean *you*. You are *incredibly* illegal, did you know? A *lusus naturae*. An abomination—" he let's the word hang in the air. "To the Council, that is."

I'm struggling to keep my face placid. "And to you?"

He hums under his breath. "Truth be told, I'm duty-bound to kill you, but... You really have no idea, do you?" he asks, cocking his head to the side and studying me with those shrewd eyes yet again.

I grind my teeth at his obvious deflection, but the only thing to do is keep playing his shitty game. "No idea of what?" I ask.

"That you are part Djinn... Oh come now, was shooting smoke from your hands the other night not a bit of a giveaway?"

"I didn't... I," my mouth moves, but I can't put anything together. That façade of composure I'd been working on completely disappears. *It* was *me. It was my magic.*

Another predatory grin slices his face, and his eyes narrow. "Say what you will about your father's proclivities, between the brilliant wards and this," he says, waving his hand around at me, "he is thorough."

Surprise shakes my nerves even more, and any hope of regaining my composure is gone. I've never met my biological father—in fact, in sixteen years, I can count the number of times he's crossed my mind on one hand—but somehow the idea that he cares enough about me to shield me from all this is both unbelievable and believable all at once. Especially if what Joaquin is saying about the Council is true. Joaquin snickers as if this is all some silly thing to him. "Oh, your father has done a *very* good job of keeping you hidden—even from yourself!" He huffs in mock amazement. "Why, I almost didn't find you myself!"

"How did you find me then?" I take a deep breath and try to center myself amid all this dizzy spinning my mind is doing. *I know he's playing one, but what is his game?* He certainly loves the sound of his own voice, and I realize that maybe if I just let him talk, he'll tell me himself.

Joaquin reclines back again, a look of sheer self-indulgence settling into his whetted features. "So glad you asked! You see a couple years ago, your adoptive Alpha had gotten himself into a bit of a pickle with the locals, and reached out to me for some... guidance. Now Silas Creek is adorable, don't get me wrong, but aside from Jon's little situation there was nothing here to really pique my interest... until I caught the faintest whiff of Djinn magic. Of course, it was gone as fast as it came, and *so* faint that at first I wasn't even sure of exactly what it was I felt. But the feeling *lingered* the whole time I was here. It would flitter from here to there, passing by my senses only to move on before I could get a bearing. And then one day, in a moment of pure serendipity, I came across three teenage girls while passing through Lunar Falls with Jon. And one of those girls," he pauses briefly and points a long, slender finger in my direction, "Had the smell on her." The sheer giddiness coming off him lets me know how proud he is of discovering me when no others had before. It makes my stomach curdle.

He continues, "It was definitely a ward, and definitely the work of a Djinn, but you see, warding is typically a powerful..." He stops again, looking thoughtful. "Probably more tradecraft than this conversation requires. Long story short, you were warded, but whoever placed said ward on you was diffusing the magical signature to different points in the surrounding country-side." He claps his hands together, and for once there's no doubt he's being genuine. "Brilliant. Absolutely brilliant!"

So, I guess my dad is a smart Djinn, then? Where was this all going? "Okay, so you found me... why didn't you turn me in to the Council?"

"Well, I had to be sure, of course. See, at maturity you half-breeds get your magic coming in full-force just like full-blooded Djinn, and that is a wave of power so strong even *these* wards couldn't hide it. And after the other night, and seeing you now here before me, I have no doubts." Joaquin waves a hand flippantly before continuing further. "Calm down, I haven't told a single soul for obvious reasons."

I frown at the man in front of me. I can't be sure if he intends to help me, or use me for something I haven't quite figured out yet. "You don't want others to find me?" I ask, trying to weave between what he's saying and what he's not.

"Precisely."

"Why?"

"Boredom? Amusement?" He leans in conspiratorially, "Prophecy? I have my reasons. And lest we forget, your father needs you to stay safe."

My fingers dig into the cushions on either side of me as my mind swirls through everything he's just told me. *Djinn don't lie*, I remind myself. But they can give you a select truth that amounts to just the same. Joaquin has plans, that much is obvious—what Djinn doesn't have their own twisted agenda—The question is, what the hell does it have to do with me?

"So, you know my father?"

Joaquin shrugs, folding his hands in his lap. "I know him, all Djinn *know* each other in a manner of speaking. You see, we're all connected to some extent. We can sense each other, feel another's joy, sadness... even when one of us blinks out of existence. But *which* Djinn he is... no, I don't know."

"Then how do you know it's my father and not my mother?"

He chuffs as his eyes roam around the living room. "Because I am Djinn. We just know things. I can smell him on you, though it's barely a trace after so many years. Not enough to pinpoint who he was obviously, but enough to know that he's the one who warded you and not your mother. She must have been a human, probably dead."

"Seriously?" I ask, and he nods once as if the words he's just inflicted upon me have no meaning. No importance.

"We're getting off-topic. The point I was trying to make a minute ago before your daddy issues cropped up was that half-breeds such as yourself are not connected the same. We can't feel you the same way we feel each other. We can only sense your magic—which is why it is very, *very* important that you do not use any magic whatsoever. If another of our kin senses you, I can't promise they'll be as understanding as I am." His head suddenly snaps toward the basement stairs, drawing my attention with it. "Your friend is awake," he says quietly, and my spine stiffens.

Shit, shit, shit! I mentally pray she stays downstairs. The last thing we need is this Djinn guy figuring out what she is. "And I think she's hungry," he says, turning back to me. Something darker and sinister shimmers in his eyes now with those words. He already knows, I realize, as a whole new wave of panic swells over me.

NINETEEN

Chloe peeks her head out from the basement stairs and I palm my face into a hand. This is bad. Very bad. "You. Are. Divine!" Joaquin says as he stands, clapping his hands together once before waving her in. "Come, come! Sit down and join us."

Chloe hesitates for a second before agreeing, then slowly makes her way over to the living room. I suck in a sharp breath, trying to run through every possible scenario before me. Either he's on my side—or just doesn't care enough—and he isn't going to try and kill her, or he kills her and there's nothing I can do to stop him. I mean, apparently I'm half-Djinn but like... I don't know how to be a damned Djinn. *Maybe it'll just happen like it did the other night?* I shift slightly in my chair, positioning myself to jump up at a moment's notice if need be and... *And what? Throw my hands in the air at him?*

Joaquin turns back towards me, his eyes narrowing over a disappointed smirk. "Don't. We *literally* just talked about this," he says, pinning me with a knowing stare. I grind my teeth to keep from telling him I hadn't planned on anything, but as soon as I open my mouth, he stops me short with a shake of his head and a raised hand. "Don't try to deny it, I felt you searching. And before you think of doing something stupid again, I'll tell you flat out that I'm not going to harm her unless she gives me cause. Using your magic would be *much* more dangerous for you and your friend here than for me."

"Because Djinn can sense my magic?" I ask tentatively, just as Chloe reaches the edge of the white carpet in the center of the room, a look of confusion and nervousness straining her normally gentle appearance. She hadn't known about me having magic. *Well, she does now.* Joaquin ignores my question and twists his right hand, turning toward Chloe. A clear bag of red liquid appears in his waiting palm as a slowly spinning mist of green dissipates. He extends the bag toward my blonde friend. "This is for you." Chloe stares at it, but doesn't take the bag. He shakes it toward her once more. "I'm sure you're starving, I know I'm always famished when I wake up. I'd really rather you not try and eat us."

Chloe visibly deflates, the fight going out of her in one stroke. The fact she managed that long surprises me. She snags the bag from his curled fingers and bites down, devouring the liquid in a matter of minutes, but Joaquin is already prepared with a second bag. She greedily drains that one, too, as Joaquin watches with anticipation, biting his lower lip. Chloe finishes sucking down the last rivulets of blood, a worryingly euphoric look of relief washing over her features. The Djinn jumps back in mock panic, his eyes darting this way and that.

"Nothing?" he questions, collapsing with disappointment. "That will be enough for now. Limiting yourself is going to be key." Joaquin turns back to me, meandering his way towards the couch once more and pats the cushion for Chloe to join.

I school my features back into a normal, calm demeanor. "You didn't answer my question," I say, trying to direct the attention off Chloe, who suddenly looks horrified with herself after licking the blood from her lips. She gives me a grateful look before darting off to the kitchen to dispose of the evidence.

"Yes, partly because we can sense your magic," Joaquin says dispassionately, checking the manicured nails on one of his hands as he settles on the couch and crosses his legs once more. "I'd hate to see all of your father's hard work ruined by an unexpected visitor. But *mostly* it's because you're untrained and still wild. Trying to use your magic would be more likely to backfire on you than it would to hurt me, all the while flashing like a beacon to the Council that you exist." Joaquin's features turn hard, his lips a thin line as he continues. "And make no mistake, if another Djinn finds you they will kill you without hesitation. But thankfully for you," he continues in a fatherly tone, "I found you first."

I ball my fists in my lap. So, I have magic, but if I *use* that magic, I die. *Fan-tastic.* Chloe makes her way back into the living room then, her face washed and every trace of the blood she just gorged on minutes before gone. Joaquin's face softens as he glances up at her and once again pats the couch beside him. She chooses the vacant recliner instead. I don't blame her. Joaquin hasn't shown any sign of being our enemy—hell, he may even be a friend—but something about his presence screams at me to stay alert. Maybe it's simply because he's Djinn. *But aren't I one, too? Well, half…* Maybe it's just him. Either way something's telling me not to let down my guard. I hope Chloe doesn't either.

"Now that you've joined us at last," Joaquin begins again, holding his attention on Chloe. "I'm assuming this," he waves his hand over her, "Happened the night of the Moon Awakening?"

Chloe nods cautiously, and Joaquin's smile grows even bigger. *Fucking Creepy.*

"So, you're brand new! And you clearly didn't drain anyone yet, so your humanity is still intact." Neither Chloe or myself say a word, but Joaquin doesn't seem as if he needs us to. "Very interesting. Very, very interesting."

I direct my best 'and' look at the Djinn. His demeanor calms as if talking about the weather.

"This transition to post-death is no doubt difficult for you, but it is important for you to know the true depth of what you are. And you are nothing short of a marvel."

"Umm… excuse me?" Chloe says then, speaking for the first time since coming upstairs, her voice timid.

"A vampire with her humanity intact! Do you know how rare that is?"

Chloe and I eye each other. How much does he know about the… Restrained? Abel knew about them—had even seen one before—and mentioned others who knew, too. Surely a Djinn would know more. He might even know where to find one of these 'nests' Abel had mentioned. Would he tell us if he did? *Djinn can't lie…* "Have you ever heard of something called a 'nest'? A safe place for… people like Chloe?" I blurt out.

Joaquin's attention snaps to me, his eyes flaring with curiosity. "Someone's been hitting the books. How did you hear about the nests?" My eyes go wide as it suddenly occurs to me that I could be mixing Abel up in all this, even more than he already was.

"I read it in a book... like you said," I babble out, hoping he doesn't press the issue.

"Sure," he replies flatly, a smirk cutting his face. "But to answer your question, as well as your next question and the one after that: yes, I've heard of them; yes, they exist; and no, I don't know where one is."

"But they do exist?" Chloe jumps in, pleading for a lifeline from Joaquin with her big, blue eyes.

"Yes. I've come across a few over the years, but they obviously like to keep a low profile. And Djinn aren't really in the vampire business anymore, so to be perfectly honest, they're really nothing more than a curiosity as far as we're concerned." He looks sadly back at Chloe, like he's taken a joke too far. "Oh, you poor thing, I'm sorry if you got your hopes up."

"Then you don't know if I'll become..." Chloe trails off, no doubt unable to admit the fear that is written in her eyes.

Joaquin shrugs. "I don't. But my hope for you is that you learn to control your hunger. It won't be easy, but imperative. You must remain pure. To kill anyone by draining them of blood will taint your very soul, and your humanity will be lost with the last drop of their blood."

Chloe's exhale reverberates around the room.

"That cannot happen," Joaquin says, pinning her with a hard stare, his forehead creasing in the middle as his eyes bore into my friend until she slowly nods her head once. That action must have been what he needed, as he relaxes once more, easing back into the cushions of the couch. A meaningful silence follows his movements, and his gaze moves back and forth between Chloe and I.

Suddenly he leans forward. "You know, I'm really starting to like this town. Here I thought it was just some quaint, little backwater with an overreaching Alpha a couple years ago, and then I find you, a warded half-Djinn," he says, that predatory grin slowly spreading across his face again as he holds me with those dark eyes. "And then you, a vampire holding onto her humanity." He shifts his gaze to Chloe, and then leans back again. "Between you two, the missing pack princess…" He trails off, shaking his head in feigned disbelief.

"You know about Blake?" I blurt out before he can continue. Did he know something about that, too?

He looks confused for a second, then answers. "Well, it's hardly a secret. And 'no,' to your next question." *Did he know I was going to ask if he knew where she was, or was he just trying to deflect before I had a chance to ask him directly?* "Curious, curious, curious," he continues, as if I had never even asked about Blake. "Even the humans in this town are interesting, 'eh Ari?" He pins us both with another stare, then stands, clapping his hands together once. "Well. I should be going," He turns those sharp eyes on me once more. "Your mate should be here soon and I'm sure he won't be too happy to see me."

"My what?" I ask, my voice spiking on the last word. Did he just say *mate*?

Joaquin ignores my question, replying with only a wide,

toothy smile, then disappears within a cloud of bright-green smoke.

Chloe's eyes linger on the spot Jaoquin disappeared from for a moment before swiveling to me. Her beautiful blue eyes are three sizes larger in her shock. "Um… I think we need to talk."

I nod sucking in a deep breath between my teeth while trying to order the thoughts running through my mind on warp speed. *I guess we haven't really talked about all this, even though we spent so long together the last couple days.* "Well… I guess a lot, um… well, there are some things we haven't really filled you in on."

"Ya' think?" Chloe asks, flopping back into her recliner and fully relaxing now that it's just the two of us. "And here I thought me turning into… Well, I thought that was the worst of it."

I shake my head slowly before diving into all the events from the night of the Moon Awakening, starting with Chad shooting at Dean and ending with Chloe and Blake being the only two on the missing persons list. When I'm finished, Chloe is no longer relaxing. Instead she's poised on the edge of her chair with her face in her hands, no doubt trying to process all the information I just threw at her. "And to think the other night my biggest worry was you ditching me at that party," I say with a laugh dripping with irony.

Chloe's eyes turn up. "About that…" she starts, and I shake my head, cutting her off.

"It's the least of my worries at the moment."

Chloe's frown deepens, her forehead creasing in thought. "Maybe, but at least it's something I can give you an answer for. All the rest of this," Chloe waves a hand in the air as if to emphasize the situation we're in rather than any particular object. "Well, I don't even know where to begin with that."

I snort with laughter, eyeing my best friend. "You and me both."

"Well... when mom texted me, she said it was important. I went to find you at the party to tell you, but you were dancing and having such a good time that I didn't want to barge in. And I knew that if I told you I was leaving you would leave, too, and you needed to stay."

I frown, keeping my eyes on the chipped polish of my finger-nails. The last couple days had seriously messed up my manicure. "I..." I start, then stop as Chloe continues over me.

"You would have left with me."

I nod, knowing she's right.

"So, I texted instead. Turns out Mom only wanted me home for Madeline." Chloe laughs at the memory. "You know how sentimental my little sis is. She wanted to watch a movie one last time before I presented. I guess now..." Chloe's words trail off with a shake of her head. I don't need her to finish to know she was going to say that now she's glad she did.

"Me, too," I reply, and the two of us slip into a comfortable silence. My mind runs over everything that's happened. Chloe leaving me at that party seems like years ago now. But she had been right—at least that was something we could work out now rather than letting it just drag up more questions like everything else. "Mate," I whisper the word under my breath as it circles back through my mind again, pulling my thoughts to Dean.

Mate.

Twenty

When Dean returns home an hour later, I am nearly unraveling at the seams. Joaquin's words are still twisting my insides into a tangled knot. The sun has set, and the house is lit with the warm glow of lamp light. Chloe is busying herself cleaning in the kitchen, no doubt trying to keep her own thoughts from spinning. But not me. I haven't left my chair—not once—as I slowly let myself sink in the frustration of all the news I've received today.

He enters, dropping his bag on the island in the center of the kitchen and makes some small talk with Chloe that I'm too busy brooding to pay attention to. "Thanks," I hear her reply faintly, probably in response to something about all the cleaning. I don't glance toward the two of them from my chair, though. My eyes are firmly held on my hands. *Mate, mate, mate!* The word repeats through my mind like a mantra I don't really want to hear. A second later, I hear Chloe whisper something to Dean and I finally pull my eyes up to the kitchen. Dean's eyes dart to mine as Chloe silently makes her way from the kitchen and down the stairs to the basement. She must have informed him about our little visitor.

Dean starts toward me, holding his hands up in peace. "So… I take it something happened while I was gone."

"You could say that," I state, my lips pulling into a hard line. Dean's discarded the jacket, now just wearing that plain gray t-shirt and jeans, and, of course, he's dripping in sex appeal. I ignore it. I specifically don't watch as his chest muscles tug against his shirt, his arms straining and pulling as he makes his way into the living room taking each step slowly as if approaching a startled animal. Or a venomous snake.

"Joaquin showed up. The Djinn."

With my words, Dean's face goes from calm to angry in two seconds flat. "What?" he growls.

"He had quite a bit of information for me, starting with the fact that I'm half Djinn and ending with the fact that I'm, apparently, your mate?"

Dean falls onto the couch, running a hand through his hair. "Shit," he says under his breath. Though his face has relaxed some, the anger is still swirling there beneath the surface. I don't blame him for being mad—I'd be pretty upset if someone had trespassed into my house without my permission, too, let alone a Djinn. They might be the ruling species, but to say any supernatural is a fan of them would be a crazy overstatement.

"Let's slide over the fact that a Djinn was in your house. No doubt you're upset about that, but I don't have time to wait for you to get over it. It's done, he left."

"Okay… so you're half-Djinn? That's how you were able to use magic the other night to stop the bullet from hitting me?"

"Yes."

"And…"

"I'm your mate," I finish for him. "I'll circle back to my being part Djinn later. Right now, I need to know this first—"Is it true?"

Dean sucks in a deep breath and leans back against the couch cushion. "Yes," he says softly after a moment.

One word, one simple word, and the whole world spins before my eyes. I have a mate. "How is that even possible? I'm not a Were."

He shrugs, and a strand of blond hair falls into his face. He doesn't move it and I can't help focusing on it. My fingers itch to brush it back into place. I slam that thought down. "I don't know, honestly. Weres don't often mate with humans, though it does happen. But Djinn… never." Dean pauses thoughtfully. "I had thought this was one of those rare occasions when a mating bond develops with a human. It's more common for tigers than wolves, but… now… I don't know."

I chew my lower lip. "How long have you known?" I ask.

"I've been drawn to you for as long as I can remember. Since we were kids I've been pulled to you. I thought…" Dean leans forwards shaking his head. "I thought you felt it, too, but the more you pulled away the less I was sure." I bite my lip even harder. I *have* always been drawn to him. I've always wondered why the Goddess was constantly shoving us into the same space, and why I couldn't help but want to be around him.

"A few months ago the feelings intensified. I couldn't stand being around another woman. I didn't want to flirt. I didn't… I tried to fight it at first, forcing myself to act like I normally had, but after a while I couldn't fight it anymore. I started to suspect that we were mates then, but still I wasn't sure. It didn't feel the same way others described it."

"Like an instantaneous attraction… As if suddenly no one else matters?" I ask, remembering what I've heard from others, and he nods.

"The closer we got to Halloween the stronger my feelings became. The harder they were to ignore. But at the Awakening—on your birthday—I took one look at you and I just knew. As if I'd been suddenly struck by a bolt of lightning. I had no doubt."

I look away, my heart pounding so loud I'm sure he can hear it from across the room. I should be overjoyed. I've always felt that pull to him, too, but *mates*? Bonded to another being forever—and a Hottie Mchottie Tiger at that. I'm only sixteen, which might make me an adult in the supernatural world, but in the human one I'm still a teenager. I have so many years of growing and dating and figuring out what I want. *I don't want to date anyone else, though*. The realization slams through my chest so hard it nearly knocks the breath from me. Holy shit. Dean is my mate.

"I started to tell you the night of the Awakening, before… everything that happened."

I think back to that night, to Dean guiding me further into the woods, into the privacy of the forest, telling me he needed to tell me something. Was this it?

I stand then, nodding once to myself. The need to leave and collect my thoughts and gather everything I've learned today is suddenly so overwhelming I can't stay here a minute longer.

My chest tugs with the need to have space. "I'm gonna go," I say finally. "I need to…" I pause, trying to decide exactly what I need. *To think this through? To run away?*

"Listen, Ari," Dean says, standing and taking a step toward me. Half of me wants to close the distance between us and the other half wants to take a step back, but the sound of my name on his lips has my feet locked in place. "A mating bond isn't set in stone without completion, and we don't have to do that right away. I guess ever… I mean if you don't want…" Dean stops and runs his hands through the soft strands of his hair. I realize he's nervous. I almost laugh at the thought. Mr. Fuck Boy of Lunar Falls is nervous about what to say to a girl. "I just mean you have plenty of time to figure out what you want. There isn't any rush."

I nod again and pull a small smile to my lips. "Thanks," I say, knowing he means every word. Dean wouldn't force me into something I don't want. He won't rush me into this and he'll accept whatever decision I make. A fuck boy he may have been—and he had definitely broken some hearts—but he'd never forced anything. "I just need some time… this is all so much," I say the last waving a hand around his house. Between Chloe and Blake, learning I have magic that I, apparently, can't use, and now hearing that Dean is my mate, I feel as if I'll explode with all the feelings rushing through my system.

"Of course," Dean replies, and I start toward his front door. He takes a single step as if he wants to follow me, but stops himself from taking another one and I'm grateful.

"I'll be back tomorrow," I say, then leave for home.

Twenty-One

The fluorescent lighting is too bright and the chatter in the halls is too loud—sleep is not letting go of me this morning. I yawn while spinning in the combination for my locker. I had tossed and turned all night long with thoughts of Dean—*my mate*—in bed right across from my bedroom window. He seemed like the kind of guy that slept in the nude... And when I wasn't imagining that, I was thinking about my magic and Joaquin. And Chloe being a vampire... and Blake.

Sadness grips my chest once more as all the thoughts from last night take hold of me all over again. Even with all the weirdness consuming my life the last few days, being here feels the strangest. How am I supposed to walk these halls without Blake and Chloe by my side like always? Blake should be right here, leaning against the lockers and explaining why Mrs. Daughtry plainly doesn't know how to teach. Chloe should be skipping down the hall to interrupt us with a report on how cute the new kid is… How am I supposed to focus on school without my two best friends with me?

My shoulders drop and I shove those thoughts away. I can't remember the last time I'd been alone at school. It had happened before, of course, pack responsibilities or the flu or… there's just something that feels *permanent* about it this time, though. *Definitely in Chloe's case*, I think with a wince. *Goddess, I hope not in Blake's*. Today is going to suck. Yanking out the books I need and stuffing my backpack inside, I shut the door and bee-line through the crowded halls to First Period.

Something slams into my shoulder making me trip on my boots. I stumble forward a step before catching myself. Lost as I am in my own thoughts, I realize I must have hit someone. "Sorry, sorry…" I say as I bend down to pick up the math book that had fallen from my arms.

"It's cool," a male voice says, the familiar tone making me pause. I pull myself back to standing, brushing off my pants and putting on a casual face. It's hard to keep it, though, when I turn to find that it *is* Chad, the handsome football player with killer blue eyes who had me and Dean at gunpoint a few days ago, standing in front of me. Reminding myself that Joaquin made him and his friends forget what they'd done, I steel myself again and put on my best poker face.

"Oh," I squeak, and apologize again.

Chad laughs, totally cool, as he digs his hands into his pockets like he doesn't have a care in the world. "Hey, so… the other night. Why'd you rush off so fast?"

I frown, he can't mean Halloween, right? "The other night?" I ask, trying to keep the worry from my voice.

"Missy's party… remember?"

"Oh right!" I say with a slight exhale, hoping I don't look as relieved as I feel. "Yeah, sorry, I had to get home. My mom was so mad." I say the last with a roll of my eyes, jutting my hip out to the side. *Chill,* I remind myself.

"Right, yeah… so, uh, you took off so fast I didn't get to ask you… but there's a party this weekend at my family's lake house. I was hoping you'd go."

Is he asking me out? "Oh, uh… I don't know, maybe."

"I mean, I know your friends won't be able to go with you, but like Missy will be there."

My eyes narrow. "Why wouldn't my friends be able to go?"

"Aren't they like sick or something?" Chad asks, his forehead creasing, though whether in worry or confusion I can't tell. How could he even know they weren't going to be here today? It's not even First Period. The pack has made it clear that what's going on is to stay within the pack for now, but I suppose they would have to let the school know *something*. They would notice a couple missing students. And Joaquin said he'd wiped their memories, but do I even trust Joaquin? *Djinn don't lie,* I remind myself, but what were his *exact* words? *Did I miss something?* There's something off about all of this.

"Right, no, I don't think they are?" I say, fighting to keep my voice casual. "But yeah, text me the address and maybe I'll be there." I tuck my hair behind my ear, batting my eyelashes. Chad seems to visibly relax. Is it because he was nervous asking me out, or because he was worried he said too much? I throw that problem on top of the pile of others I've got right now and hold my phone out toward him. *Play it cool.* Chad takes the device and adds his phone number to my contacts, then quickly hands it back. "Maybe I'll see you there," I say, turning away from him and shooting one last look over my shoulder. Hopefully, he confuses my anxiousness for interest.

"Yeah, cool," he says to my back, and I head toward class counting each step I make to keep them slow and deliberate. I can't let him see just how much that conversation has me spinning. The only way he could know that Blake and Chloe are missing is if he remembers Halloween. Or at the very least, he must know what happened on Halloween. Maybe Chloe's mom and Jon reached out to the school to say their kids were sick to cover the problem for a bit. Maybe Chad overheard it in the office or... There *are* reasonable explanations, and the way he had acted could have been because of a bunch of different things. Maybe the weight of everything the last few days has made me paranoid.

As soon as I turn the corner and am out of eyesight of Chad I dart off into the nearest bathroom. My breath is heavy, my chest is heaving, and I check to make sure no one else is in here with me. *Shit, shit, shit.* Something just isn't right, I can feel it. Between his comments at Missy's party and everything that happened the night of the Moon Awakening... *Goddess, what did Joaquin actually say?* I work on taking deep, controlled breaths as I lean against one of the sinks and pull my gaze to the mirror in front of me.

My carmel skin is flushed, my hazel eyes are bright. Quickly, I run my hand through my hair, smoothing out the black layers and hoping the action will settle my nerves.

I need to tell Dean.

I yank my phone from my back pocket and shoot off a quick text to him.

I need to talk to you.

A second later he responds. **I'll pick you up after school.**

Hours later, Dean's truck pulls up in front of the entrance to the school where I've been waiting not-so-patiently. My entire body seems to vibrate with a nervousness that has only tripled in size since I texted him this morning.

Pulling open the passenger door, I climb into the cab and lay my backpack on the floorboard by my feet before buckling myself in.

"So, what happened?" Dean asks as he puts the truck into gear and pulls away from the curb. With a huff I rush into the conversation I had with Chad before First Period.

"I know I could be totally paranoid and letting my mind work it into something it's not, but something tells me I'm right. He knows something. He has to…" Dean stays quiet the entire time I talk, listening intently and never interrupting. When I finally finish I glance out the passenger window and realize we're headed into town, not toward Lunar Falls. "Where are we going?" I ask.

Dean glances at me with his particular brand of smirk, then focuses back on the road. "We are going to get coffee, because we both need a little bit of normalcy after the last few days." My brows raise, but I don't argue. *Fair point.*

"And as for Chad, I'd be more than happy to rip out his throat just for asking you out."

I groan, "Oh, don't be an Alpha-hole."

"But I think you're right. Something feels wrong about it all. And if we *are* just being paranoid, well then treating him like he's involved and trying to find out more is the best way to exonerate him," Dean continues on with a shrug as if I hadn't said anything, then adds with a smirk, "And 'Alpha-hole?' Really?"

"Yes. That's a Blake original." *Blake.* I don't have any evidence to say Chad knows where she is, but he *at least* knows she won't be around for a few days when exceptionally few people at school could have, and his friends are the only people in this whole fucked-up situation that we didn't see that night... But why ask me out? Maybe he's trying to find out what I know, too. There are just too many 'ifs' and 'buts' for my liking.

"I'm going to that party," I say, setting my mind on it.

"And I'll be your date," Dean says, sending another smirk my way. My mouth works to argue, but he doesn't give me the time. "I'm not letting you go alone, especially if it turns out you're right and he does know something. And I'm sure as hell not letting him be your date, alpha-hole or not."

I roll my eyes, but agree all the same. Dean brings the truck to a stop in front of a small, little café, tucked into a line of cute brick buildings. "Fine. It's a date."

Twenty-Two

The café is small, but cute. Light filters in through the front windows, casting the small space in bright warmth. The smells of different coffees and espressos fill my nose. I breathe them in. It's peaceful, quiet, and exactly what I need right now.

I sit at a small table set for two, tucked in a corner beside another set of windows. Outside the trees are a perfect autumn palette of bright reds, oranges, and yellows that mix and blend in the light breeze.

The sound of footsteps heading in my direction pulls my attention away from the beautiful scene outside. Dean returns, setting a steaming, white cup in front of me. A little heart design has been etched into the foam of my latte. I smile down at the mug.

"Thanks," I say to Dean, and he takes the vacant seat across from me.

"I thought a little escape from everything in Lunar Falls might be smart right now," Dean says as he takes a sip from his own coffee. The sunlight traces through the strands of his blond hair, painting a tawny halo around his head. My fingers itch to run through the longer layers at the top. My eyes trail along the sharp lines of his face, then the corded muscles in his neck, then his shoulders... My breath hitches as I eye his chest. His pecs strain against the cotton of his white t-shirt and it feels like I have to physically pull my gaze back to his face. I'm pretty sure his hair is the only soft thing about Dean.

"I think you're right," I finally say, staring into those mint-green eyes. Looking at him now, I realize I've been more successful at avoiding him than I thought. I barely know anything of substance about the man in front of me. "Tell me something about you?"

His eyes search mine and one brow raises slowly with the question, but he doesn't argue. "Well, let's see. My favorite color is purple," His eyes almost glitter on the last word, as if he wants to remind me that my dress for the Moon Awakening was that exact color. I smile at the memory of him and I dancing under the lantern glow. "Horror movies are my favorite, and I could eat pizza every day."

"Horror movies?" I ask, and he nods. "Me, too," I admit, turning my gaze to my coffee and glancing up at him from beneath my lashes, the omission making me feel suddenly shy. What the hell is wrong with me? I've never been that shy, timid girl, but with Dean... I squirm a little in my chair. *Ugh, this is* not *normal behavior.*

Dean shifts in his chair, settling his arms on the table and wrapping his hands around the warmth of his mug. "I know."

"You know?"

"Yeah. I know a lot about you actually."

I snort. "Like what?"

"Well, for starters, you're more of a comfort-first kind of girl—jeans and hoodies over heels and skirts. You love music, or at least you almost always have your earbuds in. You enjoy walking. And I'm pretty sure autumn's your favorite season." Dean's eyes shine with each word.

"How do you know so much about me?" I ask, my whole face pinching.

He shrugs once, taking a sip of his coffee. "I pay attention." He glances out the window, as if that doesn't quite explain it all. "I don't know, it's like I'm always *aware* of you… what you're doing, what you're wearing, who you talk to." When his eyes pull back to me they're swimming in an emotion I can't quite place. *Longing?* My frown deepens. He's flirted with me for years, but I never paid much thought to it. This is a guy that could have any girl he wanted.

"Why me?" I finally ask, breaking the silence. Dean shifts in his seat, turning back to me.

"Why not you?" he fires back, and I have no idea how to answer that. He chuckles under his breath. "I'm glad it's you, though," He laughs again, this time a little fuller. "I think I've had a crush on you since we were kids getting thrown together by our parents."

I blanche, my whole body shifting with the action. "What? Why didn't you ever say anything?"

"Because you never seemed interested back."

"Has that ever stopped you before?"

Dean eyes me with a playful expression, but his eyes darken with a deeper meaning before he waves me off. "Because it was never serious with anyone else. If they rejected me it wasn't a big deal."

"Oh," is all I can get out as the thought slams through me. He cares so much more than I originally thought. He always has. The realization warms my insides, but I can't tell if it's because I'm happy to hear it or it's the pangs of regret.

"So... how's Chloe adjusting?" I ask, changing the topic. Dean seems relieved at the conversation shift, too, and his shoulders relax as he leans back in his chair. The reality is I know how she's adjusting—I've spent just about every afternoon and most of the nights at Dean's house since Halloween, keeping her up to date on the outside world. She keeps me up to date with all the different things she and Dean have figured out, like that hot coffee helps to keep her body temperature in a normal range and constant snacking helps keep the cravings down. But the most important thing is not skipping a meal. Ever.

"She's... really positive," he says, and I frown at him, my head tilting slightly. "This horrible thing has happened to her but she's really super-zen about it." He shrugs. "Most of the time I can't figure out if she wants to drain me dry or hug me for helping her with the transition."

I laugh—it's such a Chloe thing to have a whole 'Moon Goddess works in mysterious ways' approach to all this. She's always been more bubbly than the rest of us. "That definitely sounds like Chloe."

Dean nods, sipping from his mug, and I follow suit. Silence stretches between us for what feels like minutes, the only sounds coming from the café around us. A few tables over, someone's fingers fly across the keyboard of their laptop. A couple sits side-by-side at another table by the register, their heads close together, holding hands beneath the table. Steam blasts and espresso grinds behind the counter, filling the modest space with the bittersweet aroma of coffee.

"Has she mentioned talking to her family at all?" I ask suddenly, my voice somber.

Dean sighs, his brows creasing in the middle. "In a roundabout way, I suppose. Never directly. I don't know if she'll ever be able to. At least in person." His eyes are on the milky liquid in his cup. "And I don't know how they'd handle it, for that matter. She's a vampire now. How do you tell your family that you've become their worst nightmare?" Dean shakes his head before continuing on with a shrug. "She's not the type of vampire that they know, but... "

I inhale deeply, knowing he's right. I imagine the excitement at finding out she's alive... and then fear, sadness, and anger that would wreck her family to know what she's become. "If we can show them first that she's still Chloe..." I let my words trail off. It wouldn't be enough though, would it? I shake my head. "We should figure out a way to let them know she's okay, at least. Before we get her out," I finally say, the words barely a breath on my lips. I know it's what Chloe would want. She'd want to try for her family. For Madeline.

"Yeah... But," Dean starts, then takes a deep breath, "It's probably best to wait until she's already gone. And in the meantime, I'll reach back out to Abel, see if he's talked to his friend yet. Maybe he's figured out how to find one of those nests."

Dean says with a reassuring smile, but it doesn't quite reach his eyes.

"Maybe," I mumble out. My heart's too busy breaking to put any emphasis on the word. Finding a nest is Chloe's best option. Maybe her only option. Everything she had here in Lunar Falls is over, and there's nothing anyone can do. It's too much, and I change the subject again. "Should we tell Abel about Joaquin? And… me?"

"I think we should. A little extra support never hurts."

"I just… I don't want to get him wrapped up in something he never asked for. He didn't seem very enthused when we mentioned a Djinn being involved."

"Yeah, but I guarantee not even five minutes later the curiosity was eating him alive," Dean answers with a quiet chuckle, the mood lightening a bit.

"Doesn't curiosity kill cats?" I can't help but grin stupidly at my own corniness, but the question is serious enough.

"That's why we have nine lives," Dean replies with a wink. We stare each other down, then both burst out laughing. Goddess, it feels good to *really* laugh again.

Twenty-Three

"I want to go!" Chloe says with her hands firmly planted on her hips, a dangerously serious look cut into her pale features.

I lounge casually on the living room couch while Dean faces off with her, arms crossed and jaw set. I'm making mental bets as to who will win out—right now, my money is on Chloe.

"It's too dangerous," Dean argues, and Chloe rolls her eyes.

"I'm not going to eat anyone."

"Are you sure? The only two people you've been around since you turned are Ari and me, and you like us enough to stop yourself…"

"Well, I like Ari…" Chloe mumbles under her breath sarcastically.

Dean shoots her a petulant smile and continues, "There's going to be a lot more people there, and people you don't know or care about as much. And depending on what we learn, a few people there might give you a reason to get bitey, too." Dean has a point, but I also know Chloe—she wouldn't hurt a fly. The idea of hurting anyone is unthinkable to her. *Or at least it was*, I think wistfully, the intrusive thought catching me by surprise. I quickly shove it away. *No. It's still Chloe.* I know it in my core. She's still the same girl that got mad at Blake for swatting a spider instead of catching it and taking it outside.

"Well, I'm never gonna learn to *really* control it if I never go around other people," Chloe rebuts, also making a good point. I raise an eyebrow at Dean, who sends a glare my way in response.

"Not gonna help, Ari?" he asks, though it's more accusation than question. I shake my head with a small laugh. Dean huffs, then directs his attention back to my friend. "What if word gets back to the pack that someone saw you?"

"No one knows I'm "missing" outside of the pack, and the pack kids never go to these parties." Chloe argues, her voice straining with the effort to not yell. Chloe isn't one to get mad easily, but the steam coming off of her right now says she's way past that line. "They're human—they won't be able to smell me the way Weres can."

"Yeah, and speaking of Weres, we also need to sneak you out and back in through a neighborhood full of them." Dean immediately counters. It seems like he's getting just as heated now.

"You have cologne, don't you? I'll just douse myself in it and hide in the back seat under a blanket or something. Anyone who looks will just think *you* forgot to shower." Chloe fires back, jutting out her hip and pursing her lips. "I'd believe it." *Uh oh*. Dean stares back, and I can see him chewing the inside of his cheek.

But then Chloe deflates, dropping her head and letting out a long sigh. When she looks back at Dean and I, there's nothing but sincerity in her bright eyes. "Listen... I *need* to go out there with people. You can't hide me in your basement forever, Dean. It's not fair to me, and it's not fair to *you*, either. You can't live your life constantly on alert for me. At some point, I *have* to leave here. My best bet is for us to find one of these 'nests' or whatever, but even if we don't... I can't stay in Lunar Falls. I can't stay in Silas Creek. No matter how badly I want to..." She trails off with a whisper, taking both of our eyes with a pleading stare in turn. I can't bring myself to speak, and it seems neither can Dean. Chloe picks back up, her eyes damp, "I think... I think I'm starting to accept that. But either way, I *need* to do this. I need to learn to be around humans or I have *no* hope for a life outside of a basement."

Chloe sniffs and wipes her eyes, and I suddenly realize I need to do the same. Dean has his head down, looking humbled. Silence stretches, and then once again Chloe speaks up, "Besides, you could use an extra set of ears if we're gonna find out what Chad and his friends know. My hearing is even better than yours."

I wipe the remaining wetness from my cheeks and steel myself. "We could use the help. I can't use my magic—not that I'd even know how to or what to do with it—and my hearing is the same as any other human. Only you have heightened senses... and Chloe." I say to Dean, then give Chloe a glance over my shoulder. She answers me with a look of appreciation.

Dean runs his hands through his hair, turning away from the two of us. He turns after a moment with a rumbling exhale, and then nods. "Well then, it sounds like we have a party to crash..."

Two hours later we are pulling up in front of Chad's parents lake house, a secluded two-story faux cabin set deep into the mountains about half an hour outside of town. The yard is illuminated with strung lights that lead to a dock on the edge of a still lake, painted silver by moonlight. The party is already in full swing—music blares and a crowd of people surrounds a bonfire flickering almost as tall as they are. Some of them hold sticks with marshmallows on the end, others red solo cups. Their voices carry over the music even to where we're parked.

Chloe emerges from underneath a blanket in the backseat, puffing a stray strand of blonde hair out of her face. "Are we here?" she asks excitedly, her face lit up like a kid's in a candy store.

"Yeah," Dean answers flatly. He doesn't seem nearly as excited about the situation as my blonde friend. He's gone rigid while his aquamarine eyes roam the groups of people partying along the side of the lake, as if each and every one is an enemy. A few of them very well could be.

I wrap my hand around his arm, pulling myself into his side. "Relax," I say as I look up into his gorgeous face from beneath my lashes. The moon casts his face in a soft, white glow, highlighting the high points of his cheek bones and the strong line of his jaw. "It's a party."

His eyes lighten as he looks back at me and suddenly I'm lost in their minty green depths. My lips part unprompted with the want to close what little distance there is between us. I don't—I fight back my desires and jerk myself up straight, turning my attention to Chloe as I struggle to catch my breath. A low laugh rumbles from the man and now I'm forcing myself to ignore the tingles running through my stomach.

"We ready?" Chloe asks as she turns to me, her face alight in excitement.

I nod my encouragement as Dean gives her one last bit of advice. "Remember to try and open your mouth as little as possible. The last thing we need is someone catching those fangs."

Chloe brings her left hand to her lips almost nervously at the reminder of those sharp, pointed teeth. They're slight enough that if she talks fast—and doesn't smile too wide—no one will notice. Chloe, however, isn't one to keep a smile from her lips. Suddenly I'm not so sure this is a great idea anymore, but it says something that I'm more worried about her smiling than vamping out. *Too late now, anyways. We're doing this.*

The three of us set off toward the gathered groups of partiers, our plan already devised beforehand. Dean splits off from Chloe and I a few seconds later, but keeps us both in his line of sight—and hearing. I search the crowd for familiar faces, and it doesn't take long for my eyes to land on Missy, who squeals and runs straight to me as her eyes meet mine. "Hey!" she shouts over the mix of music and voices, quickly covering the short distance. "You came!"

"Yeah, Chad invited me," I answer. She frowns for a second, but it's gone as quickly as it landed. "Have you seen him?" I ask, hoping I sound casual.

"I'm pretty sure he's down near the lake, but who knows?" she says, waving me off. Dean starts casually walking off toward the dock and the lake at the periphery of my vision. "You look different," Missy says, turning to Chloe.

"Oh?" Chloe asks, running a hand nervously through her hair.

"I don't know what you did, but it looks good on you," Missy answers, and Chloe smiles carefully, keeping her lips closed. She isn't wrong. Chloe looks the same as she always had, except... *more* now. There's a noticeable difference in her beauty, which had already been striking, as if everything had been amplified. There was this innate magnetism to the roundness of her eyes and the soft contours of her cheeks, her lips, her... everything.

Chloe thanks her, and they make small-talk as I scan the faces around us, searching for a sign of Chad or one of his friends. Missy fills Chloe in on all the tea she's missed from school, and I smile and nod at what I think are all the right moments, but I can't focus on her words. We need to get eyes on Chad. Luckily, Chloe is good at keeping Missy's attention, so she doesn't notice my lack of it. I spot Dean talking with a group of people not far from the dock, still keeping Chloe and I where he can see. He locks eyes with me and nods, then turns back to engage with the group. *He found Chad. Let's do this.* "Hey, Missy?" I cut in, "Sorry, but it was kind of a long ride. There a bathroom here?"

"No worries, I get it, girl," she answers with a laugh. "Inside the house, hallway on the left."

I thank her, and Chloe jumps in behind me, "I'll join you. I should probably touch this," she says, waving a hand around her face, "up."

"There's nothing to touch up, honey," Missy laughs again. "When you guys are done come meet me at the bonfire, 'k?"

"Sure thing, we won't be long," I answer, then take Chloe's arm in mine and turn us toward the house. Determination sets in my chest. "Ready?"

"Yeah... " Chloe replies with a smile, keeping her voice low so only I can hear. "It feels *so* good to get out of the house. Even if it's for a little breaking and entering." I glance over and see the intensity in her eyes. She means every word. We were so busy trying to protect her that we never thought about how much keeping her locked up was affecting her, especially someone as outgoing and as close to their family as Chloe. The realization slams into me like a punch in the gut, just like the scene earlier in the living room. As if reading my thoughts, Chloe continues: "I never thought I'd be so close to my family and yet... so far."

I sigh, not knowing how to answer her. What I know she must be feeling, what she's going through, almost takes my breath away. We stop as we reach the porch stairs heading up to the cabin, and I wrap my arms around her shoulders. She leans into me, laying her head on my shoulder. "It's gonna be okay." She nods against me, a stray strand of hair finding its way into her face. I brush it away. "We'll find Blake and bring her home, and then we'll... figure something out with your family."

"I can't go home."

Goddess, what the hell do I even say to that? We both know she can't, but... "No. No, I guess you can't. But... maybe you can meet them somewhere away from Lunar Falls, or... We'll at least let them know that you're okay. And that you're gonna *be* okay, even if you can't see them. I don't know," I say, shaking my head. "We'll figure something out, though." I set my jaw in a determined line. Blake would know what to do. She always does. *I wish she was here.* My chest aches at the thought, just as much as it is for Chloe right now, but I'll be damned if we don't find some kind of fix—for both my friends. "We'll find a way."

Chloe closes her eyes and takes a deep breath. It looks like her features have gone to war with each other when she looks back to me, trying to compose herself. "Sorry, not the time or place. It just kind of hit me, being out together like this. Guess I wasn't ready, huh?" She laughs, brushing a strand of hair behind her ear. I don't reply, just lean in and wrap my arms around her, hugging her tight. She matches my embrace, leaning into me once more. When she finally pulls away, determination paints her face: "Let's find Blake."

Twenty-Four

Chloe and I make our way up the porch steps towards the light streaming from the open double doors of the lake house, side-stepping into the little pocket of shadow beside them. Chloe's audible exhale is in-synch with my own, and I can see her posture tighten as we both steel ourselves. "Alright. Gameplan. We go in, act casual, and try to spot any place they could be holding her—closed rooms, locked doors, whatever. You use your super-hearing and I'll use my… myself. We find her, sneak her right out the front door, and get out of here before Chad and his friends know any-thing. Sound good?" I ask, trying to fill my voice with as much confidence as I can find.

"Yep. And don't get caught."

"Right. Don't get caught."

We give each other solid nods, then walk arm-in-arm through the doors into a well-lit living area right off the porch. The music from the yard carries through the open doors and blends with the loud conversations inside to fill the open space. Mostly everyone is outside by the fire or down by the lake, but it's still a party even here. A couple guys shotgun beers in the adjoining kitchen, others are sitting at the dining room table playing a drinking game, and here and there people lounge in plush, woodsy furniture and chat. Would Chad keep Blake here, and then invite all these people? *Would anyone be able to hear her calling for help over all of this?* I suppose it would be a good cover. But then again, any one of these people could drunkenly stumble into her here. I shake my head and get my mind off the spinning merry-go-round it's on.

We move in a bit and stop near one of the brown leather couches by the porch doors, and I try to get my bearings. A few people lean against the wall beside a door in a hallway to our left, which must be the bathroom, and further past them is an open door to what looks like a guest bedroom. Past the kitchen is another bedroom, door open as well, where a few people sit and talk on the bed. People filter in and out of a second living area near the front door. The second floor looks like it's almost entirely a loft, and all the doors I can spot are open as well. I feel Chloe lean back against the arm of the couch, and I take a nonchalant stance as I scan over the house again.

Only one closed door that I can spot in the whole place, and it looks like it might lead down to a basement. *If she would be anywhere, it'd be there. It's always the basement, right?* I nudge Chloe. "Chloe... basement door, to our right." I whisper, locking my eyes on the door. No one has come in or out of it since we've entered the house that I could see. "Can you hear anything down there?" The door is next to the kitchen. If we move quickly enough, we should be able to get through it before anyone has a chance to look up from their drinks. Maybe. "Chloe?"

I finally look away from the door—Chloe looks pale and clammy, and her eyes are clasped shut in concentration. She blows out a long breath from between her painted lips, then inhales deeply through her nose. I take her hands and squeeze. "Chloe!"

Her eyes pop open and meet mine, and she seems to shiver in my hands. "I'm good. I'm good," she says finally, "There's just a lot of noise. A lot of... heartbeats." She smiles weakly back at me, but some of her color seems to be coming back. Her chest swells as she takes another deep breath, then deflates again as she gives me a stronger smile. "I've got this. Basement door. To our right." She nods at me, then scans the direction I had been looking in a moment ago. She's concentrating on the basement door now, and can't see the beaming smile I'm giving her. *She's got this. She's going to be okay.*

I give her hands one more confident squeeze. "So, anything down there?"

"It sounds quiet. No heartbeats or anything that I can tell... but maybe the walls are thicker down there because we're near the lake?" She shrugs. "I don't know. Everywhere up here seems open. Too many people. If she is here, my money," she says with a nod toward the door, "is on the basement."

"Agreed." I scan the room again. The guys in the kitchen are hotly debating football and championing their favorite teams. They should be easy enough to slip by unnoticed, but we'll be in full view of the people in the dining room and the few lounging in the living area. *Shit.* "We'll just have to look like we're supposed to be going down there. Confidence is king, right?"

"Right," Chloe says as she stands up, straightening her dress. She loops her arm through mine and we stride forward in calm, measured steps. The kitchen debate is still in full swing, and no one from the dining or living room seems to be paying any attention to us as we get to the door. I reach a hand out to turn the knob and am immediately greeted by the tell-tale jingle of a locked door. *Shit, shit, shit.*

"It's locked," I whisper to Chloe, though I have no doubt she's aware.

"Stand over here," she replies, lightly grabbing my shoulders and moving me to block the view of the door from the dining room area. She reaches down to the door knob and holds it in her hand. "Laugh. Like loudly." I raise a curious eyebrow but comply, giving my best attempt at a deep belly laugh with absolutely nothing funny going on. Chloe twists hard on the knob as I laugh obnoxiously, and a short, sharp 'snap' rings out between us. She looks at me and smiles, two little white points biting out from her top lip. "Not anymore." This time, my laugh is genuine.

I look over Chloe's shoulder to the kitchen where the guys have somehow managed to get even more animated. *All clear there.* I can see Chloe casually scanning over my shoulder as well. She looks around a bit more, then meets my eyes again and nods, opening the door as she does so. We scramble around into a dark stairwell and softly close the door behind us.

The only illumination is the light sneaking in from underneath the door, and I feel around the walls for a light switch but find none. "Can you see anything?" I whisper to Chloe. "I can't find a light switch." She takes my hand and steps down.

"I can see. Follow me." Chloe leads me down the stairs and we turn the corner into complete darkness. The floorboards creak with movement, and muffled noise from the party buzzes above us. She leads me forward a few more paces and I hear a switch flip. The room floods with light, revealing a den decorated in greens and browns. Leather furniture sits around a mahogany coffee table, and the walls are lined with mounted deer trophies. Two grayish pelts hang conspicuously beside a gas fireplace. Wolf pelts. A stocked wood and glass gun cabinet sits in the corner next to a silver stand topped with decanters. "Chad's dad was quite the hunter, huh?" Chloe says as her eyes move across the walls.

Those foreboding feelings are back again. *Deer, Rabbit... Wolves.* I remember Chad's words from Missy's party. "Yeah," I answer quietly. "Seems that way." I take a deep breath and try to regain my focus, shaking away the terrible thoughts running through my mind. *We need to find Blake.* Chloe stares intently at each of the doors leading from the den in turn. All look slightly ajar. "Anything?" I ask, desperately hoping she'll march forward to one of the doors and reveal our missing friend.

Her brows sink, and disappointment crumples her features. "Nothing," she replies, shaking her head.

"You think... Maybe they drugged her? And that's why you can't hear anything?" I ask, already knowing the answer. This close Chloe would be able to hear her, even if they had done something that would slow her heartbeat. She looks back at me with a placating smile and shakes her head. *Damn it.* Silence fills the basement while disappointment fills my chest, and I realize how much I had built this all up in my head. There was really no reason to suspect Chad was holding Blake here, aside from my own desperate hopes that that was the case. I mean, throwing a party where you're hiding a kidnapped girl is possible, I guess, but I don't think he'd be that bold. Hell, whether or not he's actually involved is still up in the air, but... I just know he is. I know it in my bones. *Goddess, where are you Blake?*

The buzzing of my phone breaks the quiet and I nearly jump out of my skin. I sniff at my jumpiness and check the screen—Dean's calling. *Uh oh.* I accept the call and put the phone to my ear. "Hello"

"Hey, not sure where you guys are at, but Chad and his friends are heading to the house."

"Shit, okay. We're almost done here," I answer, looking over to Chloe who's listening intently.

"Okay. They're almost there now. Said they were heading to the basement to grab some of the good liquor, so you should just be able to let them pass and then sneak back out to the fire."

I go quiet. It looked like there was only one way in and out of the basement. Chad is going to run right into us in what should have been a locked basement, now with a busted door knob. We're trapped. Chloe's eyes have gone wide, and she's staring towards the stairs leading back up.

"Ari?"

"We're in the basement. Gotta go." I don't catch whatever it is he's saying as I smash the end call button. "We need to get out of here!" I whisper shout over to Chloe, who's still watching the stairs.

"No time. Someone's coming. We need to hide." *Shit, shit, shit.* Chloe runs over to the wall and cuts off the lights, and once again I'm plunged into pitch black. Seconds later I feel her hand take mine and pull me along, then stop short and gently press me back against a wall. The soft creak of a door being almost shut sounds next to me while the sounds of the party suddenly fill the basement outside, and several feet sound on the steps. The basement door shuts hard, and the party turns back into white noise.

"—dumbass busted the door. I swear to god if someone came down here and messed with my Dad's shit I'm going to lose it." A tall sliver of light shoots through the inch or two gap Chloe has left open, illuminating a thin line on the back of the room where we're hiding. I press harder against the wall, trying to sink into it and keep my breath quiet and steady.

"Doesn't look like they touched anything…" Chad's voice trails off to the sound of clinking glass. Chloe presses closer to me, squeezing my hand. Liquid pours, and then another piercing *clink* rings through the room. "Cheers."

"Mmm. I can see why you hide this shit." Another familiar voice says, though I can't place which of Chad's friends it belongs to.

"Yeah, it was my dad's favorite. Only for special occasions." More footsteps, and then the puff and creak of leather furniture. "We'll have another reason to celebrate in a few weeks." That was Chad, and laughter follows his statement.

"Somethin' new to hang on the wall," a third voice this time.

"No, it's not going on the wall. It's gonna be a *gift*." Chad's voice takes on a sinister tone, and the laughter that follows this time sounds more nervous than mirthful. A gift for who? And no one else is missing. Unless… unless this is about Blake and he doesn't know she won't turn. "Maybe we'll keep some teeth as souvenirs for ourselves." More laughs. My stomach turns, and I can feel Chloe tense next to me.

A phone buzzes.

"Uh oh, Chad. Missy's lookin' for you."

"Yeah, well, I'll find her in a minute. I was hoping Ari would show up." My palms go sweaty at the mention of my name.

"Still don't know why you invited her, bro. You're asking for trouble."

"I just wanted to talk to her, that's all." A couple sniffs and snorts follow Chad's voice. *Goddess, what the shit is going on? Is he asking for trouble because of the Missy thing, or because they think I suspect them of kidnapping Blake?* "She knows something." *Well, that answers that… I think.*

A phone buzzes again, followed by a long sigh.

"Alright… I gotta go make nice with Missy before she tweaks out. C'mon." There's more movement and the sound of glass being set on a wooden table. Everything goes dark again and footsteps sound on the stairs. They're quickly washed out by the noise of the party, and then… quiet. I deflate against the wall, sucking in a deep breath, and almost fall down with the escaping tension. I feel around against the wall and flip the light switch. For some reason the soft, fluorescent light is making me feel better. Chloe is hunched over with her hands on her knees.

"That was close," she says, standing up straight with a huff.

"Yeah…" is all I can think to reply. I send a quick text to Dean to let him know they're gone and that we're okay before he does anything stupid, then sink back down to the floor. "Do you think they were talking about Blake, or are we just too wrapped up in our own conspiracy?" My phone buzzes almost immediately with a reply, but I leave it, too on edge to try and hold two conversations at once.

"I think they took her," Chloe responds quietly with her head down and her hands planted on her hips. Her arms are tense and the vein in her neck is visible. She's pissed. I nod in agreement, though I doubt Chloe sees it. They're involved, and now it sounds like this whole situation has gotten more complicated. What's in a couple weeks? And what the hell is Joaquin's game in all this. Did he just mean he wiped Chad's memories of *me* from that night? I deflate with a deep exhale and lay my head back against the wall, hoping it will stop my mind from spinning.

For the first time since turning on the lights, I really look around the room. Built-in bookcases line the walls around a thick wooden desk covered in papers and picture frames. A city map of Silas Creek hangs behind it—a city map of Silas Creek with Lunar Falls circled in red.

Twenty-Five

The bright-red circle around Lunar Falls screams at me from the other side of the room. "C-Chloe?" I say hesitantly, not turning away from the map.

"Hmm?" she answers from my right. I raise my arm and point across the room. "What the hell?" Chloe crosses my vision and moves behind the desk to stand in front of the map. I push myself up off the floor and walk around to meet her. "What was it you were you saying about conspiracies?" she mutters quietly at my side.

The large map dominates the wall behind the desk, showing every street and district in Silas Creek. Different colors highlight the different zoning areas of the town, and in the northwest corner sits a patch of light yellow labeled "Lunar Falls," circled in thick red sharpie. The area behind the neighborhood—our forest—looks colored over in green highlighter, with a large black question mark drawn in the middle. Several other buildings close to Lunar Falls are marked with red Xs as well.

A flash cuts across the map, and I turn to see Chloe with her phone up, snapping pictures. *Good Idea.* I pull my own phone out and see Dean's message at the bottom of my screen: **K. Where are you now?** I quickly reply back that we're still in the basement, we'll be out soon, and to keep his eyes on Chad. *It must be eating him alive not being here to watch out for us.* My heart sinks with the thought, but he's going to have to deal with it for now. I snap my own picture of the map and then turn to the desk.

"Chad's dad was in real estate, right?" I ask Chloe as I look over the desk. The usual office supplies are all here, though everything looks a little dusty. I doubt anyone has been here in awhile. Colored folders are stacked on the right hand side of the desk, and several pictures line the edge.

"Yeah. He was a big-time developer or something. Owned a lot of places in town," she says behind me, probably still studying the map.

I pick up one of the gold-framed pictures—A handsome man in his late thirties or so sitting with a young boy on his lap, both in matching flannel shirts. The little boy looks exactly like the older man, and leans his head back against him. They both look so happy. *Chad and his father...* I frown sadly as I set the picture down, then flip open the first folder in the pile. It looks like paperwork for a property he must have owned, but I don't recognize the address. I snap a few pictures and move to the next folder. More paperwork, but this time the address immediately jumps out at me—it's 'The Brew,' the bar Dean works at. *What the hell?* The pack owns that bar... Except this paperwork is very clearly in Clark Danvers's name. I flip through the rest of the folders, snapping more pictures as I go, but don't recognize any of the other properties.

"How long has the pack owned The Brew?" I ask over my shoulder. Chloe slides in beside me, looking down at the spread of papers on the desk.

"A couple years I think," she answers with a shrug. "Right before my dad died… It was one of his favorite spots for that last month or so before the attack." Her shoulders sag a bit and a sad smile crosses her face as memories seem to alight in her eyes. I give her hand a reassuring squeeze, then show her some of the other paperwork. "I'm not sure about any of these," she says with a quick shake of her head.

My phone buzzes, and I look down to see another notification from Dean. He's getting anxious. "We need to hurry."

"Right. I'll check the bookcases. Anything in the drawers?" Chloe asks as she moves over the shelves lining the walls. She runs her fingers down the length, scanning the titles with her eyes. I watch her movement for a moment, then start poring through the drawers. There's hardly anything of interest—mostly more office supplies, some floor-plan designs, and a half-drunk bottle of Scotch.

"Anything over there?" I ask, looking up from the desk as Chloe snaps a few more pictures.

"Well, Clark Danvers found supernatural folklore super interesting. Especially stuff about werewolves," she says flatly, an ironic smirk blooming under her blue eyes. I look back to the circled 'Lunar Falls' on the map and sniff. *Hell of a coincidence.* I turn back to the desk and open the last couple drawers.

"More than interesting," I murmur, my mouth going dry. A

polished steel revolver sits on top of some papers in the bottom drawer, which in and of itself isn't very intriguing. The silver bullets next to it, though... I grab one and hold it up for Chloe. "I'd say he was a believer."

We had done our best to casually exit the basement, though I doubt we managed it without catching anyone's attention. At this point, though, it was the least of my concerns. There was a chance Chad would figure out who the 'two girls coming out of the basement' were, but he already suspected that we—well, *me*—knew something. And while we still haven't found any 'smoking gun' that he and his friends are the ones behind Blake's disappearance, we did find one with silver bullets. Chloe, at least, is convinced. I can't say I'm not right there, too.

The temperature change as we make our way out onto the porch and back out into the night is jarring. A light breeze has picked up, coolly kissing my skin and making the music by the bonfire sound even louder than before. It's still burning high, and the space around it looks more crowded now than when we had arrived. Faces flash under the light from the lanterns and the fire, and then disappear into shadow as they move around the crowd. I search the backyard for Dean—he's supposed to be meeting us here at the back of the house—but it's difficult to pick out anyone in the chaos.

...Except for Chad, who stands with a group of guys about ten feet away from us. For the first time tonight I lay eyes on him, despite being just this close not even ten minutes ago. His dirty-blond hair is combed back, and a smile lights up his face as it tips back in a laugh at something one of his companions says. He's not with his usual lackeys, but some other people I vaguely recognize from school.

I catch Chloe's attention with a quick squeeze of her arm. "To our left," I say, and glance toward Chad. She follows my line of sight, and then we both turn back to one another.

"Can I eat him?" she asks with a voice that doesn't betray her one way or the other. I purse my lips and hit her with a deadpan stare.

"No. But he hasn't seen us yet, so…" I start to say, glancing over my shoulder in Chad's direction. We lock eyes. *Shit*. The tension in Chloe's shoulders is still there when I turn back, and the face she's making is doing nothing to put me at ease. "Is he walking this way?" I ask.

"Yup." Is all Chloe replies. That neck vein is thrumming again.

"I'll keep him busy. You go find Dean." Chloe doesn't look back at me, still focusing over my shoulder at Chad's approach. "Chloe!" I put my hands on the side of her face and turn it toward me. "Go find Dean," I say again, as soothingly as I can. Her expression apologizes but she doesn't verbalize it, then she nods and walks off toward the bonfire.

I turn away from Chloe's retreating form and face Chad. My stomach is full of butterflies that seem to grow more and more agitated the closer he gets. I breathe in and out slowly, hoping to settle my racing heart. *Get your shit together, Ari*, I think to myself, though the thought seems to have the opposite effect. I dig my hands into my back pockets to keep them from shaking.

"Hey," I say, stepping up to meet him midway. His face alights with a smile.

"You came!"

"Yeah," I say with a slight nod. Anxiousness has its claws in me, and I'm sure he can hear it in every word. I direct a slight smile at my shoes as I toe the soft grass. Maybe I can play it off as flirtatious nerves? Goddess, I hope so. *Let's see how well I can play this game.* I glance back at him, and I don't have to even try for my cheeks to heat. I know they're red and blushing.

Chad nods toward Chloe, who's disappearing into the crowd, "You brought your friend."

"Yeah." I need to think of something to say to this dude other than 'yeah.' Not a great start... "I didn't want to come alone."

Chad laughs and nods, beer sloshing over the rim of his red Solo cup. "Safer to come in a pack, eh?" he asks, and my gaze shoots to the smirk he's wearing. The gleam in his eyes is almost a challenge. *Because it is...* He wants to see my reaction, and I'm sure my face is spelling it all out for him for now.

"Right..." My word trails off and I lick my lips, wracking my brain for the right thing to say in response. I can feel his eyes pressing hard on me, analyzing my every movement. I'm not going to pass this off as nervously flirting. *Switch gears*, I decide.

Straightening my shoulders, I set my stance and cross my arms. "Where's *your* pack?" I ask, narrowing my eyes. This is a lot easier to play than the innocent, flirty girl.

"Matt and Donavan? They're over there," he says, pointing to his right. I glance in that direction and see the two guys he's usually hanging with, one with tawny skin and jet-black hair, the other with brown eyes and curls. They're almost certainly the two other voices from the basement. I spot Dean and Chloe approaching from the fire behind Chad's friends, and comfort and confidence swells in my chest. I steel my features and turn back to Chad.

"Do any hunting lately?" I ask, crossing my arms across my chest again. Chad laughs, and it seems as if a bubble has formed around us. Everyone must be spotting the clearly visible hostility rising between us. People here and there pass by with shifting eyes, but only Dean and Chloe approach—and now Matt and Donavan.

Chad alters his stance to something firmer and less casual, but his hands are still loose, one holding his cup and the other hanging casually by his side. His eyes are shifting between thoughts, as if he's deciding how best to answer, when he finally says, "Not lately, no, but we caught something nice a couple of weeks ago."

The alarms in my head are ringing at his words. *He has Blake.* He didn't say it, but I don't need him to. I can see it in the malicious gleam glowing beneath his blue irises. He has Blake. "Quite the beauty," he adds, and my blood boils.

"You should be careful. Caged animals can still bite."

Chad snorts, his head turning away for a second then back to me. "Not without teeth."

I don't need to hear any more. I turn on a heel and head straight for Dean. I can tell he's heard every word, as if they're etched into the strain of his muscles. His jaw works as he eyes Chad behind me and the look on his face says he's seconds away from ripping someone's throat out. Chloe's face is even more violent.

"We need to go," I say as soon as I reach them, taking their hands and steering them away toward the front of the house and Dean's truck. "Not here..." I whisper quietly to my friends.

We've almost made it to the front of the house when Chad's two buddies move to block our path. Chad circles around to join them, the three now standing with their arms crossed and a look of pure enjoyment settling onto their features.

"Did I say something to scare you off?" Chad asks, just as Dean's hand wraps around mine. I squeeze his palm, as if to say 'I'm here.'

"Maybe I just decided I don't care to be around you anymore," I say as Chad meets Dean's gaze. Recognition seems to light his eyes, making me pause. I watch his expression closely and wonder if he isn't quite sure where he knows Dean from, as confusion, and then frustration, lines his features. *Does he remember him from school a couple years ago, or does he remember Halloween?*

"Who's your friend?" Matt asks with a gesture to Dean.

"None of your damn business." Dean says as he straightens next to me, bringing him to his full height and putting him inches above the three men in front of us. Chad takes a single step back almost *instinctively*, and I wonder if he knows on some level what Dean is capable of, even if he doesn't remember exactly why.

"That your boyfriend?" Matt snickers. "And here Chad was hoping you came to see him."

The other boy, Donavan snorts, and gives Matt a playful shove. "Yeah, and I see your blonde friend is here too, but... where's that other girl you hang out with? She couldn't make it?"

"Oh right! What was her name again? Where's she tonight?" Matt replies, mock confusion crossing his face. My eyes narrow.

Beside me, Chloe steps forward and smiles—a dazzlingly

bright, white smile. She lunges forward a step as fast as lightning, hissing and flashing her fangs in all their glory. The three men take a step back, nearly falling over each other, all smiles gone. "What the fuck are you!" Matt exclaims, stumbling another step back, and Chloe just laughs.

"I'm Chloe. *And her name is Blake*," she says, voice sweet as honey. It's a lot more aggressive than I'm used to from Chloe, but I can't help but laugh. "Happy to help you remember." Matt and Donavan don't hesitate as they take another step away. Matt grabs Chad's jacket, pulling him along, and the three turn and run back to the party.

Twenty-Six

It's been a few days since the party at the lake house. That 'couple weeks' Chad mentioned feels like a freight train bearing down on me, but Dean, Chloe, and I are no closer to finding Blake. I groan, flopping down onto Dean's couch and glance at my phone. I still have a few hours until I need to be home. Part of me doesn't even want to go back to that house.

Every time I see my mom or dad I want to scream at them for not telling me I'm part Djinn. They had to know, right? Which then leads to the bigger question of why two werewolves are watching over the daughter of a Djinn in the first place. Between that, finding Blake, everything we found at the lake house, Joaquin, nests, and whatever the hell else I'm forgetting, I'm getting really tired of 'big questions.'

Big questions *and* revelations, like how, apparently, Chad's dad knew about werewolves, or at least believed in them enough to get silver bullets, which probably means Chad does, too. It didn't take long for us to conclude that Chad was probably referring to the next full moon when he mentioned those 'couple weeks,' but how much does he really know? It was almost like he knew Weres existed, but he also seemed to be waiting for her to shift, which isn't going to happen, but... *Ugh*.

The mental strain of wrestling with all of this has slowly turned to frustration and anger. And now, every ounce of that frustration and anger is wound like a tight coil in my stomach, and it's only getting tighter by the day. Running into Chloe's mom yesterday at the supermarket hadn't helped either. I dropped my basket right there in the middle of the aisle and ran in the opposite direction.

It hadn't been all bad news the last three days, though. We had spoken to Abel, who had heard back from his 'friend' up north. Apparently, he had a lead on a nest—or at least a general area where one might exist. Abel had also grilled me on Joaquin, now very much invested in that situation with us as well. He had asked for a rundown on our entire conversation in Dean's living room—twice—as close to exact as I could remember. I could hear his furious notetaking even over the phone, but who knows when or if he would figure anything out. It was all better than nothing, but just like Blake, maddeningly out of reach.

"I don't know how much more of this I can take," I huff out as Dean lands on the other side of the couch, handing a warm cup across to me. I take it with a smile I'm sure doesn't reach my eyes, and without taking a sip I set it back onto the coffee table. I let my head fall back into the cushions.

Chloe will be up soon now that the sun has set, but even the thought of seeing her sets my insides twisting further. Seeing her mom the other day had put a lot into an unsettling perspective.

There's no changing what she's become, and while we might—we *are*—going to get Blake back, there's no way this ends without me losing Chloe. She'll have to leave at some point so that she can actually have a life. It doesn't mean I have to like it, though. There's only so long I can indulge my selfishness—at some point, I'm going to have to accept where the universe has taken us.

Dean drags my feet onto his lap, and when I don't fight him, he takes my shoes off one by one and starts rubbing the tension from them. I sigh at the tender pressure of his rough hands. "We'll get this figured out. We *will* find her," he finally says, and I peek at him then through my half-closed eyes. His focus is on massaging my feet, but I can see the thoughts spinning though his mind as well. He can't be in any higher spirits than I am. We've spent the last day or two trying to find every bit of information we can about Chad, Matt, and Donavan, but it all amounts to mostly nothing. Chad and his friends just seem like your average teens on paper.

There was more on Chad's father, but most of it so far was all superficial—mostly things about his business exploits and his sudden heart attack while hunting a couple years ago. Everything else we had looked into, like the records we found in his office, were hard to make sense of. Unfortunately, none of us are property lawyers.

The only person we knew who could probably help on that end was Jon, and that would mean a lot of questions about what we're doing that could bring him a step closer to learning about Chloe. Between that and Abel's off-putting warnings about Jon at his house, we had decided against it. The help didn't seem to outweigh the risk.

"Chad and his friends have as good as said they have her," I say, knowing we've been over this so many times we practically have the conversation memorized. They had been careful not to *explicitly* say anything, but between all we overheard in the basement and the scene outside, I don't think any of us are uncertain anymore. My thoughts drift back to the confrontation at the party, and suddenly the image of Chad forcing pliers into Blake's mouth fills my mind. *If he really did that, I swear to the Goddess...* I shiver and shove the thought away. Dean shifts beneath my feet and turns slightly toward me without ever letting me go.

"We've searched all their houses, the lake house *again*, and even tailed Chad for an entire night. If they have her, they're doing one hell of a job of keeping her hidden."

I sigh, knowing he's right. Things are getting desperate. The pack has already stopped looking for her—and Chloe. In fact, there was going to be a small funeral for them both in two days for everyone to say their goodbyes and offer up prayers to the Moon Goddess. I'm not sure I can bring myself to attend. Blake's still alive, and Chloe... is just fine.

"Maybe we're looking in the wrong places," Chloe's voice sails up from the basement stairs. I slide my feet off of Dean's lap and we both turn toward her. "It would be too obvious for them to keep her at their houses. Besides, their parents would find her, and as far as we can tell, they have no idea."

"Then where would they be hiding her?" Dean chimes in.

Chloe shrugs, crossing to the living room. "Somewhere they can be sure she won't be found or heard. Maybe someplace else on one of their properties. Chad's family has nearly a thousand acres of land. Maybe he's got a hunting camp or something out there."

Dean turns forward once more, his eyes focused on the coffee table in front of him. Chloe shrugs again when neither Dean or I offers a response, then turns toward the kitchen, no doubt for breakfast. A few minutes later she plops herself down onto the recliner, sipping from a dark-green coffee mug. The metallic smell coming off the cup is strong, even for my nose, and I'm suddenly glad I don't have the strong sense of smell that the other two do. My nose wrinkles, and Chloe only laughs. "You get used to it," she says, raising her cup at me with another laugh. "Want a sip?" I snort at her comment. It's just like Chloe to make light of the situation, though it feels like those moments are coming less and less here lately.

"Maybe," Dean finally says, bringing us back to the topic at hand. "Something like that probably wouldn't be listed anywhere."

"That's a lot of ground, but… It's worth looking into," I say, picking up my cooling mug of coffee. "Clark Danvers was an 'avid hunter.'" My chest feels lighter at the thought of at least having a direction to move in. Chloe nods her head in agreement.

"Well, we can't cover it all tonight," Chloe says, glancing between the two of us, "And you two look like you're ready to snap… who's up for a movie?"

Dean and I turn to one another. The dark circles under his eyes are probably a mirror of my own. It does feel like I'm reaching a breaking point. There's only so many times you can run into a wall before you fall apart, and then I'd be no help to Blake. I let out a deep sigh and settle back into the couch. Dean must have come to the same conclusion, mimicking my movement and pulling my feet back onto his lap. "A scary one," he says, and I 'mhmm' in agreement.

Chloe wrinkles her nose and I laugh. She's more of a rom-com type of girl, but doesn't argue. "Fine, but I pick the next one," she says, finally settling back into her chair and handing the remote over to Dean. Quickly he pulls up a streaming site on his tv, searches for horror movies, and fifteen minutes later we've decided on a flick to watch.

On the TV a girl claws her way through the crawlspace maze of a basement, frantically searching for a way out as her kidnapper pursues her. His eerie voice follows her through turn after turn. I can't help getting sucked into the scene, my throat tightening as my brain screams for her to run, to get free. I'm praying she makes it out before her kidnapper catches her, and of course she will—she was 'good' the whole movie: no premarital sex, drugs, or rock and roll. None of the usual shenanigans that get you minced up and put in a freezer like the rest of her cohorts. "Go, go, go," Chloe chants at the TV, just as the actress pulls herself free from a vent shaft. Looking around, she recognizes where she's at: an office building in the heart of the city.

I snatch the remote from Dean's lap and pause the movie, pulling myself upright on the couch. *We* have *been looking in the wrong places.* "What if that's what Chad did with Blake!?" Dean and Chloe turn to look at me, both of their faces lined with confusion.

I huff, pointing the remote towards the TV. "What if Chad and his cronies have Blake somewhere completely obvious like this. Somewhere close enough to people that the constant noise would drown out any cries for help, but also conspicuous enough that no one would even think to look there."

Dean's face morphs into a frown that I know means he's thinking through my words. Probably playing back what we just watched on TV and piecing it together with our town. Chloe, on the other hand, still looks doubtful as she glances from me to the TV and back.

"Maybe..." Dean starts, and I hold my breath waiting for what he comes up with. "It would probably have to be somewhere downtown to have that amount of foot traffic and noise level at all hours."

I nod slowly as I glare at the TV, the image of a girl climbing from the small ventilation shaft to the street side of a massive building stares back at me. Downtown Silas Creek isn't particularly large compared to the city in the movie, but it's not tiny either. It's certainly big and busy enough that no one would hear Blake when people are out and about, and even when they weren't the streets were never really quiet. But there are so many buildings there. He could have her in any one of them. *Unless...*

"There's too many buildings downtown with deep basements. Where would we even start?" Chloe sighs, her brows wrinkling into her forehead.

"Guess we'll just have to search near them all," Dean says with an unreadable expression, though his tone is nothing but cynical. "With my sense of smell and Chloe's hearing... I mean it's possible, I guess, but..."

"Not necessarily," I say hesitantly, the thoughts still piecing together in my head. "The map in the office at the lake house. It had a bunch of places marked downtown. I know everything in there looked like it hadn't been touched in years, but if those places used to belong to Chad's dad, maybe Chad still has access to some of them." I fish my phone out of my pocket and bring up the picture, looking it over to validate my idea.

Chloe's eyes light up. "That could be it! I mean, if they're hiding her anywhere, it's probably somewhere they've got the keys to, right?"

"It's a hell of a lot better than searching blind," Dean says. Even he's looking positive. "We'll start tonight."

I glance at my phone and my shoulders sag. "I have to be home in an hour," I say, deflating.

A slow smile slips across Dean's chiseled jaw. "Sneak out after."

Twenty-Seven

wo hours later I'm leaning out of my bedroom window staring at Dean like he's lost his mind. *Clearly, he has.* He has his arms out like a cheerleader ready to catch a flier, looking a little impatient and gesturing for me to jump. I cross my arms. There's no way I'm jumping from this far up. I've never been particularly afraid of heights, but between the slope of the lawn and being two-stories up, I'm also not crazy, either.

"I'll catch you, I swear," Dean whisper-shouts, just loud enough for me to hear. He waves at me to jump again

I bite my lip, glancing behind me to the bedroom door. Going out the front is *not* an option. My parent's bedroom is on the ground floor, and the drawback of living in a family of were-wolves is their superhuman hearing. You would think being part Djinn would heighten my senses like it does for them and pretty much every other supernatural, but no. *That would actually be helpful...* That first creak of the stairs they'll be on alert. And as soon as that door opens... I'd never clear the front porch before getting sentenced to a year of house arrest.

I may be an 'adult' as far as the collective supernatural world is concerned, but that line is always a little blurry from family to family. Sneaking out past curfew for Koa and I is still a definite 'no.'

Fuck. I have no other options, I realize. Slowly, ever so carefully, I pull my legs over the window sill to sit on the edge. *He'll catch me, right? I'm his mate, and a Were's mate is life itself. He wouldn't do anything that would put me at risk like that. Right! Right?* I try to focus on my thoughts rather than my thumping heartbeat, sure that it will wake my parents any second. It's not that far of a drop either. *The worst that could happen really is I break my leg. Which would suck. I really don't want to break any bones. Unless I fell back over his arms, and landed on my neck... Shit, that's enough,* Ari. Closing my eyes, I force everything from my mind, take a deep breath, and push myself from the window.

Wind rushes through my hair as my soul tries to leave my body through my throat and gets stuck in-between my gritted teeth. My stomach, however, feels like I left it on the ledge of the window. My body slams into the hard muscles of Dean's arms before my breath has caught up. My arms wrap around his neck in a death grip as my mind races through a mental checklist of all my body parts. I don't think I've broken anything, though a bruise is definitely forming on my side where Dean's arm broke my fall.

A low laugh rumbles through his chest, giving me the courage to open my eyes. I look up into the halo of Dean's beautiful face, the edges illuminated by the light coming off the visible slice of moon. Suddenly I can't breathe for a different reason.

"And you doubted me." Dean leans down slightly and whispers into my ear. His hot breath on my skin sends heat rushing through my core. I push against him and clumsily climb from his arms, straightening my shirt and jeans and wiping away imaginary dirt in the process. I mumble a quick, shaky 'thanks' under my breath and compose myself.

"Chloe's in the truck. Let's go," Dean whispers, grabbing my hand and pulling me toward his truck. I let the nighttime, autumn air cool the heat from my skin as we cross the lawn, then climb in the passenger side as Dean pushes the button that sends the truck roaring to life. He glances at me from the side, and I can feel my skin ignite all over again. I turn away quickly, forcing my gaze out the window. How is it possible for one man to affect every part of me with a single look? *Mate*, I huff mentally. *No, definitely not going there yet.*

Soft music plays over the speaker as his truck automatically connects to his phone, but I can barely hear what's playing. It's taking every bit of my concentration to keep my eyes and mind off the man next to me. "We're out of the neighborhood," Dean announces without looking from the road after a minute or two, and Chloe pops out from under a blanket.

"Can we change this blanket out? It's starting to smell." Chloe huffs from the backseat. Dean only chuckles in response.

Outside my window, trees blur past in dark masses, lit up here and there by street lights hanging high above us. It takes us about twenty minutes to reach the edge of downtown, and then another five to find a parking spot. The streets are sparse but far from empty, even at this time of night.

The three of us climb from the truck and converge in front. "So… what's the plan?" Chloe asks, digging her hands into her pockets as her eyes follow the handful of citizens walking down the sidewalk. I wonder if she's smelling each one, hearing their blood pulse through their veins like she could at the party. I suddenly find myself examining her, hoping she's not getting overwhelmed again. As if sensing my thoughts she turns to me then: "I'm fine, I ate before we left," she assures me with a wink. *She's got this.*

"Well, we use the pictures you guys took," Dean says, looking from Chloe to I. "I'll take these on the west side, you two take these to the east over here, and we'll work our way towards the center of town and meet back in the square here." Dean gestures with his finger on the screen of his phone, stopping with a sharp poke on the small park in the center of town. I look up to Dean and Chloe, and we give each other a nod.

I wrap my coat tighter around myself. Winter is right around the corner, judging from the cold bite in the air. "Let's go find Blake."

An hour or so later, Chloe and I have hit the first several marked buildings on the east side of downtown. We hadn't talked much as we made our way from building to building, focused like we were. Each had been a small office building of some kind—old and new, tall and short, some made of brick or stone while others were more modern—and all closed for the night. We circled each, checking the exits, street accesses, and basement windows. Watching, listening, smelling… with no luck whatsoever.

"You know, it's strange," Chloe says from my right as we march toward our next target. "I wasn't sure at first, but I swear most of those buildings smelled a bit… I don't know. There was a lot going on, and my sense of smell is nothing like Dean's, but I swear something wolf-y was floating around in that mess of scents."

I stop dead in my tracks, and the look I shoot at Chloe has her stumbling over herself to explain. "No, no, no. If she was there it would have been *wayyyy* stronger, and I *definitely* didn't hear anything suspicious. It was just kind of a… general… wolf smell?"

"She's been gone for a while." I say, wrapping my arms tight against my chest to ward off the chill. "Maybe it's hers, but it's old? I suppose they could have been moving her around…"

"Dean could probably tell for sure, but I don't think so… maybe?" Chloe replies, looking curiously over her shoulder back the way we came. "That would be a good thing though, right? If they were moving her around then we're on the right trail!" She beams at me, flashing her teeth for a moment before quickly realizing and throwing a hand over her mouth. Her cheeks turn as red as the jacket she's wearing, and I snort with laughter.

Excitement fills my chest for the first time in what feels like ages. Maybe we're finally on the trail—the real, *actual*, trail to finding Blake. "C'mon, let's go," I chuckle, taking Chloe by the arm and pointing us toward the next building on the map. She pulls her hood on a little tighter, and almost skips along with me. Trees dot the sidewalks at even intervals and ball lights are strung in a zigzag fashion between the buildings, illuminating the streets in a warm, inviting glow. The wind has picked up a little bit, playfully blowing my hair back and gently swaying the tree limbs. To everyone we pass I'm sure we look like nothing more than a couple friends out for a night on the town. Here and there, couples and groups pass us, probably doing just that.

We circle two more buildings—a small tea shop and a skin-care store—with no Blake, but that lingering smell is still there according to Chloe. My heart swells with each footstep, and the *click-clack* of our boots on the sidewalk sounds like a clock ticking down to finding Blake. *Only three more buildings on this side of town.* Chloe glances down at her phone, looking over the map again. "Next one should be right around the corner, the next block up," she says excitedly, gesturing up a couple streets.

I shoot her a quick smile, and we both increase our pace. My mind drifts to Dean, and I suddenly wonder if he's been sniffing out the same thing as Chloe has. We've almost cleared our side of the city, but hadn't heard anything from him yet.

"So... mates huh?" Chloe asks, side-eyeing me with a raised brow.

I shake my head from side to side. "I'm so not ready to dissect that yet."

Chloe shrugs. "Fair," she says as our pace slows a tiny bit.

"It's just I've always been drawn to him. For as long as I can remember I wanted him... I mean he *is* f-ing gorgeous right!"

"Definitely fire."

"But now that we have this thing between us that says he doesn't just *want* me, he's my one true love... I'm terrified." I shake my head again, kicking at a loose pebble with my boot before I stop and turn to my friend. "I don't know if I'm ready for that all-consuming-I'll-destroy-the-world-to-save-you-type of love. I don't even know if I'm ready for a long-term relationship." I have to laugh at the ridiculousness of it all.

Chloe's eyes shine beneath the moonlight as empathy sparkles within the blue depths. She places a hand on each of my shoulders. "I think he would already destroy the world to save you. I mean he is kind of risking everything to keep your best friend alive even though she wants to eat people."

I chuff under my breath, sending a jacked brow in my friend's direction. "Seriously though," she says, continuing, "a mate bond doesn't have to be rushed, it can even be rejected."

"But how do I know he's the right choice? Not all mating bonds are."

Chloe drops her hands and shrugs. "It's a leap of faith. Albeit more likely to work than not because of the bond, but every relationship is—bond or not."

I nod my head slowly as we both turn back toward our destination. "The sexual tension between you two might literally set the house on fire, though. For real, you should put him out of his misery soon and at least take him for a test run."

I snort and roll my eyes. "Goddess, I want to, though." Chloe laughs, and I'm right there with her, laughing as we march arm-in-arm.

My phone buzzes, and I reach down to fish it out of my pocket. It's a text from Dean. *Does the mate bond come with telepathy, too?* I chuckle to myself, and then send a silent prayer up to the Moon Goddess. *Dean found Blake. Dean found Blake. Dean found Blake. Please.*

Does Chloe smell anything weird? It's not the response I was hoping for, and I arch a brow at my phone.

She says she smells something 'wolf-y' idk. We think they might have been moving Blake around. I think we might be on the right trail! I send back. I feel Chloe guide us around the corner as I watch the ellipses appear at the bottom of the conversation and wait for Dean's response. The wind whips up again, the chilly air burning my exposed cheeks.

It's not Blake. *What?* Cold air snakes its way down the back of my jacket, but it's Dean's brusque and blunt response that has me shivering. The ellipses appear again, and I suddenly realize we've stopped. I look over to Chloe, thinking she's been following the conversation on my phone, but she's staring at a café across the street. Her whole body is rigid, and her big doe eyes have somehow managed to grow even larger. My phone buzzes again in my hand, and I look down to Dean's next message. **I recognized some of these places. They belong to the pack.**

"Chloe?" I ask, confusion tainting my voice. She doesn't respond, and I hurriedly follow her gaze back across the street. A man sitting at one of the circular tables in the front patio of the café has stood up, adjusting his brown leather jacket and raising his chin like he's holding his nose to the wind. *Oh fuck.* Chloe's grip on my arm is threatening to cut off my circulation. The man's chin drops, and he scans the sidewalk opposite of where he stands, his eyes narrowing as he searches the length of it. His eyes stop.

"W-wolf." Chloe stammers out. She stands completely still, a deer in the headlights. Panic floods my chest, filling up the space where excitement had been just a minute ago. *We need to move.*

The man makes his way around the waist-high wrought-iron fence separating the patio from the sidewalk and steps to the edge of the street just as a car passes. Closer now, I recognize his face from pack meetings. *Shit, shit, shit.* I snatch Chloe's arm and spin her around, nearly dragging her back down the way we had come as I throw my hood up. The wind surges again, blowing at our backs as if willing us away. It might have just saved our lives… If it hadn't been blowing in the opposite direction, he would have smelled us coming before Chloe had any idea he was there.

I set a brisk pace with Chloe in tow and glance over my shoulder. He's crossed the street now. Tracking us. I pull my phone out again and shakily text Dean: **Wolves.**

His reply is almost instant. **Share your location. I'm coming.**

I fumble around with my thumb, sending Dean our location and quickening our pace. Chloe shakes beside me as we walk, and I rub her arm reassuringly. "Dean's coming," I whisper under my breath, just loud enough for her to hear. Her nod is quick and sharp, and she keeps her eyes ahead on the sidewalk. I chance another look behind us. He's keeping pace, about two streets back, weaving around the few people passing up and down the sidewalk. Following. *He wouldn't do anything in the middle of downtown. Not in public like this*, I think to myself. *Right?* I'm suddenly aware of all the dark alleys we're passing, and my mouth goes dry.

Keep moving towards 4th street. Almost there. Dean sends. I can see the signs for 4th street several blocks ahead. *Just get to 4th street and then…* And then what? What was Dean's plan? Was he going to have to attack this guy? *Oh, Goddess.* The memory of what he said all that time ago floods back, about what the pack would do to him if they found out about Chloe… Somehow more panic crowds in my core. I shake my head and clear those thoughts away. *Focus, Ari.* None of that was going to help right now. I look back over to Chloe. Her cheeks are damp.

"When we get to 4th street, we're going to turn right and run. Full speed, okay? Fuck pretending nothing's going on," I whisper to Chloe. I've got no idea if that's even a viable option, or if he'd just say 'screw it' and start running, too, but it's a hell of a lot better than just walking straight with no plan. *I have my magic.* Would it work like last time if I need it? If he just keeps coming? Would I call down the Council on me? *Goddess, I hope I don't have to find out.* I give her arm another reassuring squeeze—as much for her as for me—and she looks over to me for the first time since this started, giving me another quick nod.

The signs for 4th street are getting closer, now only two blocks away. One block. Our pursuer hasn't missed a beat. If anything he's quickening his pace. Another text from Dean flashes on my phone: **Meet back at the truck.** *What the* hell, *Dean?* The plan was to get to 4th street and now he's saying to head back to the truck? *Fuck this.* I grit my teeth, turning the anger from Dean's change of plans into determination. We pass another alley. The green sign for '4th street' flares like a beacon, shining under the hanging street lights. "Almost there. Remember, turn right and—"

A loud 'Oof' sounds behind us, and I peek over my shoulder to see the man from the café on his ass. "Oh shit, my bad man." *Dean!* Dean stands over the man, 'helping' him up but keeping a deathgrip on both sides of his jacket. "Sorry, man, I was in such a hurry I didn't even see you—" Dean's voice trails off as we reach the sign.

"Run!" I whisper harshly through my raw throat. Chloe and I turn right, bolting in the direction of Dean's truck—and safety.

Twenty-Eight

When we make it back to Dean's truck, Chloe's floodgates open. She presses back against the door with her face in her hands, her blonde hair cascading down in front of her from underneath the hood of her jacket. It hides the tears, but not the deep, gasping sobs. It feels like her cries are reverberating in my chest, and my heart hurts. With all my focus on her, it takes me a second to realize I've started crying, too. I rush forward and embrace her, holding her head to my shoulder and together we let the tears flow. And now that the high of adrenaline is slowly fading, I'm feeling sick to my stomach. *So close. So close.*

Minutes or a lifetime pass before Chloe's shakes slowly subside. She takes a few stuffy sniffs and wipes her nose, gently pushing away from me and standing up straight. Her eyes are red and puffy, and the wetness on her cheeks reflects in the soft light of the moon, now lower on the horizon. "My funeral's not supposed to be for two more days." Chloe wimpers out with a smile completely at odds with the rest of her face. I sniff and shake my head. *Still Chloe.* I can't bring myself to really laugh, though. Not with how razor-close everything had been.

The adrenaline might have worn off, but the swirl of emotions churning in my stomach is still definitely in full swing. To go from thinking we were *finally* about to find Blake to speed-walking for our lives is… jarring. That merry-go-round of hope and despair is spinning again, and I want off. Chloe sniffs again and wipes her nose with the sleeve of her jacket, then looks up over my shoulder. "Dean's coming."

I glance over my shoulder, then step to Chloe's side. It takes a minute for Dean to materialize out of the shadows and into the overhead lights of the parking lot. He walks quickly with his hands in his pockets, glancing over his shoulder once or twice more before closing the distance to where we wait at the truck. He joins in with our small huddle and deflates with an audible exhale. "I'm back…" Chloe reaches out and takes his hand, giving it a small squeeze.

"Thank you."

Dean's lips flatten and he nods. "Everyone okay?" he asks, holding Chloe's gaze for a moment before focusing his blue-green eyes on mine. The sudden want to close the distance and wrap myself in the warmth and safety of his arms is almost overwhelming, but I hold back. Now's not the time—I can fall apart again later. Right now, we need to focus. I straighten up and nod in response.

"Are you sure you lost him?" Chloe asks. Her posture is all business, but the remnants of her weeping are still everywhere on her features.

"I'm sure. And I don't think he got a good look at either of you. At least not that I could tell." One small weight lifts from my shoulders at his comment. I hadn't even thought about the fact that if I could recognize him, he could recognize us...

"You talked to him?" I ask, wondering how much talking Dean had to do to get himself out of this, and praying he hadn't somehow implicated himself in anything. *It's his life on the line, too*, I remind myself.

"I 'helped' him look for you two," Dean says flatly. "Said I smelled something funny and was following the scent, and then ran into him. His name's Jeremy. He recognized me, too." A hint of worry flashes across his face, but he steels himself in an instant. Ice-cold wind blows through, kicking up a small whirlwind of fallen leaves in the parking lot. Dean half-smirks at it, then turns his attention to Chloe. "The Goddess must have been looking out for you tonight. The wind helped muddle your trail. I'm not sure what I could have done, otherwise."

I shiver at the fear that crosses Dean's face. What would he have had to do if Chloe hadn't been hard to follow? I swallow at the implication. The wind breezes through our huddle again, as if to comfort me in response. I silently thank the Goddess for sending it.

"Yeah," Chloe says quietly, adjusting her stance and rubbing her forehead. "So, no Blake, but a lot of wolf." Judging by the look on her face, she's ready to change the subject. I don't blame her—no one wants to keep hearing about how they almost died. "These places all used to belong to Chad's dad." She lets the statement hang in the air between us.

"And now they belong to the pack. Jeremy said he was out here keeping an eye on the place for Jon. Not a stretch to assume that was what we were smelling at all these places," Dean says, looking thoughtful.

"Maybe Jon bought them all up after Chad's dad died?" Chloe shrugs. "How did we not know about all this?"

"Everyone knows Jon is in real estate… and I mean, it's not like Jon has to reveal everything he owns to the pack. Nobody asked, so he didn't tell. The only reason it seems strange to us is because of that map." Dean's brows pinch, and he gives each of us a hard look.

Another shiver from the chill takes me, and Dean shrugs out of his coat and wraps it around my shoulders. I open my mouth to protest but he cuts me off with a soft smile and a shake of his head before I can. "I don't feel it like you do." Slowly I nod, giving him a quiet thanks and pulling my arms through the jacket. I dig the toe of my black boot into the asphalt of the parking lot, puzzling over his and Chloe's words. The map. All this property belonged to Clark Danvers. Now it belongs to Jon. Chad has Blake.

"And about two years ago, Chad's dad died…" I say, involuntarily speaking my stream of thoughts aloud. An epiphany hits me so hard my knees threaten to buckle. *Joaquin said…* "Joaquin said… He said he was here two years ago to help Jon, because Jon ran into some trouble with the locals." I tremble at the thoughts falling on me like stones. "What if this was all part of that 'problem?'"

I pause, turning from Dean to Chloe and back, pinning them with my eyes. I suddenly don't feel as cold anymore. "We think Chad took Blake, but we never asked why! And… and Dean, remember what Abel said about Jon? That we don't know what he's capable of… What if Jon had something to do with Clark Danvers's death? This is revenge! Chad took Blake for revenge!" Their stretching silence is deafening. "Or have I actually broken and completely lost my mind?"

"Shit," Chloe whispers under her breath, but I can't get a read on how she's feeling. "I mean, it fits. It's motive. Clark Danvers disappears two years ago around the time Jon picks up all this property. He seemed to know about Weres, so maybe that has something to do with it all, too. But what about the vampire attack?" she asks, looking confused.

"That's right! The vampire attack… with your dad and Blake's mom… that was around the same time, too." I follow her up, then immediately feel embarrassed for sounding so excited.

"I— I meant the one on the Moon Awakening. The night they took Blake. I was wondering how that connected, if it did, but… You don't think what happened with my dad and everything is connected to all this, do you?" Chloe's face is a mess of disbelief and… anger?

"It *was* right around the same time all of this happened…" I start, trying to sound as conciliatory as possible. Joaquin, multiple suspicious deaths, Jon inheriting a ton of property… *Have I lost my mind?* "Sorry… maybe I *have* gone off the deep-end." I didn't want to push it. Obviously, it would be a touchy subject with Chloe, but… It was a hell of a coincidence that *all* of this was going on right around the same time, right? I look to Dean, who's been silent the whole time.

He leans his head to the side, as if seeing the picture I was painting. He locks eyes with me, and I know he sees the connection. "I guess… we can't rule it out." His expression turns sad then, "But even if all that's the case, it still doesn't help with the Blake situation."

"What? But it—" I'm left gaping, the realization dawning on me. Dean is staring at his shoes, hands planted on his hips. "But it doesn't get us any closer to finding Blake." *FUCK...* He's right. I feel like I need to scream. We already basically knew Chad had Blake, the problem was finding her. All this did was reveal some insanity in the background—maybe. "Well, it feels nice to have some sort of understanding of *why*, even if it might not help us find her," I say quietly, trying to rationalize everything rattling around in my head right now with the fact that we're still no closer to Blake.

"Maybe there's an answer in there somewhere," Dean says, looking at me with a reassuring smile. I can't tell if it reaches his eyes. "Let's make a timeline or something. Get all the pieces together. Maybe something new or some kind of hint will jump out at us." He shrugs. "It's more than we had five minutes ago."

"That's probably a job for tomorrow," Chloe cuts in, her voice edged with hurt. "We need to head back soon, it's only another hour or two before the sun starts to rise." Her face turns toward the descending moon off in the distance.

"Yeah. We can regroup tomorrow and see what we can puzzle out," Dean says, earning a curt nod of agreement from Chloe. We all turn on a heel and take our seats in the truck. Quiet descends on us once again. Dean brings the vehicle to life and then pulls out of the parking lot, turning us down the road toward Lunar Falls. When Dean's hand wraps around mine I don't pull away. The warmth of his skin melts through my skin, as if he's funneling the heat into me. I let the sensation course through the rest of me, and the light squeeze he gives my hand says it's all going to be okay. I glance at him, and a lump forms in my throat at the determination shining in those minty irises of his. *We will figure this out, and we will find her,* they seem to say. Straightening in the passenger seat, I give him an equally determined look, hoping he can see the reply written in my eyes just the same.

Twenty-Nine

Climbing out of Dean's truck I glance up at the traditional home in front of the three of us. I try not to let our failure or the gravity of what I had been rambling about earlier sink its claws back into my consciousness. Instead, I force a different mantra into my brain. *We will find Blake. We will save her and she will be okay.* The white paneling of the house almost glows in the moonlight and I breathe it in, as if the glow will find its way into the hollow spaces of my heart and fill it with warmth.

"I'll… you know," Chloe says, jacking a thumb over her shoulder. Her usual bright and lively voice still sounds pained. Dean glances at her for a moment then nods, turning back to his house. My brow rises in answer, but I decide not to voice the question as the two of us head into the house. Chloe takes off silently into the brush of the backyards on the street.

"She's going to check in on her family," Dean says as soon as we cross the threshold, his voice shaking through a yawn.

I jerk straight at his words. "What?" I shake my head. "And after everything tonight? She can't!"

He shuts the door behind us, helping me shuffle out of our coats. "Don't worry, she's not talking to them or anything. Just watching them from the forest behind her house." Dean shrugs, running his right hand through the blond strands of his hair. His body sags slightly and I see the rings under his eyes, the tired slump of his shoulders. He's as exhausted and stressed as I am, I realize. "I followed her the first couple nights… just to be sure. And she probably needs it more than ever tonight."

"She's *been* doing this?" I ask with a sigh. Of course, she has. While I'm running away from her family, she's running toward them—unable to talk to them, to hold them, to assure them she's okay… "What about the patrols?"

Dean shakes his head. "They're on the edges of the neighborhood. They're looking for vamps coming in, not one's already running around inside." He pins me with a smile that seems genuinely impressed. "And especially not one's who can strategize. She knows their routes and shift changes. Don't worry, she's sneaky. Tonight was… different." Worry is hiding behind that smile now, as if Dean is suddenly worried that it had all been luck up until this point.

"I guess," I say, not able to muster an argument even with the change in Dean's expression. I suppose I would be doing the same thing in her shoes, regardless of the danger. Not to mention, her mother and sister were about to lay her to rest soon. They'd be taking the first step in moving on into a life without her. In a way, there is more finality to that than her actual death. *She'll be dying for the second time…* It dawns on me once again how hard this must be for Chloe, and how incredibly strong she's been. I have to stop myself from tearing up. I am in no position to judge—she had lost almost everything, and if sneaking out to see them at night is what she needs, then I support it all the way.

I make my way to the living room couch and let the weight of everything push me down into the cushions. Two short strides later, Dean crosses the room and lands right next to me. Pulling a blanket off the back of the couch, he hands the fleece material over to me. "Thanks," I say, taking the offering and wrapping it around my front.

Dean turns his body toward me as he adjusts himself into a comfortable position. For a few minutes, we allow the silence to fill the air around us. It isn't awkward, though, and neither of us seem to mind the quiet. I'm thankful for it, really. It's so nice to *be quiet* for a little while with everything that has happened in the last few weeks. I realize we don't need words to always fill the space between us, and I smile. We both snuggle in the warmth of the couch and the comfortable silence hanging in the room.

My eyes roam over the man next to me, starting at his soft, blond hair that is longer on top and shaved on the sides, then moving down each curve of his face and jaw. Down his neck to the corded muscles of his shoulders and arms. One drapes casually over the back of the couch, the other the sofa arm. He's wearing a dark-gray t-shirt that looks soft and I want to touch the fabric to see. My fingers itch to move as my eyes outline the rise and dips of each one of his abs accentuated beneath the shirt. I suck in a sharp breath as my heart rate picks up.

"So…" I start, finally breaking the silence. "Tell me about this whole mate thing."

Dean's eyes turn to mine then, the teal shade darkening with a want so strong I can almost feel it echo in my own veins.

"What do you want to know?" Dean's words are tight, as if it's taking all his control to ask rather than show me exactly what mates do. My thighs ache at the thought.

I glance away, plucking at a loose strand of thread on the blanket to keep my hands from doing something they shouldn't. "How do you… you know, complete the bond?"

Dean smirks in that signature way of his and I snort. I can never help my reaction to that look. "We bite each other," he says, and I snap my head back at him, my mouth hanging open. *Did he just say 'bite?'*

"We do what now?"

Dean nods, his expression one of pure amusement. How did I not know this? Obviously because I never thought a mating bond would happen to me.

"It's this overwhelming need to mark one another, to claim the other as theirs. The male partially shifts, just enough for their teeth to lengthen enough for the bite."

"Oh." I frown, trying to picture his words in my mind. And I'll be damned if he doesn't make it sound hot as hell. "It sounds… primal?"

"I guess it kind of is," Dean runs a hand through his hair, messing up the perfect layers in a carefree way. I squirm a little as the heat of his gaze turns toward me again.

"Do you… feel like that?" I ask, biting my lip. While my brain hopes for denial, the ache between my legs is begging for something else entirely.

Dean shuffles in his seat before answering. "Yes… everytime I look at you a part of me wants…" his words trail off with a small shake of his head. "But it's usually at the height of sex…" His shoulders sag forward with the omission. "Or leads to sex."

This time I can't close my mouth, and I know I'm gawking. I'm not sure I want to know what he sees in my eyes right now. I don't know if they're filled with fear or something more hungry. Probably both.

He shrugs, turning his face away from me. Maybe he didn't like what he saw? "Listen, you don't have to worry about it. I'd never force you into something like that."

"I-I know," I reply, stumbling over my words as my brain tries to catch up. "I just don't know if I want that or not yet."

Dean rolls his shoulders and stands in one fluid movement. "It's late…" he lets his words trail off, and I glance down at my hands buried in the blanket bunched in my lap.

"Can I stay here tonight?" I ask, not daring to look him in the eye just yet. "I don't want to be alone." I rush the words out through my lips in barely a whisper before I finally allow myself to peek up at the man in front of me. When I do, heat ignites in my core and threads its way through my limbs with the intense gaze shining in his eyes.

"You're always welcome to stay," Dean gives me his cocky grin again before glancing toward the stairs, as if debating whether to stay here with me or go up to his own room. When he turns back to me, all nervousness or doubt is gone from his expression. Fate decides your mate. That's what the pack believes, and the Moon Goddess never makes a mistake. I don't know if I believe that, but I know that right now the idea of going next door and sleeping in my own bed is almost as depressing as cuddling with Dean on this couch is terrifying. *Be brave*, I remind myself, and pat the couch beside me where he was just sitting moments before.

Dean laughs under his breath and I pinch my lower lip between my teeth. "Only as long as you can keep your hands to yourself," Dean says, but his voice is teasing and I know he doesn't mean it. I roll my eyes as I lift the blanket for him to settle in next to me. Dean snags the remote off the table next to the couch, plopping his feet onto the coffee table as I turn and snuggle into his chest.

Thirty

A subtle shaking wakes me. I yawn and stretch, blinking my eyes open to find myself still tangled up on Dean's chest. I glance at the now blank TV and realize we must have fallen asleep during the movie at some point. I jerk upright, suddenly all too aware of Dean's hard body beneath my own. My cheeks flush as I scramble to the side of the couch, pulling my phone out to check the time. Judging from the light streaming in through the windows, I'd guess it's sometime close to noon. My phone proves me right—12:32pm. "Shit," I mumble, realizing I way overslept. At least it's the weekend.

And then I see the five missed texts from my mom. I rest my head in the palm of my hand as I start to read them one by one. They're pretty much all the same: Where are you? Did you leave early for something? Now we're starting to worry. I quickly shoot off a reply to my mom.

Hey, sorry I left early this morning for a walk and ran into Dean. Went to his house and fell asleep watching a movie. Just woke up.

It doesn't take long for Mom's reply. **Next time leave a note. We were worried.**

Sorry. I'll do that next time

Good. With everything that's been going on we need to know where you are

K mom. Love you

I send off the last text to Mom and turn back to find Dean has snuck off into the kitchen and is returning with two steaming mugs of coffee in hand. "Everything okay?" he asks, his brow creased in worry.

I nod my head. "Yeah, just replying to my mom." I answer, sipping gingerly from the mug. I savor the taste, and a pleasant warmth starts to creep through my insides. "It's all good. Did Chloe make it back last night?"

Dean stands next to the couch, quietly sipping from his own mug. "Yeah, about an hour or so after we turned the movie on. I'm pretty sure you didn't last twenty minutes," he says with a chuckle, running his free hand through his thick, blonde hair. "I'm gonna make some breakfast," he adds, gesturing at the kitchen. I meet his gaze from where he towers above me and I smile with a single dip of my head.

"Thanks," I say quietly, and he turns toward the kitchen. I follow his exit with my eyes. He stretches the sleep from his limbs as he walks, his muscles stretching and pulling beneath the thin t-shirt he's wearing. I squirm a little on the couch as heat rises between my legs. Damn, he is fucking hot. Every hormone in my body is screaming at me to take this man and do all things imaginable with him. Alarms race through my mind. 'Mate' they seem to say. *Mates are for life*—it's not like a regular relationship. If it doesn't work, you two can go your separate ways, maybe there's some bad blood, maybe you lose a house in the divorce. But you'll make it. Mate's lives are tied to one another. If one dies the other may survive, but it is *brutal*—maybe the most painful thing a Were can go through. Humans that complete the bond almost never survive a mate's death. Luckily for them, I suppose, their short lifespan means they'll likely never have to go through the pain of a mate's death. Another reason why Weres rarely mate with humans.

But I'm not human, I remind myself. According to Joaquin, I'm half Djinn, which would make me immortal right? Or close to it. That's *if* I inherit more than just magic from my dad. Maybe it makes my lifespan closer to Weres? They can live around 200 years or more. Not immortal, but still a pretty damn long time. The fact is, I had never even heard of a half Djinn before Joaquin mentioned them, so I have no clue about their lifespan, or anything else really.

I shake my head as questions pile up in my mind. I have magic—I saw and felt it on the night of the Moon Awakening—but what else had my father passed to me? Why does the Council think I'm an abomination? Was that just a… racist thing? Pride? Maybe, but when you're an all-powerful Djinn, why would you go out of your way to track half-Djinn's down and kill them? Really, it all circled around to the question of how much can I even trust that Joaquin isn't lying? Well, not lying, but definitely not telling the whole truth.

I wish Blake were here. She would know exactly what to do about all of this—the right questions to ask, the right interpretations. She's always been the smartest of the three of us. She would read Joaquin like a book. *And she wouldn't hesitate to tell me to take Dean and climb him like a tree*, I think with a small chuckle, my eyes landing on him scrambling eggs in the kitchen. *We* will *find you, Blake. I promise.*

Dean's smart home display lights up in the kitchen, and he reaches over from the stove to press an 'accept' button on the touchscreen. Confusion mixed with a bit of surprise colors his face. "Chloe?"

Chloe's voice filters out through the speaker. "Hey… I couldn't sleep. Can you hit the shades?"

"Uh, yeah. One sec…" Dean answers, hitting a few more buttons on the touchscreen. In a moment, the automatic blinds begin to slowly draw down. Soon, the living area and kitchen are shrouded in shade, the natural light replaced with the glow of light bulbs and LEDs. Aside from a few streams around the edges of the blinds and the light coming from the foyer area, all the sunlight has been hidden away. "All set," he calls through the display.

The basement door slowly opens, and Chloe's blonde head peeks out, scanning the room. She gets her bearings and exits the stairwell, shooting me a tired, half-hearted smile. "Morning." I return the greeting and watch her play a three-dimensional game of 'the floor is lava' as she carefully makes her way to the kitchen and grabs breakfast from the refrigerator. She doesn't bother with a cup this time, and downs the whole bag quickly. Dean watches her from the corner of his eye where he cooks.

"Just extra hungry or something?" Dean ventures carefully. He swirls the spatula around the frying pan a couple more times, then turns off the burner.

"No, no. I mean I was hungry, but... Like I said, I was having trouble sleeping. I couldn't turn my mind off. Last night was... a lot." Her shoulders sag and her gaze drops to her feet.

Dean 'mhmms' in agreement, nodding his head. "Well, grab another bag and come join us for breakfast," he adds with a friendly smile. He makes up two plates of eggs for me and himself, then makes his way to the living room. The couch sinks beneath his weight as he sits, and he turns and hands me a steaming plate. After a few seconds, Chloe completes her journey into the living room, taking a recliner across from us with a blood bag in hand.

"Do you... want to talk about it?" I ask after the quiet stretches for an uncomfortable amount of time. Dean's eyes rise from his plate to look between Chloe and I, his cheeks stuffed with food. Chloe daintily sips from her bag for another second or two, then meets my eyes.

"I don't know... I'm still processing so much, and then right when it feels like I'm getting a grip on *literally* anything, something new drops on me. I was getting a grip on this new 'life' I've got, and then I almost lose it last night. And speaking from experience, I don't want to die again." She sniffs to herself, but the small laugh doesn't reach her eyes. "I thought I was getting a grip on dealing with my family moving on—with me moving on—but this funeral thing tomorrow has thrown that all out of whack. I thought I had accepted what had happened to my dad, but after what you said last night..." She trails off, that hint of anger and hurt still ringing on the edge of her voice.

I look down at my barely-touched plate, suddenly unable to meet her eyes. "About that... I know I sounded... excited. But it was just because I thought we were finally on to something, especially after not finding Blake again, and…" I stop myself short of the ramble I know is coming. I look back up to find Chloe's big blue eyes looking sadly at me.

"It's okay. I get it." She smiles wistfully at me for a moment, then looks thoughtfully off to the corner of the room. "I was angry when you said it. I guess I still kind of am. I had moved on from all that. The wound had closed over, but when you said that it felt like it had been ripped right back open, and now I have to deal with his death all over again. It's not even really what you said… It's that I think you might be right."

"I didn't want to push it, but… I think I am, too," I say quietly. It's just all so much all around the same time, and it feels like all of the consequences have rippled forward to now. "It's just… it all feels related," I continue, working through the ideas as I speak. "Two years ago, something went on between Clark Danvers and Jon, Joaquin showed up, there was a vampire attack, then Clark Danvers died. Two years later, Chad Danvers kidnaps Jon's daughter, Joaquin shows up again, and there's a vampire attack." Chloe nods silently after I finish, still looking off to the corner, while Dean's green eyes stare at me over his plate of food from the other side of the couch. His brows suddenly furrow, and he puts his fork down on his plate. He takes a deep breath.

"And there's Abel… Abel helped Jon with something after the vampire attack. And for whatever he did, he got let off the leash," Dean whispers over his plate. His gaze drops, and the worry creasing his face is plain.

I sigh. "So, we have the Danvers, Jon and Blake, Abel, vampires, and Joaquin—"

Pop.

Thirty-One

Light-green smoke explodes to my left and I instinctively shy away, pressing myself into the arm of the couch. I watch it dissipate through half-closed lids to reveal the form of Joaquin sitting between Dean and I, one leg crossed over his knee, arms draped casually over the back of the couch.

Dean's already standing, gripping his fork like a weapon, while Chloe seems to have tried to melt into the back of the recliner. Joaquin's head snaps in my direction so fast I feel like I should hear a whip crack. That malevolent toothy grin cuts across his fox-like face. "You rang?"

"W-what?" I stammer out.

"You said my name three times, and so here I am," he answers with a subtle bow of his head.

"Wait, what? Is that a thing?"

Joaquin snorts with laughter. "No, of course not. But that

would be *really cool*, wouldn't it?" Dean's knuckles go white on the fork.

"Then why are you here?" he nearly growls, towering over the sitting Djinn.

"Oh, I was eavesdropping," he answers matter-of-factly, "Your detective team meeting seemed like fun, so I decided to pop in... Get it? *Pop* in? Anyone?" Joaquin looks to each of us for some kind of approval, then contorts his face into a mockery of disappointment.

Dean doesn't move from where he stands, still staring down the Djinn. Joaquin meets his gaze and continues: "Oh come now, what are you going to do? Kill me with a fork? There's very few things that can kill a Djinn..." he starts, then turns his head and winks at me. *What the fuck?* "...but I assure you, your dollar store tableware is *not* one of them. Sit, sit, sit." He pats the space next to him on the couch, staring back at Dean pleasantly. That grin returns. "*Sit.*"

Dean seems to throw himself backwards onto the couch, his arms taking a second to catch up with the rest of his body. He suddenly groans, and I spot the fork sticking out of his leg. His hand still grips it, and he makes no move to pull it out. Dean stares down at his unmoving hand, then snaps his eyes back to Joaquin. "I swear I'll..." Green smoke fills his mouth.

Joaquin *tsks* and shakes his head, then turns back to me. "Honestly, I'm not sure what you see in him." I watch Dean silently struggle against invisible bonds next to me. Joaquin turns back to him, raking his eyes over his struggling form. "Actually... I *do* think I see what you see in him. There's certainly a *lot* to look at, isn't there?" He winks again at me. I feel like I'm going to be sick.

I mentally quiet my rumbling stomach and meet his gaze. *Be brave.* "Let him go, Joaquin." His dark eyes bore into me. *Don't look away. No fear. Be brave.* His flat lips ever-so slowly curl up into his cheeks.

"As long as he behaves..." Joaquin drawls, still staring me down. *Don't look away. No fear.* After what feels like a lifetime, Joaquin 'hmpfs,' and waves his hand casually at Dean. "Fine."

A clawed hand slams through Joaquin's suddenly incorporeal form, embedding itself in the wall behind the couch. Green smoke swirls as he dematerializes, reforming next to Chloe in the recliner. Dean pulls his hand away, taking drywall with him. Chloe shies away to the arm of the chair, silently staring up at the Djinn. Joaquin deflates with a bored exhale, looking annoyed. He sniffs, "Well—"

"Why are you here, Joaquin?" I cut in before he can make any more jokes. Dean is seething across the couch from me, a small trickle of blood leaking from the top of his leg. *Attacking him head on won't work, Dean,* I try to mentally will to him. *Not when he knows it's coming.* Joaquin takes a seat at the other recliner next to Chloe's, across from me on the couch. He casually crosses his legs again and straightens the arms of his suit jacket. He looks thoughtful for a moment.

"Because I'm finding how events are unfolding quite engaging," he says with a wave of his hand. "So, I wanted to stop by and watch your 'process,' as it were. Don't let me interrupt— please continue! Something about Danvers, and Jon and Blake, and vampires, and myself... Pretend I'm not even here." He leans back in the recliner, motioning like he's locking his mouth shut.

We need to keep him talking. We can't play this game. I hold his dark eyes with mine again. *Stay strong. No Fear. Be Brave.*

"Well, since you're part of it, and you're sitting right here, why don't you join in on the 'process'? What happened two years ago?"

He scoffs. "Just reveal *everything*? And steal the thrill of discovery from you all? But you're so close! And let me just say, I have genuinely enjoyed watching you three scurry about, putting pieces of the puzzle together." He's a predator stalking the three of us again. "And the pieces are all coming together beautifully. We're so close to the end. So close..."

Something in my gut isn't sure those last words have anything to do with what happened two years ago. It's the way he says it, as if it's happening in the present. And who is the 'we.'? "So, the pieces are coming together... What happened two years ago will help lead us to Blake then?"

Joaquin's body settles into that creepy, uncomfortable stillness. His eyes never leave mine. "Putting that puzzle together will help you *understand* why your friend is missing, I suppose. You really already do, do you not? You said it yourself the other night: it's revenge. But helping you find her? Something tells me you and Chloe will find her no matter what... you three being together feels like it's meant to be. *Ordained*."

He's been watching us this whole time. He said he didn't want anyone to find me, so it would make sense, but... *Think, Ari, think!* Why is he interested? Why had he said he wanted me to stay hidden? Joaquin's words from that day drift through my mind again, the same I had told Abel when he asked about our conversation. *Boredom, amusement, prophecy.* He had said it jokingly, but... finding Blake would just happen, as if it was ordained? Did he really mean 'prophecy', or was this all just some play on words. We've barely spoken and already this conversation is becoming exhausting. *This is all a game to him*, I remind myself. *Keep him talking, focus on his words.*

Silence fills the room as I wrestle with Joaquin's statement and fail to find something else to say. Dean still stares daggers at him from the couch while Chloe seems to be working on composing herself, adjusting her position in the recliner. Joaquin sighs deeply, then starts again: "This is… this isn't fun. You all look so dour. You all should be as excited as I am! We're so close!" he says with a shake of his head. "This was supposed to be fun, watching you all work. Do you know how incredible it is to stumble across something this thrilling at my age?"

"So, this is all just entertainment to you?" Dean asks through gritted teeth across from the Djinn. He looks like he's about to rip the arm off the couch.

"This, currently?" he answers, waving his hands at the room. "Yes. But I will admit there are bigger things afoot." Joaquin sniffs, and then an excited expression takes his features. He holds a finger up, "I know! How about this? In the human stories, Djinn grant three wishes. Let's play to the legends! How about I grant you all three questions? I swear on my honor I will answer truthfully." He places his hand on his chest, looking around at the three of us.

I look back and forth to Dean and Chloe, who both meet my gaze with doubt in their eyes. Joaquin must notice this, too, and doesn't wait for an answer. "You three are so distrusting… I swear, you tell people you can *not* lie and for some reason they immediately second guess everything you say. It's enough to make you crazy." He scoffs and looks away, a caricature of disbelief on his face. He gestures openly to us: "As a sign of *good faith*, how about I untie the gordian knot of two years ago for you?" He again glances around to the three of us. "You three are just chomping at the bit over it, and it's all sort of secondary in the grand scheme of things… but I know how comforting *knowing* can be for those of the human persuasion."

It's still a game, I think to myself. We just have to ask the right questions. There's only one question that really matters right now: *Where is Blake?* "Fine," I state, nodding toward Joaquin. I force confidence into my voice, but my nerves have me readjusting myself on the couch. It's suddenly hard to get comfortable. Chloe gives a firm nod at the edge of my vision, and Dean grunts an acceptance.

"Splendid! This *will* be fun… I get to play the villain monologuing at the end of the movie!" The excitement in his voice has my stomach roiling.

"So, you *are* the villian?" I ask pointedly, pinning him as best I can with my gaze. His head snaps to attention like before, his deep-set eyes looking almost black under the shade of his brows.

"On the contrary, I'm quite certain I will be the hero of this story," he says, his voice low and airy. That toothy grin comes to life again under his sharp cheeks. "You'll see soon enough." He leans back in the recliner, settling himself into his seat. "Now, where to begin?" Joaquin strokes his chin for a moment, as if genuinely considering. My anticipation builds, and the churning in my stomach gets worse. Dean sits statue-still, but Chloe seems to be having the same issues as I am.

Finally, Joaquin begins: "Two years ago, Chad Danvers had a plan for the forest behind Lunar Falls. All that land was just *begging* to be developed—it could be a paradise of strip malls and big box stores and money. Lots of money. The problem of course, was that the forest was your pack's ancestral land, and owned by your Alpha. So, what does Clark do? He simply asks Jon to sell. Jon was doing nothing with the land anyway as far as Clark knew, so why not take the money? But Jon won't sell!" Joaquin leans forward, enraptured with his own storytelling. "Why? Why won't he sell? It's certainly a nice chunk of change, and he obviously has no plans for any of the land... So Clark starts digging. And *my* what a rabbit hole he falls down! Clark learns Lunar Falls' dirty little secret..." He leans back, a bland smirk cutting his features.

"Now, would anyone believe Clark? Of course not. But Clark *knows*, and he's gone a bit wacky with this sudden shift in how he understands the natural order. He thinks he can blackmail Jon with this information. But woe to anyone who challenges an Alpha! How *dare* this human? Your Alpha, of course, likes to style himself as an intelligent man," Joaquin continues, rolling his eyes at his last statement. "So, he comes up with his own plan. A trade! Jon will trade the forest for some of Clark's more lucrative properties downtown. All hush-hush. Clark would take a hit initially, but *long-term*... there was no way he could pass this up. Jon, of course, had no intention of trading. He was going to keep the forest *and* take Clark's properties—and make quite a lot of money in doing so. So, Jon sets *his* plan in motion.

"This is where the trouble starts, and where your handsome narrator enters the story." A devilish smile appears on the Djinn's face. "Moving properties around obviously takes time. And in the course of doing so, some members of the pack found out..." He lets silence hang in the air. "How could Jon *do* such a thing? Trade the pack's forest for profits? He was unfit to lead! A cabal forms among some of the higher-ups in the pack. It was time for a coup!"

His words hit home, and the depth of his double-talk becomes apparent. I had just assumed the 'problem with the locals' had been with Chad's dad. He had meant the 'locals' of Lunar Falls the whole time. Joaquin doesn't stop. He's on a roll now, gesturing wildly with his hands: "A replacement was chosen from a neighboring pack. Jon's stuck. If he addresses it publicly, the rest of the pack finds out about his gamble and the revolution grows. Even if everything worked out, the mere fact he did what he did would be grounds for deposition. Alpha Jon asks for help." He draws out the last word, raising his hand as if to say 'present' as he finishes.

"Around this time, Clark is… not in the best place mentally. He's about to lose almost everything, and he wants some pay-back. I understand his plight, truly I do—all he wanted was to buy some land, and now… Well, helping others is kind of my thing, and I see a way to make everyone happy. Clark will get his revenge on the evil, thieving wolves. The scheme to remove Jon goes away. All I really had to do was point Clark in the right direction, drop a little hint about the conspirator's next meeting… There's so much you can accomplish with just a little nudge," Joaquin's gaze rockets to me. "A word or phrase said in passing."

He holds a finger up. "But there's always a price. Always some sacrifice that needs to be made for what we want, as Jon would learn." His eyes drift slowly around the room, starting with Dean, then myself, until finally resting on Chloe. It seems clear enough what he's saying, but I can't bring myself to give it voice. The way his eyes bore into Chloe… She has to know what he's saying, too. Vomit feels like it's clawing up my throat.

The 'vampire' attack... Chloe's gone rigid and pale. She visibly swallows.

He holds his gaze on her, a mournful look painting his angular face. "Sometimes there are externalities we can't account for... sometimes the price is out of our control... Sometimes people are in the wrong places at the wrong times." The sadness in his features doesn't reach his eyes, and I want to slap the look off his face. Playing with her emotions like this—of all the things he's said and done this afternoon, this was by far the most gruesome. *He's enjoying this.* I want to spit.

"Clark did what Clark was want to do. And once that was done, there was no reason for Jon to let him live, and every reason for him to take his life. So, Jon did what Jon was want to do." The wild gesticulating is gone, his voice soft and melancholy. "And now, a couple years later... 'Sins of the father,' as they say."

My mind is doing somersaults. There's no comfort in knowing all this—in finding out what we *didn't know.* I'm digging gashes into my palms, my hands closed in fists. I instinctively look over to Dean to check on him. His shoulders are limp and his head sags. I see him mouth 'Abel?' Chloe is looking in her lap, too. There are tears in her eyes but her mouth twists in rage.

My friends look like they're reeling, and I can't pretend like I'm not, too, after Joaquin's story. I take a deep breath and shove every heartbreaking thought down. *We can process later*, I tell myself. I put on the best mask of calm I can manage right now. He said he'd answer questions...

The only question that matters right now: "Where is Chad keeping Blake?"

At first surprise—actual surprise—crosses his face for the

briefest of moments, and then it's quickly replaced by a sly smile. "Well, there's no rattling you, is there? Very well..." He settles back into the recliner and re-crosses his legs, dropping his chin and fixing me with those dangerous eyes under his brow. "You had the right idea the other night, but downtown Silas Creek is a little too far afield. That's not quite 'under your nose.' No, you and your friend's noses usually spend their hours elsewhere, don't they?" He pauses for what I'm sure he thinks is a dramatic effect. *And he's mentioning the three of us together again...* "She's where you think."

A weighted silence suffocates the room. *What the* fuck *kind of answer is that?* I almost laugh out loud, my body unsure of how to handle the ridiculousness of his 'answer.' Joaquin seems to take offense at my quietness.

"What? I answered true. And I've certainly given you enough to add it all together. You should be able to read exactly what I'm telling you... or is this all above your grade level?" He titters. His face seems so pleased, I want to scream. "It's no matter, really. I promise you'll find her." He starts humming under his breath... *Silver Bells?*

"You son of a b—" I start.

"It wasn't a vampire attack... It was Clark Danvers. You sent him... And Jon covered it up?" Chloe cuts in, shooting daggers with her eyes at Joaquin. But it's not just anger there. Fear rings her gaze, too. Tears well beneath her blue eyes.

"I'll take that slight inflection at the end there to mean that was a question. Essentially... yes. I mean I've never heard of vampires using silver bullets before..." Chloe looks ready to jump across the room at him.

"It was your fault…" Chloe trails off.

Joaquin shoots another mournful glance her way that I know he doesn't feel. *Asshole*. He sighs, "In a round-about way I suppose I bear some responsibility. Remember though: I may have given them a little tap, but it was Jon's ambition that set up the dominoes. As I said, some things can't be foreseen. Others? Well…" He shrugs, shifting his gaze to me. "But… by my count, that's three questions. This *was* fun! Thank you all for indulging me!"

"That was only two questions!" I nearly scream, forcing it through my clenched teeth. He counts down with his fingers, fake concentration straining his face.

"No, definitely three. As promised."

"No, only—" I deflate. I asked if he was the villain. *Son of a bitch… it was before his story, but… Should have fucking known better.* He rakes his eyes around the room once more, that predatory look returning.

"It's gotten quite tense in here, and I'm sure you all have a lot to think about… a lot to discuss…" He trails off, slapping his knees. "Big week coming up, too. I'm sure I'll see you all again very soon."

Pop.

THIRTY-TWO

Joaquin had only been half-right.

There was plenty to think about, but very little discussion after his exit. Chloe sat silently for a few more minutes, a mess of angry inhales and tears, then disappeared into the quiet of the basement. The Djinn had dropped a bomb on her, and the shockwave had rewritten her past. I couldn't blame her for wanting to be alone. Dean was better, but only slightly. He had rushed to me first to make sure I was okay despite his bloody leg, but the possibility that Abel had a hand in all of this had clearly shaken him. I was shaken, too.

Joaquin had revealed so much—especially taking into account the fact that there were probably two or three different meanings you could interpret from everything he said—but I still had endless questions. And as much as my heart ached for Dean and Chloe, few of them had anything to do with the past. What had happened, had happened. We couldn't change what had set this all in motion years ago, only deal with the conse-quences. Blake is missing *now*.

Dean's living room had felt uncomfortable after Joaquin left, as if his presence had left an acrid taint on the space. I went back home after a few largely silent hours. Dean and I had both been too lost in our own minds to talk much, and there seemed to be some sort of unspoken understanding that we both needed our space after that info-dump. Despite everything, there was a har-mony there between us that put a smile on my face, if a sad one.

When I finally laid down to sleep that night, my bed felt like it was adrift at sea. I replayed Joaquin's words on an endless loop until I could recite our conversation by memory. I went through every movement, every disgusting wink he gave me. *She's where you think*. It repeated like a mantra in my head. And the prophecy stuff, the continual mention of Blake, Chloe, and I all together… more questions that had me spinning. Round and round and round it went until I woke this morning, not remem-bering when I had actually dozed off to sleep.

And now, a few hours later, I'm dressed for a funeral. I stand in the foyer of my house with the rest of my family as we all do our pat-downs, making sure we have everything we need before heading to the Community Center. Usually these things are held in the same clearing used for the Moon Awakening, so that the deceased's spirit could be sent to the Moon Goddess in her domain. But under the circumstances… a change in venue is understandable.

My family has said little to me this morning, and even now our little group is mostly silent. Koa, who has fully recovered from the attack, hasn't spoken to me at all except to say 'I love you,' and to give me a warm hug. They don't seem to want to push any kind of conversation I might not be ready to have, though conversations lately have been few and far between. My issues with my parents hiding who I am have been on the back-burner, but the scab is still there. I don't think I can have that conversation just yet. I'm sure they've noticed the tension, too, but have likely written it off as grief over my friends. I'm sure it seems the same today, but... The truth is, I'm not entirely sure how I should feel, or more importantly, how I should act. How *do* you act at a funeral for your two best friends when they're *not* dead... kind of? Obviously, I can't be nonchalant about the whole thing, but faking despair feels very, very wrong. *Just be stoic, I guess?*

"We ready?" my dad asks at the door, a frown deepening the creases in his face as he rubs my mom's shoulder with a free hand. He looks to my mom and Koa, but I know the only answer he's waiting for is mine. I finally meet his eyes and nod.

"Yeah, let's go."

Dad holds the door and we exit one-by-one into a chilly November morning. The air is still, thankfully keeping the temperature manageable. I glance next door, hoping through some fluke Dean might be exiting at the same time and we could walk together. His truck is there, and a weathered blue jeep sits in the driveway behind it. *Abel?* Had he just shown up, or did Dean force a conversation? Either way, we needed to talk. I shoot Dean a quick text as we start making our way down the sidewalk.

We're leaving for the funeral. Where are you?

Already there. I'll meet you at the door I get back after a moment.

Abel's here?

Yeah, I called him last night. We can talk later

K. See you soon I send, looking back up to make sure I haven't walked into the road yet. *Abel...* there are questions that need answered there. The connection was clear enough—he had helped Jon cover up the attack. I'm praying he was forced into helping, that he hadn't done something so awful just so he could go off on his own. He didn't seem like that kind of person, but then neither had Jon. *Dean, apparently, hasn't killed him yet, so that's something positive I suppose...* After a moment or two, my phone buzzes again.

Have you talked to Chloe? *Strange.* She would be sleeping by now... Unless he's asking if she sent me anything before the sun came up?

No, why?

I didn't hear her come home last night. She could have used the basement door I guess, didn't want to talk to me. Probably nothing to worry about

Probably

Yeah

It probably *is* nothing to worry about. The way she had stormed off last night, it wouldn't be surprising that she didn't announce her return to Dean. News would have already spread if she had been caught, but despite that fact my chest still feels heavy. *I'll check on her tonight...*

Slowly our group becomes larger as more and more pack members join the parade toward the Community Center. The whole pack would be coming out today, and not just because the funeral was for the Alpha's daughter. Everyone might not have been close with Blake and Chloe, but they were part of the

Lunar Falls pack and deserved the respect afforded to all members, regardless of any personal relationship.

We eventually reach the back of a cluster of black-clothed figures bottlenecking at the entrance of the building, waiting for their turn to enter. Occasionally, some of their solemn faces look around and meet my gaze, and they offer some silent form of condolence. Everyone knows Blake and Chloe had a thing for the adopted human. I do my best to arrange my face into something sad, but accepting. *I'm definitely not going to be faking any tears.* I finally settle on just keeping my head down.

Inside, the Community Center is about as full as the last time I was here now that everyone has recovered. People mill about the room, conspicuously avoiding crossing an open area in the center of the hall. Too large photos of Blake and Chloe sit on easels there, hung with twisted wildwood wreaths covered in roses and wildflowers. No caskets, no urns... *It's going to be pretty wild when Blake shows back up*, I think to myself. *...She's where you think...*

The smells of sage, mint, and eucalyptus... and motor oil... drift from behind me, and I breathe them in. A firm hand lands on the small of my back, and electricity tickles my spine. "Hey," Dean says quietly, taking his place at my side. His magnetic turquoise eyes look down at me and he smiles. I melt a little. *Damn, he looks good in a suit*, I think, then immediately chastise myself. *Goddess, Ari, we're at a funeral.* But then again, are we? *What the hell has my life become?* I have to choke back a laugh.

Dean looks away to my family. "Mr. and Mrs. Maddox. Koa." Dean says each with a nod. They start exchanging pleasantries, but I've tuned them out as my attention drifts to the man standing a little ways behind Dean. Abel stands at attention, looking horribly uncomfortable in what must be one of Dean's suits. His shaggy hair is still a bit of a mess, and that 5 o'clock shadow hasn't gone anywhere.

"Abel."

"Miss Ari," he answers, bowing his head a little. He rubs the back of his neck and his lips pinch as he does so, a slight blush showing up on his cheeks. He looks like a kid who just got caught with his hand in the cookie jar. *Dean must have had that conversation with him.* I keep my face purposefully blank and turn back to where my family chats casually with Dean. We can sort that out later.

I smile absently at my parents and Koa as Dean deftly plays the boyfriend meeting the family, but my eyes are scanning the room again and— *Did I just think of him as my boyfriend?* 'Mate' flies through my mind, something becoming uncomfortably regular, and I mentally shake it away. *We're at a funeral, Ari.* My eyes land on Jon, off to the side of the cleared space in the middle of the hall.

He stands rigid with his arms behind his back, as if he's physically having to keep himself upright. His chin is slightly raised in what must be an attempt to appear strong, but it's betrayed by his posture and red, tired eyes. A new knot of emotion forms in my stomach—resentment, anger, sympathy, pity. He had lost his wife because of what he had done, and now, whether he knew it or not, he would be thinking he lost his daughter. Had he paid enough? What about Chloe's dad? He had been innocent, if Joaquin could be believed. Blake definitely is. Could he ever pay enough for his greed and pride? But then again, the torture is clear on his face... He would be paying for it all the rest of his life.

I wrestle with the thoughts as Jon's eyes meet mine. A heartbroken, compassionate smile cobbles together on his face. He bows his head politely before shifting his gaze behind me. All compassion and grief on his face is shoved away by a twinge of anger. He sniffs and shakes his head. *He's looking at Abel.* A pack member steps forward to Jon and the rage is wiped away in an instant, replaced by a practiced calm as he shakes hands with the new sympathizer. I turn back to look at Abel. Uneasiness hides in his emerald green eyes under furrowed brows. He's chewing the inside of his cheek.

"—like that, Ari?" My dad's voice saying my name snatches my attention forward. *Shit, that was a question. 50-50 shot.*

"Yeah. Yes." I smile and nod. His eyes narrow and his head tilts slightly. Dean eyes me from the side. *Wrong answer.* "Sorry, I was..." I trail off, shaking my head.

"It's okay." Understanding colors my dad's voice and smile as a hush falls over the gathered pack. We all turn toward the center of the room, where Jon stands in between the portraits of my friends. He waits calmly as the last voices die off, and lets the fresh silence hang over the room. He clears his throat.

"Thank you all for coming." Another bout of silence. "Today we are here to commend the spirits of Chloe Hanshen and... my daughter Blake," his voice cracks, and it's deafening, "to the Moon Goddess. If you all will join me in a prayer to..." His voice trails away from my hearing as that knot of emotions nearly knocks the wind out of me again. I lean into Dean's comforting, steady form beside me. What Jon had done was horrible, and yet every shaky word, every sniff, every clearing of his throat is soul-crushing. He loved her. *But there's always a price.* Joaquin's words drift through my mind, and I'm somehow feeling even sicker.

Should I feel sympathy, though? Other people were dealing with the consequences of his choices—not just his daughter. Chloe and her family had nearly been torn apart when her dad died. A husband and a father had been taken away, and for two years the only explanation was a lie... Jon is still here, still rich from his powerplay. All he has to deal with is feeling bad. The pack needs to know the truth, one way or another. People had died. There's always a price. I exhale, suddenly feeling dizzy.

I tune back into the center of the room. "And so I'd like to invite Jessica and Madeline to say a few words." Jon stretches out his hand, inviting Chloe's mom and sister to join him. A statuesque woman makes her way through the crowd, and it's clear where Chloe got those eyes from. Even from this distance, though, it's easy to make out the redness there and the raw skin underneath them. Madeline follows close behind her mom, blonde hair pinned up with a black bow. Her head never looks up from the carpeted floor.

Jon reaches out to take her hand, but Jessica refuses with a curt shake of her head. It lasts for an instant, but the look she gives him as she passes could drop an elephant. The anger is unadulterated, and Jon's hand quickly returns to his side. *What the hell was that?* She breezes past, her chin held high though she looks on the verge of crying, to stand next to the picture of her daughter. "Thank you, Jon," she begins, sounding like she's nearly choked on the words. She unfolds a small piece of paper with shaky hands and begins to read. The dam breaks, and those big, blue eyes are suddenly hazy with tears. Madeline still has her head down.

I wish Chloe could be here, somehow. To tell her mom she's okay, to take her sister's hands and tell her everything will be alright. The need to tell them what's going on grips my chest. *I'll talk to Chloe tonight*, I think. We need to let them know somehow before she leaves. They deserve that. Chloe deserves that. My anger at Jon flares up again. After all this he'd be getting Blake back—Jessica and Madeline might not ever get to see Chloe again. Dean must sense the tension rising in my back, and his arm curls around my shoulder, pulling me closer. Jessica finishes her speech with a sniff and wipes her eyes with a delicate finger. "Thank you."

Jon says a few more quiet words, then ends the ceremony. Slowly, the buzz of voices fills the space once more and people start moving about again. The majority of them head toward the center of the hall to where Jon stands. Jessica and Madeline have already moved off into the crowd. Dean squeezes my shoulder and peers down at me, those electric eyes and that smile comforting me even more than his touch somehow. "Wanna get out of here?"

"Yeah," I reply with my own smile. The ceremony wasn't long by any means, and yet I'm drained. All I want to do is sink back into bed. Staying here any longer would probably make it worse. I turn to my family and let them know I'm going to spend some time with Dean and his cousin. They don't question me, just nod and wish us well. They move off toward the press of people crowding around the Alpha.

Dean takes my hand and we move toward the exit, dodging around small knots of people and accepting nods and sympathetic waves as we go. Abel trails a pace behind us with his hands planted in his pockets. Nearly at the door, Jessica Hanshen briskly makes her way over to cut us off. It's easier to see the devastation on her face up close like this, and the smile she offers us is bittersweet.

She sniffles and takes my hand in her's. "I just wanted to make sure I thanked you for being such an amazing friend to Chloe before you left. Everything you," another sniffle, and then she takes Dean's hand as well, "did for her... and... just thank you for being there for her. *No matter what*." Her face is a war of different emotions—grief is written in the lines of her face, yet her eyes are brighter now, and there's genuine gratitude above those dark circles. Madeline quietly smiles at the two of us from behind her mother—it's the first time I've seen her hold her head up the entire afternoon. She steps forward and embraces me with a tight, comforted hug. She steps back and does the same with Dean. "We need to be seen for a bit longer, but... thank you again."

She gives another bittersweet smile, then moves back toward the crowd with Madeline in tow. Dean and I share a look. *If I didn't know any better...*

"Poor things..." Abel mutters behind us. His jaw is tense and his forehead creases. He takes a deep breath as he looks at Dean and me. "We'll get your friend squared away. Promise." I force on a blank face again, still not sure how I should feel about him.

"We need to talk."

"Yeah... Yeah, I s'pose we do."

Thirty-Three

A half-hour later, Dean, Abel, and I sit quietly in Dean's living room. A mug of fresh coffee warms my hands as I lounge on one of the recliners with my legs tucked underneath me. Dean's taken the other recliner, sitting forward elbows to knees with his hands clasped in front of him. We both have our eyes on Abel, who sits alone on the couch. He presses back against the cushions, as if the weight of our gaze is physical, and nervously picks at his fingers.

His dark-green eyes shift back and forth between Dean and I under his ruffled, blond hair. If he's waiting for one of us to speak first he's got another thing coming. I'm not sure how this conversation is going to go, but I'm definitely not going to hold his hand through it no matter how uncomfortable he looks. I take out my phone and check the time as the silence stretches— it's still a few hours to sunset. We'd need to catch Chloe before she comes upstairs. With everything she's going through, running into the guy who helped cover up her father's murder unannounced might make things... tense.

Because she's definitely downstairs. My chest tightens again just like it had when Dean sent that message. There really was no reason to worry at the moment. It was completely possible she snuck back in without saying anything and without Dean noticing—she'd been successfully sneaking around Lunar Falls this entire time. The neighborhood wasn't in an uproar over a vampire that looked strikingly like a now-deceased pack member, either. We're just being paranoid—and Mrs. Hanshen was just emotional this afternoon—that's all.

I send her a quick text anyway. **Text me as soon as you get up. Love you**

Abel must have taken me checking my phone as impatience. He sniffs and mutters something under his breath, then leans forward against the press of our eyes. "What all has Dean told you?" he asks.

"Aside from him calling you last night? Nothing."

Abel nods, then drops his head. He stares at the floor for a moment before looking back up and continuing: "Well, from what Dean and I spoke on last night, sounds like your Djinn friend has the right of it. Jon got into it with some human. Didn't know his name at the time, but... Clark Danvers killed those people. Wasn't no vampires." After Joaquin's story and what we had found in the lake house and downtown, we knew that already. Hearing it confirmed again still feels good, though. *But that's not why we're sitting here.*

Abel seems to know it, too. He leans back again, and his eyes drop back to the floor. He runs one hand through his hair while the other lies limply in his lap. Those hands squeeze into fists, and when he looks back up to meet my gaze there's determination set in his eyes.

He doesn't wait for me to ask the next question. "And I know it wasn't vamps that killed those people because I found the bodies." Abel's admission hangs in the air for a moment, and I nod.

"How?"

"Bad luck," he sniffs. "Wrong place, wrong time. Went out for a run on my usual trail and smelled…" Abel trails off for a moment and his nostrils flair. A disgusted look pinches his features. "I followed my nose and found them all. Bad luck for me. Great luck for Jon. Funny how things work like that sometimes." No laugh follows that last statement, not even a sarcastic one. He looks down again as the muscles in his shoulders go taut. His knucles turn white with his clenched fists.

Abel sniffs again, his breathing becoming heavier. "I recognized them, of course, and it was obvious what had happened. The first person I called was Jon," He looks off into the kitchen and shakes his head. "He went quiet. And then the first thing he said… the *very first thing*… was to ask if anyone was with me or if I was alone." Abel turns back, scratching at the stubble dotting his chin. He looks to Dean, who's resting his chin on his clasped hands, and then to me once more.

"Jon told me to stay put and eventually he met me out there. He cried over his wife for a bit, I'll give him that." Abel snorts and shakes his head again. "But at a certain point he stopped, and when he looked over her body to me there was nothin' in his eyes. No sadness, no grief, no anger, no… I mean not a *damn* thing." He swallows. "And then he told me what we were gonna do."

I bite my lip and sit up straighter in the chair. My sympathy for Jon feels like it's evaporating out of my skin. He mourned his wife for minutes, and then it was back to business. *An awful, bloody business.* My resolve seems to harden in that moment—after Blake and Chloe, we'd take care of Jon. The pack would know.

I look back to Abel, whose thousand-yard stare splits between Dean and I. His flat lips and set jaw projects nothing but anger, but the red edge to his eyes and the suddenly visible crow's feet scream that he's in pain. The steady rise of his chest gets heavier. "With my profession and all... So I..." He starts again, his voice cracking a bit. "So, I helped..." He stops, taking in a deep breath. His fists clench so hard I'm worried his knuckles might crack. "I helped him pass it all off as a vampire attack. Like I said, good luck for Jon." Abel leaves it there, and doesn't elaborate any further. There's so much intensity radiating from him that he's almost difficult to look at. He suddenly unclenches his fists and stretches his fingers, then rubs the back of his hands.

I'm chewing my lip again. Part of my mind is begging me not to, but I need to ask. "Why?" I can taste bile. Dean's forehead rests on his hands now, and there's visible anger in the press of his lips. Abel is looking at the floor again.

"I was alone in those woods with him... and Jon is Alpha for a reason," he says soberly. "I didn't have anything other than my word at the time, and the Alpha's cult of personality would've taken care of what the pack would believe." He looks up and pins me with a stare. "And there was Dean and Eli and their parents to think about..." The implication there is clear. I snap my head toward Dean. His whole body has gone rigid—he and his family had been threatened for the past two years, and none of them knew. Dean's head comes back up like he can feel my stare, and he forces a small, strained smile at me. He probably thinks it's comforting, but I can see the anger simmering in the depths of his blue-green eyes.

My chest is thick with that anger, too. I can physically feel the last of the empathy I had for Jon leave my body. He could argue he never wanted any of this to happen, that he never meant for it, that he was in an impossible situation. But it was a situation he created and refused to own. Abel had done something horrible, too. But at the very least he could say he had stumbled into it, and then had his and his family's lives held over his head to keep quiet. I'm not sure what I would do in his shoes. *That* was an impossible situation.

"You can call me a coward if you want, but—" Abel starts.

"You're not a coward, Abel. Jon's just an evil piece of shit." Dean growls. He's sitting straighter now, and that anger he held is out in the open. I nod in agreement, and Abel seems to visibly relax. "And before this is all done, we'll make sure everyone knows." Dean's confidence fills me up, and I nod again at the two men. The 'this' he's talking about is finding Blake and getting Chloe out, though… *Goddess, what about Blake?* How would she take this? Would she believe it? What would it all mean for her with the rest of the pack? *One problem at a time…* And then there was Chloe. Would any amount of explanation or reasoning be enough for her to accept or forgive Abel?

"We need to be… delicate… about this when Chloe comes up," I say after a moment.

"I might have a peace offering. Kind of," Abel offers up from the couch.

"What's that?"

"Savannah."

"Like, the city?" I ask, the worry and anger of moments ago giving way to a trickle of hope. "Did you find a Nest?"

"Not quite." Abel answers, and that trickle threatens to dry up immediately. "I don't think that's how it works. After a few days of playing telephone with contacts of contacts of contacts… I'm almost certain there's one operating out of downtown there. But they're professional shadows. We wouldn't find them, they'd find us." He shrugs. The slow stream of hope returns, but there's a bitter taste to it, like oil slicking on water.

Finding a Nest is the best bet for Chloe and her safety, but it also means losing a friend. And with the amount of secrecy, apparently, involved with these guys, it probably means losing her for good. I know that, and I know that I will need to accept it. Apparently, I 'm not quite ready yet. I frown, wondering if Chloe is even ready for that transition. It suddenly occurs to me that we've been avoiding that conversation for a while now. *One more thing to talk about tonight.*

"So, we just… drop her off and cross our fingers?" I question, dragging my mind back to the present. Abel's head tilts to the side as he considers.

"Well, we did find *something*. Have you ever heard of Hobo Codes?"

"Huh?" I look to Dean, who only raises an eyebrow at this cousin.

"Hobos? The guys who would ride in train cars from town to town. You know, with a bindle on a stick and…" He trails off, motioning with his hands as if it might help ring a bell for us.

"We know what hobos are, Abel. What's the code part mean?" Dean asks beside me, trying to speed his cousin to the point.

"Right. So, in the late 1800s there was this sort of urban legend that started about a secret code that hobos used to let other hobos know important stuff about where they were heading, like where they could get a free meal or if there was somewhere they needed to avoid." He leans forward on the couch, totally engrossed in his lecture. I can't help the little smile growing on my face. As heavy as things had been a little while ago, it's nice to see the real Abel again. "They would carve the symbols into wooden posts or on trees or write them in chalk or...whatever. It turns out it was all kind of made up to sell magazines and newspapers when hobos were like a pop culture thing in the U.S. but..." He slows down, and looks back and forth between Dean and I. "Which is all to say that, apparently, there's a hobo vampire code."

Abel holds up a finger, then stands and heads to the island in the kitchen. A battered, dark-blue duffle bag is laid there, and he digs through it for a few moments before retrieving a stack of manilla folders and returning to the couch. He drops back into the cushions hard and I can see Dean wince from the corner of my eye as it slides back with a metallic creak. Abel doesn't seem to notice as he flips through the pages of the top folder. He abruptly grunts and reaches across the coffee table, holding out a piece of paper. "That's what we're looking for," he says finally, a giant grin threatening to push his cheeks off of his face.

I reach across and take the paper. Dean gets up from his recliner and moves to stand next to me, lowering himself until I can feel his warmth over my shoulder. A black marker line drawing of a rudimentary house sits in the middle of a paper creased from folds. An upside down 'V' makes its roof, the ends hanging slightly over the lines for the two walls, and a floor. Inside at the top, just under the apex of the 'roof' sits a semi-circle over top of a slighly curved line with smaller lines coming down from it—a closed eye, I realize. Beneath that, three plus signs sit arranged in an upside down triangle.

"There are other symbols we think we found, too," Abel says across from us as he taps the top of the first folder. The excitement is rolling off of him in waves. "But that one... means Safety. Or Safehouse. Safe shelter? I suppose there are several different ways one could interpret it. It makes me wonder if there are dialects... like do Cei Reținuți in the North have slightly different symbols than Cei Reținuți in the South or out West? Is there some proto-symbology from the Old World that you can trace it all back to or—" I eye him from over top the paper in my hands. He smiles, his cheeks going a little red. "That's what we're looking for."

I take another look at the symbol, committing it to memory, then nod at Abel. "Okay. So, we look for this symbol... anything that can help guide us to it?"

"Uhhh... maybe? Probably. We haven't really decoded it all, and that *is* assuming everything we've put together is legit, but... That's why I said they'd find us before we ever found them."

"I thought they didn't want to be found? Why would they mark their buildings then?" Dean asks from my side.

"I mean, I doubt it's like their headquarters or something," he says with a sniff. "More than likely it's just a place to hide, and probably something they would keep an eye on. Just a hint or some help for other Restrained. Like a hobo code." Abel pauses and looks us both in the eye. I think it's your friend's best shot."

As little as it is, he's right. What are the other options? Staying here is out of the question. And just smuggling her out and dropping her off somewhere with no resources seems insane. If we can find a Nest, or rather have one find us, they can take care of her, show her how to survive. She'd never be safe, but... *safer* is better than whatever the hell we're doing here.

It'll be a new adventure for her, I try to convince myself, but it falls flat. Hope and happiness is flowing instead of trickling through me for Chloe now, but that oil slick hasn't gone away. *It's for the best. She'll be okay.* I deflate with a sigh, and feel the press of Dean's hands caress my shoulders. I soften under his touch and my head lolls. I close my eyes, embracing the feeling for a moment. I suppose it is one thing off the list. We can figure out the logistics—and the goodbyes—later, but Chloe has a direction now. A way out. That just leaves Blake... *She's where you think.*

"We can fill Chloe in when she gets up here," I say finally, looking back at Abel. "I don't know if that'll smooth everything over, but... hopefully, it helps." Abel's eyebrows gather together and his lips pinch. He 'mhmms' and looks back down to his folders regretfully. *That's a lot of paperwork.* "Are all those symbols?" I ask, pointing to the stack in his lap.

His head shoots up, and the expression he wears immediately sets off my alarm bells. "No. No, uhh... This is about your Djinn friend. I think I know what game he's playing."

Thirty-Four

What game is Joaquin playing? Looking at Abel's stack of folders, I'm suddenly aware of how little I had thought about what his role is in all of this. It's for sure always a question, but it has taken a backseat to wrapping my head around where Blake might be. Figuring out what went on two years ago has all been in pursuit of Blake, and last night I had spent my time trying to decipher his words—to find out where Blake is. *She's where you think.*

Joaquin's focus seemed to be centered on the three of us... and prophecy? There's a reason he wants me to stay hidden, and why he didn't kill me like he's, apparently, duty-bound to do. Could that be it? I mentally wince... Joaquin is frustration incarnate. Is he an enemy? Is he helping us in his own twisted way? Is it all really just an amusing little thing to watch for him? My stomach follows my brain's lead and somersaults. I give Dean's hand on my shoulder a squeeze and then lean forward, rubbing my temples. "Prophecy?" I venture.

"I thin— Yeah… yeah, how did you…?" Abel stutters out. His head is cocked and he narrows his eyes on me.

"He said it explicitly once, in that conversation we talked about. And when we talked yesterday he kept talking about Blake, Chloe, and I together… Always the three of us. And that he thought we would find each other no matter what. I believe the exact word he used was *ordained*." I sigh, still not fully believing what I'm saying. "It crossed my mind before, but it sort of sunk in as a real possibility yesterday. He's insane, right?"

Dean chuckles and moves back to the other recliner, taking a seat and sinking back. Abel shrugs. "Not really. Relatively speaking, that is. Wild shit like this is pretty much a Djinn's default setting," he says with a smirk. "And unfortunately it doesn't matter if he's insane or not if *he* believes it. Sorta leaves us in the same situation."

"Yeah, I guess so. Though I suppose it's nice to know that I'll find Blake no matter what, right?" I choke out a sarcastic 'hah', but no one seems to find it very funny. But will I? We've been stumbling around all this time learning about everything except where Chad has hidden Blake—aside from Joaquin's bullshit riddles. So much back and forth, hope and despair spinning round and round. I feel that anger building up again. If it is *ordained*, like Joaquin said, I would think it would have happened by now. I'm tired of waiting.

"Did you have a particular prophecy or foretelling in mind?" Abel asks. "I started looking through some of the bigger ones that float around in the supernatural community and… were you thinking of the 'Verhaal van Mevrouw Snijder,' too? It's the only one I could make fit."

"Verhaal van what, Abel?"

"Gonna have to translate that one buddy," Dean adds in sardonically from where he lazes in the recliner.

"The Telling of Madame Snijder. I figured— doesn't matter. Short version: Madame Snijder was a Dutch settler in the Michigan Territory in the early 1800s. Also a witch. Had a vision of the fall of the Djinn and wrote it down. Het Verhaal van Mevrouw Snijder." Abel rapid-fires out, then crosses his arms and sinks back into the couch with a satisfied grin. "How was that?"

Dean snorts beside me and I can't help laughing, too. "That was great Abel, but… how does it fit with us? Why does he think we're fulfilling some prophecy?" *A prophecy about the fall of the Djinn.* Every muscle in my body stiffens and I go cold. That friend or foe question just got a lot more serious. Abel's too busy searching through his papers to notice, but Dean gives me a concerned look from my right. Before I can give him an explanation, Abel shoves a paper between us.

"Here. This is the best English translation we have," he says, shaking the paper for effect. Dean and I swivel our recliners toward one another and each grab one side of the page, holding it between us. I start to read aloud:

"Three of two of fallen sires,
    Of the blood and not the blood,
  Of fur and frost, blood and desire, and
    Power and magick
Three of two bonded,
    Bound to consecrated days
To bloom beneath a glowing hunter

Hidden and hunted,
　　To hunt
Beneath argent bells
Set forth by one from without
To bring low those from without,
　　And now above.
Three of two to stand
　　Three of two to fall."

I finish the last stanza and bite my lip. It wouldn't take much to make this fit with my friends and I, but some of it just didn't seem to match up. "Joaquin thinks this is about us? I mean, maybe some of it, but... look at this first line: 'Three of two of fallen sires.' We're the three, obviously, but what's the 'of two' part? And 'fallen sires'? Chloe's dad is dead, but Jon's still here and my dad is alive somewhere, as far as I know..." I trail off, wrestling my thoughts.

"There's more than one way to fall." Dean says to my right, eyes still fixed on the page. "Jon's definitely 'fallen' in my book... and we really don't know much about your dad." He shrugs.

"The 'of two' part in Joaquin's mind probably refers to how you all are kind of half supernatural, half human. You're a half-Djinn, Chloe's a vamp with humanity, and Blake is a wolf who doesn't shift. *Of* two," Abel offers, who's now moved closer and sits on the coffee table. I shake my head, still not sure what to think about all of this.

"Yeah, but I bet we could make every one of these lines fit if we tried hard enough," I murmur as I reread Mrs. Snijder's vision. The 'fur and frost' line seems out of place for Blake, but the next two certainly fit with Chloe and I. Consecrated days? The Moon Awakening... Glowing Hunter? A full moon in October is called a hunter's moon... I was hidden by my dad and kept that way, supposedly, by Joaquin. Chloe is hidden by us. We are hunting Blake, who is being kept hidden by Chad...

"Joaquin seems to think they do. And to be fair, Miss Ari, it's pretty easy to see why he might think that, especially in your case," Abel says, leaning forward with his hands on his knees. Dean sniffs beside me. My stomach flips again and my throat feels tight. He's right. You really didn't have to force the pieces much to fit. *But...*

"Why *especially* me?"

"Because you're a half-Djinn," Abel answers. Confusion colors his features.

"Sure. Sure. Which means...?"

"Throw us some context man," Dean chimes in.

"Well, it's about the fall of the Djinn, and you're like their boogeyman," he says, looking at Dean and I like that should explain everything. His lips pinch at our silence, and he continues: "Djinn are like pure magic. They can use it, feel it... that's why they can feel each other. And they feed on it, too, but they can't feed off the power of other Djinn. You don't have that restriction. So, not only are you hard for them to find, you can eat 'em, too. Like the boogeyman."

"Well, that is definitely some context..." I mutter. So, I can be a weapon against full-blooded Djinn. *Good to know.* That explains why half-Djinn are hunted down and killed, I suppose. But then why had Joaquin let me live? Is he using us for some kind of play for power? *Goddess, what about my dad?* Had he hid me away and warded me because he cared, or did he want me safe because he had something similar in mind? I shove my daddy issues away with a groan.

So, I have the ability to steal a Djinn's power... The only question is how. I would need to use my magic to learn. But if I do that, other Djinn might find me. *Better learn quickly.* But without learning, I'm just as helpless as if I had never learned in the first place. My mind is starting to feel as dizzy as my stomach. *Unless...* Joaquin wants me hidden. Would he remove my dad's ward? He knew when I used magic the night of the Moon Awakening, but he was already watching us. *If I'm still warded, then maybe...* I file the thought away for later and focus back on the page in front of me.

"So then, the ones from 'without,' that's the Djinn?" I question. Abel had been pretty clear about who this was about, but I have never heard them referred to like that.

"Well, yeah. Djinn ain't from here," Abel answers, motioning with his hands. "Not sure *where* exactly, just that it's not here. They keep that one close to the chest."

"So, it's saying this will all be started by Djinn, then?" I look up from the page to meet Abel's eyes.

"Seems that way."

"Joaquin did say he 'bears some responsibility' for all of this," Dean says, looking up at the two of us. "He was talking about Danvers attacking the meeting, but maybe he was talking about something else? Double-talk or something. " He shakes his head and exhales with his whole chest.

Something tickles in the back of my skull, but I can't quite put my finger on it to itch. *There's something there I'm not putting together*, I think to myself. I realize I'm chewing my lip again. I lick my lips to stop myself and read through the annoyingly poetic and vague vision again.

Beneath argent bells… The line grips my attention and won't let go. Argent, like silver. Beneath *silver* bells. *She's where you think*. Joaquin was humming 'Silver Bells' when he told me about Blake. My grip on the paper tightens, and I have to force my fingers to loosen before I tear right through it. I tap the line, pointing it out to Dean. "Silver Bells. Joaquin was humming 'Silver Bells' when he told us where Blake is!"

Dean's eyebrows scrunch in thought, and then his minty eyes go wide. "He was, wasn't he?" His smile draws down almost as fast as it appears. "But we were already trying to think of something that fits that, and…" He shrugs.

"Well, yeah, but… if Joaquin thinks this is true, and he knows where Blake is, then that kind of confirms that it's a real clue." *But it's still only a clue, not an answer.*

Abel's eyebrows raise. "Joaquin told you where she was?"

"Yeah. She's *where I think*," I answer flatly. "With silver bells, apparently." Abel laughs out loud.

"What an ass… Obviously it's a riddle, but still…" His chuckles trail off and he rubs the back of his neck. "Not that funny really, but…"

It isn't funny. I'm tired of Joaquin's clues and riddles. He said he 'bears some responsibility' for putting this all in motion. It feels like he's some kind of fucked up puppetmaster that's been making us dance on his strings, though. At *best* he's using us for his own gain, and at worst who the hell knows. Either way, he's enjoying himself along the way. Toying with us. *She's where you think*. We've kept digging into things that never bring us any closer to finding Blake, when I've had the answer the whole time. It's time to stop playing by Joaquin's rules. I saved Dean's life, I can save Blake's, too. *And if I'm still warded…*

Fuck his riddle.

THIRTY-FIVE

"Actually…" I say, sitting upright in the recliner. Resolve grows and hardens in my core. We've been going in circles for too long.

Abel pauses mid-sentence and looks up at me. "What? Is it… funny?" he questions, cocking an eyebrow at me.

"No." I shake my head. I pull myself from the recliner and pace toward the kitchen. "What's funny is that this whole time I've been following Joaquin's lead. We all have. But I'm his boogeyman, right? I can drain a Djinn's magic… because I have magic."

Dean raises a brow but doesn't reply. My smile grows as I elaborate. "I used it to stop a bullet. Can't I use it to find Blake?"

"Wouldn't that call down the Council on you?" Dean asks, suddenly sitting upright himself. He grips the arms of the chair as the worry grows on his face.

"According to Joaquin. And maybe it is true," I say with a shrug, still pacing. "But if the ward my dad put on me is still active…"

"That's a big *If*, Ari," Dean shoots back as he stands.

"Tracking Blake can't possibly use a lot of magic. Probably won't even take more than a minute, and then we'll know where she's at."

Dean steps toward me and crosses his arms. "And you know this from your vast magical experience?" His piercing eyes take mine, and I almost forget what we're arguing about. I shake it away and stand my ground.

"I used magic on Halloween and no one's killed me yet." I roll my eyes. "And all that info is coming from Joaquin, so how much can we actually trust that what he said is what he actually means? Besides, isn't it worth the risk if we can find Blake?"

Dean plants himself solidly in front of me. He pauses, as if thinking through all of this—thoughtfulness and worry cloud his features. My back straightens. I don't need his permission. I would prefer him on my side, but I'll do it with or without him. He turns toward his cousin. "Abel?"

Abel throws his hands up. "Woah. Uhh… well, she did use magic, and the Council hasn't dropped in yet—"

"Thank you, Abel." I state firmly, staring Dean down the whole time. His lips twitch.

"But just because something hasn't happened yet don't mean it won't in the future, and—"

"Thank you, Abel." Dean fires back with a smile that sets my blood boiling.

"But you haven't had any luck with anything else. Might be worth a shot," Abel says the words hesitantly, as if waiting for another interruption. I throw a hand out toward him and cock my head.

"Ari..."

"Dean."

I hold his gaze, not letting those electric-green eyes turn away. He might think he's stubborn, but he's about to learn how deep I can dig my heels in. Nothing else has worked and that full moon deadline is coming. This is happening, one way or another. I'm tired of running. Abel shifts uncomfortably in my periphery as the standoff continues. And then, finally, Dean relents. His arms drop to his sides and he looks away for a moment, then turns back. "Fine." He takes my hands in his and looks down with open eyes. Concern still lights their depths, but there's understanding there now, too. "Just... be careful. The Council's not the only thing to worry about."

I give him the best reassuring smile I can, and he pulls me close. The hard line of his jaw flexes. There seems to be a thousand things he wants to say, but he remains quiet, rubbing the back of my hands with his thumbs. He slowly lets go, holding my gaze for a moment longer, then motions for me to take a seat on the nearby stool at the island in the kitchen. I move Abel's bag aside, then plop down into the soft cushion and flex my fingers. Dean's still not keen on the idea, but I have to try, even if it brings the Council down on me. If I can find Blake, it will make it all worth it. Besides, I can just drain their magic then, right? And if the magic backfires on me, well... we'll cross that bridge when we get there.

I close my eyes and grip the charms of the necklace I'm wearing, as if the small metal discs will breathe some encouragement into me. They can't, but something about holding them tight makes me feel more secure.

Inhaling a deep breath in through my nose and then slowly releasing it out through my mouth, I try to picture Blake in my mind. Her black hair, long and curled as it hangs over her shoulders. The take-no-shit look she always has in her amber eyes. The highlights on the dark tones of her skin under the afternoon sun. *Where are you, Blake?* I ask myself mentally. I focus again on my breathing and wait. *Where are you, Blake?* And nothing happens.

Sagging down with my arms on the countertop, I peek one eye open to find Dean's gaze set intently on me from where he stands. His shoulders are rigid with tension. I huff. "Nothing," I say with a groan. "I guess it's a little more difficult than just visualization, huh?" I hadn't even felt a tingle. On Halloween, it felt like my veins were full and vibrating so badly I worried I might split apart from the force. But now... nothing, not even a spark. *What's different?*

"Okay, well, on Halloween, when you used your magic... How did it start?" Dean asks. Abel leans forward from his seat on the coffee table, staring intently.

Rubbing my face with both hands I try to think back. "I don't know. I panicked."

"That's a place to start, I guess. Talk me through it."

I peek at him from between my fingers. His face is a hard, serious mask. No trace of the amusing smirk he normally wears—he's invested now. I drop my hands. "Okay," I say, and stretch my neck from side to side. "When Chad had that gun pointed at you, I just… I was so afraid of losing you." I shift away, unable to look at him as I spill all my emotions from that night. "One minute I was reeling from your kiss, and the next I was… terrified. It's like all I could see was the gun pointed at us—at you. And then you shifted. I knew you wouldn't be able to stop yourself with the full moon and everything, it was inevitable. But I also knew that if Chad saw you transform into a tiger he would freak out. Even if he knew about werewolves from his dad, knowing something and seeing something are two very different things, and you aren't just a wolf… you're a tiger." Wringing my hands in front of me, I struggle to force the rest of the words through my lips.

When Dean's hand lands on top of mine the tension evaporates from my spine. That single touch is everything I need. "And then you shifted, and exactly what I was afraid of happened. When the gun went off… I don't know… I just knew I couldn't lose you, and then suddenly my entire body tingled like I was being electrocuted. It was almost painful. There were pink tendrils of smoke or mist or something all around you and Chad, and it felt like my veins might burst and…" I let the words trail off.

"I don't remember any smoke, but I do remember it felt like I was being held in place by something. And then that 'something' released us and we fell to the ground. His bullet got held in place, too. Never reached me at all. I remember I was staring right at it in front of my chest," he says with a light laugh.

I nod slowly. Dean 'hmms' under his breath as I turn back to look up at him. His eyes are focused across the kitchen toward the window above the sink. I can almost see the gears turning in his mind.

"I can shoot something at Dean if you think it'll help?" Abel cuts in, and I can't tell if he's joking or if he seriously thinks that might be a good way to spark my magic again. He stands and walks over to join us in the kitchen.

"We can't exactly reenact that night," Dean says as he shoots a sarcastic smile at Abel. "But maybe if you're afraid for Blake, it might set off something."

"You mean if I make myself afraid enough maybe the magic will kick in…" My mouth parts as I try to piece together how to make that happen.

"Worth a shot," Dean says with a shrug.

I stretch my hands out in front of me, flexing my fingers once again. I can do this. I *will* do this. "Okay," I finally say, and close my eyes once more. I force my mind to clear, emptying it of everything except for an open black space, like a mental stage. *Good thing I like horror movies…* I imagine all the worst case scenarios—Blake tied up, bloodied and beaten, tossed into some dark, dank hole in the ground, starved and cold. One after another the scenes play out in my mind. Pain shoots through my palm, and I realize I've got a death grip on my necklace again. Tears well up in the corners of my eyes, but I force myself to keep going. Worse and worse and worse. Every scene from every horror movie plays out in my mind's eye, but with Blake as the victim. *Blake…*

The tingles start, but slowly. I chew at my lip as I focus on the awful image in my mind, letting the sensation fill me up. It's a wildly different experience this time, though… On Halloween, it felt like a geyser coming from inside me and forcing its way out. This time it feels external somehow, like some sort of ambient energy is being drawn inward through my pores.

We can analyze that bit later, I decide, forcing my attention back on the image of Blake. The scene becomes... more solid? The airiness of the mental images I had been imagining begin to steady. The colors become clearer, and the edges of everything start to lose their wispy quality. Blake's figure becomes real. "I see her," I say to Dean. "She's tied to a chair. It's dark."

"Good, keep going. What else do you see? Can you feel anything?" Dean's voice floats down to me from somewhere outside... I'm in the room with Blake.

My feet are on hard, flat ground—concrete? I inhale deeply, and take in the musty scent of the room. "It's dank... wet smelling. And humid. There's something else there, too. Like a bitter, sour... gas smell? An old furnace room, maybe? It's dark," I say in two places at once. The mugginess of the room mingles with the pleasant chill of Dean's home in a confusing way. The acrid smell of the room fades in and out. Blake shifts in the chair, and my chest aches from the sight of her.

"Ari?" Dean's voice is right behind my ear and miles away.

"She's still wearing her Moon Awakening gown...her face is bloody and..." I stumble over my words as despair struggles to overwhelm me. I breathe in and out slowly. My lungs fill with fresh air tainted with mildew. *Focus. Where are you?* I look around Blake, trying to make sense of what little bit I can see. "There's a small window across the room. Too small to bring in much light. But... I think..." Light shines in from the small rectangular window to my left in the basement. The darkness behind my closed eyes lightens from the kitchen light above. "We're behind a chain-link fence. There's lots of old shelves. It's all dusty. Some sort of maintenance room?" I shake my head. "I can't get a feel of where she's at." My voice fills the room, and echoes elsewhere.

"Ari, what's go—?" Dean's voice fades out. His hand is solid on my shoulder. His hand passes through me. I sigh as the warmth of it fills me, and push my mind to single out any detail I can.

"There's... old desks crammed in a corner I think. Chairs piled up, too. Dammit I can't—" Blake shifts again, and her head lolls back. She strains to pull it back up. Her eyes narrow and her brows furrow. Dried blood cracks and flakes off of her forehead.

"A-Ari?" Her voice sounds like someone walking on dry leaves.

"Blake! Blake wher—?" A point in the center of my back pinches, cutting off my voice. My stomach lurches and the air is sucked from my lungs as I'm ripped backwards and up, arms and legs flailing in the air in front of me. Back through the fence. Back through the wall.

Faster.

I pass up through a floor into a hallway. Doors line its silver walls. White terrazzo floors. A box with a silver bell is on the wall. I'm there for less than half a second before I'm flying through double doors.

Faster.

Objects and shapes are gone. The world is nothing but streaks of color.

Faster.

Feeling leaves me except for that single point on my back, pulling until it feels like it could rip loose at any moment.

Faster.

I can't breathe. The edges of my vision dim.

Faster.

Faster.

I slam into... myself? Feeling returns in force and every inch of me aches to my bones. Dean's kitchen fills my sight once more, and then is quickly replaced by his ceiling. I'm falling backwards but don't have the air to cry out.

Something warm and solid meets my back, and suddenly Dean's face is looking down on me, bursting with shock and concern. "Are you okay?! You..." he trails off, shaking his head.

"You were... like a... foggy hologram or somethin' there for a minute. Fading in and out and..." Abel says with a laugh behind me somewhere, but there's definitely no humor behind it.

"I lost it. I was there with her, and I lost it," I murmur, letting my body sink into Dean's solid embrace. My head shakes from side to side as I let the tears fall. "If that was really her she's.... She looks like she's been tortured. She's hurt Dean." I whisper, barely able to push the words through my lips as some invisible fist has my lungs in a vice grip.

Dean cups my face and wipes away a tear with his thumb, pulling me in tighter. "Alright, let's... think through the details..." Dean starts slowly.

Pop.

My eyes shoot wide as I twist in Dean's arms, looking for the Djinn I know comes with that sound, but find nothing.

"Ari," Dean says cautiously as I turn back to see him pull a small piece of paper off the island. I bite my lip as I take the tan parchment from him and read it out loud:

Bi-locating is an exceedingly difficult—and dangerous—enterprise, even with practice. Please don't kill yourself before we have the chance to meet. And no magic, not even if it is mine. You still need that ward. — Dad.

My forehead crinkles and I wipe my eyes. I look from the paper to Dean and back. "What the actual *fuck*," I say.

"Guess your dad wants you to heed Joaquin's warning as well." Dean says with an audible exhale. My frown deepens. Did he mean I was drawing magic from the ward he put on me? Was that what I was feeling? *Well, no more magic I guess...* at least for now.

Dean sits me and the stool back up with a sad smile. His hand goes to the small of my back, and comfort radiates from the small circles he makes. "Was there anything you saw that could help?"

Was there? That room she was locked in could be any old storage or boiler room in the city. But above it? White terrazzo... silver walls broken up by doors. A silver bell. *Not* silver walls. Silver *lockers*. I nearly choke. *She's where you think. Can you* read *what I'm telling you? Can you* add *it together...* "Fucking asshole," I whisper. I'm laughing despite myself. My chest hurts. "What a *fucking asshole.*"

Dean and Abel's confused faces both turn to me as I slowly shake my head.

"I know where she is..."

Thirty-Six

My bare feet wear into the carpet as I pace from side to side in Dean's living room. I glance down at my phone for like the hundredth time. No replies yet. "She's usually up by now," I say to no one in particular. It's nearly 8 p.m. The sun set a couple hours ago and waiting for Chloe is killing me. "I'm just gonna go knock on the door," I say, shoving the device back into my pocket.

"She *is* usually up by now," Dean says quietly from where he sits. Abel has returned to the couch, and sits poring over his notes and papers.

I nod once and head to the basement door. Dean spins the recliner toward the door and sits forward, watching. I hesitate for half a heartbeat before pounding on it, loud bangs carrying through the quiet house. "Chloe, get up! We know where Blake is," I shout through the door. My feet tap anxiously and I cross my arms to stop them from fidgeting. When I get no answer, Dean steps forward and swings the door open.

More quiet meets us, and I shout down again. "Chloe! We found Blake, c'mon!" Silence. Dean and I take the steps down two at a time to the makeshift bedroom he's set up in the basement and he flips on the lights. It's empty. Chloe is nowhere to be found as we move around the room, ridiculously checking closets and corners. Dean plants his hands on his hips and looks around the room from where he stands.

"Shit," he says, running a hand through his hair. "I guess she didn't come back last night." His jaw tenses and it looks like he might leave marks where his fingers dig into his sides.

Fear snakes its way into my already twisted stomach, coiling the knots even tighter. "Do you think…?" I shake my head. Her mom had acted so strangely earlier… I pull my phone out and check my messages again. The text I sent earlier is marked read. *Oh hell no, Chloe. I don't think so.* I fire off another text.

I know you saw my message Chloe. Where are you? The seconds stretch as I wait for a reply. Dean paces in the middle of the room, watching me stare at my phone. After a lifetime the ellipses appear.

I'm alright, don't worry. I just had to take care of something last night and never went back to Dean's. It was important, I promise. I'll check in later, ok? Finding out she's okay does exactly nothing to calm me down. How could she just disappear on us like that without saying anything? Did she not trust us to be okay with it? Though I suppose if she had gone to see her mom, maybe we wouldn't have been. *Save it for later*, I tell myself, pushing all those thoughts away. *We need to rescue Blake.*

You need to check in now. We found Blake The ellipses appear, disappear, and then come back. I'm tapping my foot again. Anxiety and hope spin in a sickening mixture in my stomach.

Where? Holy shit...

School. We're going to get her tonight. She's hurt Chloe

Another few seconds pass. Dean has made his way over to me, looking down at my phone as the message comes through. **I'm already out and about. I'm finishing something up really quick and then I'll meet you there** What did she mean about already being out? Was she out in the neighborhood, or had she gone out to the city? That anxiety I was feeling is slowly overpowering the hope. Dean and I share a glance. He shrugs, and I look back down to my phone. *Ugh*, I'm ready to throw it across the room. Why is she being so vague? *We need to rescue Blake.*

Fine, we'll talk later. I'll text you when we leave

K

Anger shoulders its way into the fight between anxiety and hope. 'K'? "If she gets herself killed, I'm gonna kill her. Again." I huff with a shake of my head. I cross my arms and stomp my way to the basement stairs. I'm almost to their base when Dean's hand wraps around my waist.

"Ari, wait."

I turn on a heel, ready to throw every bit of my fear and anger at him, when the calm, soothing look in his eyes stops me. "She'll be okay," he says.

Dean tugs against me, pulling me into his chest, and I deflate against him. Just the simple action of his embrace has all of my walls crumbling. I lean into him and he tightens his hold against me. All the emotions catch up with me, and suddenly tears are trailing a slow path down my cheeks. I wobble out a semblance of a sentence. "I just... Blake's hurt and needs us. Chloe's out running around with no one to watch her back, and..."

"They'll both be okay. We're gonna go to the school and

Chloe will meet us there. By the end of the night you three will be together again," he whispers into my hair, and I pray that he's right. "But we can't just rush down there. Especially if it's just the two—well, three—of us. We need to think through how to do this." I nod against the soft cotton of his dark t-shirt. I stay there in his arms for another minute as one of his hands runs through my hair before finally pulling back and wiping the wetness from my face.

"Okay," I say. "What's the plan?"

An hour later Dean, Abel, and I are piling into his pickup truck after I shoot Chloe a quick text. Now armed with some semblance of a plan, I'm feeling a little better about the situation. My nerves are still wound up tighter than a child's toy, though. I wrap my arms tight around myself hoping the pressure will settle the anxiety wracking my insides. It all makes sense that Blake would be at the school—and for the same reasons we thought she might be downtown. It's too loud to hear her from the basement, too public to be an obvious hiding place, and yet that room probably never gets used. From the look of it, I doubt anyone has used it in decades.

And then there's Joaquin's words… It makes so much sense now that I can't believe I didn't put it together earlier. I want to kick myself. What matters now, though, is that Blake's alive and we're going to get her. I can beat myself up later.

The truck suddenly slows. I feel Abel's hands grab my seat as he presses toward the window to get a better look. A small crowd is gathered in the front yard of a home—Jon's home—and they're all staring and pointing. 'MURDERER' is written in bright-red paint across the façade and front door of the house, the porch light illuminating it for anyone passing by to see. "Well, damn…" Abel mutters from the backseat. I don't see any bodies, and they got the whole word done before anyone could stop them. Jon's car is missing from the driveway… He wasn't home, which is probably the only way whoever graffitied his house got away with it. The way my brain is using 'whoever' makes me snort with laughter, earning a confused look from Dean.

"Sorry, it's not funny, it's just… Bold, even for Chloe." I shake my head. It was stupid and dangerous, too, but I can't help but admire her for it. We were already committed to exposing Jon, but it seems like she wanted to get a headstart. This would certainly have everyone talking… But where is Jon?

"You think it was Chloe?" Dean asks, still peering out the passenger window as we crawl past.

"Who else would it have been? She said she was finishing something when we talked. It wasn't one of us and I doubt he suddenly felt guilty and did it to himself," I sniff. "This has Chloe written all over it," I finish with a smile.

Dean 'hmpfs' and we slowly speed up again, cruising out of Lunar Falls. Night has fully taken over as we navigate the familiar route to Silas Creek High. The soft-white light from the truck's headlights mingle with the illumination of the waxing orange moon. The mix is unnerving, edging the lit-up world in a rusty, reddish-brown color and making everything seem… off. It reminds me of dried blood. What is going to happen if Chad and his cronies are at the school tonight? What if they're armed? We know Chad has silver bullets… I peek a glance over at Dean. He drives with one hand clutching the steering wheel so hard it looks like he might grind off the leather. His eyes never leave the road. I wonder if he's thinking about the same thing but keep silent.

I focus back on the road and wrap my arms around myself again to try to get a grip on my nerves. If it comes down to it, Dean won't hesitate. He was ready to kill Chad to protect me on the night of the Moon Awakening. But Dean has killed before—granted, it was vampires, but it was still a kill. Will I be able to do the same? They kidnapped Blake… hurt her badly. They'll probably try to kill us, too. It should be simple. It *is* simple. But thinking about it and *actually* taking a life are two different things. Bile stings the back of my throat, but my mind resolves. If they don't let us take Blake out of there, if they don't let us walk away… then whatever happens is on them. We're all coming home, one way or another.

The large campus finally appears ahead of us, cutting an imposing figure in the orange glow of the moon as Dean pulls the truck off onto a side road. I climb down from the passenger side as he cuts the engine and climbs from the driver's seat. Abel scrambles out a moment later and stretches his legs. I pull the black hoodie Dean lent me over my head. I breathe deeply, and for a moment I'm frozen in the smell of him. Sage and eucalyptus. An overwhelming sense of home seeps into my bones, and every bit of me wants to collapse into the feeling. *Ugh, get your head in the game, Ari.*

"What's that look for?" Dean asks, stopping just in front of me. His hands dig into his pockets, his hair mussed in the autumn wind. I smile, hoping it's filled with the confidence I don't actually have.

"Nothing," I say, turning my face toward the school. I've been attending Silas Creek High School for the last two years. I've walked those halls so often I know them like the back of my hand. The idea that Chad—pretty-boy football player Chad—is the villain who kidnapped Blake and hid her in some unknown storage room under that school I know so well is almost too much to believe. How did I not see him for what he is before? Hell, weeks ago I even wanted to get to know him when I was trying out the whole 'regular human' thing. It turns out neither of us were just 'regular.' "Let's go get Blake," I say, squaring my shoulders. The image of Blake tied to a chair in her tattered gown and covered in dried blood clouds my mind. My lips thin into a stark line as determination rises in my chest, pushing out the fear and nervousness. She's coming home *tonight*.

"Ari, wait," Dean's words are barely a whisper as I take a step toward the school. Dean's hand wraps around my waist and turns me back toward him. Warmth and strength seeps into me with his nearness as he rests both his hands on either of my hips. "Just in case," he says, closing the distance between us. Dean leans down and kisses me.

His lips are hard and firm against mine. Not hesitant or unsure like our first kiss, but deep and intense—as if every emotion swirling between the two of us can be summed up in the feel of his mouth on mine. My back presses into the door of his truck and I realize I'm trapped between it and the hard lines of Dean's body, and there's nowhere else I'd rather be. The thought should sober me, but all I do is lean in for more.

The world around us disappears as he snakes his hand into my hair. It's only him and me and this electric charge that has us both ensnared. He cradles the back of my neck, angling me for a deeper kiss. I moan against him, my lips parting eagerly. He takes the invitation and slides his tongue against mine with teasing, expert strokes that have me clenching his chest. My hand grips the material of his shirt and pulls him in to close what space is left between us. The need to be closer, the desire to have more of him, fills my every sense.

Suddenly, I can't remember why I've tried so hard to distance myself from this man. Why did I ever think that anything could be better than this—the feel of him, the taste of him? I kiss him back with everything I have, sucking on his lower lip and scraping my teeth over him. I feel thoroughly devoured and explored and then he sucks my tongue into his mouth so I can do the same. His other hand finds my lower back and presses my hips forward to his. The heat of him against me has my knees weak and I sink further into him. My hands are finally in his hair and I grip hard, pulling him deeper.

This is insane. It's absolute madness and yet I can't stop. I can't get enough. I could live forever in this little bubble of delirium if it means keeping his mouth on mine. I never thought I could be so out of control over a single kiss as I am right now—so consumed with the feel of another human being. It's exhilarating and terrifying at the same time, and I know in this moment it has the power to consume me.

And I'd let it.

Dean breaks the kiss with a sharp gasp and I'm left panting and flushed. When my eyes open, his gaze is scorching heat that echoes everything my body is begging for. "I needed to do that."

"Yeah," I force the word out in a stumble through my still swollen lips. He pulls away and I'm already missing the feel of his arms around me. The cold air pierces through my hoodie with the lack of his body heat. I lick my lips and try to clear my head, thinking to take a step back but there's nowhere to go against the truck. An electrical current is pulling me back to him and I have to desperately fight the urge with everything in me... *We have a job to do first.*

"Later," I say. "We'll explore this later." I gesture between the two of us.

Dean smirks in that way of his, and I melt. I'm a complete puddle on the ground before him. His answering laugh is barely a rumble from his chest, as if he knows exactly what he's doing to me. "Ari... if we don't..."

I raise a finger to his lips, stopping him mid sentence. "After," I say, narrowing my gaze on him. "Because there *will* be an after."

Abel crosses my vision over Dean's shoulder, pointedly not looking in our direction. "So, uhhh... we ready?"

THIRTY-SEVEN

We headed into the school grounds from the woods to avoid the well-lit entrances around the main parking areas. From my too-successful attempt at tracking Blake we know she is definitely underneath classrooms somewhere, and there are only two buildings on campus old enough to have a completely forgotten storage area underneath them—Buildings C and D. Abel had broken off to look through C Building while Dean and I climbed our way up the small hill to D Building. I had taken Mrs. Davidson's Art class last semester in that very building, and she loved to open her windows for some fresh air. Luckily for us, she also always forgets to lock them back up.

Climbing through the open window had been easy enough, and now Dean and I make our way through the deathly quiet building. The hallways are almost completely dark except for the moonlight that fights its way through the small windows in the classroom doors. It casts pitch-black shadows around the hall that have my heart racing. They seem to leap at me from every angle as we walk, and I investigate each dark corner as if Chad and his friends might jump out at any moment for an ambush. I try to mirror Dean's heel-toe strides as he stalks forward, attempting to keep my footsteps as silent as his against the hard, terrazzo floor. A knot forms in my throat from the effort.

"Here," Dean whispers, pulling me toward a door marked 'Staff Only.' He gingerly reaches out and tests the knob. It's blessedly silent and unlocked. Dean pulls the door open gently, revealing a stairwell into utter darkness. I let out the breath I had been holding and take my phone out to message Chloe again.

Heading down to the basement of D Building.

K, almost there she replies quickly, and I stash my phone away to hide the light. Dean's eyes—still bright even in this lighting—meet mine, and he takes my hand.

"Ready?" His strong voice is barely audible. I take a deep breath and nod, not trusting my voice. He turns and guides me down the steps, one at a time. I can't see a thing as we descend, and if it were any quieter I think I would be able to hear what Dean's thinking. The touch of him and his patient pull forward is my only anchor. I reach forward and take his arm with my other hand, desperate to be closer to something real in this oppressive nothing. We hit flat ground, and for a moment I think we've reached the bottom, but Dean keeps moving. Every step forward has me clutching his arm harder. "One more set of stairs." Dean's whisper drifts back from just ahead of me.

We descend the last flight down in a matter of heartbeats, and Dean lightly pulls me forward to lean against what feels like a brick wall. The rough, solid press of the wall against my body is as comforting as Dean's hand still on mine, and I exhale some of the anxiety that has been gripping my chest. I hear him test another door knob somewhere to my right, and the subtle squeak of its turning sounds like a train derailing in this quiet. Every muscle I have goes rigid and I wait for some sort of signal that we've been heard. The seconds stretch on, but… nothing.

"Unlocked…" Dean squeezes out softly, but I can hear the concern even at that volume. There's no reason this door should be unlocked, especially if Blake's being kept in one of these rooms. Someone is down here. *Do they know we're coming?* My heart skips a beat as another possibility slams into me: *Someone's down here and* wants *us to reach Blake.* Either Chad and his friends have been careless, or this could be a trap. I send up a silent prayer to the Goddess that it's the former. Dean must be thinking the same thing—his muscles have gone taut under my hand. Is there anything we can even do, though? We can't turn back now, this is happening.

"Trap?" I whisper wordlessly to Dean.

"Maybe." I feel Dean press forward into the door, and I'm pulled along with him as he slowly pads into a long hallway. Darkness fills the space, but a small amount of light drifts in from the side rooms through what must be the small, rectangular windows surrounding the bottom of the building. It's not much, but compared to the stairwell we might as well be standing on the Sun. The outline of Dean's shape takes form in front of me and I let out a quiet exhale of relief. *At least it's something.*

I peer forward over his shoulder into the hallway. Several small rooms line the wall to my right, while it looks like only a few larger rooms sit behind the left. It had been hard to tell the size of the room from my brief visit with Blake, but if I had to guess, she'd be in one of those larger rooms. I tug on Dean's arm to get his attention, and nod my head in that direction. His head moves up and down in agreement, and he turns and sniffs the air. A low rumble sounds from his throat. "This way."

I can't smell what Dean does, but my nose is flooded with that same acrid, wet-earth smell that had been overwhelming when I found Blake. *This is the place. Blake is here.* I take a deep breath. Excitement and hope crowd their way into the place anxiety has been filling in my chest. *Blake!* Dean glides silently forward in a low crouch, and I follow a few paces behind. I take each step with care, and peer through the small windows in the doors to my right. More storage areas, empty and disused. The quiet becomes deafening, and I strain my ears for anything of use. They find nothing but the pounding of my heart and more quiet.

We reach the first door on our left and Dean drops to almost a crawl. He moves forward underneath the small window of the door and I follow suit, keeping low. Slowly and wordlessly we move forward. We pass beneath the window of the second door. At the third and final door, Dean moves past then presses himself against the wall. I slide in behind him and deflate against the wall. Dean turns to look at me and nods toward the door. *This is it. Blake's here.* I pull out my phone and angle away from the door, then send a message to Chloe and Abel. **D Building basement. She's here**. Dean turns toward me and leans in, the heat of his breath warms my ear and sends a shiver down my back.

"I'm gonna throw the door open. Then we wait and see what happens." He's worried it might be a trap, too, then. *Well, let's see if we can spring it.* I nod silently against him. He moves back and cups my cheek, lightly kissing my forehead, then turns back toward the door. I bite my lip as his hand reaches out to the door knob and takes hold. He brings his other hand up to me and raises a finger. *One.* Another. *Two.* His third finger rises and he turns hard on the knob, then throws the door open before pressing back against the wall. The hinges groan from neglect and the force of his push. The solid door slams against the inside of the room with an echoing bang that shatters the quiet of the basement. And then…

…Nothing.

Silence. Not even a whisper from inside. We keep ourselves pressed against the outside wall for what feels like hours. Dean is nearly vibrating with impatience next to me. The door continues to creak as it sways back and forth from the violent opening until it too goes quiet.

That horrible, ringing silence fills the basement again.

Fabric shuffles and something scrapes against concrete. A crumbling, feminine groan wafts from the room and punches me in the stomach. *Blake!* I rush forward to turn the corner, but a heavy arm keeps me in place. Dean gives me a gruff shake of his head and holds me back. He mouths the word 'wait.' I can see the torment painting his face even in the dim light. The groan sounds again and my heart shatters. I won't wait any longer. I *can't* wait any longer. I fix Dean with a stare that I hope lets him know where he can stick his arm. He holds my gaze without flinching, his minty green eyes seemingly draw in the light. His jaw grinds and then he finally relents. "Me first," he nearly growls. He turns to face the opening in the wall and takes a deep breath, then darts low into the room. Shifting.

I suck in my own ration of air and move to follow. Lights flicker on as I go to turn the corner, and the sudden shift from near-darkness has me almost blind. The hiss of rope being pulled and an eerie rattling of metal pierces through the quiet. *No, no, no...* The door slams in my face almost as hard as my shock.

Thirty-Eight

"*D* *ean!*" I scream, pounding on the closed door in front me. *Shit, shit, shit.* I try the handle and it turns only half an inch before painfully stopping. I can hear laughter in the room. *I swear to the Goddess I will paint the walls with them.* Voices float through the closed door.

"—said they'd be here tonight." That was Chad. I take a few steps back and then throw myself into the door—it barely budges and I'm thrown back from the force of my own charge. Pain explodes from my shoulder and my arm suddenly feels useless and numb. I collapse against the door. "Don't worry, you'll get it next time." More laughter.

A tiger growls and metal rattles. Feet shuffle back. More laughter. "Can you believe it? A tiger?" Donavan.

"Definitely a surprise… bet. How badass is that pelt gonna look?" Chad again. Fear and despair bubbles in my stomach, but the rage building inside of me keeps them both at bay. It floods my veins and vibrates through me—almost animalistic. *If they touch a single hair on him… If they hurt my… my mate…* Mate. Dean's my mate. The pain in my shoulder begins to subside, and sensation returns tingling to my right arm. *Unless…*

"Leave… him… alone," a dry, cracking voice barely above a whisper sounds behind the doors. Even those three words sounded painful. *Oh Goddess, Blake!* The tingling in my right arm spreads to my chest and down my other arm. What feels like a light breeze tickles my skin, blowing in from all sides. I breathe it in.

"Shut the hell up!" Feet stomp and wood crashes onto the floor. Blake whimpers. The tiger roars. Another laugh. "Aww, did that upset the little kitty?" The tingling reaches my toes. It tickles my scalp. The anger running through me is primal.

"Can't be upset if he's dead." Matt's muffled voice sounds through the wood of the door.

"True enough." Chad again. Footsteps, and then the unmistakable cocking of a hammer on a pistol. The tiger roars again.

Fuck. This. My chest swells as I breathe deeply. The light breeze has become a gale. *Sorry, Dad.* I need to get in that room. I won't lose Dean. I won't lose Blake. If it means calling the Council down on me then I'll fight them, too. Chad has to be stopped. The vibrations build, and I imagine myself past the door. Not like last time—not one place looking in on another. I *am* on the other side of that door.

I feel… wet. Like I've just stepped out of the shower. The slickness on my skin seeps inside of me, down to my bones. The world around me turns hazy and blurs. The solid press of the ground underneath my feet evaporates. The entirety of my physical experience swirls down and collapses into a single point on my chest—just like it had on my back the other day. And then I disappear.

Pop! I stumble forward through a haze of pink smoke, landing on my hands and knees. One hand instinctively flies to cover my mouth, and I fight back the urge to vomit. The tingles aren't as strong as they had been and the pain in my shoulder is returning with a vengeance. It's hard to think. Audible gasps sound to my right, and Chad looks down at me with wide eyes from where he stands with his gun raised. "W-what the f…" Chad mumbles out. I try to stand, but I'm finding it hard to reorient. The solidness of the ground feels strange underneath me. I can't seem to shake the fog clouding my mind away. I manage to make it up on one knee.

They have Dean trapped in some sort of cage. Its metal walls are held up by ropes attached to a pulley in the ceiling. Chad stands with a gun in his hand underneath the small window I had seen earlier, while Matt and Donavan cower off to my right. Behind them, Blake is still tied to the same chair I saw her in before. It's on its side, and Blake's head rests against the hard, concrete floor. One of her eyes is swollen shut, but the other meets my gaze. She smiles. It's weak and barely lasts a second before she winces and a single tear streams down her cheek. My eyes glaze with wetness, but in my daze and confusion I can't decide if it's from happiness that she's alive or anger at what they've done to her. Maybe it's both.

I grit my teeth and struggle to stand up again. My legs wobble underneath me as my senses adjust from returning to something physical. I dig deep through the clearing mental haze I'm lost in and find the strength to stabilize myself. "That's enough!" I shout with all the grit and courage I can muster. Chad looks shell-shocked and his eyes dart from me, to the cage, to his friends, and back. "Drop the fucking gun, Chad, or I swear I'll—"

"You swear you'll do what, huh?" Chad licks his lips and adjusts his grip on the pistol, aiming right at me. "I don't know what you are, but you can get it, too, you hear me!" Dean rages at his threat and slams against the cage. Chad stumbles back despite the cage and the distance between them. His eyes fly wide with rage and he raises the gun at the tiger. "But you can get it first."

Dean! I raise my arm to do something... anything... The tingling grows but the pain lacing from my shoulder drops my arm just as quickly as I raise it. Chad plants his back leg. I try again, fighting through the pain and the sickening sound of my shoulder joint grinding. He takes aim, and his finger twitches on the trigger. "*STOP!*" I scream, but nothing comes...

Glass shatters.

The gun fires.

There's a race of movement, and suddenly a figure stands in between Chad and the cage. The light reflects off their long, blonde hair. *Chloe!* She reaches a hand up to her shoulder and blood stains her fingertips when she pulls them away. "This is cashmere," she huffs, pulling at the edge of her sleeve. "Dick. Move."

Chad mutters something unintelligible and takes a few steps backwards. "You're supposed to die!" He fires again. "Die!" And again. Chloe's body rocks with each impact, but she stays standing. Chad is shaking as Chloe raises her big blue eyes toward him.

"I'm not a Were, silly," she says with a smile, flashing her fangs. Chad makes a pathetic noise and takes another step backward. The front of his pants are wet. He manages to get one more shot off before Chloe has closed the distance and has him by the front of his jacket. "You're lucky I ate before I left," She tilts her head, as if considering something for a moment, and her eyes narrow. She smiles again. "But I'm a petty bitch and you took my friends." She sinks her fangs into Chad's neck.

Chad writhes in her grip, beating at her with the butt of the pistol, but Chloe doesn't budge. A hoarse cry forces its way out of his mouth and Chloe only pulls him in tighter. Sickness is clawing up my throat. *She won't... She can't...* The gun drops to the floor. "Chloe... stop..." My mouth is open, but it's not my voice. "That's enough..." Blake pushes out through heavy breaths on the floor. Chloe pulls away at the sound. Her exhale is a thing of pure ecstasy. Bright-red blood shines against the dim lighting and drips from the corners of her mouth.

"Better than you deserve," Chloe spits, looking Chad in the eyes. She tosses him aside like a ragdoll and wipes her hands on her jacket. Chad slides to a stop against the wall and groans, gripping his neck tightly. His eyes are wide with shock and he takes deep, gasping breaths. "Don't worry, he's got plenty left," Chloe announces to the room.

The cage rattles again to our left, drawing everyone's attention. Abel has entered the room and climbed one of the metal cage walls, sawing at the rope to free Dean. The last thread rips free and the wall falls forward with a resounding clang that echoes throughout the basement room. Dean strides forward with a low growl and I shuffle over to meet him, strength and clarity finally returning to me. I take his massive head in my hands and nuzzle up against his coarse fur. *Thank the Goddess you're okay.*

Relief floods through me... The tingles start to subside. Everyone's here, Chad and his friends are out of commission, and we have Blake... I close my eyes and breathe the smell of this massive animal into me. He still somehow hints of sage and mint and eucalyptus, and I almost laugh out loud. I deflate against him, lost in the feeling of him. *Let's get Blake and go home.*

Dean rumbles underneath me and suddenly presses forward from my grip. A door sounds like it's been popped open somewhere in the distance and wood scrapes against concrete. Abel and Chloe both step forward with Dean, and I turn to face the direction they walk toward. Matt has Blake propped upright again, and he holds Chad's gun to her head. She whimpers silently while he pushes the cold barrel into her temple.

No, no, no. This is *not* happening. Not after all this. The back and forth of the last hour has my stomach spinning and my throat dry. Dean prowls forward a few steps while Chloe and Abel slowly stalk toward the sides of the room. Matt's shaking and looks ready to snap with fear. *They're going to get her killed...* I push forward past Dean and throw up my hands like a white flag. "Let's just calm down, Matt," I announce, then shift my gaze to everyone else in the room. "Let's all just calm down." Abel and Chloe eye me from the walls but hesitate and hold where they are. Donavan scrambles over to where Matt holds the gun on Blake. Dean tenses beside me. "How about you let us take our friend home, and we all go our separate ways, huh?"

"N-n-no… You'll just kill us when we walk away from her," Matt stammers, pressing the gun into Blake's head even harder. She winces at its touch. "Y-you all just leave. Just leave, and-and we'll let her go. I promise."

I take another step forward, hands outstretched. "We can't do that, Matt… we need to get her out of here. She needs a doctor. You haven't killed anyone yet, Matt," I say slowly and deliberately. Chloe and the Weres supernatural speed wouldn't be enough to save Blake. Adrenaline surges through me and the tingling starts ripping through my limbs again. Would my magic work? Do I trust it enough to try? A light breeze tickles my skin. *We have to try talking him down first…*

"No! You can come back for her! L-leave and then we'll leave and th-then you can come back for her." Matt's yells sound more like pleas. His cheeks are wet.

"C'mon, buddy, let's play this smart, alright," Abel offers up from my right. "Let's put down the gun and then everyone goes home, okay?" Matt whips the gun in his direction.

"Th-that's right! I have the g-gun, and I'm telling you to go home!" Blake twitches in the chair and the gun is back to her temple in a heartbeat.

"Okay, okay…" Abel trails off with his hands in the air, taking a step back.

The breeze against me picks up as I feel Dean rumble beside my hip. Chloe lets out a sharp, quiet gasp and her gaze falls somewhere behind Matt. Two glowing yellow eyes float in the darkness at the end of the room. My breath catches, and a new knot forms in my core. Chad's friends are too worked up to notice they're not the center of attention anymore. The two yellow orbs slowly get larger. "Matt... I really, *really* think you need to lower the gun," I force out quietly.

The eyes get larger, and the outline of snout pushes through the darkness. Black fur curls around a soundlessly snarling mouth. "Of course, you do! You—"

"Matt, you need to drop the gun. Now." I cut him off, clipping each word and filling it with as much emphasis as I can. Dean's growl clicks low beside me, and I can see Chloe and Abel both take a step backward in my periphery.

"No! Leave, now! P-please!" Matt takes the gun from Blake's head and waves it at the open door.

"Matt—"

It's too late. A massive, black shape lunges from the shadows and a colossal paw slams into Matt's outstretched arm with a sickening *crack*. The gun clatters away as the lower half of his arm dangles uselessly. Only the beginnings of a yelp escape his throat before they're replaced by wet gurgles as the jaws of the biggest wolf I've ever seen sink into his neck. A spray of red washes over Blake and Donavan as Matt is taken to the floor. Donavon presses himself into the wall with a soundless scream while Blake shakes in her chair, unable to see what's happening behind her. The giant wolf clamps down twice more into Matt's neck with a snarl, then pulls away from his twitching body. Its growl seems to shake the room as it stalks around Blake's chair to face us.

Those giant yellow eyes scan the room, seeming to take in each of us one by one. His snarl reverberates in my bones. "Jon, we came to help her..." I breathe in the breeze around me, and my veins feel like they're ready to burst. The corded muscles of the wolf go taut and his teeth gnash. *Not in front of Blake, Jon. Please...*

Pop!

The room chokes with green smoke.

Thirty-Nine

The smoke clears lazily from the dimly lit room—but not completely. Green ribbons of mist circle and swirl around my midsection, keeping my arms pinned firmly to my sides. A high, sing-song laugh titters from the center of the room.

"You've got to be kidding me," Joaquin strides forward in his always immaculate suit, his arms crossed as he scans the room. Chloe and Abel hang ensnared and struggling like me, while the swirling green bonds are locked underneath Dean and Jon's front legs. They both rage and howl. "Not one!" Joaquin starts again, holding up a finger on each hand, "But *two* surprise entrances!" Another finger jumps up. He sniffs and folds his arms behind his back, then strides lightly toward Chloe. "That was stunning, Chloe! Popping in just in the nick of time to save our friend Dean, here..." He spins on one foot like a ballerina to face the large wolf, hands held up like mock claws. "And then Jon out of nowhere with the *GRRR* and the *RWRR!* It stretches credulity! I mean, who's writing this thing, huh?" He laughs again and shakes his head.

I struggle against the green mist that coils around me, straining against it to no avail. I grit my teeth and push, but I might as well be trying to break out of steel bars. I give up the effort. *Think, Ari, think.* My body still feels full and my insides are on fire. That gale against my skin has become a hurricane and the room buzzes with energy, yet the air is still. I can feel Joaquin's magic in a physical sense, and it makes my skin crawl and my stomach turn. *If I can draw it in… Get him talking,* I think to myself. "We're not going to let you use us, Joaquin. We're not your puppets."

His head snaps in my direction in that eerily focused way, and that sinister, toothy grin cuts across his face. "Use you?" he questions. "Use you for what, dear?" He smoothly glides forward to me, tilting his head and peering up at where I hang suspended with eyes as dark as pitch.

"Use us against the Council," I nearly spit through clenched teeth. Even if that wasn't his real intention he won't be able to shut up about it, and while he talks… I draw in a deep breath and energy soaks into me. It throbs and prickles through every inch of my body. Joaquin's eye twitches and I hold my breath to dam the flow.

"I see," he says, his eyes boring into my own. "You've heard the Telling, then…" He 'hmpfs' and paces away to the center of the room. "Yes, you can see how everyone at home was in quite a tizzy over that." When he turns around to face me, the smile is back. He stares me down underneath his brows. "So, you can see then why your deaths are a matter of… national security, as it were." He waves a hand dismissively in the air. "As I told you, I'm duty-bound to kill you as a loyal subject of the Council. And in doing so, I will elevate myself *to* that Council. So, in a sense, yes, I do plan to use you. Or your deaths, at least."

It had been a possibility, and yet hearing it out loud still sends a shock coursing through my already fraying nerves. Then why all the games? Why not kill us when he had every chance to earlier? I raise my mental gate a hair, drawing in a little more of the swirling energy in the room as subtly as I can. Joaquin's eyes narrow and he scans the room. I slam it shut. "Why wait so long then? Why not pick us off one by one?" I ask. *Keep talking, Joaquin…*

His eyes cross the room one last time before his attention snaps back to me. His face is serene malice once again. "Three to stand and one, two, three," he says, pointing us out in turn, "to fall. I wasn't sure if that part was literal or not, but why not let prophecy take its course and have all three of you together for the last hurrah, hmm?" He shrugs.

"It doesn't fit, you know that, right? You're wrong," I snarl. My body is starting to ache from the sickly-sweet magic I've been bottling up inside of myself. My stomach clenches. *Just a bit more…*

His lips thin, showing the first sign of frustration I think I've ever seen from him. "Your kind are so rare. To run across one such as yourself, and warded no less, is not a small thing. And then to find out about her two best friends, all to be raised to adulthood under the same moon?" He sniffs. "Granted, only two of you fit at the time—you and your friend Blake here: a half-

Djinn and a wolf, wolves being inexorably tied to Christmas…" he says, sweeping a hand to where Blake sits tied to her chair, head and shoulders sagging. *That must be the fur and frost… Oh Goddess, is that true? But how could he know about Chloe?* He turns and strides toward her then, the top half of him staying eerily still as he walks. "But, as I have *also* told you… it's amazing what you can accomplish with a little nudge."

The realization slams into me and threatens to knock the wind from my lungs. Joaquin had sent the vampires the night of the Moon Awakening. Chloe's face has gone red with rage, and she thrashes in her bonds above him. "You son of a bitch! I will eviscerate you!" she shrieks, kicking out toward him. Joaquin doesn't move.

"A little experiment. If you're not the right three, well, then… Oops, sorry the party was a bummer." He shrugs. "But if you *are* the right three, well… here we are. Things were to be put in motion by a Djinn's own hand, and I've fulfilled that now doubly so," He stares up at Chloe and I can only imagine the look on his face. He had taken everything from her as a test. She screams down at him, and he has the nerve to laugh. It echoes through the basement and resounds within me, just like the rage and energy vibrating through my entire being. Joaquin's magic, his life-force, swirls through the room and calls to me. The urge to drink it in is almost becoming overwhelming.

"It wasn't prophecy or fate, it was you! You're wrong Joaquin!"

"The exercise of fate is a matter of perspective… Perhaps I'm an agent of fate." His smile is sickening.

I draw in a bit more, the intensity in my veins building. Dean and Jon are in a fit of roars and growls off to the side that seems to distract Joaquin for a moment. A tangle of anger cuts across his sharp features as he turns to them. "That's enough! I can barely hear myself think!" He waves his hand and green smoke fills the Weres' mouths. Something is changing in the Djinn. His carefree, always-in-control demeanor is slipping away with each sip of his magic I take. Frustration is painting his face again. *Good. Asshole.* He shakes it away and faces Chad.

"I had wanted to be a bit more hands-free, especially with an enterprising young man like Chad here," He growls, turning back towards the rest of us. "This whole endeavor was his idea—the kidnapping and whatnot—and I had hoped to stay on the sidelines while he and his boys took care of business. But it seems you can't trust a human to get the job done, ehh, Chad? And even after I told you they'd be here tonight," Joaquin scoffs in disgust as Chad tries to crawl up the wall away from him.

"It was y-you who sent the text?" Chad stammers out.

Joaquin ignores his question. "This was the best you could do... No, you and your friends," He pauses and looks to Matt's still twitching form. Disgust mars his face. "*That* was a little much, Jon. My word... You and your *friend* are going to stay here so we can have a chat after class." At the Djinn's words, Donavan scrambles up from the ground and races for the door. Joaquin turns with a snarl, and the kid erupts into red mist as he passes through the door frame. The Djinn snaps his head back around to Chad and he shakes it with a deep sigh. "*You* are going to stay after class for a chat."

Dean thrashes in the air, slamming a paw into a metal shelf behind him and sending its contents rattling. Joaquin's dark eyes fix on the tiger, and I draw more of his magic in. The vibrations coursing through me have me visibly shaking now, and I'm clenching my teeth so hard I worry they might shatter. My insides feel like they might rip apart. *I can't keep this down much longer… it needs out…* The bitter, acidic taste of it makes me want to vomit.

"Enough!" Joaquin shouts, stealing my thoughts back to the room in front of me. His voice has lost its high, airy quality. It's deeper now—almost inhuman—as if two voices are speaking at once. His smooth, fox-like features seem more weathered and worn. "I. Tire. Of. Your. Incessant. Struggling… Jon!" he pinches out through gritted teeth as a veil of green glazes over the wolf's eyes. "Kill the kittens… I know you have a thing for the older one." The swirling green mist and smoke around the Weres blows away in a nonexistent wind. Abel is already shifting as he drops, and an almost-white tiger joins Dean where he paces in front of the massive, snarling figure of Jon.

Joaquin squeezes his eyes closed and rubs his temples. His breathing is heavy and irate, visible even under the layers of his tailored suit. Behind him, Jon lunges forward and takes Abel down in a vicious tackle, sending my heart into my throat. Dean takes Jon's back with claws and teeth, just barely able to get the massive wolf away before its cruel teeth can lock down onto Abel's neck. *I need to stop this… I need to stop Joaquin…* Dean goes in for another strike, but a savage claw swats him away, sending him tumbling and bloody to the floor. I draw in more of Joaquin's magic and try to materialize what I want—out of these bonds, the Djinn's energy becoming my own… The raging storm within and around me batters my focus. *Almost there… almost…*

"YOU!" The Djinn rages, spinning toward me. He marches to where I hang in the air, extends his hand and pulls. I float down to him, as if he is holding an imaginary leash. He pulls my face in inches from his. His thin lips are pulled into a sneer over eyes filled with pitch. The nostrils of his pinched nose flare as he leans in close. "What was the plan, half-breed? Take a little here, take a little there?" He strokes my cheek with long-nailed fingers, his corrosive touch making me recoil. "It hurts, doesn't it? Holding all that power in… But you're not quite sure how to consume it or release it, are you?" He pauses and rakes his eyes over me. "You're trembling, child. Close to bursting." He leans in closer, until his humid breath stings my ear. "I warned you. You're untrained, and now your father's negligence has led you here…"

He pulls away slightly, but his face still blocks my vision. He's not wrong. There's an out of control fire running wild through my body. The vibrations rattle my bones. This has to go somewhere… Anywhere. Behind Joaquin, something heavy slams into a shelf. An animal whimpers. Joaquin doesn't let up, though. "You'll burn alive from the inside out or you'll bring the building down on yourself. Lesson learned, either way." He gives me one last sneer before gliding back to the center of the room. The Weres have backed off from each other for the moment, panting heavily and yet still circling. Dark red has bloomed all across the tigers' fur, and the massive, dark wolf is covered in wet splotches that shine in the light. Abel is limping. *Abel!*

"Speaking of lessons," Joaquin is nearly shouting. "Chad, do you know why silver bullets didn't work on that one?" The lightness and humor is back in his voice. He speaks to Chad, but his eyes never leave mine. "Because she's a vampire…" He holds his right hand to the side. Green smoke coils in his palm. "There are a couple things you can do, but… Classics are classics for a reason." His eyes flare and a wooden stake materializes in his hand. It levitates over his outstretched palm, the sharpened point spinning to face Chloe. "Aim for the heart of course…"

I fall off the edge from Joaquin's threat. The pain coursing through me reaches a fever pitch. Time seems to slow. The stake leaves Joaquin's hand as if moving through a pool. The colossal wolf is sinking its teeth into Dean's side in a slow-motion spray of red while Abel's battered and shredded form ever so slowly plows into its flank. Chloe's mouth is wide in a silent scream of defiance. The room buzzes and sings. I breathe it in. Burn from the inside or bring down the building? *Well, if I only have two options…*

I focus on the object of my rage—the Djinn standing before me.

My skin feels like it's lifting away from my body… everything I've been taking from him wants to go… somewhere.

Out. Get out…

I'm not sure what I do, but I *do* something.

I scream, and the room erupts.

My hearing comes back before my vision, though only as a harsh ringing. Slowly, the dimness clouding my sight fades away from the center of my view. The room is in chaos. Joaquin is down on one knee, staring at the floor. His eyes are wide and shock creases his sharp features. Smoke rises in dancing wisps from him, and here and there, patches of his suit smolder. Behind him, the wolf is just now staggering back to standing. Dean digs his head underneath Abel's tiger body and lifts, helping him back up on his paws, while Chloe crouches with her hand on the floor. Chad crawls across the floor while Blake lies against the wall, the wooden chair she was tied to smashed to pieces, but she's moving, barely.

My hands go to my stomach as it threatens to force its way out of my mouth and my head lolls back to the hard brick wall behind me. The intensity in my veins—the fullness—has subsided, though it floats in the background. I still feel uncomfortably warm... The air tickles my skin, and the feel of Joaquin's magic zipping through the room calls to me. I breathe in and out methodically, hoping it will still my racing heart and calm my nerves. *Everyone's okay, though...* My eyes scan the room again, landing on Joaquin and Chad once more. *Unfortunately.*

The sounds of the room steadily edge out the ringing in my ears. It's shockingly quiet—no screams or curses, no howls or roars. Soft groans and heavy breathing command the space. Something heavy falls above us, and dust snows from the ceiling. Part of the brick façade of the wall crumbles slightly. *I guess he wasn't exaggerating...* I press down with my arms, trying to stand, and they immediately give way. The old pain lacing my shoulder is back in exquisite detail. New pain blossoms in my lower back. I work my feet underneath me and press back against the wall for leverage, creeping my way upright. I grit my teeth through the pain.

"-ri! Ari!" Chloe's waist appears in front of me as I rise up. Her arms reach down to take mine. "C'mon, I've got you," her voice floats above the ringing. The pain in my back intensifies, and my eyes squeeze shut of their own accord with the effort to stand. The growls and roars have started again. There's no way the three of them can keep this up much longer. *If you die on me, Dean, I swear to the Goddess...* "C'mon, we've got to get—" Chloe cuts off, and something wet hits my face. I look up into Chloe's big blue eyes. Her face is frozen with confusion.

A sharpened end of wood juts from her chest. "Ari?" Chloe's voice is a whimper. Blood dribbles from the corners of her mouth. The confusion in her eyes gives way to pain, and then her blue irises flare wide with fear. A tear slides down her cheek while red flowers bloom around the wooden stake on the white fabric of her shirt.

It spreads.

Fear grips hold of me as her weight presses down on me. I'm shaking her. *Chloe!* My mouth forms her name but the sounds never leave my lips.

"Ar-Ari... Ari, it hurts..." The words fall from her mouth in a tearful whisper as her blue eyes lose their light. She collapses into my arms, pushing us both against the wall as I cradle her against my chest. I hold onto her with all the strength I have, ignoring the death grip seizing my heart. *This isn't happening!* Her pale skin blisters and chars. In moments I'm holding nothing but ash, slipping through my shaking fingers.

No, no, no... Chloe! "Chloe!" I scream the last. The basement shakes and groans like it's weeping, too. She can't be gone... she... she has to watch movies with Madeline again. She never really got to talk to Eli. He's a tiger, too, he might understand... She... she has to go to Savannah where she's safe. *Safe.* My chest is on fire and I'm gasping for air I can't seem to find. The buzzing energy of the room suddenly drowns everything out. My skin prickles as I draw it all into my core until I'm ready to burst. I'm burning again. I fall to my knees and start to gather the ashes into a pile... *I have magic. She's not gone. She can't be.* I press my hands down and will all the energy coursing through me into the pile at my fingertips. *I can fix this... I can fix—*

Joaquin's laugh grabs me by the throat, and I look in its direction through eyes hazy with tears. The Djinn stands in his charred suit, arm still extended in our direction. His hollow eyes lock onto mine and that malicious grin slashes across his horrible face. "Poof!" He convulses with laughter. "That's how it's done, Chad! Did you see that? Chad, my boy, were you taking notes?"

His cackling voice fades out as the buzzing grows in my ears and vibrations shake my bones. I press down into the pile of ash at my knees again. *Out! Out and into her! Put her back together!* Small, wet craters appear in the pallid dust beneath me. *My tears*, I realize. *I can... I can... I can't.* My body is wracked with gasping sobs, and the droplets at my knees multiply. *I can't fix this... She's gone. Oh Goddess, Chloe...* Joaquin's voice cuts through the din in my head.

"There are some things even Djinn magic can't fix, child," The mockery of sympathy in his voice has me choking back bile. "Some deaths are final. Ashes to... well, ashes." He titters as he finishes. Anger starts to pry away the fist of sadness gripping my heart. *Evil, callous...* My thoughts cloud with rage. *Some deaths are final, huh?* I push myself to stand as the energy I had taken in races through my being. The pain in my shoulder and back feels miles away. My body tingles to the point of numbness. My vision clears.

Blake pushes herself up on hands and knees behind Joaquin, freed from her binds now that the chair was destroyed. She shakes her head, seemingly trying to get her bearings. Jon and the Tigers are still locked in combat, but their movements are slow and lethargic. Dean's body sags to one side, and Abel hobbles with one paw held up to his side. All three are a mess of blood, their panting ragged. Chad stands to the side, raising his arm...

A gunshot reverberates through the basement, then another.

A third.

Blake's scream pierces the air as the massive wolf yelps, shifting as it drops into the form of a man. Jon's naked body rolls over to stare lifelessly at the ceiling, sickly dark veins streaking away from the three wounds in his chest. Another heavy fall above us shakes the room, sending dust raining down. Blake lets loose another scream while Joaquin claps excitedly. Heartbreak cuts through my anger for a moment, clouding my eyes with tears again. Blake doesn't know a bit about anything that's happened. That was still her father... the only parent she had left. She starts to crawl toward Jon's body.

Chad looks completely unhinged. His eyes are glazed over, and his face is a mess of conflicting emotion that I can't even begin to separate. He raises the gun again and my breath catches despite the energy raging inside me. Abel staggers forward toward the delirious teen, his lips curled back over his fangs in contempt. A low, weak growl rolls through his throat.

He leaps forward, and Chad pulls the trigger.

Another shot echoes through the room, followed immediately by a scream—it's hard to tell who it belongs to. Dean's clawed paws bring Chad to the ground and pin him hard to the concrete floor. He doesn't get a chance to make another sound before Dean's heavy canines close on his neck. He twists hard, and Chad's flails end with a frightening *snap*. Dean drops his tiger guise as he rushes to where a now human-looking Abel lays writhing, legs kicking weakly off to the side. They're both a mass of bloody cuts and black-and-blue blemishes, and a vicious wound leaks from Dean's naked hip.

Joaquin pouts in the center of the room. "Well, I suppose we've come full circle there. Revenge," he says, sighing deeply, "But at what cost, hmm?" Abel lets out a blood-curdling shriek as Dean digs into his shoulder with a broken piece of metal shelf, dark lines snaking away from the wound. Joaquin's head snaps in my direction. "Well, I do believe we're just about wrapped up here." The room shakes again, and a corner of the roof collapses. "And with little time to spare! I'll just end the fallen Alpha's line real quick, and then your head and I will take a trip to Katingir. Sound good?" A malevolent smirk flashes across his face, and he turns to where Blake looks up at him through teary eyes on the ground.

Green smoke roils and churns in his hand, and Blake rises from the ground as if someone was holding her up by the throat. *No. Not after all this. Not after Chloe.* "No!" My scream is guttural and rakes my throat as it rips from my mouth. "No more, Joaquin." The hurricane of energy in the room scours my skin. I pluck a strand of Joaquin's magic in the maelstrom and breathe it in… through my nose, through my skin, through my very being.

Joaquin's eyes go wide with rage. "You dare? You *DARE* try this again?" His other arm swings wide. Metal clangs to the floor as Dean's naked form is wrenched to hang in the air beside the Djinn, opposite Blake. She's turning blue and clawing at her throat while Dean gasps and kicks. "Then you'll watch them both die!" His voice is savage and cruel, and there's nothing but murder in his eyes.

The rage in me builds like the storm, and I pull harder on the thread. It feels like my skin is straining to hold together. "No. More. Joaquin." I throw my arms up in front of me. *Bound. Bound like we were.* A churning cloud of pink smoke erupts from my open palms at the Djinn and races across the space between us to coil around his arms like a snake, smashing away the green mist in his hands. I squeeze my fists closed and pull down, and the Djinn's arms snap to his sides. Dean and Blake fall to the ground, gulping in air through ragged coughs.

Joaquin lets out a frenzied cackle. The room shakes again with more falling debris. "Ignorant... half... breed," he spits out through heavy breaths. I pull harder on his thread, taking in more of the magic that is his life-force. The *feel* of him turns my stomach. The pressure in me is building again. "It's not that... simple," he rages. His face is creasing with wrinkles where there had been nothing but ageless smoothness before. A furious scream rips from his throat, and the pink smoke binding his arms evaporates with a shockwave that rattles the walls. Green smoke tears from his outstretched hand, slamming me back against the wall and knocking the breath from my lungs.

It swirls and roils around me, squeezing. I nearly lose the thread of him. I move to raise my arm and he mirrors my movement—my left hand crashes backwards into the brick, and I feel something break. Pain rockets through my already throbbing arm. "Disgusting... Half-breed," he hisses through ragged breaths. My other hand is crushed back against the wall. *Hold onto the thread*, I scream at myself, gritting my teeth through the agony wracking my body. *Hold onto the thread...* "You can...

die first... then." He hobbles forward a step, closing his hand. The turbulent smoke around my midsection tightens. "Do you... feel that? That's your... ribs—"

His painful shriek is earsplitting. Blake's hand grips a piece of wood buried in Joaquin's knee from where she crawls on the ground. Joaquin drops to his other knee, misery torturing his features. "B-bitch!" He waves a hand and Blake flies back into the wall, crashing into a disused shelf. I drop from the wall, barely managing to keep myself upright. I look to Blake, who stirs where she's fallen. *She's alive. Hold onto the thread...* Joaquin howls as he pulls the splintering piece of wood slowly from his leaking knee.

I throw my arms forward again, expending some of the raging power in me to fasten the Djinn's legs to the cold floor. And then I pull. I pull as hard as I can, drawing all that he is inside of me. The new wrinkles in his face deepen. His cheeks start to sink into his face. An inferno rages inside me, but I deny it. I pull harder. "Do *you* feel that, Joaquin? That's your magic becoming mine. Your *life* is mine." I straighten up despite the pain and pace forward. "For all that you've done... For Chloe..."

I raise my hand toward him as I walk, drawing more of his life-force in. *His life is mine. His magic... is mine.* It's mine... to do with as I please. The realization washes over me and damp-ens the fire burning in my core. The *pressure* of it still remains, but the pain subsides some. His magic isn't some outside force I have to contain until it tears me apart—I pull harder and let it fill me... I take what I need, and let the excess fade away. *It's mine to control.* It evaporates from my skin as I stride toward the Djinn's struggling form, trailing smoke.

Joaquin screams with delirious rage from a throat rough with age. His sunken eyes are filled with unadulterated hate. He raises an arm, green smoke pooling in his palm. "Then... we can... all go!" His laugh is pure insanity. The roiling tendrils of smoke grow while he cackles, spittle flying from his mouth. A growl sounds from behind him.

A heavy paw crashes down into his arm, claws sinking deep and wrenching it backwards while two heavy fangs sink into the Djinn's shoulder. His cry is soundless, and the smoke in his palm begins to fade. I stand over him now, pulling and pulling at his thread. His cheeks sink deeper, the wrinkles growing. His suit suddenly looks ridiculous with how loose it's become. His hair turns white and then falls away. The healthy glow of his skin fades and darkens as it stretches taut over his bones. Dean pulls away as Joaquin sinks back, his arms hanging limply at his sides. "Goodbye, Joaquin."

One last gasp leaves his throat, and then the mummified Djinn falls forward at my feet. He shatters like glass into dust, which smokes away on some invisible wind. *He's gone. It's over...* I fall to my knees, smoke still dissipating from my body. The storm raging inside me quiets, then fades away. The pain in my shoulder, back, and hand that I had pushed away surge back to fill the vacuum, along with pure exhaustion...

And then the pain of losing Chloe returns to hit me like a freight train. Tears are streaming down my cheeks, and I do nothing to stop them as I shake with sobs. Dean's face appears above me then, and I'm vaguely aware of his arms pulling me into his chest. Warmth slowly starts to seep into my skin as I lean into him. "She's gone..." I say, the words barely more than a breath of air, and Dean's hold on me tightens.

"But not Blake, not Abel…" he says, and a tiny light shines into my heart.

"No," I whisper. "And not you." What's left of my concentration evaporates, and I allow myself to completely collapse against him. The building rumbles again, and Dean searches the ceiling.

"Let's go home."

Epilogue

Christmas Day

Cold soaks through my supposedly insulated pants as I kneel in the smooth white of days-old snow. The clearing the pack uses for the Moon Awakening is always beautiful, but there's something about the shape and color of it this time of year that makes it especially gorgeous. I can't help the smile that pushes back my cheeks, and I breathe in the cool, clean air as I admire the scene. *So pretty... it's just for you.* I turn my attention back to the tangled wood and wildflower memorial in front of me and finish adjusting the holly branches and poinsettias. A little crumb of magic has kept it all preserved in the winter weather.

Chloe loved Christmas. She'd have come back and haunted me if I hadn't added some holiday flair to her cairn. *Would that be so bad?* I smile sadly. "Merry Christmas, Chloe."

I push up and start my slow walk back home through the half-foot or so of snow that blankets Lunar Falls. Older sets of footprints guide my way back out through the woods—one small and one large. Jessica and Madeline had been here earlier, no doubt. Breaking the news to them had been... rough. I've used the phrase 'worst night of my life' way too often the last couple months—I need to make a Top Ten list—and that night is at least in the top three. Not even the steady, comforting presence of Dean next to me had been enough to keep me from breaking down, and I don't think Madeline's face will ever leave me.

We had built the memorial the next day. There was no funeral like before, only our small little group to truly remember Chloe and all she had been. *Every*thing she had been. A vampire with humanity, but more importantly a daughter, a sister, and a best friend. Mrs. Hanshen had eventually revealed it to the pack with Abel's support, but it mostly fell on deaf ears. Most of the pack probably wrote it off as the words of a grieving mother, but even if only a couple seeds of doubt were planted... maybe some things would change eventually. Maybe one day we could paint the 'Safe Haven' symbol on the entrance to Lunar Falls.

Abel and Jessica had gotten really close lately. They had taken it upon themselves to reveal Jon's sins. Between Abel's testimony, Jessica's story from Chloe, and the paperwork we had discovered, it was hard for the pack to dispute. Others who had heard of the backroom dealings had spoken up in support as well. It was a painful week for the pack, but after a week of sadness and confusion—and more than a little bit of anger—a young new Alpha was brought in from a neighboring pack to lead Lunar Falls. The son, ironically enough, of the Alpha who was to take over after Jon was deposed.

Blake had taken this all… badly. How else could she? Jon had been a monster, but to Blake… He had loved her, that was undeniable. I sigh, my exhale taking form in the cold air as I round the corner to the street I live on. I shake my head at the thoughts of my friend. If I haven't been able to process all those feelings, I can't imagine how hard it is for Blake… It was the reason she had left Lunar Falls around the beginning of December. To 'travel' and collect her thoughts. She had been kidnapped and tortured, lost a best friend and father, her dad's legacy was soiled beyond cleaning… I suppose I can't blame her. Her world had collapsed like D Building.

Chad and his friends were listed as being killed in the collapse, and pack connections with the local police had removed Jon's name and body from the investigation. *It's amazing what you can accomplish with a little nudge…* Even after a month or so, I can't bring myself to feel sorry for them. *Should I?* All these moral questions were getting uncomfortable, whether they were about Chad or Jon or my friends.

In a way, I suppose I had lost both of my best friends, and in a way I suppose I hadn't. I visit Chloe's memorial every week to talk, and postcards from Blake come regularly as she travels north. *All because of a lunatic Djinn.* Bitterness grips me for a moment, and I exhale it away. I still haven't decided if the Telling was about me and my friends, but I suppose Fate would let me know one way or another. There is something calming and terrifying about that thought all at the same time.

Calming and terrifying really does sum up the last month or so. Time doesn't necessarily heal all wounds… it mostly just scabs them over. So much has changed, and yet some things have stayed the same. Like Dean. He had been my rock through all of this. When the flood of emotions was sweeping me away, Dean had been my stable ground. My partner in crime. My *mate*. A smile blooms on my face.

I reach the door of my house and enter into its comforting warmth. I shake out of my winter gear and head to the living room, where garland and stockings hang above the mantle. A seven foot Christmas tree sits in the corner, bedecked in multicolored lights, glass baubles, and various other ornaments. The hearth crackles with the warm glow of an evening fire as Christmas carols play through the house.

"Sleigh bells ring... are you listening..." My mom's voice travels to me from the kitchen as she sings along with the tune while shuffling around the island. Fresh baked rolls and roasted ham waft through the house, stealing my attention from the rest of my family all gathered in the living room.

"Speed is the key, son," my dad explains to Koa, a hint of fatherly frustration creeping into his voice.

"Yeah, I know, but I can't get enough momentum to make the rotation," my brother replies, referring to some fighting technique or another that I'm clueless about. Knowing them, they've probably been at it for the last hour or so, discussing the best maneuvers to take down their prey. *Vampires.* I've had to remind myself about a dozen times over the last few weeks that they're not talking about Chloe. They hadn't quite taken to Jessica and Abel's explanations. As angry as it made me, I understood, even if I don't agree with their close-mindedness. It takes a lot to completely reorient your understanding of the world. They hadn't seen what we had, but they *had* watched friends get mauled in vampire attacks—Jessica and Abel's word wouldn't be enough. I have to hope that with enough time, that might change. *Baby steps*. I push the thought aside and start toward the kitchen just as the front door bell rings.

"That's probably Dean," I announce, turning on a heel to answer it.

I cover the short distance in a matter of seconds and pull open the door. Just as I predicted, Dean stands in the doorway taking up most of the frame. He smirks and my thighs ache with the want to climb him right there on my front porch. His arched brow tells me he knows exactly what I'm thinking. I bite my lip, pressing my back against the open door to allow him to pass. He doesn't, though. Instead, he pulls me to him and presses his lips to mine.

"Merry Christmas," Dean growls the words against my lips then pulls away. "My mate," he finishes with a whisper. The way he says 'mate' is enough to make my toes curl. That's exactly what I want him to call me from now on. He leans in for another kiss. It's short—way too short—but the snickers behind me from my dad and brother make me suddenly glad it was barely a peck.

"Merry Christmas," I reply, bringing my hand to my lips as if to memorize the feel of his kiss. We still haven't made the whole *mate* part official, with the mark and all that. Tonight, maybe… I shove the thought back. My face heats with the knowledge that I'm currently surrounded by my family and should not be thinking of those types of things right in front of them. The twinkle in Dean's eye lets me know his thoughts mirror my own, and now I'm wishing we were alone.

"Merry Christmas," someone awkwardly says from behind Dean, and I stretch to peer around him. Abel waves with his right arm, a subtle wince flashing across his face. His left arm hangs limply in a sling. Dean had managed to get the slug out of his shoulder before the silver reached his heart, but the damage was extensive. He would probably never use that arm again. I smile sadly and return the wave, then motion for the cousins to come inside.

"C'mon, guys. Dinner's almost ready." I rub the small of Dean's back as he passes and motion for Abel to follow. The subtle crunching of snow draws my eyes back out to the street and Jessica and Madeline pad their way through the snow to our door. Abel pushes inside and Dean stands at my back as Chloe's family makes their way to the door. We say nothing, and Jessica embraces me with a deep hug. We pull away and share a smile. Madeline waves from Jessica's waist.

"Merry Christmas, Ari." She squeaks, waving a tiny hand.

I kneel down and take her in another hug. "Merry Christmas, girlie."

"Come in, come in! You're letting all the cold air in, guys!" my dad calls from inside the house, and Madeline and I giggle, releasing one another. I roll my eyes as I turn to see my mom pulling Dean in for a bone-crushing hug of her own. We all jumble into the house quickly, everyone shrugging out of coats and scarfs. Hugs and slaps on the back are passed from person to person before mom drags us all to the kitchen, shoving things into our hands to set the table while barking orders. I take the stack of plates she's thrust on me while Koa has the silverware. Dean starts on the drinks. "You're the bartender after all," Mom tells him while shaking the spatula she hasn't let go of at him.

Minutes later, we're all seated around the large formal dining room table, the one we only use on holidays like this. Conversation swirls, wine is poured, and the feast before us is quickly devoured. My gaze shifts from person to person and my smile falls a little. Christmas this year isn't any different besides the added company of Dean, Abel, and the Hanshens, but I can't help the ache of knowing the reason for the added company is loss.

"You okay?" Dean whispers into my ear from beside me. The warmth of his breath tickles my ear and I nod, but I know he can tell it's a lie. It's like he sees right through me now, ever since that night. Maybe he always had, even if it was subliminal. I had been in and out of it the few days following the fight in the school basement. Between the magic and the vicious slams, my body had taken a beating. Unfortunately, half-Djinn don't seem to be gifted with miraculous healing like everyone else in the supernatural world. It took time, most of which I had been passed out for. I woke up to find Dean posted up beside my bed. He hadn't left my side once, according to Mom. There was no hiding what had happened. I was a mess, and Dean probably looked like he had taken a hard fall off a mountain. And that was before everything else came to light. She had been a puddle of loving thankfulness that I was alive. That gave way quickly, of course, to her being livid over the fact that I'd been in danger at all. Risking my life to save my friends, not informing the pack...

That's when I confronted her about her not telling me I'm half-Djinn. That halted the argument *real* fast, and suddenly Mom was back-pedaling. I glance over at my mom now, just as she pats my dad's hand beside her while laughing at some thread of conversation. I'm not angry with them any more. At first I was... So much angrier than I had ever really realized until I let it all out. But now...

She explained the deal they made with my Djinn father to shelter me and raise me as their own. In exchange, the Djinn would save my brother's life. Before Koa, Mom had gone through several miscarriages, and things weren't looking good this time around either. Magic was used to seal the deal, and it wouldn't allow them to say a word to anyone—not even me—until my sixteenth birthday. With everything that had happened that day, they didn't know how to bring it up. I suppose a lot *was* going on.

Really, it doesn't matter now. That dark-haired, dark skinned man in a suit is no one to me past that slip of paper he sent about the magic and his ward. Which I guess, in the end, had helped save my life. I can't deny that, but Mom and Dad and Koa... they're my real family.

And now Dean.

"I love you," I say, turning to Dean on my left. He smiles, tilting his head to bump against my forehead.

"I know," he whispers back, and I laugh. *Just like that*. I suppose it really is a Merry Christmas.

Mate... *my* mate. The title is as hot as the two teeth marks that Dean left on the right side of my neck. The fact that he has a matching set has my thighs aching all over again. I'm not entirely sure how the magic works, but I am here for it. He is *mine*.

"And you are mine," Dean says, his voice husky as he nuzzles his face into my neck trailing kisses along my collar bone. A low moan escapes past my lips as my skin enflames from his touch. More. I need *more*. "Mhmmm," Dean purrs and nods his agreement without stopping.

"I didn't say anything," I mumble out, and suddenly I'm not so sure. It's hard to think past the magic he's trailing against my body at the moment.

"You thought it."

I freeze as his words wash over me, my hands gripping his shoulders and making him pause. He groans, dragging his face up to mine as if I'd just taken away his favorite toy. I almost laugh at the look of mock disappointment on his face. "What do you mean I thought it?"

Dean sighs, sitting up and pulling the blankets with him. His fingertips slide a trail from my hip up to my neck as he does and it's almost enough to make me forget my question all together.

"Mates can sense each other's emotions."

"What!"

Dean laughs, then explains: "It's all a part of the bond... it allows us to always be in-tune to one another. We can't hear each other's thoughts exactly, but I can sort of *feel* them out. You can, however, block me out, of course. But not entirely." He says the last with a devilish grin and heat rises in my core.

"Seriously?"

"Yes, now can I go back to worshiping you like the goddess you are?" he asks, and I jump at the feel of his desire mingling with my own at his words.

"Veryyyyy cool," I say, wrapping my hand around the back of his neck and pulling him down to me in the bed. His thumbs strokes the soft skin under my ear, and his gaze drops to my mouth. His eyes catch fire. Suddenly the inches between us feel like miles and the need to close the space is all consuming. As if reading my mind, Dean closes the distance and we're a tangle of tongues and teeth, devouring lips and clawing hands. His hips rock into mine, and I groan against his lips at the delicious friction. He breaks the kiss, sliding his mouth across my jaw, my neck… I'll do anything to keep him here with me. His mouth can claim anything it wants.

Need pulses between my thighs and I arch into him. There's literally nothing he could do that I wouldn't welcome. The knowledge has my body responding in kind. I want him.

Only him. Here. Now. Anywhere. Everywhere.

I surrender completely, melting into him. My body goes pliant beneath his expert hands…

The doorbell rings.

Dean pulls back and turns his head toward the bedroom door. The doorbell sounds again and we both eye one another. "Expecting someone?" I ask him, and he shakes his head. "Amazing timing…"

In one fluid motion Dean is up and out from the bed, his naked body glistening in the glow shining through the bedroom window. The sight of the hard lines of his body edged in moonlight has me biting my lip and desperate to pull him back, but another ring of the door bell gives me my answer. With a pouting groan I grab the blankets around me and drag myself from the bed. Dean flicks on the bedroom light, and I blink away the sudden onslaught of recessed fixtures. After a few moments of letting my eyes adjust I search the messy pile beside the bed for my clothes. Picking up a piece here and a piece there—and ultimately settling on Dean's discarded shirt—I turn to find him leaning against the doorframe, raking me with his eyes. His smirk screams 'To be continued.'

I return the look and he takes a step toward me just in time for the doorbell ring again, as if our unwanted visitor can tell we're one fiery look away from ignoring them. Another ring, and we're making our way down the stairs. I start to wonder if I should be worried. Most people would have given up by now. I throw the thought away. No reason to borrow tomorrow's trouble for tonight.

"Someone better be dying!" Dean shouts just as he reaches the door and yanks it open. A blonde girl stands just outside the threshold, her hand raised as if she were about to ring the bell again, but it drops to her side. She's tall and blonde with some of the bluest eyes I've ever seen—supermodel gorgeous. The thought floats through my mind that maybe she's one of Dean's exes, if you can even call any of his conquests real exes. The craziest pang of jealousy crawls up my spine. And then something else…

It hits me like a slam to the chest, nearly knocking the air from my lungs. She feels *other*. It radiates from her in the same way it has from all supernaturals since that night in the basement. She *feels* like Chloe.

"You're a vampire," I say. It's not a question. She doesn't have the decaying scent and the tell-tale red eyes of your typical junkie vamp… but that feeling is there. Not quite the same, but… close enough.

She doesn't answer. Her head turns and she quickly scans the street behind her, then her attention snaps back to Dean and I. "I'm Lindsey," her voice is feminine and lilting, tinged with fear. "Your father sent me."

Acknowledgements

I want to start by thanking my husband Kyle for literally all the things. Not only have you given me so much patience and encouragement through all the craziness that comes with being a writer, but you also dedicated so much of your time, love, and superpowers into developing this story with me. You formatted this insanity into a masterpiece because you know how extra I am, and you genuinely cared as much as I do that this book was not just good, but everything I wanted it to be: Epic! It couldn't have been done without you.

To Jon and Shelley, aka Mom and Dad: Thank you for being the inspiration for Ari's loving parents. The constant love and respect you two have in your marriage is everything Kyle and I strive for! I know your unconditional hearts get you hurt much more than not, but it's one of things I cherish the most about you both.

Elizabeth—girl, I miss you every single day. This story began with you and I throwing shit at the wall to see what stuck and it ended up being all the missing links I needed for the Winter's Series!

To C. A. Varian: thank you for giving me so much advice on my Kickstarter and TikTok shop with this release. And thank you for sharing the shit out of it and becoming a bestie along the way!

To Cara North: thank you for talking me into doing this whole Kickstarter insanity! You were right! I loved it!

To Lisa Klass: thank you for letting me drone on and on relentlessly sometimes about this story, my struggles, triumphs, and fears.

To my book club girlies—Cordelia, Grey, Belinda, Tiffany, Jaqueline, Kyra, and Leya. Thank you so much for listening to me freak out over this release and Kickstarter, and encouraging me to do it anyway! Thank you for spraying books and packing endless boxes with me! I don't know what I'd do without you guys!

To all my friends and family: seriously, every single one of you that listen to my constant babble about my books and cheer me on with each new release. Y'all either seriously love me or seriously need medication, but either way, I f'n love you for it.

Thank you to Michelle for being the final call on all things grammar because you know none of that makes any sense to me. This would be a mess without you. Thank you to Trish of Burning Phoenix Covers for designing this gorgeous cover you made so long ago and then rushing to transform it into a full wrap all this time later because it took me a lifetime to have this book ready for the world!

To all the amazing readers that supported this as a Kickstarter! Thank you! Many of you have never even read my books before and took a chance on a new author. Y'all literally made this thing a reality and blew my mind in the process. I seriously have no words for all the gratitude and feels I have! Thank you for being such a huge part of this journey with me!

Jensa Brenna	Yvette	Jule Hayes
Shelley J. Weichman	Nichole Crowley	Somer Kemble
Ashley	Elisha Padilla	Nicole Rinn
Katrina (Roxy)	Megan Kell	Sherry Mock
Alexandra Corrison	Kayla Poe	Bianca Tatjana
Deissy	Lisa L.	Megan Astell
Jacquelin Dooley	Lauren Luick	Gayle Lazur
Lexi	C. A. Varian	Chanel H.
Tamara M. Staten	Hanna Wilkinson	Kalin Nabiof
Billye Herndon	April Miller	Elizabeth W.
Tonya-Cara	Kimberly B.	Michelle Martin
Andretta Schellinger	Michelle Fortune	Jackie Fitzpatrick
Stephanie	J.P. Sina	Jenna
Leesha	Amy Murdock	Marie
Amanda Eschmeyer	Michelle Day	Karoline Farley
Kristen Bellio	PunkARTchick	Tanya Young
Cheyenne Thompson	Ruthinia	Stella
Regina Ussery	George the Girl	Melissa MacKinnon
Dori	Francesco Tehrani	Kim Prytherch
Elise Faber	Morgan G.	Tonel
Angie Nickerson	Tamye	Emily Shore
Lynn Hollibaugh	Christina Meisenhelter	Jenn Bigelow
Sarah Hoy	Amanda L. Garrison	Cassie
Lisa Klass	Kat Parkins	Lisa Watson
Maria Maija	Storm	Rica Bonin

And to you, the reader! Thank you for turning the pages on Ari's epic adventure of magic, fangs, and falling in love.

I have the best tribe around me, and without all of you, this being-an-author-thing wouldn't work, and for that I'm forever grateful.

XOXO

— Breezy

Epilogue

CHRISTMAS DAY

Cold soaks through my supposedly insulated pants as I kneel in the smooth white of days-old snow. The clearing the pack uses for the Moon Awakening is always beautiful, but there's something about the shape and color of it this time of year that makes it especially gorgeous. I can't help the smile that pushes back my cheeks, and I breathe in the cool, clean air as I admire the scene. *So pretty… it's just for you.* I turn my attention back to the tangled wood and wildflower memorial in front of me and finish adjusting the holly branches and poinsettias. A little crumb of magic has kept it all preserved in the winter weather.

Chloe loved Christmas. She'd have come back and haunted me if I hadn't added some holiday flair to her cairn. *Would that be so bad?* I smile sadly. "Merry Christmas, Chloe."

I push up and start my slow walk back home through the half-foot or so of snow that blankets Lunar Falls. Older sets of footprints guide my way back out through the woods—one small and one large. Jessica and Madeline had been here earlier, no doubt. Breaking the news to them had been... rough. I've used the phrase 'worst night of my life' way too often the last couple months—I need to make a Top Ten list—and that night is at least in the top three. Not even the steady, comforting presence of Dean next to me had been enough to keep me from breaking down, and I don't think Madeline's face will ever leave me.

We had built the memorial the next day. There was no funeral like before, only our small little group to truly remember Chloe and all she had been. *Every*thing she had been. A vampire with humanity, but more importantly a daughter, a sister, and a best friend. Mrs. Hanshen had eventually revealed it to the pack with Abel's support, but it mostly fell on deaf ears. Most of the pack probably wrote it off as the words of a grieving mother, but even if only a couple seeds of doubt were planted... maybe some things would change eventually. Maybe one day we could paint the 'Safe Haven' symbol on the entrance to Lunar Falls.

Abel and Jessica had gotten really close lately. They had taken it upon themselves to reveal Jon's sins. Between Abel's testimony, Jessica's story from Chloe, and the paperwork we had discovered, it was hard for the pack to dispute. Others who had heard of the backroom dealings had spoken up in support as well. It was a painful week for the pack, but after a week of sadness and confusion—and more than a little bit of anger—a young new Alpha was brought in from a neighboring pack to lead Lunar Falls. The son, ironically enough, of the Alpha who was to take over after Jon was deposed.

Blake had taken this all… badly. How else could she? Jon had been a monster, but to Blake… He had loved her, that was undeniable. I sigh, my exhale taking form in the cold air as I round the corner to the street I live on. I shake my head at the thoughts of my friend. If I haven't been able to process all those feelings, I can't imagine how hard it is for Blake… It was the reason she had left Lunar Falls around the beginning of December. To 'travel' and collect her thoughts. She had been kidnapped and tortured, lost a best friend and father, her dad's legacy was soiled beyond cleaning… I suppose I can't blame her. Her world had collapsed like D Building.

Chad and his friends were listed as being killed in the collapse, and pack connections with the local police had removed Jon's name and body from the investigation. *It's amazing what you can accomplish with a little nudge…* Even after a month or so, I can't bring myself to feel sorry for them. *Should I?* All these moral questions were getting uncomfortable, whether they were about Chad or Jon or my friends.

In a way, I suppose I had lost both of my best friends, and in a way I suppose I hadn't. I visit Chloe's memorial every week to talk, and postcards from Blake come regularly as she travels north. *All because of a lunatic Djinn.* Bitterness grips me for a moment, and I exhale it away. I still haven't decided if the Telling was about me and my friends, but I suppose Fate would let me know one way or another. There is something calming and terrifying about that thought all at the same time.

Calming and terrifying really does sum up the last month or so. Time doesn't necessarily heal all wounds… it mostly just scabs them over. So much has changed, and yet some things have stayed the same. Like Dean. He had been my rock through all of this. When the flood of emotions was sweeping me away, Dean had been my stable ground. My partner in crime. My *mate*. A smile blooms on my face.

I reach the door of my house and enter into its comforting warmth. I shake out of my winter gear and head to the living room, where garland and stockings hang above the mantle. A seven foot Christmas tree sits in the corner, bedecked in multi-colored lights, glass baubles, and various other ornaments. The hearth crackles with the warm glow of an evening fire as Christmas carols play through the house.

"Sleigh bells ring... are you listening..." My mom's voice travels to me from the kitchen as she sings along with the tune while shuffling around the island. Fresh baked rolls and roasted ham waft through the house, stealing my attention from the rest of my family all gathered in the living room.

"Speed is the key, son," my dad explains to Koa, a hint of fatherly frustration creeping into his voice.

"Yeah, I know, but I can't get enough momentum to make the rotation," my brother replies, referring to some fighting technique or another that I'm clueless about. Knowing them, they've probably been at it for the last hour or so, discussing the best maneuvers to take down their prey. *Vampires.* I've had to remind myself about a dozen times over the last few weeks that they're not talking about Chloe. They hadn't quite taken to Jessica and Abel's explanations. As angry as it made me, I understood, even if I don't agree with their close-mindedness. It takes a lot to completely reorient your understanding of the world. They hadn't seen what we had, but they *had* watched friends get mauled in vampire attacks—Jessica and Abel's word wouldn't be enough. I have to hope that with enough time, that might change. *Baby steps.* I push the thought aside and start toward the kitchen just as the front door bell rings.

"That's probably Dean," I announce, turning on a heel to answer it.

I cover the short distance in a matter of seconds and pull open the door. Just as I predicted, Dean stands in the doorway taking up most of the frame. He smirks and my thighs ache with the want to climb him right there on my front porch. His arched brow tells me he knows exactly what I'm thinking. I bite my lip, pressing my back against the open door to allow him to pass. He doesn't, though. Instead, he pulls me to him and presses his lips to mine.

"Merry Christmas," Dean growls the words against my lips then pulls away. "My mate," he finishes with a whisper. The way he says 'mate' is enough to make my toes curl. That's exactly what I want him to call me from now on. He leans in for another kiss. It's short—way too short—but the snickers behind me from my dad and brother make me suddenly glad it was barely a peck.

"Merry Christmas," I reply, bringing my hand to my lips as if to memorize the feel of his kiss. We still haven't made the whole *mate* part official, with the mark and all that. Tonight, maybe… I shove the thought back. My face heats with the knowledge that I'm currently surrounded by my family and should not be thinking of those types of things right in front of them. The twinkle in Dean's eye lets me know his thoughts mirror my own, and now I'm wishing we were alone.

"Merry Christmas," someone awkwardly says from behind Dean, and I stretch to peer around him. Abel waves with his right arm, a subtle wince flashing across his face. His left arm hangs limply in a sling. Dean had managed to get the slug out of his shoulder before the silver reached his heart, but the damage was extensive. He would probably never use that arm again. I smile sadly and return the wave, then motion for the cousins to come inside.

"C'mon, guys. Dinner's almost ready." I rub the small of Dean's back as he passes and motion for Abel to follow. The subtle crunching of snow draws my eyes back out to the street and Jessica and Madeline pad their way through the snow to our door. Abel pushes inside and Dean stands at my back as Chloe's family makes their way to the door. We say nothing, and Jessica embraces me with a deep hug. We pull away and share a smile. Madeline waves from Jessica's waist.

"Merry Christmas, Ari." She squeaks, waving a tiny hand.

I kneel down and take her in another hug. "Merry Christmas, girlie."

"Come in, come in! You're letting all the cold air in, guys!" my dad calls from inside the house, and Madeline and I giggle, releasing one another. I roll my eyes as I turn to see my mom pulling Dean in for a bone-crushing hug of her own. We all jumble into the house quickly, everyone shrugging out of coats and scarfs. Hugs and slaps on the back are passed from person to person before mom drags us all to the kitchen, shoving things into our hands to set the table while barking orders. I take the stack of plates she's thrust on me while Koa has the silverware. Dean starts on the drinks. "You're the bartender after all," Mom tells him while shaking the spatula she hasn't let go of at him.

Minutes later, we're all seated around the large formal dining room table, the one we only use on holidays like this. Conversation swirls, wine is poured, and the feast before us is quickly devoured. My gaze shifts from person to person and my smile falls a little. Christmas this year isn't any different besides the added company of Dean, Abel, and the Hanshens, but I can't help the ache of knowing the reason for the added company is loss.

"You okay?" Dean whispers into my ear from beside me. The warmth of his breath tickles my ear and I nod, but I know he can tell it's a lie. It's like he sees right through me now, ever since that night. Maybe he always had, even if it was subliminal. I had been in and out of it the few days following the fight in the school basement. Between the magic and the vicious slams, my body had taken a beating. Unfortunately, half-Djinn don't seem to be gifted with miraculous healing like everyone else in the supernatural world. It took time, most of which I had been passed out for. I woke up to find Dean posted up beside my bed. He hadn't left my side once, according to Mom. There was no hiding what had happened. I was a mess, and Dean probably looked like he had taken a hard fall off a mountain. And that was before everything else came to light. She had been a puddle of loving thankfulness that I was alive. That gave way quickly, of course, to her being livid over the fact that I'd been in danger at all. Risking my life to save my friends, not informing the pack…

That's when I confronted her about her not telling me I'm half-Djinn. That halted the argument *real* fast, and suddenly Mom was back-pedaling. I glance over at my mom now, just as she pats my dad's hand beside her while laughing at some thread of conversation. I'm not angry with them any more. At first I was… So much angrier than I had ever really realized until I let it all out. But now…

This whole conversation plagued me throughout writing this book. I knew I needed it in here, but not where to put it! I played with so many different places, but it finally ended up here.

355

She explained the deal they made with my Djinn father to shelter me and raise me as their own. In exchange, the Djinn would save my brother's life. Before Koa, Mom had gone through several miscarriages, and things weren't looking good this time around either. Magic was used to seal the deal, and it wouldn't allow them to say a word to anyone—not even me—until my sixteenth birthday. With everything that had happened that day, they didn't know how to bring it up. I suppose a lot *was* going on.

Really, it doesn't matter now. That dark-haired, dark skinned man in a suit is no one to me past that slip of paper he sent about the magic and his ward. Which I guess, in the end, had helped save my life. I can't deny that, but Mom and Dad and Koa... they're my real family.

And now Dean.

"I love you," I say, turning to Dean on my left. He smiles, tilting his head to bump against my forehead.

"I know," he whispers back, and I laugh. *Just like that.* I suppose it really is a Merry Christmas.

Mate... *my* mate. The title is as hot as the two teeth marks that Dean left on the right side of my neck. The fact that he has a matching set has my thighs aching all over again. I'm not entirely sure how the magic works, but I am here for it. He is *mine*.

"And you are mine," Dean says, his voice husky as he nuzzles his face into my neck trailing kisses along my collar bone. A low moan escapes past my lips as my skin enflames from his touch. More. I need *more*. "Mhmmm," Dean purrs and nods his agreement without stopping.

"I didn't say anything," I mumble out, and suddenly I'm not so sure. It's hard to think past the magic he's trailing against my body at the moment.

"You thought it."

I freeze as his words wash over me, my hands gripping his shoulders and making him pause. He groans, dragging his face up to mine as if I'd just taken away his favorite toy. I almost laugh at the look of mock disappointment on his face. "What do you mean I thought it?"

Dean sighs, sitting up and pulling the blankets with him. His fingertips slide a trail from my hip up to my neck as he does and it's almost enough to make me forget my question all together.

"Mates can sense each other's emotions."

"What!"

Dean laughs, then explains: "It's all a part of the bond… it allows us to always be in-tune to one another. We can't hear each other's thoughts exactly, but I can sort of *feel* them out. You can, however, block me out, of course. But not entirely." He says the last with a devilish grin and heat rises in my core.

"Seriously?"

"Yes, now can I go back to worshiping you like the goddess you are?" he asks, and I jump at the feel of his desire mingling with my own at his words.

"Veryyyyy cool," I say, wrapping my hand around the back of his neck and pulling him down to me in the bed. His thumbs strokes the soft skin under my ear, and his gaze drops to my mouth. His eyes catch fire. Suddenly the inches between us feel like miles and the need to close the space is all consuming. As if reading my mind, Dean closes the distance and we're a tangle of tongues and teeth, devouring lips and clawing hands. His hips

Originally I had them able to actually speak mind-to-mind, but I really just didn't like it. I decided to nix that idea and have them be connected in more of an emotional way.

rock into mine, and I groan against his lips at the delicious friction. He breaks the kiss, sliding his mouth across my jaw, my neck… I'll do anything to keep him here with me. His mouth can claim anything it wants.

Need pulses between my thighs and I arch into him. There's literally nothing he could do that I wouldn't welcome. The knowledge has my body responding in kind. I want him.

Only him. Here. Now. Anywhere. Everywhere.

I surrender completely, melting into him. My body goes pliant beneath his expert hands…

The doorbell rings.

Dean pulls back and turns his head toward the bedroom door. The doorbell sounds again and we both eye one another. "Expecting someone?" I ask him, and he shakes his head. "Amazing timing…"

In one fluid motion Dean is up and out from the bed, his naked body glistening in the glow shining through the bedroom window. The sight of the hard lines of his body edged in moonlight has me biting my lip and desperate to pull him back, but another ring of the door bell gives me my answer. With a pouting groan I grab the blankets around me and drag myself from the bed. Dean flicks on the bedroom light, and I blink away the sudden onslaught of recessed fixtures. After a few moments of letting my eyes adjust I search the messy pile beside the bed for my clothes. Picking up a piece here and a piece there—and ultimately settling on Dean's discarded shirt—I turn to find him leaning against the doorframe, raking me with his eyes. His smirk screams 'To be continued.'

I return the look and he takes a step toward me just in time for the doorbell ring again, as if our unwanted visitor can tell we're one fiery look away from ignoring them. Another ring, and we're making our way down the stairs. I start to wonder if I should be worried. Most people would have given up by now. I throw the thought away. No reason to borrow tomorrow's trouble for tonight.

"Someone better be dying!" Dean shouts just as he reaches the door and yanks it open. A blonde girl stands just outside the threshold, her hand raised as if she were about to ring the bell again, but it drops to her side. She's tall and blonde with some of the bluest eyes I've ever seen—supermodel gorgeous. The thought floats through my mind that maybe she's one of Dean's exes, if you can even call any of his conquests real exes. The craziest pang of jealousy crawls up my spine. And then something else...

It hits me like a slam to the chest, nearly knocking the air from my lungs. She feels *other*. It radiates from her in the same way it has from all supernaturals since that night in the basement. She *feels* like Chloe.

"You're a vampire," I say. It's not a question. She doesn't have the decaying scent and the tell-tale red eyes of your typical junkie vamp... but that feeling is there. Not quite the same, but... close enough.

She doesn't answer. Her head turns and she quickly scans the street behind her, then her attention snaps back to Dean and I. "I'm Lindsey," her voice is feminine and lilting, tinged with fear. "Your father sent me."

I knew this character introduction would end the story from the starting gate.

About the Author

Breezy lives in Winston-Salem, NC, with her husband, daughter, son and two fur babies, as a stay-at-home mom. She loves all things pink and glitter. Christmas is a part of her very soul, and you can't tell her Santa isn't real. He is.

If you ask what first got her into writing, she'll tell you it was the ending of *Divergent*. She remembers laughing at the first person to suggest that she could write a book, English was her worst subject in school. But she chose to give it a shot.

When she's not writing, Breezy splits her time among her many hobbies: reading, makeup and graphic design, just to name a few. These things don't come without a cost—coffee and wine. While writing hasn't always been her goal, she has fallen in love with building a world from nothing and watching it flourish.

Don't miss the first installment in the Winter's Series:

Available Now!

9 798869 310637